C000132129

About the Author

Maureen Child is the author of more than 130 romance novels and novellas that routinely appear on bestseller lists and have won numerous awards, including the National Reader's Choice Award. Maureen is a seven-time nominee for the prestigious *RITA*® award from Romance Writers of America, and one of her books was made into a CBS-TV movie called *The Soul Collector*. Maureen recently moved from California to the mountains of Utah and is trying to get used to snow.

Award-winning author **Zuri Day** snuck her first Mills & Boon romance from her older sister's collection and was hooked from page one. Knights in shining armour and happily-ever-afters spurred a lifelong love of reading. Zuri now creates these stories as a full-time author. Splitting her time between the stunning Caribbean islands and southern California, and always busy writing her next novel, Zuri still loves to connect with readers via Zuri@ZuriDay.com

New York Times and *USA Today* bestselling author **Cathryn Fox** is a wife, mum, sister, daughter, aunt, and friend. She loves dogs, sunny weather, anything chocolate – she never says no to a brownie – pizza, and red wine. Cathryn lives in beautiful Nova Scotia with her husband, who is convinced he can turn her into a mixed martial arts fan. When not writing, Cathryn can be found Skyping with her son, who lives in Seattle (could he have moved any farther away?), shopping with her daughter in the city, watching a big action flick with her husband, or hanging out and laughing with friends.

Sins and Seduction

Sins and Seduction:

Tempting the Boss

MAUREEN CHILD

ZURI DAY

CATHRYN FOX

MILLS & BOON

First Published in Great Britain 2023
by Mills & Boon, an imprint of HarperCollins*Publishers* Ltd,
1 London Bridge Street, London, SE1 9GF

www.harpercollins.co.uk

HarperCollins*Publishers*
Macken House, 39/40 Mayor Street Upper,
Dublin 1, D01 C9W8, Ireland

ISBN: 978-0-263-31897-5

MIX
Paper | Supporting
responsible forestry
FSC™ C007454

BOMBSHELL FOR THE BOSS

MAUREEN CHILD

To my cousin Timarie – steadfast and strong, beautiful
and brave. She faced the dragon and won.
We're all so proud.

One

"We already talked about this." Ethan Hart leaned back and stared across the desk at his younger brother. Elbows propped on the arms of his chair, Ethan steepled his fingers and narrowed his gaze. Irritation simmered inside him. How often did they have to go through this? Not for the first time, Ethan wondered if having his little brother on the board was a good idea.

Gabriel Hart pushed up from the visitor's chair and shoved both hands into his slacks pockets. "No, Ethan. *We* didn't discuss anything. *You* commanded."

One eyebrow winged up as Ethan lifted his gaze to meet Gabe's. "Since you remember our last conversation so well, I wonder why you're here trying to go over it all again."

"Because even as stubborn as you are, Ethan, I keep hoping that I'll manage to get through to you."

"I'm stubborn?" Ethan laughed and shook his head. "That's funny, coming from you."

"Damn it, I'm trying to do something important," Gabe argued. "Not just for me, but for the company."

And he believed that, Ethan knew. Gabriel had always been the one to try new things, to push envelopes. Well, that was no problem for himself. But for this company? Trying something new wasn't worth risking a reputation it had taken generations to build.

This was an old argument, getting older by the second. Ever since Gabe had taken his place in the Hart family chocolate company, the brothers had been doing battle. Ethan regretted that, because he and his younger brother had always been close. But the bottom line was Ethan was in charge and it was Ethan who would make the final call about the direction their company would take. And Gabriel was just going to have to find a way to live with that.

Standing up, he faced his brother. "Reality is, Gabe, we sold thirty-one *million* pounds of chocolate last year. The company is doing fine. We don't need to take risks."

"Damn it, Ethan, taking risks is how our great-grandfather started this company in the first place."

"True. Joshua Hart started the business," Ethan said tightly. "And each generation has kept our reputation a sterling one. We're one of the top five chocolate companies in the world. Why in the hell would I want to take risks now?"

"To be number *one*," Gabriel snapped. Clearly frustrated, he shoved a hand through his black hair. "Times change, Ethan. Tastes change. We can keep making the same great chocolate *and* we can add to our lists. Bring in new tastes and textures. Attract different customers, younger customers who'll stick with us for decades."

Ethan looked at his brother and felt twin tugs of affection and irritation. It had always been like this between them. Ethan had been looking out for his younger brother most of their lives. Gabriel was the wild one. The one who wanted to try new things, see new places. He was a risk taker and Ethan had rescued him from more than one escapade over the years. And that was fine, Ethan supposed, until it came to business. There, Ethan wasn't going to buck traditions that had built his family company into a worldwide giant.

"You want to start your own company," Ethan said softly, "and sell oregano chocolate or whatever, help yourself. Heart Chocolates will remain at the top of its game by giving our customers exactly what they want and expect from us."

"Very safe," Gabriel muttered, shaking his head. "And boring."

Ethan snorted. "Success is *boring*? We do what works, Gabe. We always have."

Gabe slapped both hands down on Ethan's desk and leaned in. "I'm a part of this company, Ethan. We're brothers. This is *our* family business. Dad left it to both of us. And I want a say in how it runs."

"You get a say," Ethan said, as irritation simmered even hotter, becoming a ball of anger in the pit of his stomach.

"And you get the final vote."

"Damn straight I do. The company was left to both of us, but I'm in charge." Ethan met his brother's gaze and tried to ease the hot knot of fury that settled inside him. He understood what was driving Gabriel. His younger brother wanted to make his mark on the family company. But that didn't mean Ethan was going to gamble everything they'd built on his brother's risky ideas.

Yes. They could introduce new flavors, new types of chocolates with strange fillings and flavors that bucked every traditional norm. But their current customers wouldn't be interested—they knew what they wanted and counted on Heart Chocolates to provide it.

"Never let me forget that, do you?" Gabriel pushed off the desk, then stuffed his hands into his pockets.

"Look, Gabe, I get what you're trying to do, but it's my responsibility to protect the reputation we've spent generations building."

"You think I'm trying to wreck it?" Gabe stared at him, astonished.

"No. You're just not considering all the angles of this idea." Ethan's patience was so strained now he felt as if he were holding on to the last remaining threads of a rope from which he was dangling over the edge of a cliff. So he tried a different tactic. "Introducing a new line of chocolates, hoping to reel in new customers, would require a huge publicity campaign well beyond what we already have in place."

"Pam says the campaign could be run within the plan that we're already using."

One of Ethan's eyebrows lifted. "Pam, huh? Who's she?"

Gabriel took a deep breath and looked as though he regretted letting that name slip. "Pam Cassini," he said. "She's smart as hell. She's setting up her own PR firm and she's got some great ideas."

"And you're sleeping with her," Ethan added for

him. Did this explain Gabriel's latest attempt to change things up? Was his new girlfriend behind it all?

"What's that got to do with anything?"

Before he could answer, Ethan heard a brisk knock on the door, then it swung open and his assistant, Sadie Matthews, poked her head inside. Her big blue eyes shifted from him to Gabe and back again before she asked, "War over?"

"Not even close," Gabriel said.

Ethan scowled at him. "What is it, Sadie?"

"The shouts are starting to drift out onto the floor," she said, stepping into the room and closing the door behind her.

For just a second, Ethan took a long, hard look at her.

Sadie had been his executive assistant for five years. Tall, she had short, curly blond hair, dark blue eyes and it seemed to him that a smile was always tugging at her mouth. She was efficient, beautiful, smart, sexy, and completely off-limits. Over the years, he'd actually had to train himself to not react to her as he would if she didn't work for him. It wasn't easy. Hell, one look at her curves would bring any red-blooded man to his knees.

Her mouth was a temptation and that spark of barely restrained rebellion in her eyes had always intrigued him. Early on, he'd even considered firing her just so he could try for a taste. But she was too damn good at her job.

Walking toward his desk, she said, "I actually heard a couple people placing bets on which one of you would win this round."

"Who?" Ethan demanded with another hard look at his brother.

She looked surprised at the question and shook her head. "I'm not going to tell you."

"What the hell, Sadie…"

She ignored him and looked at Gabriel. "The new distributor is waiting in your office for that meeting you have scheduled. If you'd rather, I could tell him you're in a heated battle with your brother…"

Gabriel gritted his teeth, but nodded. "Fine. I'll go." He looked at his brother. "But this isn't over, Ethan."

"Never thought it was," he said with a sigh.

When Gabriel was gone, Ethan asked, "Did you bet on me?"

She grinned. "How do you know I placed a bet?"

"You're too smart *not* to bet on me."

"Wow, a compliment for me and a pat on your own back all at the same time. Impressive."

"Is the distributor really in Gabe's office or did you do that just to break up the war?"

"Oh, he's really there," she said, walking toward the bank of windows. "But I did want to break up the argument, so I would have made something up if I'd had to."

"He's driving me crazy." Ethan turned and moved to stand beside her at the windows overlooking the Pacific Ocean. January could be cold and gray in Southern California, but winter seas had their own magic. The water was as dark as the sky, with waves rolling relentlessly toward shore. Surfers posed on their boards, waiting for the perfect wave, and a few boats with brightly colored sails skimmed the water's surface. The scene should have calmed him—it usually did. But this thing with Gabriel was getting more irritating every time it came up.

"He still wants to make some changes to the chocolate line, doesn't he."

Ethan glanced at Sadie. "And now he's got some woman helping him wage his campaign."

"It's not a completely crazy idea," she said with a shrug.

He stared at her. "Not you, too."

Sadie shrugged again. "Change isn't always a bad thing, Ethan."

"In my experience, it is," he argued. He took her shoulders, ignored the leap of heat inside, then turned her to face him. Once she was, he released her and stepped back before saying, "People always talk about changing their lives. New car, new house, new hair color, hell, new beliefs. Well, there's something to be said for stasis. For finding what works and sticking with it."

"Okay, but sometimes change is the only route left open to you."

"Not this time," he muttered. Turning his back on her and the view, he headed to his desk, sat down and reached for the latest marketing report. He gave her a quick glance. "Sadie, if you're going to side with Gabriel on this, I don't want to hear it. I'm not in the mood to have another argument for change."

"Right. Well, we all have to do things we don't want to do."

"What?" He looked up at her.

She blew out a breath and handed him a single sheet of paper. "I'm quitting my job."

"You can't quit. We have a meeting in twenty minutes."

"And yet…"

Ethan just stared at her, not really sure he'd heard her correctly. This was coming out of the blue and made absolutely no sense. "No, you're not."

She waved the paper. "Read the letter, Ethan."

He snatched it from her and skimmed the neatly typed lines. "This is ridiculous." He held it out to her. "I'm not accepting this."

Sadie put her hands behind her back so she wouldn't be at all tempted to take the letter and pretend none of this had happened. Oh, she had known quitting was going to be hard. Had known that Ethan would fight her on this, and she was a little worried he might convince her to stay. Because she didn't really want to leave Heart Chocolates.

But, she reminded herself, she really didn't want to spend the next five years of her life as she'd spent the previous five. Hopelessly in love with a boss who saw her as nothing more than an efficient piece of office furniture.

"You can't quit," he argued. When she refused to take back her letter of resignation, he tossed it face-down onto his desk, as if he couldn't bring himself to even see it again. "We've got the spring campaign to finalize, the rehab at the factory—"

"And all of it will get done without me," Sadie said, and hoped he didn't hear the nearly wistful tone in her voice.

"Why?" he demanded, scowling at her. "Is this about a raise? Fine. You have it."

"It's not about money, Ethan," she said tightly. She already made more money than she would at any other job. Ethan was generous with his employees. That wasn't the issue at all.

He stood up. "All right, an extra two weeks of vacation a year, *plus* the raise."

She laughed at the idea and suddenly relaxed her guard. Really, for being such a good boss, he was also completely clueless sometimes. "Ethan, I don't take my vacation *now*. What good is two more weeks to me?"

"You're being unreasonable."

"I'm being pragmatic."

"I disagree."

"I'm sorry about that," she said, and she really was. Sadie didn't *want* to leave. Didn't *want* to never see him again. In fact, that thought opened up a dark, empty pit in the bottom of her stomach. Which told her she simply had no other choice.

"Then what's this about?"

"I want a life," she said, and hated how desperate those four words sounded.

But she'd spent the last eight years of her life working for *Heart* chocolates, the last five of which she'd been Ethan's assistant. She worked outrageous hours, hardly ever saw her family, and the houseplants in the condo she'd purchased the year before were dried-out sticks because she was never there often enough to water them.

She wanted romance. Sex. Maybe a family of her own before she was too old to get any of that.

"You have a life," he said, clearly affronted at the accusation that he'd somehow cheated her. "You're integral to this business. To *me*."

If only.

The real problem here was that she'd been in love

with Ethan for years now. It was empty, completely one-sided and guaranteed to leave her a bitter old woman one day. Nope. For her own sake, she had to quit.

Shaking her head, she said, "That's work, Ethan, and there's more to life than work."

"Not that I've noticed," he complained.

"That's part of the problem," she argued. "Don't you get it? We work hideously long hours, come in on weekends, and last year you even called me in from my cousin's wedding to help you cover that mix-up with the Mother's Day shipment."

"It was important," he reminded her.

"So was Megan's wedding," she told him, shaking her head. "No, I have to do this. It's time for a change."

"Change again," he muttered, standing up and coming around the desk to stop right in front of her. "I'm really getting sick of that word."

"Change isn't always bad."

"Or good," he pointed out. "When things are working, why screw it up?"

"I knew you'd hate this and maybe it was bad timing coming in to talk to you right after your latest battle with Gabe. But yes. I need a change." She stared up into his grass-green eyes and felt a pang of regret that she was leaving. His dark brown hair was mussed, no doubt because he'd been stabbing his fingers through it again while arguing with Gabe. His tie was loosened and that alone was so damn sexy, her breath caught in her throat.

What was it about this man that hit her on so many levels? It wasn't just how gorgeous he was or the way he made her yearn with just a glance. He was strong and smart and tough and the combination was a constant temptation to her. So resigning was really her only choice.

How could she want him so badly and stay in a position that guaranteed she'd never have him?

"Damn it, Sadie what is it you want changed, exactly?"

"My *life*," she said, looking up into his eyes and willing him to see *her*, not just his always professional assistant. But he never would. She was like the fax machine or a new computer. There to do a job. "Do you know my brother, Mike, and his wife, Gina, just had their *third* baby?"

Confusion shone in his eyes. "So? What's that got to do with you?"

"Mike's wife is two years younger than me." She threw her hands up in disgust. "She has three kids. I have four dead plants."

"What the hell does *that* mean?"

She sighed a little. She'd known going in that quitting wouldn't be easy. That Ethan would try to keep her by offering raises, promotions, vacations. But she hadn't realized how hard it would be to tell him what was bothering her. What was driving her to leave. Heck, she'd only recently figured it out for herself.

"I want a family, Ethan. I want a man to love me…" *You*, her brain whispered, but she shut that inner voice down fast. "I want kids, Ethan. I'm almost thirty."

"Seriously?" He pushed the edges of his jacket back and stuffed both hands into his pants pockets. "That's what this is about? A biological clock moment?"

"Not just a moment," she told him. "I've been thinking about this for a while. Ethan, we work fifteen-hour days, sometimes more. I haven't been on a date in for-ever and haven't had *sex* in three *years*."

He blinked.

She winced. Okay, she hadn't meant to tell him that. Bad enough that *Sadie* knew the pitiful truth. Down-right embarrassing for Ethan to know it. "My point is, I don't want to look back when I'm old and gray and all alone—except for a cat and I don't even like cats—and have the only thing I can say about my life be, *Boy, I really was a good assistant. Kept that office running smoothly, didn't I?*"

"Doesn't sound like a bad thing."

Exasperated, Sadie stabbed her index finger at him. "That's because *you* don't have a life, either." Yes, it had been forever since she'd been with anyone. But he was no better. "You bury yourself in your work. You never talk to anyone but me or Gabe. You own a damn mansion in Dana Point, but you're never there. You eat takeout at your desk and pour everything you have into charts and ledgers, and that's not healthy."

One dark eyebrow arched. "Thanks very much."

Sadie took a step back, mostly because standing so close to him was hard on her nerve endings. He smelled good. His jaw was tight, his eyes flashing and he looked...too tempting. Not for the first time, she wondered what would happen if she threw herself at his chest and wrapped her arms around his neck. Would he hold her back? Kiss her senseless?

Or would he be horrified and toss her to one side?

Since she was quitting, she could easily find out the answers. But the truth was, she wasn't sure she wanted to know. Sometimes a really good fantasy was way bet-ter than reality.

"This isn't about me and my life," he pointed out.

"In a way it is," she said. "Maybe if you hire an assistant who insists on a nine-to-five schedule, you'll get out of this office once in a while."

"Fine." He jumped on her statement. "You want nine to five, we can do that."

Sadie laughed. "No, we can't. Remember Megan's wedding?" Her cousin had been hurt that Sadie had slipped out of the chapel and missed the whole thing. And Sadie hadn't liked it, either. "I'm really sorry, Ethan, but I have to quit. I'll stay for two weeks, train a replacement."

"Who?" He crossed his arms over his chest and dared her with his eyes to come up with a suitable replacement.

"Vicki in Marketing."

"You're kidding."

"What's wrong with her?"

"She *hums*. Constantly."

Okay, she had to give him that one. He wasn't the only one to complain about Vicki. Worse, Sadie was pretty sure the woman was tone deaf. "Fine. Beth in Payroll."

"No." He shook his head. "Her perfume is an assault on the senses."

Typical, she thought. Of course he would find something wrong with everyone she suggested. He might be young, gorgeous and a sex-on-a-stick walking fantasy, but he had the resistance to change of a ninety-year-old.

Good thing she'd been prepared for this. "How about Rick? He's been working here for two years. He knows the business."

If anything, his jaw got tighter. "Rick agrees with

Gabriel. I'm not going to spend every day arguing with my assistant."

True. So it came down to this. To *him* suggesting her replacement. "Who do you suggest, then?"

"You." He was frowning and somehow that only made him look sexier.

What was *wrong* with her?

"We're a team, Sadie. A good one. Why break that up?"

Though she loved the fact that he didn't want her to leave, she knew she had to go for her own peace of mind. How could she ever look for love somewhere else when she was too wrapped up in Ethan Hart? God, how pitiful did that sound?

"I'll find someone," she said firmly.

He didn't look happy at that, but he jerked a nod. "And you agree not to leave until a replacement is trained."

She narrowed her eyes on him, because she saw the trap. If he never agreed to a replacement, she'd never get that person trained and thus, never leave. "And you agree to accept the replacement."

He shrugged. "If this nameless person can do the job, of course."

"You sound so reasonable." Sadie tipped her head to one side and watched him closely. "Why don't I believe you?"

"Suspicious nature?"

His eyes flashed and her insides skittered in response. Seriously, from the moment she'd taken this job with Ethan Hart, Sadie had been half in love with him. And over the years, she'd taken the full-on tumble. She still wasn't sure why. Ethan wasn't anywhere near her ideal man.

She'd put a lot of time and thought into what she wanted. Yes, Ethan was gorgeous. Really way *too* handsome. Women were always tripping over themselves trying to get close to him. Yes, he was successful, but he was driven by his work to the exclusion of everything else in his life. She didn't know if he liked children because he was never around any. She didn't know if he was an amazing lover—though she'd had quite a few dreams in which he was the ultimate sex god. He had a sense of humor but he didn't use it often, and he was entirely too spoiled. Too used to getting his own way.

No, Ethan Hart was not the man for her and if she ever hoped to find that elusive lover, then she had to leave this job.

"I have reason to be suspicious," she said.

"Why would I lie?" he asked, feigning astonishment at the very idea.

"To get what you want."

"You know me so well, Sadie," he said, shaking his head. "Just one more reason why we make a good team."

They really did. Damn it. She hated having to leave and couldn't stand staying.

"Ethan, I'm serious," she said, lifting her chin and meeting his gaze squarely. "I'm quitting."

He looked at her for a long, silent minute. "Fine."

Just like that, his walls went up and his eyes went blank. "Wow, you're good at that."

"What?"

"Going from hot to cold in a blink."

"I don't know what you're talking about."

"Of course you do," Sadie said, staring into those beautiful eyes of his. "It's your signature move. Whenever a conversation or a negotiation starts going in a direction you don't approve of, up come the defenses. And now that I've officially resigned, I can tell you that I don't like it when you do it."

He frowned. "Is that right?"

"Yes." Sadie planted both hands on her hips. "You know, it's pretty great being able to just say what I'm thinking."

"I've never known you not to," he pointed out.

"Oh," she said with a laugh, "you have *no* idea the restraint I've shown over the years. Well, until now."

Those grass-green eyes narrowed on her. "Feeling pretty sure of yourself now, are you?"

"I'm always sure of myself, I just don't usually tell you everything I'm thinking. I have to admit," she added, "this is very freeing." Sure, she'd miss her job. And she'd *really* miss Ethan. But this was the best thing for her, and since she had to leave anyway, she was going to allow herself to enjoy her last two weeks with him. She'd be completely honest and hold nothing back. *Well, she wasn't about to admit she loved him or anything, but other than that...* "Also, I hate your coffee."

Now he looked insulted. "That's the world's finest Sumatra blend. I have a supply flown in every two months."

"Yes, and it's awful. It tastes like the finest Sumatran dirt."

"I don't think I care for this new blunt honesty policy."

Sadie grinned. She'd surprised him, something that was nearly impossible to do because Ethan Hart was always thinking two or three steps ahead of everyone else in the world. "Well, I think I like it."

"I could just fire you and be done with it," he warned.

"Oh, we both know you won't do that. You don't like change, remember?" She shook her head. If nothing else, she was completely confident in saying, "Never going to happen."

When a knock at the door sounded, they both turned and Ethan ordered, "Come in."

She was going to miss that bark of command.

"Mr. Hart? Ethan Hart?" A woman walked into the room carrying a baby that looked about six months old.

Instantly, Sadie's heart melted. The tiny girl was beautiful, with big brown eyes and wispy, black hair. She was chewing on her fist as the woman holding her crossed the room.

"Yes, I'm Ethan Hart. And you are?" The icy king-of-the-universe tone was back in his voice.

"Melissa Gable." She swung a black diaper bag off her shoulder and dropped it onto the visitor's chair. Digging into it one-handed, she came up with a manila envelope and handed it to Ethan. "I'm from Child Services. I'm here to deliver Emma Baker to you."

"Who's Emma Baker?" he asked warily.

"She is." And Ms. Gable handed the baby to Ethan.

Two

Not too long after his argument with Ethan, Gabriel was at his girlfriend Pam Cassini's house and his frustration felt as if it had a life of its own.

After the futile meeting with his brother, he'd hated walking back to his office, knowing everyone there had heard the argument and had known he'd lost. Gabe hated that Ethan wouldn't listen to reason and he hated having been born second. If Gabe had been the older brother, things at Heart Chocolates would be done differently.

"Instead," he mumbled, "I'll always be the little brother."

The junior partner, forced to fight for every scrap of recognition. Maybe he should have just gone home to the penthouse apartment he kept in Huntington Beach. He rented out half the top floor of the best hotel in the city and enjoyed the views and the convenience of twenty-four-hour room service and housekeeping.

Today he was in a foul mood, so he should have gone off by himself. But he didn't want to be alone, either.

"Oh hell, just admit it. You wanted to see Pam. Talk to her."

In the last six months, Pam Cassini had become more important to him than Gabriel was comfortable admitting. He hadn't been looking for any long-term relationship when he met her. And maybe that's why he'd fallen into one. He was no stranger to women wanting to hook up with one of the Hart brothers. But Pam was different. She was strong and smart and ambitious. She had her own career and she was as passionate about it as he was about his. He admired that.

Pam's tiny condo on a quiet street in Seal Beach was warm, welcoming, even to its bright yellow door flanked by terra-cotta pots filled with cheerful splashes of pink and white flowers. You could fit the whole damn place inside his apartment twice over, but there was something here his own place lacked. Pam.

He knocked and stalked the small porch while he waited. When she opened the door, Gabe blurted out, "My brother has a head like concrete."

Pam sighed, gave him a sympathetic look and opened the door wider. As Gabriel stomped past her, she asked, "He's still not willing to try a new line?"

He walked right into the living room and stopped in front of her small, white-brick gas fireplace, hissing with a few flames dancing over artificial logs. "He reacted like a vampire to garlic."

Shaking his head, Gabe turned around to face her in the narrow living room. He hardly noticed the comfortable furniture or the fresh coffee scenting the air. But as she walked toward him, even his fury with Ethan couldn't keep him from taking a moment to simply enjoy the view of *her*.

Pam was short, with a lush and curvy body that drove Gabe mad with hunger. Today she wore a tight, white T-shirt that clung to her breasts, and a pair of black yoga pants that defined every line of her butt, hips and legs. Her feet were bare and her toes were painted a deep scarlet.

She also had long black hair, the warmest brown eyes he'd ever seen and a wide, full mouth that had tempted him from the moment he first met her, more than six months ago. That was at a chocolate convention. He'd been there representing Heart Chocolates, of course, and Pam was handing out cards for her burgeoning PR business.

They'd had dinner that night, and by the end of the week they were inseparable. They'd been together ever since. In that short amount of time, Pam had become a kind of touchstone to him. She listened to his plans, liked his ideas and encouraged him to stand up to Ethan and fight for his own plans and ambitions. For all the good it was doing him.

She put one hand on his arm and looked up at him. "Trying to convince Ethan to change his mind isn't working. I told you, Gabe, all we really need is the chocolate recipe."

She'd been saying that for weeks now, and still Gabe hesitated. A chocolate recipe was sacred to a chocolatier. As ridiculous as it sounded, there actually were corporate spies out there, eager to steal a competitor's recipe. They could use it themselves, sell it, post it online or simply find a way to ruin it.

The Hart family had guarded their basic recipe for generations, just like every other chocolatier. And Gabe was hesitant to be the first member of the Hart family to trust an outsider with it.

"Think about it, Gabe," Pam was saying. "I know a great chocolate chef we can trust. With the recipe, we can have my guy make up samples of the new flavors and present them to Ethan as a done deal. Once he's tasted them, he'll see you're right and he'll jump on board."

A nice fantasy, Gabriel conceded, but hardly based in reality. He snorted. "You don't know Ethan."

"But I know you," she said softly, her voice dropping to the deep, breathless, sultry tone that always drove him crazy. "You're determined and when you believe in something, you just never quit. You don't give up, Gabe. You get what you go after. You got me, didn't you?"

In spite of everything, he smiled. How could he not, with this gorgeous woman looking up at him with hunger in her eyes? "We got each other."

"Ooh, good answer." Pam licked her lips, gave him a slow smile as she wrapped her arms around his neck and laid that luscious mouth over his. He went hard as stone instantly and gave himself up to the need she quickened inside him. He'd never known a fire like he felt with her. And a part of him wondered just how long that fire could last.

Then he stopped thinking entirely. Frustration, anger, everything else in the world simply faded away at the touch of her mouth to his. And as they moved together, in a rhythm that seared his blood and stole his breath, he knew there was nowhere else he wanted to be.

"Um," Sadie said, looking at the baby in Ethan's arms. "Is there anything you want to tell me?"

"It's not mine, if that's what you mean." He glared at her. He'd always been careful. He had no children and didn't plan on any. "I think I'd know if I'd made a baby. Besides, you just told me I don't have a life. How could it be mine?"

Sadie sighed. "First, not an 'it'. It's a girl."

"Fine. *She's* not mine."

"She is now," Sadie reminded him. Glancing through the paperwork the social worker had left behind, she said, "Bill and Maggie Baker were her parents. Ring a bell?"

He frowned and then frowned deeper when the baby kicked impossibly small legs, screwed up her face and let out a howl a werewolf would have been proud of. "What's wrong with it?"

"Being called *it*, probably," Sadie muttered, and snatched the baby from him. Positioning her on one hip, Sadie bounced and swayed in place until the child stopped crying.

Ethan took a step back just for good measure. The damn social worker had done her job. She'd handed off the baby, a car seat and a diaper bag, then left so quickly he hadn't had time to argue about anything. But he was ready to now. He couldn't take care of a damn baby. The idea was ludicrous. Who would have made *him* a guardian? Ethan had never been around a baby. He didn't even own a dog.

Baker. Bill Baker. Why did that sound familiar?

Ethan glanced at Sadie and, in spite of the situation, felt a hot rush of heat jolt through his system and settle in his groin. He'd worked with this woman for five years and he'd been fighting his instincts about her for every second of that time. It hadn't gotten any easier.

Hell, there she was, holding an infant and he *still* burned for her. She smiled at the baby, then kissed her forehead, and Ethan's belly jumped. He wanted her badly, and now that she'd resigned, he could have finally made a move on her. But if he did that and then was able to coax her into not quitting her job, after all, there'd be nothing but complications. So no move. He gritted his teeth, hissed in a breath and wished to hell for a cold shower.

Deliberately pushing thoughts of hot, steamy, incredible sex out of his mind, he went back to "Baker. Why do I know that name?" Then it hit him. Ethan stared at the baby, then Sadie. "Hell. I did know him. In college. We were roommates, for God's sake." As more of the past rushed into his mind, Ethan cursed under his breath and slapped one hand down on his desk. "We made a deal. A stupid deal."

"Involving children, I'm guessing."

"Funny." He glared at her, noticed the child watching him through wide, watery eyes, and looked away quickly. What was that ribbon of panic? Nothing scared him. But one look at that child and he was ready to run for the hills. That realization was humiliating.

"Yes," he said tightly, as memories crowded his mind. "It did involve children, obviously. Bill didn't have family. He and Maggie were engaged and she had been a foster child herself, so no family there, either. He asked me to be legal guardian to his kids if anything ever happened to him."

"And you did it?" The surprise in Sadie's voice jabbed at him.

The fact that he now regretted what he'd done so long ago didn't come into it. Instead, he was insulted that Sadie was incredulous that he would offer to help a friend. Did she really think so little of him? And because he *was* regretting it, Ethan had to ask himself if she wasn't right. Irritating.

"He was my friend." Offended at her tone, and the insinuation, he snapped, "I was twenty. Of course I agreed." Looking back now, faced with the consequences of that promise, Ethan couldn't believe he'd agreed. But in his defense, he added, "I never thought anything would come of it. At that age, you pretty much think you're immortal, anyway. Hell, he's the same age I am. Who would expect him to die?"

"Certainly not him, I think," Sadie said, skimming the paperwork again. "They were on a road trip to Colorado. The car went off the road, hit a tree. The authorities believe Bill fell asleep driving. Bill and Maggie were killed instantly." She turned to look at the baby. "It's a miracle she didn't die, too."

"Miracle." He pulled in a breath and blew it out again. From where he was standing the baby's survival looked like a damn tragedy. She'd lost both her parents in a blink and now found herself with a stranger who didn't have the first clue what to do with her. "What the hell am I supposed to do now?"

Sadie gave him a quizzical look, as if she couldn't believe he'd even asked the question. "You raise her."

"You say that like it's so simple."

"Ethan," Sadie said patiently, "she doesn't have any-one else. She needs you."

Well, that didn't sound good. He didn't want to be needed. Hell, he'd gone out of his way all these years to *avoid* any kind of connection with anyone. Except for his all-too-brief marriage. But that had turned out to be an excellent life lesson. Ethan had learned that he sucked at being a husband. He simply wasn't the *hearth and home* kind of man.

"You just told me I don't have a life," Ethan argued fiercely. "How am I supposed to give her one?"

At his rising voice, the baby started whimpering and Sadie rocked her a little more firmly. "I guess you're going to have to make some changes, Ethan."

There was that word again. Change usually screwed everything up. He liked his life just the way it was. He worked hard to keep his life unencumbered, rolling along on an expected road. And now...change.

Shaking his head, he backed up farther, as if he could actually maneuver his way out of this. And even as he argued for it, Ethan knew he couldn't. Stupidly or not, he'd made a promise, and when he gave his word he damn well kept it. When the blind panic lifted enough that he could begin to think clearly again, he said, "I don't need a life. I need a nanny."

"Oh, Ethan."

"What else should I do?" he demanded. "Get *mar-ried*? No. A nanny is the answer. All I have to do is find the right person. Someone qualified—" He broke off, checked his watch. "We're supposed to be in a meeting on the Donatello acquisition right now."

"Yes, well, we can't be." She looked at the baby as if to remind him of the hell his life had suddenly become.

"I can tell you that Richard Donatello hasn't changed his mind about selling out to you."

"He will," Ethan said. "You could take care of her while I handle business."

"No." Sadie shook her head firmly. "I'm not your babysitter, I'm your assistant. Plus, I just quit, remember?"

"I remember you gave two weeks' notice. So you're still on the payroll."

"As an assistant."

"So assist me!" That came out as a desperate shout and he hated it. So did the baby. She started howling again and Ethan winced.

"Shh, shh," Sadie whispered, bouncing the baby and patting her back. Firing Ethan a hard look, she said, "Cancel the meeting, Ethan."

Damn it. She was right. The meeting had to wait. Fine. Meeting canceled. Sadie quits. Baby arrives. *Change is not good*, he reminded himself. And sometimes you simply had no choice but to adjust. Still, he told himself as something occurred to him, that didn't mean he couldn't help himself out. At least, temporarily. Before he could think better of it, Ethan blurted out, "I'll pay you one hundred thousand dollars if you stay for an extra month."

"What?" Her eyes went wide and her jaw dropped.

Of course he'd surprised her. Hell, he'd surprised himself. "A hundred thousand dollars," he repeated, then added, "on the condition you help me with…" He waved one hand at the baby.

"Her name is Emma," Sadie said wryly.

"Good. You already know that, so you're ahead of

the game." Nodding to himself at the brilliance of his solution, he demanded, "Well? What do you say?"

"I think you're crazy," Sadie said. "But yes, I'll stay for a month. Help you find a nanny."

"And help me take care of it until then."

"Her."

"Right. *Her.*" He reached for his phone, punched a couple buttons and waited for a second. "Kelly. Tell the team the meeting's postponed until tomorrow. Something's…" he looked at Sadie and the baby "…come up." Huge understatement.

When he hung up, he looked at Sadie and deliberately shoved his hands into his slacks pockets so he couldn't be forced to hold the baby again. "Call Alice at the house, tell her what's happened. Have her get a room ready for the kid—order whatever she needs and offer a big cash bonus for quick delivery and setup."

"Ethan—"

"You still work for me, Sadie. Get it done." Then he walked to his desk, sat down and started working. He avoided looking at Sadie again and told himself it was for the best. Hell, the baby wouldn't want to be held by him, anyway.

A few hours later, Sadie and Ethan, along with the baby, were at Target, staring at a wall of baby supplies.

"How does anyone know what to get?" he asked of no one in particular.

"Well, here I've got a little experience," Sadie admitted. "On those rare Sundays off, I've been shopping with Gina, my sister-in-law."

"You're elected as guide, then."

Sadie noticed that he looked completely out of place

in the perpetually crowded store. In his elegantly cut suit, he would have been much more at home in his meeting, or in a five-star restaurant, or even just sitting in his sleek black convertible. But here in Target, Ethan Hart was enough out of the ordinary that every woman who passed him paused to stare. Of course, that happened everywhere. The man practically oozed sex and success.

But at the moment, he was devoting himself to staying as far away from the big red cart and the baby strapped into it as humanly possible. Sadie gritted her teeth. She'd promised to *help* him with the baby, not do everything herself. Not even for a hundred-thousand-dollar bonus. This was Ethan's chance to step outside the carefully built path he'd designed for himself, and Sadie wanted to see him do it. But now wasn't the time for that argument. Pretty soon, the baby would be hungry. Or wet again. Or tired. Sadie would rather avoid the inevitable meltdown that she'd witnessed with her infant nephew just a couple weeks ago.

"Okay," she said abruptly. "First, we need diapers."

"Right." Ethan instantly turned to the task at hand. "But what size? There's a million of them." He scanned the shelves, looking like a blind man trying to feel his way through a forest.

"You held her. How much do you think she weighs?"

He pushed one hand through his hair. "Twenty pounds?"

"Okay," she said. "Start there. I'll get some formula and bottles and...*everything*."

Yes, she'd been shopping with Gina, stocking up on baby supplies, but that was just adding a few things to an already well-stocked house. *This* was starting from scratch, and she was overwhelmed with deciding what Ethan might need to care for Emma. He was right—there were just too many *things*.

While the baby slapped her hands on the cart and Ethan stayed at the end of the aisle, reading the descriptions on every bag of diapers, Sadie loaded in whatever she thought might be useful. Toys, a stuffed bear that Emma grabbed hold of and refused to release, bottles, bibs, nipples, pacifiers... The cart was pretty much full when Ethan turned and dropped a single package of diapers on top of it.

"One?" she asked, stunned. "Really? You think one package will do it?"

"How the hell do I know? You're the expert here."

"Ooh," Sadie said with a grin. "That had to have been hard for you to say. Ethan Hart, the man who's never wrong and must be obeyed at all costs."

He scowled. "I don't remember you being this sarcastic over the last five years."

"That's because I muttered most of it," she admitted. "Get two more packages to start and that should hold us."

"For what? The apocalypse?" He stared at the cart. "She doesn't really need all of that, does she?"

The baby frowned, as if she understood what Ethan had said and disapproved. Sadie almost laughed, but she was afraid it might sound hysterical, so she swallowed it. Busy shoppers rushed past them as music pumped through the store speakers. "Do you really want to find out in the middle of the night that you need something and you don't have it?"

"Oh, hell no. Fine. We'll take it all." He started to walk away, but Sadie stopped him.

"She needs clothes, too, Ethan."

He goggled at her. "This is incredible. How do people do this?"

"Well, most people don't have to do an entire stock-up run all in one day..."

"Right." He looked over the aisles they had just been picking clean and said, "You know, the chocolate business makes billions, but turns out, that's just peanuts. The *real* money is in baby junk. How can someone who can't even talk possibly need so much stuff?"

She almost felt sorry for him. Almost. This was a huge disruption in the placid lake that was his life. But hey, sink or swim. "It's a mystery. Come on. Baby clothes."

He followed after her, grumbling under his breath, and Sadie looked into Emma's eyes and grinned. In the five years she'd worked for the man, Sadie had never seen Ethan completely out of his element. And it was sort of endearing. She didn't need another reason to be drawn to him, though, so she really tried to dismiss what she was feeling.

Then he did it to her again when he picked up baby pajamas and discarded the penguins in favor of the ones covered in teddy bears. When he caught her looking at him quizzically, he shrugged and tossed the jammies into the cart. Then, pointing at the baby now chewing fiercely on the stuffed bear's ear, he said simply, "She likes bears."

Sadie took a deep breath to still the jolt of her heartbeat. He didn't want the baby, but he was doing everything he could to make sure she was cared for. He didn't like change, but he was so far accepting a huge one in his life. He didn't belong in Target, but here he stood. And God knew he shouldn't look so damn sexy, but there it was. Even as she thought it, she spotted a woman staring at Ethan with open admiration.

Sadie told herself to get past it. Get over it. She was going to leave Ethan behind so she could find the right man for her. No matter how she felt about Ethan, no matter how her blood burned when she looked at him, going after him was a catastrophe waiting to happen.

He wasn't the man for her and trying to pretend otherwise was just setting herself up for a crash. So she busied herself by concentrating on the shopping and promising herself that one day, she'd be doing this for her own family.

The sad part of that dream was Ethan wouldn't be a part of it.

Three

By the time they were finished and checked out, Sadie was stunned by just how much Ethan had bought—and that wasn't even counting the baby furniture ordered and hopefully already delivered to his house. Sadie took Emma in her car while Ethan loaded all the bags and boxes into his. They'd taken both cars so Sadie could leave once he was settled in with his new charge.

With Emma in her car seat, Sadie headed for Dana Point, barely keeping up with Ethan as he hurtled down Pacific Coast Highway. If she hadn't known better, she would have thought he was trying to lose her. But that couldn't be true, because she already knew where he lived.

Sadie had been to Ethan's house before, bringing him papers or running one of the parties he threw for distributors, but today felt different. They weren't there for business and it sort of colored how she looked at the house itself.

It was Spanish-style and gigantic, even by mansion standards. The red tiled roof made the white walls seem even brighter than they normally would have. The grounds, from the sweeping lawns to the flower beds and climbing roses over the pergola in the backyard, were lovingly tended by a team of gardeners and the floor-to-ceiling windows glinted in the winter sunlight. Behind the house, she knew, was a sloping yard that ran down to the cliffs where waves beat a constant rhythm against the rocks.

The view was majestic and the house itself was breathtaking. Every room was huge, open and appealing in an earthy, masculine way. Brown leather furniture and burnished wood decorated every room and the dark red ceramic tiles in the halls were a dramatic statement. Sadie's favorite spot was the Spanish-style, enclosed courtyard. Three sides of the house surrounded an outdoor living area, complete with comfortable furniture, a bar and kitchen. Terra-cotta pots held a wide variety of plants and the area provided a wonderful view of the ocean.

Today, though, she really didn't have the time to luxuriate in the place itself. She had a cranky baby in the backseat and a ton of things to unload.

Ethan came around and opened her car door. The baby chose that moment to scream her fury and Ethan winced. "How does she hit those notes?"

"It's a gift."

"Why don't you take her inside? I'll get the gardener and some of his guys to empty out the cars."

Huffing out a breath, Sadie accused, "You're just trying to avoid touching her, aren't you?"

"See why I hired you?" he countered. "You're smart."

"Right." This did not bode well for Ethan and Emma. If he avoided the baby every chance he got, he'd never adapt to the new situation. Yes, he'd paid Sadie a lot of money to hang around until he got things settled. But she was going to make sure that he did at least half the baby care.

She got the little girl out of the car seat, plopped her on one hip and headed for the front door. Ethan wasn't too far behind her, but when she opened the front door and walked inside, they all stopped dead.

Alice, Ethan's housekeeper, was standing in the entryway, arms folded across her abundant chest and a frown etched deeply into her features. Really, Alice defied stereotypical logic. Looking at her round body and bright blue eyes, most people would have guessed her to be as kind as Mrs. Claus. Nothing could be further from the truth. Sadie had never understood why Ethan kept such an unpleasant woman working for him. It probably helped that he was rarely at home and so wasn't exposed to her much.

Alice's eyes narrowed accusingly on the baby. "I'm the housekeeper," she said flatly. "I don't take care of children."

"Fine," Ethan said, pushing Sadie farther inside so he could step past her.

"I mean it." Alice lifted her chins and sniffed. "I've got my routine and I won't have it upset by an infant."

Sadie had never really liked Alice. No surprise there, since the woman was cold and distant. On those rare occasions when Ethan was here, in his own house, Alice behaved like he was an interloper. Normally, she had the run of the mansion on the cliffs. She was alone here more often than not and Sadie had a feeling it was only Ethan's inherent hatred of change that had kept him from firing the woman.

"I said fine," Ethan repeated. "Fernando and some of his guys are bringing the baby's food and—" he waved a hand to indicate everything else they'd dragged along "—stuff to the kitchen. Did the furniture for her room show up?"

"It did," Alice said, her mouth flattening into a grim line of displeasure. "Those men tracked dirt all over my floors and made a racket for nearly an hour."

Ethan just looked at her. "So her room's ready."

"It is, just don't expect me to clean up after an infant."

Sadie took a breath and clamped her mouth shut to avoid telling Alice exactly what she thought of her. Holding the baby a little closer as if to protect her from the nastiness, she watched Ethan and saw a flash of anger in his eyes. It was a wonder Alice didn't bother to notice it, as well.

"I'm a housekeeper, not a babysitter," Alice said again.

"I heard you the first time," Ethan said, and Sadie heard the warning in his tone.

"As long as you remember it," the woman snapped. "Now, I'll be having my dinner in my kitchen. As I didn't know you'd be home, or bringing along company—" her gaze swept over Sadie and the baby dismissively "—I didn't prepare a meal for you. I'm not a babysitter and I'm not a cook."

"Here's something else you're not," Ethan interrupted. "Employed."

"I beg your pardon?" Alice bleated.

"You should," Ethan retorted, "but I doubt you really are. You're fired. Get your stuff and get out."

"What?" Sadie said.

She couldn't believe this. For years, she'd thought he should get rid of Alice. But to do it today? When everything was already in turmoil? What had happened to "change is bad"?

Alice's whole body stiffened as if someone had shoved a pole down the back of her grim black dress. Clearly indignant, she lifted her chin and glared at Ethan. "I see no reason for this—"

Ethan took a step closer to her and the woman backed up. Alice was in no physical danger and she had to know that, but seeing Ethan's temper was so rare, it was startling when it finally appeared.

"This is my house, Alice. Not yours," he said. "Something you seem to have forgotten over the years."

"I don't know what you mean…"

"Yes, you do." Ethan loomed over her, using his height as an intimidation factor. "Do you really think I haven't noticed that you've crowned yourself queen of *my* house?"

The woman's eyes darted from side to side as if looking for an escape—but she didn't find one.

"I've been willing to put up with your attitude because, frankly, you didn't matter enough to make a change. But that ends now," Ethan told her. "This is *my* house. And I'll run it however the hell I want to run it. And I'll hire someone who's more concerned with her job than she is with pretending she's the lady of the manor."

Alice sputtered and Sadie ducked her head to hide a smile. She really shouldn't be pleased about this, but Alice had had this coming for a long time. Plus, Ethan was the sexiest show she'd ever seen. Anger rippled off him in hot waves, yet he spoke so quietly, so coolly. It was the contrast, really, that was making Sadie feel as if her nerve endings were electrified.

Well, that and the look in his eyes. The man was so hot that smoke should have been lifting off the top of his head. He was definitely her weakness.

"You owe me two weeks' salary," Alice snapped.

"You're right." Ethan started for the stairs, already putting the awful woman in the past. "Leave an address on the entry table and I'll mail you a check and a severance bonus."

"A bonus?" Sadie said quietly, as she followed after him.

"It's worth it," Ethan muttered.

"See?" Sadie countered, her voice as quiet as his. "Like I told you. Not all change is bad."

He shot her a look. "Save it."

By the time they got the baby settled in her room, Ethan was even more on edge. He'd fired his housekeeper, been saddled with a baby and his assistant had resigned.

"Hell of a day," he muttered.

"A long one, anyway," Sadie agreed. "At least the baby's room looks beautiful. Well, except for that beige paint. That should be changed to something a little more girlie."

"I'm not having a pink room in my house," he argued, walking down the stairs behind her. His gaze dropped to the curve of her butt and his hands itched to grab hold and squeeze. Actually, what he really wanted to do was get her out of her work clothes, stretch her out on the floor in front of the fire and explore every square inch of that tidy body.

"I didn't say pink," she said, tossing him a look over her shoulder. "That's a little sexist, don't you think?"

"I didn't know a color *could* be sexist."

"Well," she quipped, "now you do. I was thinking something cheerful, bright. Pale yellow, maybe, or a soft green. With pictures and maybe a mural. Something to stimulate her."

He snorted a laugh. "The way she screamed when you put her in the crib tells me she's already plenty stimulated."

At the bottom of the stairs, Sadie stopped and turned around to look at him. "She's lost her parents, been thrown at people she doesn't know and forced to sleep in a bed she doesn't recognize. I'd like to see how well either of us would handle that situation."

There were actual sparks in her eyes as she glared at him. Ethan held up both hands. "You're right."

Astonishment flashed across her features. "Wow. I'm right. A banner day indeed."

"There's that sarcasm again. What does it say that I'm starting to enjoy it?"

"That you're a glutton for punishment?" She grinned, turned around and marched across the foyer to the front table, which held a massive crystal vase and a fall flower arrangement. She picked up her brown leather bag and slung it over her shoulder.

Suspicion washed over him as he demanded, "What are you doing?"

"I'm going home."

A feeling he didn't want to describe as "panic" washed over him. He glanced down at the baby monitor in his hand as if it were a live grenade. "You can't leave."

"Sure I can." She gave him a smile that punched at his insides. "Don't worry, thanks to that bonus, I'm staying for an extra month, remember? I'll see you tomorrow."

He threw a quick look at the stairs behind him. There was a baby on the second floor and if Sadie left, *he* was the only one here to take care of it. *Her.*

Unacceptable.

How had this happened to him? He, who so carefully regimented the world around him. This morning, his life had been just as he wanted it. A successful business, an efficient assistant, no bumps or twists on a road that lay before him, straight and narrow. And now…everything was a tangled mess and damned if he'd suffer through this alone. "Stay."

"I am."

"No," he said tightly, knowing she was referring to staying on at the office, and helping him find a damn nanny. He meant so much more. "Stay here. At the house."

A flash of something interesting darted across her eyes and was gone again in a blink. "You want me to stay the night?"

"No," he corrected, making sure she understood. "I want you to stay here at the house with me. Help me with that baby until I find a damn nanny or hire a housekeeper who isn't allergic to children."

She laughed a little and shook her head hard enough to send those loose blond curls into a dance around her head. "Not a chance."

Her laughter was both erotic and extremely annoying. Sadie was about to walk out that door, leaving him alone in the house with a child. Cowardly or not, Ethan had no problem acknowledging that he did *not* want to be alone with that baby.

Earlier that day, he'd given Sadie a lot of money to get her to stay an extra month. Maybe all he really needed to do here was offer even more. Hell, money was easy for him—asking for help wasn't.

"I'll pay you fifty thousand dollars extra to move in here temporarily."

"What?" She stared at him.

"You heard me." At least he had her attention. She hadn't left yet, and that was good.

"I did. I just don't believe it."

"Well, believe it." Ethan pushed one hand through his hair briefly. "Look, I don't like admitting this, but when it comes to that baby I'm out of my depth. I need your help."

Her head snapped back and a small smile curved her mouth. At any other time, he would have enjoyed that soft smile.

"You're saying that there's something Ethan Hart can't handle."

He scowled at her. "You're enjoying this, aren't you?"

"A little."

This was new territory for Ethan. He was self-sufficient. In charge. Yet now, an infant had reduced him to admitting his failings. "Fine. Yes. I need your help. So what do you say?"

She tipped her head to one side and her short blond curls fell lazily with the movement. "For fifty thousand dollars, of course I'll stay."

Pleased, but a little surprised that she'd given in so easily, he wondered why money was such a motivator for her. Was there something going on in her life that he didn't know about? "I didn't expect you to agree so quickly. Who knew you were so mercenary?"

She laughed shortly. "Mercenary? That may be how it looks to you, but I've got news for you. Maybe it's not the same for gazillionaires, but the rest of us peons have to make mortgage payments, car payments, buy, you know, *food*. This money will let me take my time finding a new job. Help me get a new car, maybe fix the plumbing in my condo..."

He didn't much care for the "finding a new job" thing, but for the rest, he realized he hadn't taken any interest in Sadie's life before now. He should have. The car she had strapped the baby into was a nearly fifteen-year-old sedan. Why was she driving such an old car? And her condo had plumbing issues? Hell, until today he didn't know she *owned* a condo.

They'd worked together closely for five years and she was a mystery to him. His own fault, he told himself. He'd been so attracted to her that he'd treated her as if she were invisible. He hadn't taken an interest in her because he couldn't *afford* to. Since she'd turned in her resignation a few hours ago, it was as if he were meeting her for the first time.

The desire was there and stronger than ever—but

there was also something new. Damned if he didn't *like* her.

Well he felt like an ass. It didn't happen often, thank God, but Ethan could admit to it when it did. At least to himself. Offering her money had been a last-ditch effort for him to keep her in her job. To keep her here, where she could help him out with that baby. He hadn't even realized how important that money could be to her. He paid his employees well and never really thought about it otherwise. He'd grown up wealthy and intended to stay that way. So when you were used to a lot of money being readily available, you didn't often stop to think that money might be an issue for someone else.

She was still watching him. Waiting. Finally, he said, "Fine. I admit it. You're the hero of the working class and I'm a cold money grubber."

"That sounds about right." She grinned and that smile punched him in the solar plexus so hard he had to fight for air. "I mean, come on. You're paying me a hundred and fifty thousand dollars to help you out for a month. Normal people don't do that."

"Now I'm not normal?"

She laughed again and it irritated him just how much he enjoyed the sound.

"Of course you're not."

"Thanks very much," he muttered darkly.

"I didn't say you were *abnormal*," she said. Digging into her purse, she pulled her keys out and jangled them in her palm. "For example. Most people don't live in mansions."

"I know that."

"Do you?" She tipped her head to one side again and Ethan realized just how often she did that when talking to him. And he also realized how fascinated he was with those loose blond curls and how they moved. He wondered how they would feel sliding across his skin.

"You realize the bonus you offered me today is more than most people make in a year."

He frowned and shook himself out of the distraction of her hair. Focusing, he said, "I'm not completely clueless, Sadie." Then he noticed the car keys in her hand. "Where are you going? You just agreed to stay *here*."

"Not without clothes."

Okay, that short sentence opened up a world of images in his mind. Sadie, walking through his house naked. Sadie in the shower, water sliding down her skin. Sadie stretched out across his bed, holding her arms up to him. Sadie beneath him, crying out his name as he slammed his body into hers.

Ethan swallowed hard, took a breath and blew it out again. Man, once he'd unleashed all the sexual thoughts about her he'd been suppressing for years, they were almost too much to take. He came back to the present in time to see her headed for the door. She paused and looked back over her shoulder. "I'm going home to pack a bag. I'll be back."

He couldn't stop himself from shooting a worried glance at the staircase that led to the ticking time bomb upstairs. Shifting his gaze back to Sadie's, he said, "An extra twenty-five thousand if you make it back before she wakes up and starts screaming again."

"Stop throwing money at me." She laughed and the sound bubbled through his bloodstream like champagne. "You're really off your game, aren't you?"

"Will it get you back here fast if I say yes?"

"Relax. I'll be back in an hour or so." She opened

the door, stepped onto the porch, then added, "Emma's not going to kill you, Ethan."

When she left, closing the door behind her, Ethan muttered, "Don't bet on it."

"I'm still not sure about this."

Gabriel stood outside the Heart Chocolates offices and looked up at the building as if he'd never seen it before. He'd done a lot of thinking about this plan and he was still torn about what to do.

Not surprising, really. He was a Hart, after all, even if he was the younger brother. He'd grown up with the same family stories Ethan had heard. He'd been taught to respect what had come before and build on the traditions already set in stone.

But wasn't that what he was trying to do? Build on what had been left to them? If they went Ethan's route, they would continue to be successful—at least in the short term. But if they didn't grow and build on what had been left in their care, would they be doing justice to the great-grandfather who had started it all?

Behind him, on Pacific Coast Highway, traffic whizzed past in a never-ending stream. He turned to watch the life pulsing on the street and the cold, January wind slapped his face. Winter nights came early, but that didn't mean people avoided coming to the beach. Out on the sand tonight there would be flames dancing in fire pits, barbecues and music pumping into the night.

When he was a kid, he'd been a member of the never-ending party at the beach. But right here, right now, all Gabe could think about was what he was about to do.

For generations, his family had guarded their chocolate recipe like the Holy Grail. Was he really willing to be the first Hart to share that recipe with an outsider?

"Gabe…" Pam took his hand and gave it a squeeze, as if she could sense his uncertainty. "You're not betraying anyone. You're trying to help. To make a difference."

"Yeah," he mused wryly, "not sure Ethan would see it like that."

"This isn't about Ethan," she said softly. "But honestly, if you don't feel right about this, then don't do it."

He looked down into her brown eyes. The streetlights threw shadows across her face and made her eyes seem even deeper, darker, than they usually were. Gabe held on to her hand like a lifeline. "No, I have to. But trust me, once Ethan finds out what I did. This could tear us so far apart we might never find our way back to each other. And yeah, I know he's a pain in the ass, but he's my brother."

A cold, damp wind rushed past them, lifting Pam's hair into twisting black strands. A rush of heat and something more filled Gabe, and he held on to it, to distract him from what he was about to do. He read the sympathy on her face and held on to that, as well.

He tried to make her understand how he was feeling about all of this. As much as Gabe wanted to try out his ideas, to push his brother into stepping into the twenty-first century, it went against everything he was to sneak into the office and take that recipe. His whole life, he'd been raised with the notion that family was more important than anything. That their family legacy was to be honored. Defended. But essentially, wasn't that what he was trying to do?

Rubbing one hand across his eyes, Gabriel murmured, "You know, Ethan's been the head of the family since our dad died. He's taken care of everything. Put me through college and worked here, running everything by himself until I was ready to come on board."

"And the minute you did, his thumb came down on top of you," she reminded him. "I can't remember how many times you've told me about Ethan squashing your ideas."

Gabe winced. It did feel like that sometimes, but he knew what Ethan dealt with. It wasn't just about maintaining the Hart family legacy… It was dealing with buyers, merchants, marketing, and God knew what else, just to keep moving forward. If Gabe went through with this tonight, what else could it be but a betrayal?

"Maybe I made it sound worse than it is," he mused.

"I know all about family, Gabe. And yes, my brother drives me nuts, too. But really, this comes down to you. You're having second thoughts," Pam said, holding his hand between both of hers.

"And third and fourth," he said, agreeing with her as he took an even longer look at the building that held his family's heritage.

It was brick, which made it stand out in the middle of Newport Beach. Probably not a good idea to build with brick in earthquake country, Gabe silently admitted. But his grandfather had insisted the brick looked sturdy. Dependable. As he wanted their then-fledgling company to be. And Gabe had to admit he must have been onto something because but for a few falling bricks and a couple cracked windows in the last big quake, the building was still standing. Just like the Hart family itself.

But would the family connection survive Gabe going behind Ethan's back to prove a point? And if he didn't go through with this, see his own ideas through, would Gabe eventually resent Ethan enough to destroy their relationship completely?

Questions he wished he had answers to.

"Gabe?" Pam's voice cut into his thoughts and he could have kissed her for it.

"Yeah?"

"You're not doing this *to* Ethan. You're doing it *for* Ethan."

His mouth quirked briefly. He knew damn well his big brother wouldn't see it like that.

She wasn't finished, though. "Like I said before, I understand family loyalty, Gabe. I really do. But sometimes, you have to do what you know is right, whether the family agrees or not. This is your chance to prove something—not just to Ethan, but to yourself."

Pam was right and Gabe knew it, though he wasn't thrilled about it. Still, if he didn't try making up those new flavors, following through on his idea, he'd always regret it. He had to know that he'd done what he could to make his own vision a reality. After all, if *he* didn't have faith in his vision, how could he hope to convince Ethan?

Pam reached up and cupped his cheek in the palm of her hand. "But if you don't want to do this…"

"I really don't," he said, bending down to give her a quick, hard kiss that scrambled his brain cells even as it steadied him. "But I also don't have a choice."

"Are you sure, Gabe?" she asked, biting her bottom lip in a sure sign that she was anxious. "I'll back you either way. You could even wait for a better time. I didn't mean to rush you into this by suggesting we take the recipe to a chocolate chef I know."

"You didn't push me into this," he assured her. "Don't think that. The idea to make up some of the new flavors was a good one. But I'm doing this for me, Pam. If I don't try, I'll never know."

She studied him for a long minute, then nodded. "Okay, then. I'm with you."

"Yeah," he said, smiling. "You really are."

He slung one arm around her shoulders and hugged her tight before steering her toward the glass doors. Gabe already knew Ethan wasn't at the office. His car wasn't in the parking lot, so the coast, as they said in old movies, was clear.

The security guard in the foyer leaped to his feet to unlock the door as Gabriel approached. Once they were inside, the door was closed and locked again. Light streamed down on the gleaming, honey-toned wood floor. The walls were splashed with colorful pictures of their chocolates.

"Evening, Mr. Hart," the guard said. "Didn't expect to see you back here tonight."

"I won't be long, Joe," he said, and guided Pam to the elevator. "Just have to go get something from the office."

"Yes, sir." The older man went back to his desk and wasn't even looking at them when the elevator doors hissed closed.

The office was too quiet. It felt as if they were walking through an upscale abandoned building. Their shoes on the hardwood floors clacked noisily in the stillness. The lights were dimmed and in every shadow, Gabe imagined he could see his great-grandfather and all the other Harts who'd come before him watching with disapproval. But he shook that off and continued into Ethan's office.

The original recipe had, of course, been scanned into the computer and was kept in an encrypted file that only Ethan and Gabriel could access. It was also stored on flash drives kept in several different places, for security's sake. And because he was Ethan, Gabriel's big brother kept the original recipe in a bank box, and a copy of it in a wall safe. He did it because their father had done it that way, too. As if keeping that recipe close would continue the company's growth.

Though it wasn't a plea to the universe for luck. It was more of a family talisman.

And Gabriel was about to set it free.

Four

Sadie was running late, but she stopped at her brother's house, anyway. She told herself it was sort of on the way to Dana Point from her condo in Long Beach, so it wasn't as if she'd gone very far out of her way. Fine, it was *way* out of the way. But the truth was, she just wanted to talk to Gina.

Mike and Gina's house was in a subdivision in Foothill Ranch. The houses were big, but rooms were small. The neighborhoods were laid out in curving, twisting streets and the houses sat practically on the curb. No room for a front yard or a driveway. The backyards were small, too, but the streets were crowded with herds of children. Which was really why her brother and his wife were still in the house they were outgrowing.

Still, every time she turned onto their street, with the cookie-cutter houses lined up like pale beige soldiers, Sadie thought of the opening shots of the old movie *Poltergeist*.

"Hey! Nice surprise!" Gina opened the front door, reached out to hug her, then dragged Sadie into the house. "How did you escape your captor?"

Sadie laughed. Mike and Gina were not big fans of Ethan. "There've been a lot of surprises today. That's why I'm here. Had to talk to you about it."

"Oh, now I'm intrigued." Gina grinned and tucked her shoulder-length black hair behind her ears. She wore faded jeans, one of Mike's long-sleeved white shirts that, on Gina, hung down past her thighs, and she was barefoot. Her daughter was only three weeks old and already Gina looked fabulous. "Come on in, sit by the fire and spill your guts."

"Lovely invitation." Sadie glanced at the stairs. "The kids in bed already?"

"Don't jinx me," Gina warned, holding up one finger to her lips. "I wore the boys out at the park today and the baby's in one of her four-hour sleep jags. So let's take advantage of it. You want some wine?"

"So much." Sadie dropped her purse on the dining room table and followed Gina into the kitchen. Through the wall of windows behind the sink, Sadie looked out at the greenbelt and the yellow lab, Einstein, who was sprawled across the grass, taking a nap.

The house, this place, was cozy. There were toys on the patio, a trampoline in one corner of the yard and tiny sneakers kicked off beside the back door. It was family. It was exactly what Sadie wanted for herself. And finally, she'd set herself on the path toward getting it.

"What's going on?" Gina handed her a glass of wine,

took one for herself, then led the way to the couch lined up in front of a gas fireplace that was hissing merrily.

Sadie told her. All of it. As she talked, she watched Gina's reactions and was glad to see that most of them matched what she'd been feeling herself.

"I don't know what to comment on first," Gina finally said, when Sadie ran down.

"Dealer's choice." Sadie took a long sip, then got up to grab a bag of chips from the pantry.

"Okay, *wow* on the money front. I mean, whether he knows it or not, Ethan just helped you quit."

"I know." Sadie plopped down beside her friend. "I don't think he realizes that yet."

"Eventually he will and he won't be happy." Gina reached out and patted Sadie's hand. "But honey, this is great. You'll be able to take some time before you jump back into another job. And get a new car before the one you have breaks down around you and you're left sitting on the street clutching a steering wheel."

Sad, but true. "That's what I was thinking."

"Plus you won't be held hostage at a chocolate factory anymore, so maybe we could set you up with Mike's friend Josh." Gina grinned and winked at her. "He's really great. Gorgeous. Beautiful eyes, fantastic butt."

"Aren't you married to my brother?"

"Please. Was I struck blind lately?" Gina rolled her eyes. "Anyway, Josh joined the fire department a month ago and Mike really likes him."

Mike was a firefighter, which meant he was gone for four days, then home for four days. Since they all spent so much time together, Mike got to know the guys at his station really well. But this was the first time he and Gina had tried to set Sadie up with one of them.

"Wow. A setup. That's a first."

"Well, come on, what would have been the point before?" Gina shook her head slowly. "You were always working. Why bother setting you up? Heck, you walked out of Megan's wedding for your job."

Sadie winced. "I just reminded Ethan of that today."

Gina curled her legs up under her and leaned back on the couch. "Sweetie, this is your chance to have a life. What're you looking so worried about?"

"Do I?"

"Your forehead's all wrinkled up. You should stop that."

Instinctively Sadie reached up and smoothed her fingers across her brow. "I'm not worried. I'm…" She sighed. "I don't know what I am. It's been a weird day."

"You could say that," Gina said with a laugh. "Resigned, helping take care of a baby, poor little thing, and lots of cash."

"And," Sadie mused, "once I quit, Ethan looked at me differently."

Gina snorted. "You mean he noticed you were female?"

"Exactly." Sophie took another sip of the cold white wine. "It was…exciting."

Gina slapped one hand to her forehead. "Oh, God."

"What?"

"Sadie, the whole point of quitting was so you could find a life, right?" Gina reached out, grabbed her hand and shook it. "Didn't you tell me two weeks ago that you want to find the right guy for you and give up on the fantasy of Ethan?"

God, it was humiliating to have her own words tossed back at her. But this was why she'd come to Gina. To get the truth. Hard as it was to hear. Mike and Gina had the kind of relationship that Sadie wanted for herself. They were partners. They laughed. They fought. They loved and always had each other's back. And Sadie wasn't blind. She'd seen the looks her brother gave his wife when he thought no one was watching.

She wanted to be wanted like that.

"Yeah, I did." Sadie looked down into her wine. "But..."

"Do you still have your list?" Gina asked.

"Of course." Sadie had been working on that list for the last two years.

"How many qualifications are on it now?"

"Five," Sadie said, staring down into her glass. When she first made up the list of what she wanted in a man, there'd been more than twenty items on it. Over time, though, she'd whittled it down to the top five.

"Let's hear them."

Sadie knew what her sister-in-law was up to. She wanted to remind Sadie that Ethan was *not* the man for her. And maybe Gina was right. Today had been fun. Watching Ethan's panic, sharing things outside the job with him. Seeing him fire Alice and take charge of a child he hadn't wanted. It was as if they'd been a team of a different sort today. Not the work thing, where they each knew their roles and acted them out effortlessly.

This had been different. Today they'd been simply Ethan and Sadie. Man and woman. And she'd enjoyed it way too much. So it would probably be a good thing if she reminded *herself* about her list.

"Fine." She ticked them off on her fingers. "Sexy.

Adventurous. Sense of humor. Spending time with me. Loves kids."

"Uh-huh," Gina mused. "And how many of those fit Ethan?"

"Sexy..." Her voice trailed off, because she couldn't say more. "Okay, fine. He's not the man on my list."

"Thank you." Nodding at her, Gina said with some sympathy, "Sadie, I know you're nuts about the man, but you deserve someone to be nuts about *you*."

"Yeah. I know. But—"

"No buts," Gina interrupted, holding up one hand to keep her quiet. "Ethan's not going to give you what you want."

"What if all I want is hot sex?"

Gina laughed and set her glass down. "Who doesn't want that? But it's not *all* you want."

"No, it's not." But oh boy, it was a great idea. Just imagining hot, wild sex with Ethan set off tiny fires inside her. She took a drink of the cold wine, hoping to smooth things out. It didn't work.

"Still, not a bad idea." Gina shrugged and took another sip of her own wine. "If you think it'll help, get the hot sex from Ethan, then when you finally leave your job, you walk with no regrets. No what-if's running through your head. Sadie, it's long past time to look out for yourself."

More heat rushed through Sadie at the thought of hot sex with Ethan. But then, she'd been feeling that rush for five years. Was Gina right? Should she take advantage of her "resigned but still with him" situation? She *really* wanted to. Even if her future wouldn't include the man she'd loved for so long...the present could be pretty great.

"Good," Gina said. "You're thinking about it. And from what I can see, you like the idea. But don't think too long," she warned. "Sometimes you think yourself right out of doing what you want to do."

Sadie fell back against the couch. "It's really annoying that you know me so well."

"That's so sweet."

Sadie laughed just as a baby's wail drifted through the monitor sitting on the coffee table. Gina sighed. "Playtime's over. You sure you don't want to stay here tonight and go rescue Ethan in the morning? Mike's shift won't be over for two more days and I could use the company."

"Tempting," Sadie said, "but Ethan offered me another twenty-five thousand if I made it back before Emma woke up."

Gina's laugh rolled out loud and hard. "The man's really desperate, isn't he? Okay, fine. But once you're really out of a job, your nephews would love to spend some time with you."

"Disneyland trip on me," Sadie promised, then leaned in to give Gina a hug. "Then I'll camp out here with you when Mike's on shift."

"Good, that sounds great."

"Thanks," Sadie said. "Seriously."

"I didn't do much."

"You married my dumb brother just because you knew I needed a sister," Sadie teased.

"Yeah, that's why I did it. And the hot sex, of course."

"Well, naturally."

If she hadn't been so damn efficient, Sadie could have been on the road toward Ethan's house. Instead, she was stopping by the office to pick up the file on the Donatello acquisition. Since the meeting had been postponed until tomorrow, she and Ethan could go over the basics again tonight.

Joe let her in the front door and she headed straight for the elevators. Time was ticking. She'd stayed too long with Gina, but it had felt good to have her sister-in-law back her up. Of course, no surprise there. Gina had been after Sadie to quit her job for the last two years so she could have a life outside the office.

And Gina was right. Sadie knew it, even though she didn't like it. Stepping off the elevator, Sadie looked around the place that had pretty much been her world for the last five years. It wasn't the first time she'd been in the building long after everyone else had left for the day. She couldn't count how many times she and Ethan had worked late, just the two of them in the quiet.

This time, it felt different to her. Not only because she was here alone, but because now she knew she wouldn't be here much longer. In another month or so, she'd be gone from her job, this office, Ethan's life. She felt a small pang of regret at that thought, but leaving was really her only choice if she wanted more for herself than a good-paying job.

She started walking toward Ethan's office. The lights were dim, cubicles quiet and the air still smelled of the day's coffee. It was empty, of course, but for the memories that crowded around her. "It's going to be weird to not come here every day," she whispered, and shivered a little as her voice dissolved in the silence.

Sadie shook off the thought and her own mixed feelings as she opened Ethan's office door and said, "Gabe? What're you doing here?"

Startled, Gabriel jumped, then laughed shortly. "God, you scared the hell out of me."

The woman with him was pretty, with long black hair and big brown eyes. As Sadie watched, she moved in closer to Gabe, standing beside the bank of wide windows. "Hi," she said. "I'm Pam. Pam Cassini."

"Right, sorry." Gabe shook his head and dropped one arm around Pam's shoulders. "Seriously, Sadie, you move so quietly I didn't hear you coming in. What're you doing here?"

"I wanted to pick up a file to take to Ethan's."

He looked confused. "You're going to Ethan's house?"

"Yeah," she said, walking across the room to the wall of wooden cabinets. Opening the top one, she flipped through the files inside until she found Donatello's and pulled it out before shutting the cabinet again. Sure, they had all the files on computers and backed up by the cloud, and any number of other security measures. But they still kept hard copies, too. So much easier to read through.

"It's a long story," she said, "so I'll let Ethan tell you about it. But bottom line, he's been named guardian of a six-month-old girl."

"Ethan?" Gabriel's shock was understandable. Ethan wasn't exactly father-of-the-year material. "My brother's taking care of an infant?"

Sadie laughed a little. "With my help. But why are you guys here?"

Gabe looked at Pam briefly, then shrugged and said, "I wanted to show Pam around and Ethan's office has the best view."

It did. But not at night. Odd, but it wasn't her business why one of the owners might be in the office after closing. After all, *she* was there, right?

"Okay. Well," she said, waving the file, "I'd better get moving. I'll see you tomorrow, Gabe. Nice meeting you," she added to Pam, who smiled and nodded.

She was in the lobby, still wondering what was going on with Gabriel, when her cell phone rang. "Thanks, Joe," she said, slipping out the door before glancing at the phone screen.

Grinning to herself, she answered. "Hello, Ethan."

"Are you on your way back?" he demanded. "She's making noises. I think she's waking up."

"On my way." This situation was really far more entertaining than it should be. But Sadie couldn't help enjoying seeing the man who was always calm, cool and in charge suddenly thrown off balance by a baby. She unlocked her car, slid in and fired it up. "Be there in twenty minutes, and don't offer me more money if I can get there in fifteen."

"Just get here."

Still smiling to herself, Sadie shook her head and steered into the never-ending traffic on Pacific Coast Highway.

"She's asleep again," Sadie told him a half hour later. "I just patted her back for a while and she drifted off."

"Good." Ethan grabbed a beer out of the fridge. "Do you want anything?"

Oh, so many things, Sadie thought. Starting with, of course, that hot sex she'd been talking about with Gina. Looking at him now, she found it astonishing to realize just how sexy the man looked in a pair of jeans and an untucked blue dress shirt. She'd only ever seen him in one of the elegant suits Sadie had sort of assumed he had been born in.

God knew he was sexy as sin in one of his suits, but seeing him here, dressed so casually, put a whole new spin on her fantasies. Her mouth watered and her heartbeat kicked up a notch. Then she took a breath, pushed her fantasy aside and said, "Food, Ethan. I want food."

He nodded. "I had Chinese delivered. It's in the oven."

"Perfect." Sadie got it and set everything out on the table, then opened a half-dozen cabinets before she found plates.

Ethan found silverware, opened a bottle of wine and got each of them water besides. In a few minutes, they were sitting opposite each other in the soft, overhead light. The kitchen, like the rest of the house, was huge.

It was white—boring—with gray cabinets and a mile and a half of black granite counters. They were so tidy it looked as though no one used the room at all, and that was probably true. Alice had said herself she wasn't a cook, and Sadie was willing to bet that though he could order takeout, Ethan wouldn't have the first clue how to cook for himself.

The table sat in front of windows that overlooked the backyard and the ocean beyond. At night, though, like now, there were solar-powered lights shining beneath bushes, under trees and along a path that led down the slope toward the cliff's edge.

As she thought of that, Sadie said, "You're going to have to put a fence in at the end of the yard. Once Emma starts getting around, it won't be safe the way it is."

"Already thought of that," he said, helping himself to a serving of cashew chicken. "While you were gone,

I called the contractor who did the remodel here a couple of years ago. He's coming out tomorrow to do the measurements."

Impressed, Sadie said, "That was quick."

Wryly, Ethan responded, "I may not know how to diaper a child, but I do know how to keep it safe."

"Her."

"Her." He took a bite, glared at Sadie and said, "What took you so long?"

She dived into her beef and broccoli—that was a point for Ethan. He remembered her favorite from all those times they'd had dinner in his office while they worked. "After I got my stuff, I stopped at my brother's house to talk to Gina."

"To tell her you resigned?"

"Yes," she said, "and other things." She wasn't about to admit to him that Gina had suggested using him for hot monkey sex. Although now that the thought had settled into her mind again, the suggestion was sounding better and better.

"And was Gina happy to hear it?"

Sadie looked up and met his eyes. The overhead lamp shone down on his face, creating shadows, but strangely, it also illuminated. Everything inside her turned upside down. It had always been that way with Ethan. One look from him and she was quivering inside. It was humiliating to admit, even to herself, since he seemed completely unaware of her as a person—let alone a *woman*.

"Yeah," she finally said, taking a sip of wine before digging into the fried rice. "She was glad I quit."

"Nice that your family's happy about you being unemployed."

Her eyebrows lifted. "That's because she knows I

won't be for long. What they're happy about is that maybe now they'll get to see me occasionally."

He dropped his fork and it clattered onto the fine china plate. "You make it sound as if you were an indentured servant. It wasn't that bad."

"Megan's wedding," she said.

"One time," he countered.

"Hardly. I couldn't get to the hospital for any of Mike and Gina's kids' births, either," she reminded him.

"And this is all my fault." His tone clearly said he didn't think so.

"Partly," Sadie said, reaching for her glass of water. She took a long drink, then said, "Mostly mine, though." Meeting his gaze across the table, she continued. "I could have said no to you. I could have told you that I wouldn't work all hours. Or that I wouldn't leave Megan's wedding."

He studied her and she wished she could tell what he was thinking. But he'd sat back in his chair and now his eyes were shadowed, too, hiding what he was feeling.

"I didn't, though, because I liked my job, Ethan." Well, that was true as far as it went. But it wasn't what had caused her to come running whenever Ethan called. That was something else.

Wanting to be with him, around him, working and talking with him.

She didn't mind the late nights because she and Ethan were together, solving problems, making plans for the company's future. She'd fooled herself into believing there was more between them than there was. Her own imagination and desires had convinced her that one day he would notice her.

Well, that had never happened.

"And," she went on, "since I liked it, I sort of let it take over my life."

"Thanks for that, anyway," he muttered.

"Wasn't finished," she added, waving her fork at him. "You do the same thing, Ethan. You don't have a life outside the business."

"So you said earlier." He pushed the plate in front of him to one side. "But my life is just how I like it."

She looked around the kitchen, which was so tidy it could have been in an empty model home. "Really? You like being one man living in a house big enough for ten or twenty people?"

"I like the quiet."

"Right." She laughed shortly and pushed her own plate aside. Here in the darkness, it felt intimate, sitting so close to him. With no one to interrupt, she felt as though she could actually say a few things that she'd wanted to over the years. "You're hiding, Ethan."

"Hiding? From whom?" A bark of laughter shot from his throat. "That's ridiculous."

She shook her head slowly. "No, it's not. Ever since your divorce, you shut yourself off from everything."

Even in the dim light she could see his features freeze up. His laughter abruptly ended, and his mouth flattened into a grim line. "We're not talking about that."

"Of course not. You never have." Forearms braced on the table, she leaned toward him. "This time, though, you don't have to. I will," she said with a shrug.

"You're full of yourself after turning in that resignation," he said.

She nodded. "That's fair. Like I said, it's very freeing."

He didn't smile. "Think you can say anything you want, and I suppose you can. But I don't have to listen."

Her head tipped to one side. "Hiding again?"

"Not hiding," he said shortly. "Just not interested in *sharing*."

She sat back. Picking up her wine, Sadie took a sip, then asked, "What are you interested in, Ethan?"

"My company."

"And?"

"And what? That's it," he said, and stood up. He carried his plate to the sink, turned around and looked at her. "My family started this business more than a hundred years ago and it's up to me to keep it at the top. To protect it. And since when do the two of us talk about this stuff?"

"Since I quit and I don't have to worry about my boss firing me." Sadie carried her plate to the sink, too, and stood beside him.

"I can still tell you to get out."

"But you won't." She pointed to the baby monitor standing in the center of the black granite island.

He gritted his teeth so hard the muscle in his jaw twitched. "Think you're safe, do you?"

"Actually, yes, I do." Turning around, she leaned back against the counter, bracing her hands on the cold, hard edge. She tilted her head to one side and noticed a brief flash of something in his eyes.

"You realize you're still working for me for the next month…"

"Sure," she said, "but that's unofficial."

"I'm paying a lot of money for 'unofficial'."

"I'm worth it," she quipped, and saw that flash in his eyes again. However briefly it had appeared, it set off a similar flash inside her. Sadie felt heat puddle in the pit of her stomach and then slide slowly south. A deep throbbing began at her core as she stared up into his eyes, and it took every bit of her self-control to keep from moving to try to ease that ache.

"I suppose you are." His words came in a whisper and his eyes looked suddenly deep, dark and filled with emotions she couldn't read.

Sadie would have given a lot to know what he was thinking, but in the next moment, she got her first clue.

"It's strange," he said.

"There's been a lot of strange today," she said softly. "Can you be more specific?"

"Okay. I think this is the first time I've ever seen you out of your work clothes…"

Sadie glanced down. She wore black jeans, a long-sleeved red T-shirt and black ballet flats. Hardly an outfit worth putting that look of interest on his face, but there it was.

"And you're barefoot, wearing jeans. I didn't know you *owned* jeans," she said. God, he was barefoot. That was sexy, too. *Get a grip, Sadie.* "It's the first time we've been together when we're *not* working."

"Not true." He put his hands on either side of her and loomed in close. "There was that trip to Dublin last summer."

"A business trip," she murmured, and felt his heat drifting toward her. He was doing this on purpose. Why was he doing this? And oh, she hoped he didn't stop.

"What about when we had a drink in that pub after the meeting?"

"Still work," she said, and she had to look up to meet his gaze as he loomed over her. Her brain instantly painted another picture where he would be looking down at her. Where his body would cover hers. Where his mouth would be on hers as they came together in the most intimate way possible.

"And the singing?" he asked, and she dragged her focus back to the conversation at hand.

"Work but fun," she said, remembering that night in Ireland as one of the best out of the last five years.

"So you can at least admit you had fun that night."

"Never said I didn't."

"Uh-huh. Are you having fun *now*?" he asked, bending his head a little closer to hers.

"I could be, if I knew what you were up to," Sadie admitted, staring into his eyes and trying to decipher what was behind all this. "But I think *you* are having fun."

"Oh, I am," he assured her, as his gaze moved over her features.

"Why are you doing this?" she asked, and could have kicked herself. Did it really matter *why*? Having his mouth just a breath from hers, having his gaze locked on her, was something she'd thought about for years, and now that it was happening she questioned it? What was *wrong* with her?

"Am I making you nervous?" Ethan asked in response.

"If you were?"

"Then I'd stop."

"Then I'm not nervous."

"Glad to hear it." Suddenly any trace of humor was gone from his eyes. His features were taut as he stared at her as if seeing her for the first time. When he leaned in closer, so did Sadie.

Her breath was gone. And she didn't care. She could hear her own heart pounding, felt it hammering in her chest, but breathing was simply off the table. Her blood rushed through her veins, then headed south to set up camp in her groin. Heated throbbing took over, along with an ache she knew all too well. She wanted him, and now it looked like she might have him, and her body was reacting with bursts of internal joy.

"I've thought about doing this," he whispered.

"Me, too," Sadie said softly.

"Yeah?" One corner of his mouth lifted. "I didn't because you worked for me. But now you don't."

"Good point," she agreed. She stared into his eyes, lowered her gaze to his mouth and then back up again. "So, are you going to kiss me or what?"

"Stop talking, Sadie." Then he kissed her.

Five

That first touch of his lips to hers was electric. Sadie's whole body lit up like a neon festival. He cupped her face with his hands, tilted her head and took more. He parted her lips with his tongue and she met that intimate caress with eagerness. It was everything she'd thought it would be and more.

Pulling her close, Ethan held her pressed against his chest as his hands moved to stroke her, touch her. Everywhere. He grabbed hold of her behind and squeezed, sending new tendrils of excitement scattering through her cells.

She moved in even closer to him, twined her arms around his neck and held on while their mouths met and danced and promised each other more.

Hot sex with Ethan.

That one thought blazed across her mind and she

groaned as Ethan tore his mouth from hers to drag his lips and tongue along the line of her throat.

This was really going to happen. She was going to have sex with Ethan. She was going to actually live out her fantasies.

And then it ended with a screech.

Breaking apart, they stared at each other while they struggled for breath. Ethan looked down at her and his expression told Sadie he was as stunned as she felt. Even in her wildest imaginings, Sadie had never expected to react to him as she had. It wasn't like she was a vestal virgin or something, either. She'd had sex. Plenty of times. But even the best of those nights couldn't hold a candle to what she felt when Ethan kissed her.

Then the baby cried again, that shriek coming through the baby monitor on the counter. Emma was demanding attention and there would be no ignoring her.

"I should go check on her," Sadie said brokenly.

"Yeah. Yeah, we should." Ethan let her go and took a step back.

Sadie had never felt colder in her life. Strange how the heat enveloping her dissipated instantly the moment she wasn't being held against him.

And strange that she didn't know whether to be disappointed or grateful that the baby had interrupted them.

Hot sex, sure. But now that her blood was cooling off, she could think about the possible pitfalls of this. He'd paid her to stay for another month. If they were having sex all month—and didn't *that* sound great— would it be too weird? Did she care? And that was why she should be grateful, Sadie told herself. Her brain was confused enough already.

Little Emma had unwittingly given Ethan and Sadie more time to think. To look at every angle of what might happen and really decide if this was what they wanted— oh boy, she really wanted it. And she hoped he did, too.

"Okay, we'll…"

"Talk about this," he finished for her.

Nodding, she walked out of the kitchen, headed for the stairs and Emma. Ethan was right behind her and she was almost surprised that he was willing to do his part in taking care of the baby.

But a bigger part of her was wondering if their "talk" would turn into something else.

A few days later, they were already settling into a "routine." One that Ethan had never wanted. Having an infant in his house was unsettling enough, but seeing Sadie every day and every night was harder to deal with than he'd imagined. He'd been thinking about that kiss for days. Wanting more, knowing he shouldn't have it.

And still, he knew exactly what he wanted.

Sadie.

Funny how a few days could change everything. And this was one change he could completely get behind. Sadie was living in his house, in the room across from his. He'd tasted her and hadn't been able to sleep since for thinking about it. About *her*.

Neither of them had talked about it since, but the tension was there and building. Need pumped through him with a vengeance almost constantly, and damn it, it showed no signs of fading away. If anything, his desire for her had only grown since that one seductive kiss.

Five years. Five years he'd worked with her, known her and had never guessed what he might find if he kissed her. Just as well, he told himself. If he'd had any idea at all, he would have fired her years ago and seduced her on the spot.

Shaking his head, he tried to turn his mind back to work, but it was surprising how little the Mother's Day marketing campaign interested him at the moment. "Which is why you need to concentrate on it."

There were too many damn distractions in his life right now. They'd interviewed two would-be housekeepers and neither of them were right for the job. He and Sadie were bringing Emma to the in-house day care every day, but that couldn't keep going on. Ethan wasn't going to be driving a child back and forth to work every morning and evening. He needed space. Time to think. He needed his life to get back into order.

As much as he wanted Sadie, as much as he wanted this day to be over and the two of them alone together back at the house, Ethan knew that being with her would open up all kinds of problems. What if she took sex the wrong way? What if she expected a relationship? What if she started looking at the two of them plus the baby as a family? No, he wasn't going down that road again.

He'd tried marriage once, completely screwed it up and had learned his lesson. He was no good at it. He liked his space and wasn't interested in being seen at the "best" parties, either. His ex-wife had made it plain when she walked out that he was less-than-stellar husband material.

When they married, Marcy had thought marrying a billionaire would mean great trips, big parties, celebrity friends. But that wasn't Ethan, and she hadn't bothered to hide her disappointment. He hadn't fought the divorce. What would have been the point? Marcy had been unhappy, so why try to keep her where she didn't want to be?

Besides, that brief marriage had taught Ethan an important lesson. He was better off on his own. He didn't like failure and so had no plans to set himself up for another disaster. He liked women, but he didn't want one permanently. Not even one who could make him feel what Sadie had.

As much as he burned to have her—under him, over him; didn't matter, he wasn't picky—he'd seen Sadie's eyes when she looked at the baby. When she held Emma, Sadie got a soft look about her, as if she were wrapping herself emotionally around that child. She clearly wanted kids. A marriage. A family.

What he wanted could be solved in a few hot, steamy nights.

"That does it," he muttered, and lunged out of his chair. He couldn't keep thinking about this. About *her*. It would drive him even crazier than he was feeling at the moment. Walking to the bank of windows behind his desk, he stared out at the ocean, hoping the view would ease the knots tightening inside him. He pushed one hand through his hair and wasn't the least bit surprised when Sadie's image rose to the front of his mind again.

When someone knocked, then opened his office door, he didn't bother to turn around.

"Ethan?"

He closed his eyes briefly. Even the sound of her voice now hit him with a visceral punch. "What is it, Sadie?"

"I just wanted to bring you the Donatello file. The meeting's in an hour, so…"

He glanced at her over his shoulder.

She shrugged and walked toward his desk. She dropped the file on top, then said, "You know, I stopped by here that first night to pick up the file, thinking we could review it before the meeting... Then it got postponed again and I just forgot about it. Well, to be honest, I forgot about it that night. At the house. When we..."

He knew why, too. Hell, looking at her right now, he'd come up blank if anyone asked him anything about business. His gaze locked on hers and he felt a quick jolt of white-hot need that shot from his suddenly tight throat down to his groin, where it flashed into fire that felt as if it would consume him.

"Guess we both forgot things that night."

"And we haven't talked about why, yet."

He laughed shortly. "You really think *talking* is going to solve this?"

"I didn't know anything needed solving."

"Sadie..." He took a breath, blew it out and said, "You know damn well that what happened that night changed things."

"I do." She bit her lip and he flinched.

But he didn't want to talk. He wanted to taste. To touch. To explore. So he turned back to his desk, glanced at the file and added, "Thanks. I'll look it over before the meeting."

"Sure." She didn't leave.

"Is there something else?"

"Yes." She walked closer to the desk and stood opposite him. "What's going on?"

"I don't know what you mean." Yes, he did.

"Yes you do." She was wearing black slacks, a white shirt and a short red jacket that managed to draw his attention straight to her breasts. He'd almost had his hands on them last night and his palms itched to do it right now.

"Just leave it alone, Sadie," he ground out through gritted teeth. "This isn't the time."

"I don't think so. We said we'd talk. It's been days. It's past time. And I'm ready to talk."

"Here?"

"It's where we always are, Ethan," she pointed out.

"We can talk at the house tonight."

"Tonight we'll have the baby to take care of. At the moment, Emma's in day care, so we don't have any interruptions."

She folded her arms across her chest, lifting her breasts even higher, and Ethan wondered if she was doing it on purpose just to keep him off his game.

"Fine." He came around the desk, then perched on the edge of it so that they were nearly eye to eye. "Talk."

"Okay," she started, letting her arms fall to her sides. "I've done some thinking the last few nights. Actually, I did a *lot* of thinking."

"Me, too." Especially since he hadn't been able to sleep. Sadie's image had kept rising up in his mind. Her taste had lingered in his mouth, flavoring every breath.

"Good. I think that's good." She looked not nervous, but as if she were searching for every word. "So what I need to know is if you're thinking what I'm thinking."

"Which is?" He held his breath. If she said no to sex, he wasn't going back to the house. How the hell could he live across the hall from her and *not* have her?

"It's probably a really bad idea for us to sleep together."

"Wasn't thinking at all about *sleeping*," he told her.

"Yeah, me, either." She took a breath, licked her bottom lip and unknowingly sent arrows of heat darting through him. "But—"

There was a "but."

"—it's probably not a good idea," she said.

"Yeah." His chest felt tight. "That's what I think, too."

"Oh." She looked disappointed. "But the thing is, I also think we should do it, anyway."

He came off the desk in a blink, had her wrapped up in his arms and pressed along the length of him in seconds. "I agree," he said, then took her mouth with all the hunger that had haunted him through what felt like forever.

It was just like the first time. Ethan half expected to see actual flames licking up his body. He'd never known this flash-fire need before. Ethan had tried to tell himself that his reaction to Sadie was simply because it had been too long since he was with a woman. Any woman. He devoted so much of himself to work, there was rarely time to think about anything else.

But the truth was it was Sadie doing this to him. He'd never experienced such a mindless rush of desire before. Ethan wanted to believe his hunger for her would be eased by having her, but something told him it was only going to build. He didn't care.

Tasting her, stroking his tongue against hers, feeling her breasts crushed against his chest… This was all about *Sadie*. And beyond satisfying what he was feeling at the moment, he didn't want to think about what that might mean.

He couldn't touch her enough. Feel her enough. Her mouth joined to his, her tongue stroked his and Ethan felt those flames rising, growing more powerful. He had to have her. Her hands swept up his back to his shoulders, where her fingers curled in and held on. That simple action went straight to his groin and tightened his erection to the point of pain. Desire pumped wildly through his system, shutting down all thought beyond this moment. This had never happened to Ethan before. This complete loss of control. All he could think about was getting his hands on her.

With that thought in mind, he tore his mouth free of hers, looked down and quickly opened that bright red jacket. Then the buttons on her shirt.

"Ethan…"

"Have to feel you under my hands," he murmured.

"Oh, good…"

He gave her a quick grin, pleased that she was as torn up as he was. Relieved that she hadn't said "stop." Stopping now might kill him. Ethan spread the fabric of her shirt apart and looked at her pale pink bra. "Pretty. But in my way."

"It unhooks in the front."

"Good news." He flicked the hook and eye open and her beautiful breasts spilled into his waiting hands. At the first touch of his skin to hers, she inhaled sharply. His thumbs and fingers worked her nipples as they jumped into life, going rigid with the need swamping her.

Ethan watched her eyes glaze over as he tugged on those twin sensitive points. He felt her reaction as if it were his own. She rocked her hips helplessly against him and he smiled again. Desire was alive and burning in the room, heat swirling around them like hot air from a blast furnace.

He did a quick turn, lifted Sadie and plopped her on the desk, then bent his head and took first one nipple, then the other into his mouth. Her taste filled him, her scent surrounded him and his mind was a fog from the physical demands crowding his body.

"Ethan…" Her voice was a strained whisper as she threaded her fingers through his hair, her short, neat nails scraping along his scalp. He licked and nibbled and suckled at her breasts, drawing her deep into his mouth as the rush of heat building between them became all encompassing.

This. This was what he'd needed. To indulge himself in her. For years, he'd fought to ignore her, to bury his desire for her, until now it felt as if he were breaking free from the chains he'd wrapped around himself.

"Ethan," she choked out, "whatever you do, don't stop."

"Not the plan," he answered in a murmur. Again and again, he drew on her breasts, his mouth working her tender skin until she was writhing on the desk, helpless against the rising tension inside her. And he knew what he could do to help that.

He dropped one hand to the junction of her thighs and cupped her. At his first touch, she gasped, threw her head back and moved into him. Her slacks were in his way… That was all he could think. He wanted to touch her heat. Push his fingers inside and stroke her until he felt her climax pump through her.

But he couldn't stop long enough to give either of them that gift. For now, he stroked and rubbed and tasted and nibbled until she was a writhing mass of desire. Her response fueled his own. They both fought for air as the most basic of needs overtook everything else.

The first ripples of release hit her and Sadie leaned forward, burying her face in his shoulder. He heard the harsh, keening sound she made, but he knew she'd muffled it purposely so no one else in the building would guess what was happening here. Finally, she stopped, and Ethan took a breath and straightened up. Pulling away from her, he stepped back. Her eyes tracked him as she fought for air.

"What're you doing?"

"I'll be right back," he ground out, and congratulated himself silently on being able to speak at all.

"You're *leaving*?" She sounded outraged and he couldn't blame her. Hell, he could barely move for the pain in his hard, aching groin.

"No." He walked across the office, flipped the lock on the door and came back to her in a blink. "I'm making sure no one's going to walk in before we're finished."

"Oh, good. We're not finished."

"Not even close."

She nodded, licked her lips and sent a jolt of electricity to his dick. "Then locking the door was a good idea."

"I thought so." He walked to the other side of his desk, pulled open a middle drawer and took out the box of condoms he'd bought that morning when they'd stopped to get more diapers for Emma. Sadie was still watching him, and this time, she smiled. "I love a man who's prepared for any situation."

He disregarded the *L* word and went with what they were both feeling. "I bought these today. In case we actually did what we were working up to."

"Good call."

"But I don't want to wait until tonight." It cost him,

this fight for control. His voice was thin, strained as he looked at her.

Her curls tumbled around her face. Her breasts were displayed in all their glory and her delicious lips parted as she slowly, deliberately, licked them again. This time, he could see, in anticipation.

"Neither do I." She scooted off the edge of the desk and shrugged her shirt and bra off. "Now, Ethan. We can talk later, but right now, I need you inside me before I explode."

"It's *when* I'm inside you that you're going to explode."

"Show me."

He tore the box, grabbed a condom and ripped the foil package open.

"Let me help," she whispered, holding out one hand for the sheer latex covering.

He moved in closer and handed it to her. Her nimble fingers undid his slacks, pulled the zipper down, then reached into his shorts to free him.

The minute her fingers curled around him, Ethan groaned. *Too long*, he told himself. It had been too long. Instantly, he realized that he was doing it again. Trying to explain away what he felt with Sadie by dismissing it. The truth was, he'd *never* reacted like this to a simple touch. Sadie's fingers curled around his length and stroked him slowly in a tantalizing motion that had him reaching for the ragged ends of his control.

Her thumb traced the tip of him, wiping away a single bead of moisture before sliding that, too, along the length of him. Her gaze was locked on his, so he saw the flash of desire burning in her eyes. Felt a similar burn within himself. "Put it on me, Sadie. I can't hold out much longer…"

She smiled at his admission and he saw that powerful look all women got when a man was at their mercy cross her features. Then it was gone and there was only desire again. She smoothed the condom down his length, making sure her fingers did another long tease of him as she did. By the time she was finished, Ethan was breathing hard and aching in every inch of his body. Need was a pulsing beast crouched inside him. And Ethan was done holding it back.

"That's it," he said, in what was more a growl of frustration than a simple statement. He undid her slacks and pushed them and her pale pink panties down her legs. She kicked them and her shoes off.

Then he dropped one hand to her hot, damp core again and she trembled, groaning out his name. One finger, then two, slid inside her, stroking, rubbing, exploring. His thumb smoothed across her core and she jolted in his arms, spreading her legs farther apart to accommodate him.

Ethan stared into her eyes, watching emotions flash and burn one after the other as she rocked her hips into his hand wildly. Then she came again in a sudden, hot rush of satisfaction. She bit down hard on her bottom lip to keep from crying out—still keeping quiet to protect them both from discovery.

He admired her control, but he wanted to break it. Wanted to hear her crying out his name, screaming it. He wanted—needed—more.

When the last of the tremors died away, Ethan reached out and swept everything off his desk to fly out and land on the hand-tied rug that lay across the wooden floor. Then he turned her around, laid her out across his desk and whispered, "Hold on."

He looked at her like she was a feast laid out before a starving man. And that was how it felt. Sunlight poured through the wall of windows and made her skin seem to glow. Ethan kept his gaze locked on her as he stripped his own clothes off and tossed them aside.

She curled her fingers around the edge of the desk, glanced back over her shoulder at him and parted her thighs. Then she whispered, "I'm ready, Ethan. I mean, *really* ready."

So was he. Ethan filled his gaze with her. Her bare butt was beautiful and waiting for him. He rubbed her behind hard, squeezing her flesh until she moaned and twisted her hips in response. She threw him a hot look and muttered, "Ethan, *now*."

"Now," he agreed, and pushed his body home. In one long stroke, he was buried deep inside her heat. Her body moved and rocked to accommodate him and Ethan groaned at the satisfaction rippling through him.

He lost himself in the rush of finally joining with her. Of feeling her take him in. Her hips moved as her breath crashed in and out of her lungs. He couldn't stop looking at her. Looking at *them*, together.

Heart racing, Ethan felt her response, deep inside as her muscles contracted around him. Her climax hit hard and Sadie bit down on her lip again to keep from crying out. But he'd seen her reaction. Knew what they were doing to each other, and a moment later, Ethan gritted his teeth to muffle the sounds of his own surrender as he gave himself up to her.

A few minutes—or hours—later, when his heartbeat stopped thundering in his ears, Ethan was stunned at what they'd just done. Hell, he'd *never* had sex in his office before. Five minutes alone with Sadie and that record was smashed. Hell, he didn't know how he'd ever get any work done in here again. He would forever be seeing her stretched across his desk, deliciously naked.

Shaking his head, he carefully stepped back from Sadie, then helped her up. She moaned a little as she stood, and Ethan winced. "Damn it, Sadie, did I hurt you?"

She threw those blond curls out of her eyes and looked up at him with a wide grin. "Are you kidding? I feel fantastic!"

Just like that, he wanted her again. How had he not guessed all these years what kind of woman Sadie Matthews was? He'd thought of her as efficient and she was. But she was so much more, too.

This was going to be trouble.

She scrambled to get back into her clothes, so Ethan did the same. Once they were dressed, though, he took hold of her shoulders. "That was crazy."

"I know," she said, still giving him that wide smile. "Honestly, it was crazy *and* amazing."

He scrubbed one hand across the back of his neck and watched her. "That talk we were supposed to have? I think it's time we had it."

"Okay." She stared up into his eyes and Ethan's mind went blank for a long second or two. Hell, he'd completely lost focus. Another first.

All he could think about was what had just happened between them and how badly he wanted to do it again.

"You start," she said, and walked around him. She squatted down to pick up the scattered papers and pens he'd pushed off his desk.

Irritated somehow, Ethan snapped, "You don't have to do that."

She glanced up at him. "I do still work here, Ethan. Relax."

His brain was racing and she was telling him to relax. Not going to happen. When she'd gathered everything, he reached down for her arm and helped her up. She set it all down on the desk, then gave the wood a soft pat.

"I'm going to have real affection for this desk from now on."

He didn't know what to make of her. They'd worked together closely for five years and Ethan felt like he didn't know her at all. She wasn't horrified or regretful or even embarrassed. She reveled in what had happened between them and Ethan envied that. Because he wasn't at all sure they hadn't made a huge mistake. He really hated this uncertain feeling. Ethan always knew what to do, what to say, in any given situation. This off-balance sensation was unsettling.

"You're still worried and you don't have to be," she said softly. Walking up to him, she laid one hand on his chest and looked up into his eyes. "What happened here is because we both wanted it to happen. You don't owe me anything and I'm not asking for anything, so you can get that slightly panicked look off your face."

Offended somehow, he instantly smoothed out his features. "I'm not panicked. I just don't want you to think that this means more than what it was."

Now she laughed shortly and gave his chest a pat. "Ethan, I've known you for five years. If anyone knows you're not a relationship person, it's *me*. Besides, I quit, remember?" She threaded her fingers through her curls, then said, "In four weeks, I'll be gone and you won't have to worry about any of this."

Then she walked across the room and opened the door. Giving him a finger wave, she slipped through and he was alone again. The room was still humming with sexual energy and all Ethan could think about was what she'd said.

In four weeks, I'll be gone.

And damn it, he already knew that four weeks wouldn't be enough.

Six

Gabriel had it all worked out.

A chef at Heart Chocolates would be making the samples of the new flavors. This was the best idea all around. Not only did Jeff Garret already work for him as an assistant chocolate chef, he was looking to advance his career. Plus, Gabriel didn't have to take the recipe out of the company fold. A win—win. All he had to do was find a professional kitchen he could rent for a couple nights.

"I still don't understand why you didn't use the chef I arranged," Pam said, anger clear in her tone.

And Gabe didn't understand why she was so pissed. But she had been ever since he'd told her the new plan. "Because I don't know him."

"I do," she argued.

"That's great," Gabe said, "but Jeff's a chef with my

company. He's studied with the top chocolatier in Belgium and he wants more responsibility at the company. This is his chance to prove himself." Gabe stopped, laughed a little and said, "I guess Jeff and I have a lot in common in this."

She scowled at him. "This isn't funny, Gabe. Not to me."

"Yeah, I can see that." He studied her for a second or two. "What I don't know is *why*?"

She shook her head, obviously thinking about it briefly, and said, "We were doing this together, and now all of a sudden we're not. What am I supposed to tell my friend?"

Now she was concerned that her chef friend would have his feelings hurt? His professional pride? Well, that really wasn't one of Gabe's big concerns.

"Tell him the truth," Gabe countered. "That this is my family's recipe and I can't trust it to just anyone."

"I'm 'just anyone'? Good to know." Pam whirled away so fast her long dark hair swung out around her shoulders like a cape. Then she spun back to look up at him. "You weren't trusting my chef, Gabe. You were supposed to be trusting *me*."

She turned again and this time walked away from him.

Gabe caught up with her quickly. Grabbing her arm, he whirled her around and looked down into her big brown eyes. "I do trust you."

"Sure." Her gaze slid from his. "I'm convinced."

He was getting more confused by the minute. Ever since he'd told her about using one of the Heart chefs, she'd been irritated and hadn't bothered to hide it.

They were in his penthouse apartment at the hotel.

They were supposed to be celebrating with a great dinner and an icy cold bottle of champagne he'd ordered from one of the best restaurants in the city. But the dinner was uneaten and the champagne was rapidly going flat.

This was not how Gabe had thought the evening would go. He'd planned the great dinner and then figured on having some celebrational sex when they were finished. Looked like that was out the window.

When Pam stormed through the living room and out onto the balcony overlooking the ocean, Gabe followed her. This was the first time he'd ever seen her temper. And though it was impressive, he also found it sexy as hell. He liked a woman with fire in her eyes. He'd just like to know what had caused all this.

"I don't understand why you didn't stick to the plan," she said.

"Because this plan's better. I told you. This way the family recipe stays in the family." He looked at her, and even in profile he could see the suppressed anger on her face. Well, he wasn't too far behind her on that front.

"I'm sorry," she said suddenly and just like that, his own temper drained away. "I was just surprised, Gabe. You didn't even tell me you were changing the plan."

"Hey." He took her arm, turned her around to face him. "Honestly, I didn't think it would bug you so much. This isn't about trust, Pam."

"Isn't it?" She pulled free of his grasp and took a step back. Holding on to the wrought-iron railing with one hand, she pushed her windblown hair out of her eyes with the other.

He threw both hands high in exasperation. How did this go sideways so fast? "We're a team, Pam. Nothing has changed."

"Doesn't feel like it." She shook her head. "Not anymore."

"What the hell, Pam?" He shoved his hands into his jeans pockets. "Where's all the fury coming from? I don't know your chef from a hole in the ground. Why wouldn't I use one I already know? The guy's insanely talented. And he already works for me."

"Fine." She waved a hand at him, effectively dismissing that argument. "But now I have to explain to my chef why he can't be in on the ground floor of a new chocolate line."

"He wouldn't have been, anyway," Gabe argued. "He was going to make samples. That's as far as his involvement went. But if this goes well, then Jeff will get a promotion and I'll have the satisfaction of hearing Ethan apologize and admit he was wrong for the first damn time ever."

She didn't look like she cared much.

"This is making zero sense," Gabe said, his own frustration building. "And damned if I'm going to apologize for protecting my family even while I'm sneaking around behind their backs."

"Hey," she said quickly. "Nobody's *forcing* you to do anything. You *wanted* to do this," she reminded him. "I didn't talk you into it. In fact, I told you that you didn't *have* to do it at all."

He stepped up closer, laid both hands on her shoulders and could practically feel her vibrating with anger. The woman was making him crazy. "Babe, I know that.

This whole thing is on me. Which is why I'm doing it my way. You said you understood family loyalty."

"I do."

"Then you should get why I'm doing it like this."

She considered that, then took a breath and huffed it out again. "I get it, Gabe. I just don't know why you kept it from me."

"I only finalized it today," he argued. "Hell, I didn't see you until a half hour ago. When was I going to tell you?"

"When you started thinking about changing the plan?"

There was more going on here than anger over a plan changing. Something else was bugging her. He just had no idea what it was. "What's really going on here, Pam?"

Below, the ocean was dark, but the waves were topped with froth that stood out in the moonlight. Couples strolled the sand at the water's edge and a few bonfires winked in the blackness of the beach.

"What do you mean?"

"This is about more than using a different chef," he said, as suspicion slipped through his mind. He didn't like the feeling. But what the hell else was he supposed to think when her reaction to all of this was so damn irrational?

Pam was the one he could count on. Talk to. She'd been his sounding board for months. Always supportive. Always ready to listen. If something had changed, he wanted to know what it was. "So tell me what's happening."

"There's nothing to tell," she said, then pulled her phone from her back pocket to check the time. "I've got to go. It's my father's birthday and the whole family's gathering at their house."

"You didn't say anything before."

"Well, I am now," she murmured.

"But we've got dinner. Champagne."

"Yeah, I don't feel much like celebrating."

She slipped out of his grasp and his hands felt empty, cold. "Damn it, Pam, tell me what's going on with you."

"It's nothing."

Before he could say anything else, she was walking back into the main room and snatching her purse up off the couch. The table, set for an intimate dinner, complete with candles, was ignored. "Pam."

She stopped, turned and looked at him. In her eyes he could see disappointment still shining there. Her mouth was tight and flat, and her spine was stiff. "What?"

He didn't know what had gone wrong here, so he didn't know how to fix it. That was an irritation, too. Looking at her now, he could see that though she was standing right there, she was miles away emotionally. But until she was willing to talk to him about what was bothering her there wasn't a hell of a lot he could do about it.

"Are you going to be there when we make the new chocolates?"

Her mouth curved though her eyes remained the same—dark, closed off. "Of course I will. I want to see this through with you."

"Good," he said. "I'll call you tomorrow."

"Sure, Gabe. Tomorrow." Then she left and he wondered if this idea was going to ruin his and Pam's relationship as surely as it would his and Ethan's.

* * *

"They're holding out for more money." Ethan sat back in his desk chair a few days later and looked up at Sadie.

Her breath caught in her throat. Not so long ago, she'd been sprawled across that desk like the main course at a feast. And the memory of it sent a quick ripple of excitement along her spine. Hard to keep your mind on work when all you could think about was…

"Sadie? Are you listening?"

"What?" She snapped back. "Yes. Of course. They want more money."

"I thought we were close to finalizing. The old man, he wants to sell, but his adult children are making him have second thoughts." Ethan tossed a pen onto his desktop and pushed himself to his feet. "The lawyers, ours and theirs, are trying to hammer out a deal, but—"

"Why don't you do it personally?" Sadie asked.

He shifted to look at her. "I don't do the negotiating. That's why I pay the lawyers."

She chuckled and shook her head. "That's the way we usually do it, yes. But Donatello's might be different."

"How?"

He'd tucked the edges of his suit jacket back and had his hands tucked into his pockets. He looked the epitome of the high-powered businessman. And yet, looking at him, she could see him as he was when they were together, and that sent heat waves rocketing through her body.

"Sadie?"

Wow, she really had to concentrate. "Okay, um, I mean that Donatello's is a family business."

"Yeah, I know. I just told you. It's the kids who are

fighting this buyout. They're the ones demanding more money, and at the same time, telling their father not to sell at all." He scowled fiercely. "If they'd just butt out, we could have this done. I don't know why they're being so difficult, anyway. We're offering a fair price."

Funny that he couldn't see the similarities between the Hart family and the Donatello family. Richard Donatello's adult children were fighting for their legacy, their own family's traditions, just as Ethan was. As important as the chocolate company was to him, he should understand what the Donatello kids were going through.

"Right." Sadie shrugged. "Well, you know how you feel about the Hart family business. We both know you would do whatever it took to keep this company thriving. So just for a minute, put yourself in their place."

He snorted. "Not the same. Not by a long shot. Yes, Donatello's has a great reputation, but they're still a small, one-shop business."

"Just how Heart Chocolates started."

"A long time ago," he pointed out.

Honestly, sometimes Sadie felt like beating her own head against a brick wall. It would certainly be more satisfying than trying to convince Ethan that he was wrong about *anything*.

"Donatello's has been around for almost fifty years." He frowned.

"And it's successful enough that you want to buy it."

"Well, yes," he argued. "Because they have a great web presence, an excellent location in Laguna and their customer list is phenomenal."

"All good points," she said, wondering why he still wasn't getting it. Really, was it possible that once you reached success, you actually *forgot* how it had happened? "What I'm saying is that the Donatello chocolate shop is where yours started out a hundred years ago. Hardworking. A family. Building a reputation."

He frowned again, but she could see that he was considering what she was saying. It was a start, Sadie told herself, so she went on.

"Is offering him more money such a horrible thing?" she asked. "Hasn't he earned it? Richard Donatello built a company that you badly want. Maybe if the kids see that you treated their father well, they'll back off."

"Maybe." He nodded thoughtfully.

"And think about it, Ethan...you paid me an extra hundred and fifty thousand for one month."

"Yeah," he said tightly, "that was personal. This is business."

He had the wide windows behind him, where gray, January clouds scuttled across the horizon, hovering over a sea the color of steel.

"Not completely," she argued, and watched one of his eyebrows arch. "Business, sure. But it's also about family. Their family, Ethan. A legacy as important to them as yours is to you."

A couple long, tense seconds passed before he nodded again. "All right. You've made your point. I'll give it some thought."

Sadie knew when to leave well enough alone. "Okay, good. Now back to the personal front—"

"I don't have time for a quickie today, Sadie."

She blinked and her head jerked back as if she'd been slapped. Staring at him, she could see that he wished he hadn't said that, but it was enough to know that he was thinking it. "I don't remember asking for one."

"No, you didn't." He sighed, shook his head and rubbed the back of his neck. "I'm sorry. That didn't come out right."

"Oh, I don't know. You made yourself pretty clear," she said stiffly. And she'd really love to know what had brought on such an insult to her—to both of them. What they'd shared had been far more than a "quickie." There'd been emotions involved as well as their bodies, but apparently, Ethan didn't want to admit that to her or himself. "As it happens, I wasn't talking about sex, Ethan. I was going to tell you the agency is sending over another housekeeper to be interviewed tonight."

"Oh." He frowned. "Fine."

Apparently he was going to pretend he didn't say anything, and she was supposed to pretend she hadn't heard it. Well, fine. She could do avoidance and pretense as well as anyone. Hadn't she been hiding her love for this idiot man for five long years?

"Her name is Julie Cochran. She's a single mother of a five-year-old. She's a good cook, has no issues with also looking after a baby, and she really needs the job."

His jaw dropped and his eyes went wide. "You want to move *another* child into my house?"

Sadie almost sighed. She'd really thought they'd been making progress over the last few days. Hearing him now was more than disappointing. "I'm sure the little girl doesn't have the plague or anything, so you should be safe."

"That's not funny."

"No," she agreed. "None of this is funny. But Julie is a single mom who needs work. The agency says she's one of their best—"

"Then why is she out of work?"

"Because the woman she worked for was elderly and recently died."

He frowned. "Oh."

"Ethan, you want someone good with kids. Well, Julie is. The housekeeper's quarters are big enough for her and her daughter, *and* she's a cook, as well." She shouldn't have to work so hard to sell him on this. "She pretty much hits every point you needed."

"I didn't need another child," Ethan ground out. "Hell, I didn't want the one I've got."

"Wow." Sadie just stared at him. For some reason, she'd thought he was coming around a little. He was helping take care of Emma. He'd fed her and bathed her the night before. The two of them together had tucked the baby in for the night. So what was the problem?

"Damn it, don't look at me like that."

"How?" she asked. "Horrified? Disappointed?"

"Either," he muttered. "Both."

"I don't know who I'm more insulted for," she admitted. "Me or Emma."

"I'm not trying to insult either one of you."

"Well, congratulations then," she said tightly. "You appear to be so gifted with insults you don't need to try."

"Damn it, Sadie—"

"I'm not talking about me now, Ethan. This is about Emma. You've only had her a little more than a week," she said, reminding herself as well as him of that fact. Maybe he'd need more time to get used to having Emma in his house. But what kind of excuse was she supposed to make to cover the insult he'd delivered to *her*? "Give it a chance."

"I am, aren't I?"

"Are you?" she countered. "Honestly, I thought you were. You're really good with Emma, but hearing you now, I don't know if you're doing the right thing in keeping her."

He stared at her, surprised. "What else can I do? I promised her father I'd be her guardian."

"A guardian is more than a place to live and a housekeeper to make sure the child is fed and clean." Sadie stared him down. "A decade-old promise isn't enough reason to keep her, Ethan. Emma needs more than your duty. Heck, she *deserves* more than that. She deserves to be loved. If you can't do that, maybe you should consider giving her up for adoption to someone who can."

Now he looked stunned. "You really think I'd do that?"

"Before the last five minutes, no," she admitted. "But listening to you complain is pretty convincing."

"That's great. Thanks." He paced behind his desk and she thought he looked like a tiger in a too-small cage. "Good to know I have your support."

"Like I have yours?" she countered just as hotly. "What was that you said about a *quickie*?"

He stopped pacing and threw her a look that was both apologetic and irritated. Amazing that he could conflate the two. "You know damn well I didn't mean anything by that."

"Do I?"

"You sure as hell should," he snapped. "We've known each other too long for you to take one stupid comment and build a case on it."

There was more going on here than just the baby and

the housekeeper and the constant change in a life that had been so rooted in routine that it was more of a rut than a path forward. And maybe it was time he told her what was bothering him.

"What's going on with you, Ethan?" she asked quietly.

"Nothing."

"Right." She crossed her arms over her chest. "You've barely spoken to me since we were together. You leave every morning without a word, and when you are forced to talk to me at work, you're cold and distant. And let's just add, as of today, insulting."

"I said I was sorry."

"Well, all better then." She uncrossed her arms, then set her hands at her hips. "Why are you avoiding me?"

"I've been busy."

"Hey, me, too," she said, walking toward him. "And I'm also the one who took Emma to the day care. The one who checked on her at lunch, and I'm guessing I will be the one driving her back to the house. You've been ignoring both of us, Ethan. Why?"

He glared at her, then looked away. "Because things are different since we had sex."

Surprised, she asked, "Different how?"

He snapped her a look. "Hell, it changed everything. I've thought about it and realized that what we did was a mistake."

Sadie flushed and felt both rage and embarrassment rise up inside her. Strange, she hadn't been embarrassed at all while she was laid out in front of him. But hearing him dismiss what they'd shared was enough to color her own memories of it. "Is that right?"

"It is," he said tightly, and locked his gaze on hers. "There's too much going on right now and I don't think we should let that happen again."

"How long have you been working on that speech?"

"What?"

Sadie was furious. This was why he'd been ignoring her? He had regrets over what they'd done, and like the lord of the manor, he was going to put everything right again. Men were just idiots sometimes. He thought insulting her, ignoring her, would be enough to keep her at a distance. Clearly, he didn't know her as well as he thought he did.

"*You* don't think," she said, keeping her voice as calm as possible. "You've decided. Thank you, Ethan. How very kind of you to figure all of this out without any input from me."

He winced a little. "If you'll just listen…"

"Now you're ready to talk and I should just, what? Sit down and listen as you lay out your plans?"

"I didn't say that…"

"Let me ask you, Ethan, do I get a vote in any of this?"

"Of course you get a vote," he practically snarled, and came to a stop behind his desk, as if he needed that heavy piece of mahogany furniture as a barrier between them.

But only a few days ago it had been so much more than that.

"Well, that's very democratic of you, Ethan."

He frowned and watched her warily. "The words sound right, but the tone is off."

"Good catch," she said. "But the real question is,

why didn't you talk to me about this before you made up your new rules?"

He scrubbed one hand across his jaw. "It's complicated."

"No, it isn't." Sadie was frustrated and her fury was beginning to ease back down into extreme irritation. "For heaven's sake, Ethan, it doesn't have to be complicated unless you make it so. Whatever you're thinking, just stop it."

He laughed shortly. "Sure. I'll stop thinking."

"You overthink, Ethan. That's the problem." Shaking her head, Sadie stepped forward, laid both hands on the edge of the desk and said, "We had each other, right here."

His eyes flashed.

"Why can't you just let it be what it was?" she asked. "Two adults enjoying each other."

"You said that then."

"And will again tomorrow if I have to," Sadie said, folding her arms across her chest again and giving him a hot stare. "And I probably will, because you don't seem to be listening. I didn't ask you for anything, Ethan, remember? You don't owe me anything and I don't need you to protect me from big bad you."

He reached up and shoved both hands through his hair. "I don't want this—whatever it is we've got going on here—getting messy."

"It will."

His head snapped up and his eyes fired.

She sighed. "Life gets messy, Ethan. It just happens. But relax. I won't be crawling at your feet, begging for scraps of attention."

"I never said you would," he said in his own defense.

"And you're perfectly safe from a proposal, too," Sadie reassured him. "Trust me when I say you are not the man for me."

He actually looked offended. "What's that supposed to mean?"

"It means," she told him, "that I have a list of qualifications for the man I want and you only meet one of them." She stopped, thought about the impromptu hot sex on the desk in the middle of the day and had to admit that he was not only *sexy*, but had proved himself to be *adventurous*, too. "Okay, two. But that's not enough."

"How many points are on this dubious list?" he asked, frowning.

"Five," she said. "And two out of five is not nearly good enough for me. So believe me when I say you're completely safe."

"Great." He was still frowning, and if anything, the offended expression on his features had deepened.

Not a bad thing, she told herself. Maybe it was good that Ethan find out he wasn't the prime catch he thought he was.

"So, if you're okay now, I'm going back to work." She turned for the door and stopped. "You will be at the house tonight to interview Julie?"

"Yeah."

"Good. And once you've completely recovered from this conversation, maybe we could try out a bed next time…"

She didn't wait to hear his answer.

She didn't need to.

She left and stood with her back to the closed door. The office was bustling, phones were ringing and fingers clacked on keyboards. But she wasn't paying attention to any of it.

Instead, her mind was on the man she would soon be walking away from. Forever.

Seven

"So what do you think?"

Ethan looked over at Sadie and saw the gleam of triumph in her eyes. He couldn't blame her. "I think you were right. Julie will work out."

"Wow. *I was right.* I like hearing that."

One of his eyebrows lifted. "Don't get used to it."

She laughed and, God, the sound of it slammed into the center of his chest and tightened everything inside him. After their conversation that afternoon, he would have bet every penny he had that Sadie would make him pay, by dishing out silence and cold, hard stares. It was how every other woman he'd ever known had gone about payback. About making sure he understood just how wrong he'd been in whatever personal situation was happening at the time.

He should have known that Sadie would be different here, too. She was behaving like they hadn't had an argument at all.

"I don't know," she said with a grin. "I think I'm on a roll. You're offering Donatello's more money. You hired Julie in spite of her little girl..."

True, he had upped his offer for the Laguna chocolate shop. He hadn't heard anything yet, but Sadie had made a good point that he hadn't thought about before. Donatello's was a small shop, but they'd been in their location for forty-five years. They'd built a family business just as his own family had. That was something to respect, and a part of Ethan was ashamed that until Sadie spoke up, he hadn't noticed. Hadn't *let* himself notice. And that admission was a hard one to make.

As for Julie, that had turned out to be the easiest damn decision he'd ever made. Yes, there was now *another* child in his house, but even Ethan had to admit, at least to himself, that Alli was a cute kid. Didn't mean he was getting soft. Only that he had eyes, he assured himself.

"It was her chicken dinner that sold me," he admitted.

"Can't blame you for that. It was delicious. Now you know why she insisted on cooking for us. To prove she knows her way around a kitchen." Sadie leaned back on the couch and propped her feet up on the low table in front of her. She had tiny feet. Why was that sexy? He shook his head to clear out distracting thoughts.

"Yeah," he said, remembering the dinner Julie had fixed for them. "Makes me wonder why I put up with Alice all those years."

"Because you hate change?"

He looked at her and caught the impish gleam in her

eyes. "Must be it," he agreed. Though for a man who hated change as much as he did, there'd been plenty of it in his life lately.

Most of it revolving around the woman smiling at him. But then, so much of his life over the last five years had revolved around Sadie. She'd been a constant in his daily life. At work, which was really the only life he had, she was irreplaceable. And he was only just now figuring that out. So what did that say about him?

Frowning, he glanced around the empty room, then back to where Sadie was reclining on the deeply cushioned couch. Suddenly, he realized that they were alone in the house but for baby Emma. Julie and her daughter wouldn't be moving in until the following day.

And in spite of everything he'd said only that afternoon, he wanted Sadie so badly it was an ache inside him. To hell with rules. Plans. If she wanted him, too, why shouldn't they have each other again?

"So with Julie willing to watch Emma, I guess you don't really need me to stay the full month, right?"

Startled, he realized *that* hadn't occurred to him. The firelight streaming from the hearth danced across her features and shifted in shadows that seemed to settle in her blue eyes. Why hadn't he thought of that? He had almost three more weeks to go with Sadie and damn it, he wanted them.

He'd already wasted too much time, worried about consequences when she clearly wasn't.

"We still need to find a nanny," he said firmly.

"Yes, but Julie will be able to watch Emma until you do, so…"

Ethan pushed up off the far end of the leather sofa and walked over to her. Reaching down, he pulled her from the couch, and when she was standing right in front of him, he said, "Yeah, I paid you to stay a month. I still need you here."

"Why?" She looked up into his eyes and he found he couldn't look away.

He told her the honest truth. "Because I'm not ready for you to leave yet."

"Why?" She smiled and that simple curve of her mouth tugged at something inside him.

He gave her a reluctant smile. "Going to make me say it?"

She tipped her head to one side in that move he was so fond of, and said, "Yes. I think I am."

"Fine." He nodded, swallowed hard and let the desire pumping inside him have free rein. His body tightened; his heartbeat thundered in his chest. "You're right about this, too. I want you, Sadie. I want you all the damn time. Every time I have you it only makes me want more."

"And that's a good thing, right?" she asked, and made her only reference to what they'd talked about just that afternoon.

Best thing that had ever happened to him, not that Ethan was going to be admitting that anytime soon.

"It's a damn gift is what it is," he ground out.

She wrapped her arms around his neck and said, "Well, what're we standing here for?"

"Good question."

He swept her up into his arms and Sadie felt a bone-deep thrill rush through her. He held her close to his chest, looked down into her eyes, and she read the hunger shining there. Clearly, he was done trying to pretend that what was between them could be ignored or pushed aside. That hunger radiating from Ethan fed what she was feeling, making her tremble with reaction.

It had been days since they'd been together and Sadie had wondered if they ever would be again. She knew Ethan so well and had realized that over the last few days, he'd questioned himself, what had happened, and tried to work out every possibility, up to and including never touching her again. He was a man with a hard inner line that he didn't cross on a whim. But here he was, holding her, looking down at her with a promise of what was to come, and Sadie silently acknowledged that she still loved him. Would always love him. And it wouldn't matter if she left. Didn't matter if she tried to find someone else to make a life with.

A part of her would always be here. With Ethan.

"You accused me of overthinking, but I can see the wheels in your mind turning," he said as he walked toward the stairs. "Changing your mind?"

"Not at all." Caught, she scrambled for something to say that wouldn't give away what she was feeling. So she went with humor. "I was just wondering how quickly you could take the stairs…"

"We're about to find out," he said with a grin, and made it to the second floor in seconds.

"Impressive," she said, and dragged her nails against the back of his neck.

He inhaled sharply and turned toward the master bedroom. "I'm just getting started impressing you."

A sizzling knot of anticipation settled in the pit of her stomach and made her blood fizz like champagne. Reaching up, she stroked his cheek and he gritted his teeth in response.

There was no sound from the baby's room, thank goodness, because Sadie didn't want an interruption. Not even from the cutest baby in the world. All she wanted now was Ethan. She would always want Ethan.

When he carried her into his bedroom, Sadie took a moment to look around. In all the time she'd known him, she'd never seen it before. Over the years, when she'd come to his house, it was for business, and she'd worked with him in his office downstairs or in the main room or even outside on the patio.

Now, it was personal, and she felt as if she were being given a glimpse into the man.

The room was massive, of course, as she'd expected for being in a mansion. There was a huge TV hanging on the wall opposite the bed. A wide bank of windows looked out over the backyard and the ocean beyond. She guessed that in daylight, the view would be gorgeous. Now, though, she saw only the dark with the pale wash of solar lights on the lawn.

Beneath the TV was a fireplace, cold now, and twin comfy chairs pulled up in front of it. There was a long, low dresser on another wall and tables on either side of a gigantic bed that was covered in a navy blue duvet and mounded with pillows in shades of blue and gray.

"It's nice," she said, and knew that sounded lame, but really, she'd been lucky to squeeze those two words out of her tight throat. The room was lovely, but impersonal. There were no hints to the inner thoughts of Ethan Hart. It was as if this were a palatial hotel room. And actually, that's what it was. Though Ethan owned this beautiful home, until the last week or so, he'd spent almost no time in it. At most, it was a place to sleep and to store his clothes.

There were no family photos in the room, no scattered coins on the dresser or keys casually discarded. Sadie realized that outside of his office, his company, Ethan had less of a life than she'd guessed. But maybe she could help him change that while she was there.

"Thanks," he said, "glad you like it." He gave her a wry smile, walked to the bed and dropped her onto the mattress.

Sadie yelped in surprise, then grinned as she bounced. "Very suave."

"Again. Thanks."

She toed off her shoes and let them hit the floor with a thud. Then her fingers went to the buttons on her shirt. He was watching every move she made and Sadie loved the flash of heat she saw in his eyes.

"Trying to make me crazy by undoing those buttons extra slowly?"

"Is it working?" She knew it was. She could feel his impatience building as quickly as her own. It felt like forever since she'd touched him. Since he'd been inside her.

"Way too well," he said tightly, and tore off his own shirt, sending buttons skittering across the hardwood floor.

She drew in a fast, deep breath. He must have a gym somewhere in this palace, Sadie told herself, because the man's body was sharply defined muscles that made her fingers itch to touch him. He undid his slacks, stepped out of them and his shorts, and then he was standing in front of her and her heartbeat jumped into a gallop. His chest wasn't the only impressive physical trait the man possessed.

"You're overdressed," he murmured, leaning forward

to unhook her jeans and pull them down and off her legs. Then he gave her a smile of appreciation. "If I'd known you were wearing black lace, it might not have taken us so long to get here."

In the heat of his gaze, Sadie felt beautiful. Powerful. Her stomach swirled as she sat up, undid her shirt and shrugged it off to display the matching black lace bra.

"You are a picture," he whispered. "But you're still overdressed."

She smiled up at him. "Why don't you see what you can do about that?"

He reached for her and she rose up to meet him. His fingers flicked the clasp of her bra free and his eyes fired even as he filled his hands with her breasts and rubbed her pebbled nipples with his thumbs.

Sadie's head fell back as a buzz of awareness swirled through her, tightening into a coil in the pit of her stomach. It felt so good. *He* felt so good. His hands were strong and gentle and oh so talented.

She opened her eyes to look up at him and saw her own desire reflected in his gaze. "I've missed you," she admitted.

"I missed you, too," he said softly, "and I didn't want to."

Sadie almost laughed. That was so Ethan. "Then it's twice as nice to hear," she said, and took his face in her palms to kiss him.

Instantly, he levered her back onto the bed and covered her body with his. His mouth latched on to hers and their tongues twisted together in a sensual dance that began slowly and in seconds became breathless, frenzied. Sadie ran her hands up and down his arms, up to his broad shoulders. She curled her fingers in, holding on to him as if to keep him right where he was. His hands swept up and down her body; his fingers hooked around the thin elastic of her panties and pushed them down. She lifted her hips, helping him. She wanted nothing between them, not even that tiny scrap of lace.

He dipped his head to her breast and Sadie took a harsh breath at the sensation of him drawing her body into his mouth. He suckled her, drawing and pulling until it felt as if he would tear her soul from her and into him. And while she sighed and writhed beneath him, he touched her core, dipping his fingers into her heat as he had once before, and this time it was even better.

Because they were here, in his house, and she could shout if she wanted to? Because she'd finally accepted that the love she felt for him wasn't going anywhere?

Did it matter why? No. All that mattered was his next kiss. The next touch. The next breathless anticipation. In the next instant, she pushed every thought aside. Nothing mattered but this moment. She wanted it to go on forever. The feeling of his body against hers. His hands on her skin.

"God, you smell good," he whispered, tracking his lips and tongue along her skin, up to her throat, where he nibbled at her pulse beat.

She tipped her head to one side to give him better access and slid her hands up and down his back. "And oh, you feel good."

He lifted his head, looked down at her and smiled. "I really do feel good, thanks."

She laughed and realized that until this time with him, she'd almost never seen his sense of humor. Sadie enjoyed this closeness between them. Beyond the sex, beyond their bodies coming together, this link was everything she'd ever hoped for. This easiness between them was worth everything.

The smiles, the laughter, the shared sighs and the breathless need all combined to make Sadie feel as if she and Ethan really were connecting on a much deeper level than simply physically.

He sat up and pulled away then, reaching for the bedside table. She knew what he was doing and she was all for it. "Hurry up, Ethan."

He shot her a grin. "We have all night, Sadie. No need to hurry."

All night. Didn't that sound wonderful? But for now, she had an ache demanding to be satisfied. She went up on her elbows and tossed her hair back out of her face. "Hurry now, take our time later."

He sheathed himself with a condom, turned back to her and said softly, "Yes, ma'am."

Grabbing hold of her butt, he pulled her closer, lifted her legs and draped them over his shoulders. Sadie shifted, writhed, wiggled her hips, anything she could do to entice him to get on with it. She felt as if she were wired so tightly she might just explode, and nobody wanted that.

Then she almost did, the moment his mouth covered her core. She was helpless in his grasp. All she could do was moan and shout and beg for the release he kept just out of reach. Sadie watched him, reached down and ran her fingers through his hair, then held him to her. He licked her, nibbled at her, scoring her center lightly with the edges of his teeth. Again and again, his tongue claimed her, stirring that one sensitive bud until it felt as if it were electrified.

She rocked her hips because it was the only move

available to her. He took her higher, faster, than he had before, and Sadie fought for air. She didn't want to pass out and miss anything about this moment. She couldn't tear her gaze from him.

His hands kneaded her butt while his mouth tormented her. He didn't stop, not even when her climax erupted and turned her into a writhing, screaming mess, trying to hold on to the world so she wouldn't fall off.

Before the last ripple had coursed through her, Ethan dropped her to the mattress and claimed her body in one long, hard stroke. Sadie felt shattered. As if she'd come apart and now he was tormenting the jagged pieces. And she moved into him to make him go faster, deeper.

He set a rhythm designed to drive her insane. Caught, held in place by his strength, she lifted her hips, rocking high to take him deep. Sadie curled her fingers into the silky duvet and held on tight.

"Ethan!"

"Come on," he ordered harshly, his voice hardly more than a scrape of sound. "Come again, Sadie. Come for me."

She shook her head. If she climaxed again, she might never be put back together again. And yet there was no stopping it. She screamed his name again and relished the feeling of his body slamming into hers, over and over again.

She felt it coming, so she opened her eyes so she could look at him when he pushed her over the edge. His eyes burned as his gaze locked on her. He moved faster, harder, and Sadie rushed to meet that crashing release. And when it claimed her, she shouted his name like a prayer.

Once again, Ethan didn't give her body time to stop shaking, shivering, before he moved and changed the game again. Smoothly, he shifted to lay on his back, taking her with him. Sadie straddled him then and braced her hands on his hard, sculpted chest.

He was embedded so deeply inside her now, she wanted to savor that feeling, keep it with her always. His hands came down on her hips and Sadie smiled at him. "Your turn, Ethan."

She moved on him, and this time it was *her* setting the pace, her driving the action and creating a rhythm that drove Ethan to the edge of madness. She watched him, saw his eyes glaze with passion, felt the strength of his hands tighten on her hips. She swiveled on him, deepening their contact, driving them both now. Sadie knew another orgasm was coming and she held it back, wanting to reach that peak with Ethan this time.

And when he was ready, she took his surrender and gave him her own. Seconds, minutes, maybe hours ticked past as their bodies exploded in tandem. Then she crashed down onto his chest and was cradled in his arms.

"That was…" Sadie said with an exhausted, yet exhilarated sigh.

"Yeah, it was." Ethan dragged his hands up and down her spine, keeping her right where she was, sprawled on top of him.

"I don't think I can move," she admitted. Never in her life had Sadie experienced anything like what she had with Ethan.

He was the man she'd looked for her whole life. And he was the one man she couldn't have.

Her heart broke a little even though her body was content, practically humming.

"That's good," Ethan said. "I really don't want you to move."

She laughed a little and turned her face into his chest. "We can't stay like this, Ethan. We'll starve."

"We can call out for pizza," he said. "I can reach the phone from here."

"And the delivery guy will bring it to us here?" She lifted her head and looked into his eyes. "A little embarrassing, don't you think?"

He grinned. "I'll toss the duvet over your excellent ass."

Her heart turned over in her chest. "Excellent? Thanks."

"Absolutely," he said, as he dropped one hand to her behind and squeezed. "Nobody sees that ass but me."

She thrilled to that and her too eager heart started celebrating. But she knew he didn't mean anything by it. He wasn't talking about permanence. Heck, he might not even really like her butt. It could all be the kind of things he said to every woman he took to bed. It would be foolish to build something out of nothing. And yet...

Sadie pushed those thoughts aside to examine later. For now, she kept her gaze fixed on his. "Your bed's a lot more comfortable than the desk."

She saw a flash in his green eyes and his hands on her butt tightened. "I've got a real fondness for that desk, now."

"Me, too," she admitted, then shivered.

"You cold?"

"A little," she said, then whooped when he rolled them over, covering her body with his.

"Better?"

"Better," she assured him, then gasped when he bent his head to taste one of her nipples again. "Okay," Sadie whispered, "not cold anymore."

He lifted his head to wink at her. "Glad to hear it. Now, let's get even warmer."

She swallowed hard, told her heart to slow down so it wouldn't simply explode out of her chest, and let herself slide into the feelings Ethan engendered in her. His hands were everywhere. He moved and she sighed. He touched and she moaned. He kissed and she hungered.

With her eyes closed, it was strictly a sensory world. She heard the bedside table drawer open again. Heard foil being ripped. Heard him sigh as he sheathed himself, and then he was turning her onto her belly, lifting her hips and pushing her legs apart. She turned her face to one side as she reached up to hold on to the padded, gray leather headboard. Then Sadie looked over her shoulder at him, saw him poised at her center and felt everything inside her melt into a puddle of need and love and desire so thick and heavy, her body ached with it.

How could she need him again so quickly?

She licked her lips and whispered, "Do it, Ethan. Take me."

His green eyes burned. His jaw was tight. Desire rippled off of his body in waves that washed over her and nearly took her under. Then he pushed himself home and she forgot everything.

She moved back into him, rocking, pushing. He ran his hands over her butt, then swept one down to touch her core as he drove into her from behind. Again and again, he was relentless, tireless. He pushed her, demanding she give him all she was, while he gave and took all at once. Their bodies slapped together and the heat in the room was breathless.

He was all. He was everything. What he could do to her. What she did to him. The magic they created together shone around them like fireworks raining down from the ceiling. He stroked her hard, pushing down on that tight, hard nub with his thumb, and Sadie shattered again. She screamed his name and only moments later, he shouted in triumph and emptied himself into her.

Bodies burning, hearts crashing, they curled up together, her back to his front, and dropped into exhausted sleep.

For Ethan, the next few days were…challenging. Not only did he have a new housekeeper and her five-year-old daughter living at the house, but he and Sadie had crossed the barriers separating them. She spent every night in his room, because what was the point of going in and out of the guest room?

Every night, they made love with a frantic fierceness that seemed to only get stronger. He couldn't stop touching her. Wanting her. He woke up in the middle of the night and reached for her. She'd become…essential. Ethan wasn't sure when that had happened or even *how* it had.

He'd wakened this morning to realize there were lotions and makeup lined up like tiny soldiers on his bathroom counter. In the shower, her shampoo sat beside his and made the whole damn room smell like lemons. Her clothes were in his closet, her shoes lined up alongside his, and when he'd finally noticed all this, he'd had one brief moment of panic.

It had been a long time since he'd shared any part of his home, his life, with a woman. And that had ended so badly, he'd promised himself he would never risk it again. But this was different, he assured himself. This situation with Sadie was temporary. This wasn't a mark of a relationship beginning, but of a business partnership ending.

"And I don't care for that, either." They still had almost three weeks on their deal and neither of them had spoken again about the fact that now that Julie was working for him, and willing to care for the baby, he didn't really need a nanny. At least, there wasn't a huge rush for one.

So why had he asked Sadie to stay? Why hadn't he told her that she could move out of his house?

"Because," he muttered, turning in his chair to stare out at the ocean, "you don't want her to leave."

Sure, it worried him to see how much she was settling into his home, his bedroom. But the nights with her were addictive. The more he had her, the more he wanted her. If she left, he might never get her back in his bed again, and Ethan wasn't ready to give that up yet.

And then there was Emma.

The tiny girl was carving out a place for herself in his heart and that was shocking, as well. He'd never expected to feel something for the baby. Care for her, sure. He owed Bill and his wife that. Ethan had made a promise and he intended to keep it. But he'd never been around kids much and he'd liked it that way.

Now Emma was opening his eyes to the idea that just maybe he'd been...wrong. It didn't happen often, which was why he hadn't recognized it right away. But he was a big enough man, he hoped, to admit when the unthinkable happened.

Only the night before, he'd been struck by just how the changes in his life had affected him. He'd heard Emma stirring on the baby monitor and got up before Sadie could wake. In the dark, quiet house, he'd walked into Emma's room and crossed to the crib. The little girl opened her eyes, looked up at him and *smiled*. She knew him. Trusted him. Was happy to see him.

And in that instant, a bubble of warmth had spread through his chest and settled around his heart. He hadn't expected it, wasn't prepared for what it was going to mean to his life, but he also couldn't deny it.

Emma. Sadie. They were changing everything and it was quickly coming to the point where he couldn't remember what it had been like without them in his house. In his mind.

All he had left of his once orderly world was work. His company. And even that was under constant assault from Gabriel, though Ethan hadn't heard another word from his brother about changes. Which should worry him, he supposed. On the other hand, he'd take the break where he could.

Then a knock on the door sounded and Sadie poked her head inside. "Ethan. Ms. Gable from Child Services is here."

Well, that break didn't last long. He wondered if this was a routine check or if the woman had some idea of taking Emma from him. If that was her plan, she would be disappointed.

Emma and Sadie were his and Ethan wasn't ready to give either of them up.

Eight

"Send her in, Sadie."

Melissa Gable walked into his office with long, purposeful strides. Ethan silently gave her points for an in-
timidating presence. In her black suit jacket, starched
white shirt and knee-length black skirt and sky-high
heels, she looked all business. He supposed most people might wither and quietly panic beneath her steady
stare. But Ethan wasn't worried. Ms. Gable wouldn't
get anything he wasn't willing to give.

She carried a black bag the size of Montana on
her left shoulder, and as he rose to greet her, Ms.
Gable reached into the bag and pulled out a manila
file folder.

They shook hands, then she took a seat opposite his
desk. He sat down, too, studied her, waiting. He didn't
wait long.

"I've already been to your day care here in the building to check in on Emma, see how she's doing."

"How did you know she wouldn't be at home with a nanny?" Just curious, he told himself.

"I didn't," she said. "But it's my job to be thorough, so I checked the day care first."

"And?" He offered nothing. He'd learned long ago that the secret to successful negotiations was remembering that he who speaks first loses power.

"She appears to be happy and healthy," Ms. Gable allowed. "And as a side note, I have to commend you on your in-house day care, as well. Unfortunately, there aren't enough employers farsighted enough to realize that a well-run day care is imperative in this day and age."

"Agreed." He nodded. "It pays to keep your employees happy, and when they don't have to worry about their kids, they're more productive." Well damn, that sounded cold even to him. Maybe that *was* why he'd begun the day care in the first place. But since Emma had arrived in his life, he'd realized just how important it was for people to be able to check on their children during the day. He'd been downstairs a few times himself.

"Yes. Well." She checked her notes, then looked at him again. "I've spoken to the day care operators, who tell me Emma is well fed, clean and obviously well cared for."

That irritated him beyond measure. "You expected she wouldn't be?"

"No, but even the most well-meaning people don't often pull things together as quickly as you seem to have." She flipped through to another page, scanned it, then said, "I went by your house earlier and your house-keeper showed me Emma's room. I approve of what you've done there and…" She checked again. "Julie, is it? She assured me that the baby is cared for and happy."

"Again," he said, tapping his fingers now against the desk. The desk where he and Sadie had taken each other for the very first time. Odd, but that stray thought eased the temper building within. "You're surprised?"

Ms. Gable closed the file, tucked it into her bag and said, "Forgive me, Mr. Hart, but you seemed less than happy when you discovered Emma had been left in your charge."

He winced internally at that, because she made a good point. He hadn't wanted the baby. Had resented that Bill had remembered that long-ago promise Ethan had made. But whether he'd wanted them to or not, things had changed. That baby girl had started out as nothing more than his responsibility. Now she was more. Now she was *his*.

Just then, he recalled Sadie telling him, "If you can't love Emma, maybe you should give her up to someone who can." And he thought about that. Thought about that tiny girl. How it felt when she curled her fingers around his. How *he* felt when she laid her head down on his shoulder. How right it was when he checked on her at night and saw her smile at him with delight.

He did love her.

Might not have wanted to. Might not have counted on this ever happening to him, but Emma was important to him now. And he'd give her up to no one.

"Mr. Hart?"

"Emma stays with me," he said flatly, coming out of his thoughts. "I'm looking for a nanny now and until

I find one, my housekeeper, Julie, is helping us care for her."

"Us?"

"My assistant, Sadie Matthews, is assisting me with Emma, as well."

"I see." Nodding to herself, she stood up, held out her hand and waited for him to shake it. "Well then, from what I can see, you have this situation well in hand. I'll make my report to my superiors and recommend the guardianship become permanent. If you care to eventually legally adopt Emma, I'd be happy to help you in any way I can."

Surprised, but pleased, Ethan stood up and nodded. "I appreciate that."

Once the woman was gone, Sadie slipped into the room and closed the door, leaning back against it. "Well? What did she say? Do? Think?"

He laughed a little. Sadie's enthusiasm was contagious.

"Emma stays with me," he said.

"Really?" Sadie smiled at him and approval shone in her eyes. Strange how good it felt to know she was proud of him and what he'd done.

"I'm glad, Ethan."

"Why?" he asked, his gaze sliding over every square inch of her.

"Because I think Emma's good for you."

One eyebrow arched. "More direct honesty?"

Sadie shrugged. "A little late to change that now. Besides, would you prefer lies?"

"No," he said, his gaze locked on her. She was wearing what he'd always thought of as her "work uniform." Black slacks, dress shirt and short black jacket. And she looked sexier than any other woman would have in diaphanous lace or a skimpy bikini. Just looking at Sadie hit him on so many levels he couldn't have counted them all.

He wanted her.

As he did every moment of every damn day.

It didn't matter if she was laughing with him or her eyes were snapping with fury. Sadie Matthews was the one thing in Ethan's world he couldn't predict. Couldn't control. And he enjoyed knowing that more than he would have thought possible.

"It's not as scary as you thought, is it?"

Could she read his mind now?

"What's that?"

"Love."

The way she said that word sent a chill along his spine. He stiffened and his voice went deep and gruff as he demanded, "Who said anything about love?"

Her head tipped to one side, delighting him, even as her expression screamed disappointment. "I did. But you should. Ethan, you love that baby."

"I care for her, sure," he hedged. He wasn't going to use the *L* word because it didn't matter. He'd made Emma a part of his world, his life. He would take care of her, make sure she was happy. Wasn't that enough, for God's sake?

"Is it really beyond you to admit you know how to love?"

"It's not that I don't know how," he said tightly. "It's that I choose not to."

"And that's immeasurably sad."

He ground out, "Thanks so much."

"Ethan…" She took a step toward him and stopped.

"I'll only be here a couple more weeks. When I leave, what then?"

A couple more weeks. Well hell, he didn't want to think about *that*. Time was moving too quickly. It wasn't only Emma who had invaded his life, it was Sadie, as well, and knowing she would be gone soon was like a thorn constantly jabbing at him. Ethan wanted to find a way to keep her with him; he just hadn't come up with anything yet. But damned if he'd lose Sadie now.

Marriage was, of course, out of the question. He'd already failed spectacularly at that institution and he had no interest in repeating the mistake.

"You don't have to leave."

"We've been over this, Ethan."

"I don't want you to leave," he said abruptly.

"What?" She stared at him, shocked. "What are you saying?"

"I'm saying we're good together, Sadie." He came forward, took both her hands in his and held on tightly, stroking his thumbs across her knuckles. "We're a hell of a team. Why should we end it?"

"Ethan…" Her eyes shone and she licked her lips as if they'd gone suddenly dry.

"Things have changed between us, Sadie. You know it as well as I do. We have more together now." The thought of losing it was unacceptable. "You don't have to go, Sadie."

She looked as though she might be considering it, so he continued. "In the last couple of weeks, we've been more flexible with work time, right?"

"Work time." She frowned.

"Yes." He held her hands tighter when she tried to pull free. "You can work whatever hours you want. You can take your vacations and I won't call you out of family gatherings."

"I see…"

"And we can be together," he finished, pulling her up against him.

"Like we have been," she said softly.

"Exactly." He looked down into her eyes. "Sadie, the last couple of weeks have worked for both of us, haven't they?"

"Yes."

"So why change it?"

She gave him a small smile and shook her head. Ethan didn't like what he was reading in her eyes.

"Because I want more in my life than great sex and work," she said.

"What else is there?" Ethan demanded, though he knew damn well what her answer would be.

"*Love*, Ethan," she said, meeting his gaze with an intensity that almost slapped at him. "I want someone to love. I want to *be* loved. I want a family of my own."

"You have Emma," he countered, thinking of how close she'd become to the baby over the last couple weeks. "We both know you love that baby. I can see it whenever you hold her."

"I do. I really do. But she's not mine, Ethan," she said, shaking her head again. "She's a darling, but she's your baby. To her, I'll never be more than someone who comes and goes from her house. Like a visiting aunt."

"Then live there with us," he argued.

She took a breath, blew it out and said, "You want me to live with you, have sex with you, help you raise Emma and work here for you."

"Is that so bad?" The demand rolled from him in

deep, tight tones. "For God's sake, Sadie, we're doing all of that now. Why not keep doing it?"

"Because it's not enough."

"It is for me," he countered.

"Not for me." She swallowed hard and added, "If I'm going to have my own life, have what's important to me, I have to leave. To you, I'll never be more than your lover."

"And that's bad?" He released her hands and didn't let himself think how empty his hands felt.

"For me, yes," she said. "I need more, Ethan. I deserve more."

He couldn't argue with that, because she did deserve everything she wanted. But he couldn't give it to her. Wouldn't get married again.

"Fine." Nodding, he stepped back behind the desk, as if pulling on a suit of armor. "Well then, you'd better get busy finding your replacement here. And I'll still need a nanny for Emma."

"Ethan, I wish—"

He ignored that. "Get me marketing, will you? I want to have another look at the Mother's Day campaign before it's set in stone."

"All right."

"And bring me some coffee when you get a minute."

"Sure." Her heels tapped against the floor as she left the office.

When she was gone, he sat back in his chair and told himself to get used to that empty sensation. It was going to be with him for a long time.

"You had sex."

"I did," Sadie said, and picked up the wine Gina had poured for her. "Many times."

"Finally." Gina sighed happily, took a sip of her own wine and demanded, "Who's the lucky guy?"

"Ethan."

Gina choked on her wine, slapped one hand to her own chest and coughed until her eyes ran. Feeling a little guilty, Sadie tried to help, but Gina shook her head and waved one hand at her. When she could finally breathe again, she cried, "What do you mean, many times? Are you crazy?"

Sadie had been asking herself that for almost two weeks now. And the answer was still the same. If she *was* crazy, she didn't care. "No. He's—"

"Don't. Don't even say it," Gina told her, and took a cautious sip of her wine. "Honey, I know I told you to have sex with him, but that was to get him out of your system, not to dig him in even deeper."

That's just what had happened, though. Even after the scene this afternoon at the office, Sadie couldn't regret what she'd had with Ethan. Yes, he'd made it plain that he wasn't interested in love. That he didn't want to give more than he had or risk more than he dared. And maybe she could understand why, even though she wanted to throttle him to make him see what they could have together if only he'd believe.

She'd left the office right after their...*meeting* and come to Gina's. Ethan was perfectly capable of driving Emma home and seeing that she had dinner. It would be good for him to do it himself. To see what it would be like without Sadie around to help. And oh, that thought broke her heart. She wouldn't be there to watch Emma grow up. Wouldn't be sleeping with Ethan. Or having sex with him. Or waking up snuggled next to him. She wouldn't even be working with him anymore, and boy, his absence in her life was going to leave a huge, gaping hole.

"I need cookies." Gina got up to rummage in a cupboard and came up with a bag of chocolate-covered marshmallow cookies. "This is my private stash. None of the kids know. Not even Mike has found them yet. But I'm willing to share with you."

"You're a saint." Sadie grinned and took a cookie for herself. Biting in, she took a quick look around. Gina's kitchen was bright and cheerful. White walls, red cupboards and black granite counters. There were sippy cups on the drain board and a row of baby bottles waiting to be filled. It was homey and cozy and light-years from Ethan's showplace kitchen. But, Sadie reminded herself, now that Julie was working at his house, she'd made some changes to the sterile atmosphere that could almost make it this warm.

"If I were a saint I wouldn't have told you to sleep with Ethan."

Sadie looked at her sister-in-law. "You couldn't have stopped me, either."

"Well, don't tell Mike that. I have him convinced I'm all powerful."

Sadie laughed and took another bite of cookie. "I can't help what I feel, Gina."

"But you're hoping this is going to turn into a fairy tale or something," the other woman said. "I can see it in your eyes."

"Well, that's annoying," Sadie admitted. Because of course that's what she'd been hoping for. Even knowing the chances of it happening were practically zip. And today had pretty much tied that up in a bow. Yet still, she hadn't completely given up. "Okay, yes, I'm hoping, but the more rational part of me knows this isn't going anywhere. But Gina, he's hitting most of the points on my list now."

"Really…" Gina ate another cookie and washed it down with wine.

Sadie ticked them off. "Sexy, oh yeah. Adventurous…" Thinking of the night before in the shower, she flushed with pleasure. "Boy howdy. He's spending time with me and he loves Emma."

"Has he actually said so?"

"No, but I can tell." He didn't want to say the word, but that didn't mean he wasn't feeling the emotion. The more time Ethan spent with the baby, the easier he was with her. Emma had wormed her way into the man's heart against his will and it was wonderful to watch. Whether Ethan knew it or not, he was opening up to the world. To possibilities. Why couldn't one of those possibilities be *her*?

"And sense of humor?"

"He has that, too," she insisted. "He doesn't show it often, but it's there."

"Sadie, that list was there to prove to you that Ethan wasn't the man for you. Instead, you're fiddling with it to make sure he meets all the criteria you have. That's not a good thing."

"I know." Restless, Sadie set her wine down and walked across the kitchen, picked up one of the baby's bottles and turned it in her hands. She wanted children of her own. A husband. A job she loved. Was that really too much to ask?

Not looking at Gina, she said, "We're still hunting for a nanny. When we find one, I'll go."

"I know you don't want to," Gina said.

"I really don't." Looking at her from across the room, Sadie gave her sister-in-law a sad smile. "I just love him. Like you love Mike."

"I know. But sweetie, setting yourself up for heartbreak isn't the smartest thing you've ever done."

"True. But honestly, if there is no happy ending here, at least I had this time with him."

"It won't be enough."

Sadie set the bottle down. "It'll have to be."

Gabriel watched as the chef made up the samples that they'd present to Ethan.

Making fine chocolates was more a science than an art, though most people didn't realize it. Of course, there was plenty of art involved, as well.

Tempering the chocolate itself to the right temperature, where it would set up glossy and hard enough to *snap* when you bit into it. Mixing the ganache to the perfect texture before infusing it with the flavors Gabriel was hoping would convince Ethan to open his mind and try something new. Once the ganache was ready, the truffles and other assorted fillings had to be hand rolled into a uniform size and perfectly rounded or squared. Sometimes they used molds to get the right shapes, but here, in this rented kitchen, Jeff Garrett would be rolling the chocolates by hand.

As an assistant chef at Heart, Jeff was talented and eager to move up the ladder. Tonight was his chance at excellence, as well as Gabe's. Jeff already had the chocolates—milk, white and dark—tempered and waiting. The cold marble slab held rows of perfectly rounded truffles and ganache and were just waiting for Jeff to hand dip them and then stamp and decorate. Now that most of the basics were done, the chef as artist would take over. With talent and style, a good chocolate chef would make his creations shine like jewels.

"It smells great in here, doesn't it?" Gabe murmured, not wanting to disturb Jeff as he mixed the last of the spices into the final ganache.

"It does," Pam whispered, her gaze never leaving the chef and the chocolates laid out on the marble slab in front of him. "Do you still have the recipe with you?" she asked. "Just in case he has to start over, I mean."

"Don't even say it." Gabe shuddered and checked his watch. "Jeff's already been at it for hours. If we have to start over…"

"But the recipe's safe, right?"

He looked at her. "Yeah. Of course. Don't worry so much."

"I just…know how much this means to you, that's all." Pam watched as Jeff used a candy fork to hand dip a lavender truffle into the white chocolate melt. He carefully lifted it out, laid it on the cool marble, then swirled the chocolate on top by twisting the candy fork over it. He did the same with five more truffles until he had a tidy row laid out.

On another slab were pieces of what would be dark chocolate raspberry coconut bark drizzled with white chocolate.

Earl Grey tea truffles coated in cocoa powder were resting alongside white chocolate lemon blackberry bonbons. The last offering was a dark chocolate ganache infused with Sumatran coffee—Ethan's favorite—and orange liqueur.

The samples were flavorful and beautiful, as Jeff

concentrated now on decorating each piece until it shone.

"The chef I was going to have you use would have made the bark white chocolate with dark chocolate drizzle. To showcase the red of the raspberry." Pam sniffed a little.

Gabe slanted her a puzzled look. "Jeff's creations look perfect."

"Oh, they're very nice." She shrugged. "I just think a more experienced chef might have done an even better job."

Okay, he thought, she'd been a little off ever since their first fight about the chef and she was still off tonight. Not really angry, but not herself, either. He'd wanted her there with him because it had really all started out as Pam's idea. The two of them together, facing down Ethan. But ever since Gabe had decided to use Jeff, Pam had been...different.

"What's going on with you, Pam?" Gabe asked. "Jeff studied with master chocolatiers in Belgium. He's been with Heart Chocolates for four years. He's worked his way up to being an assistant chef and he wants this almost as badly as I do."

"All true," she said with a shrug, "but you never even gave my guy a tryout."

"I didn't need to," he said, impatient now. After all, this might have started out as her idea, but this was his life. His company. She didn't have a horse in the race, so she had nothing to lose.

She flashed him a hard look and interrupted him. "I keep telling you, I thought we were in this together, Gabe. *We* were making decisions, and then suddenly, you changed the rules and I'm cut out. How do you think I should feel?"

He blew out a breath and tried to see it from her point of view. Gabe guessed he would have been pretty pissed if the tables were turned. But bottom line, this was his life. Not Pam's.

"I know you wanted to help," he said, striving for patience. He loved Pam, But damned if he understood her. "I do trust you. But this is my company. I've got to do what I think is best for it."

"I know, Gabe. Really. And I love you. I'm just…" she shrugged again. She shifted her gaze to Jeff.

Gabe watched as the man used an airbrush pencil to dazzle the white chocolate with rainbow colors in swirled patterns. As those colors began to set up, Jeff switched cartridges to paint a stylized red heart on top of the dark honey-infused caramels coated in a thick layer of milk chocolate.

"They all look great," Gabe said.

Jeff paused to glance up at him and smile. "Thanks, boss. The dark chocolate raspberry and chipotle chili are going to be coated in an extra layer of dark, then streaked with the milk in a heart pattern." He glanced around at his creations. "Then I think we'll be ready."

Ready to face down Ethan and demand he take a chance on the future. Hell, Gabe was betting everything on this as a win. Ethan's head would explode when he found out Gabe had taken the family recipe from the safe. So these chocolates had better damn well convince Ethan that Gabe was right, or working with his older brother from now on was going to be a living nightmare.

"When will you take these to Ethan?" Pam asked.

"Tomorrow," Gabe said firmly, nodding to himself. "You ready for it, Jeff?"

"So ready," the chef said, concentrating on the last of the chocolates he was creating. "I've got the boxes here. When they're finished setting up, I'll box them for tomorrow."

"In the morning. Be at my office at ten. With the chocolates. We'll face Ethan down together." He turned to Pam. "Are you going to be there?"

"Sure." She lifted her chin and met his gaze. "I told you before, Gabe. I'm with you."

Gabe dropped one arm around her shoulders. She was tense and stiff for a couple seconds, then she moved into him and leaned her head against his shoulder. He smiled to himself. Whatever was going on, they'd get past it. Once this was settled, he'd sit down with Pam and not let up until he found the answers he wanted. But for now, he had to focus on the plan he'd put everything into. He knew this was a step toward the future for Heart and damned if he wouldn't find a way to convince Ethan.

Gabe believed that. He had to. Because if he failed, he wouldn't lose only this chance at making a mark on the company. He might lose his brother.

Ethan was already in a crappy mood when Gabriel walked into his office the next morning. He hadn't slept all night because he hadn't had Sadie with him. For the first time since moving in with him, she'd slept in the guest room. Annoying to realize how much he'd come to count on having her there beside him.

She'd been right across the hall and yet she might as well have been hundreds of miles away. He knew what it would take to get her to come to him. And he couldn't give it to her.

Wouldn't, he corrected silently. She wanted a relationship. Something permanent. A family. A commitment.

Hell, he'd changed enough lately, hadn't he? He'd taken her into his house, into his bedroom. He'd been with her now longer than he had been with anyone else other than his ex. Ethan already knew he hadn't been a good husband. Why would he even *think* about trying that again? He liked Sadie. Liked being with her, so why would he risk making her miserable by marrying her? No. She might think he was being a selfish bastard by pulling away, but the truth was, he assured himself, he was doing this for her own good.

Let her find another man. His insides twisted at the thought. One who would hold her at night, make her belly swell with a child. He gritted his teeth and fisted both hands helplessly. Some other man would be the one to get her smiles, her kisses, her—

"Ethan," Gabriel said, splintering his thoughts, "we have to talk."

"Looks like more of a meeting than a conversation," Ethan observed. He looked from his younger brother to Sadie, to Jeff Garrett, one of their top chocolate chefs. A cold, suspicious feeling snaked along Ethan's spine and colored his tone when he demanded, "What's this about, Gabe?"

"Jeff and I have something we want you to try." Gabe motioned to the chef, who stepped up and set three small candy boxes on Ethan's desk.

His temper bubbled, but Ethan kept it tamped down. Gabe had done it. Gone behind his back and made up samples of the candies he wanted to incorporate into the company's product line.

Standing up behind his desk, Ethan looked at Sadie. "Did you know about this?"

"Nope," she said, and shot Gabe a hard look.

"Don't give Sadie a bad time. She didn't know a thing," Gabe said, and faced off against Ethan. Bracing his legs wide apart as if readying for a fight, he folded his arms across his chest and said, "This was my idea. Well, mine and Pam's."

He turned to hold out one hand toward a woman hovering near the doorway. "Come on in, honey. It's game time."

Ethan watched her walk to his brother and he frowned slightly. "Who's this?"

"Pam Cassini," Gabe said. "She's with me."

Amazing. He'd brought his new girlfriend in on this? Ethan studied the woman. She looked familiar somehow, but he couldn't put his finger on why. Frowning, Ethan set that niggling worry aside a second later because damned if he didn't have bigger issues at the moment.

Sadie walked up and stood beside him. Thankful for the support, he gave her a quick nod, then looked back to his brother.

Gabe was standing in a slash of sunlight pouring through the tinted windows at Ethan's back. He stood like a man waiting to hear a sentence pronounced. Well, he wouldn't have to wait long. "What the hell have you done?"

Nine

Gabe lifted his chin and met Ethan glare for glare. "I rented a professional kitchen and Jeff made up some samples of a few of the flavors I was talking to you about."

Ethan's gaze shifted to Jeff, who looked a lot more worried than Gabe did. As he should. "You know I could fire you for this," he said tightly.

Jeff swallowed hard. "Yes, sir, I know. But I agree with Gabe. It's time to push outside the box."

Astounded, feeling cornered, Ethan lifted his eyebrows. "In a box? You think Heart Chocolates is boring? Is that it?"

"No, he didn't say that," Gabe interrupted. "And don't come down on him, either, Ethan. He can't fight back."

"But you can," Ethan said, and his voice was so controlled, so quiet, Gabe should have been wary. Instead, his brother looked defiant, rebellious. Situation normal as far as Gabe's attitude went.

Sadie caught Ethan's reaction, though, and silently slid her hand into his and gave it a squeeze. With that single touch, she dialed down his temper, his frustration, and helped him focus.

"What exactly did you do?" Ethan asked, and thought he was remaining remarkably calm, all things considered.

"I told you."

"Yes. But how did you make up the chocolate?" Ethan studied his brother. "For these 'samples' to be a true representation of Heart, you'd have to have access to the recipe."

The minute the words left his mouth, Ethan saw the truth on his brother's features. And his calm dissolved into a pit of white-hot fury. "You *took* the recipe?"

"I'm a Hart, too, Ethan," Gabriel argued, meeting fire with fire. "Yes, I took *our* recipe. I made a copy of the one in your safe."

Ethan actually saw red. That recipe never left the safe. It had been copied and protected and kept in a separate place, but the original... "How did you—"

Sadie tugged on his hand and he looked down at her. "I ran into Pam and Gabe here in your office the night Emma arrived. I didn't mention it because I didn't think anything of it."

Could his head actually explode? Ethan stared into Sadie's big blue eyes and read a plea for patience. She was asking a lot. But for her, he'd try. He took a long, deep breath, glared at his brother and demanded, "What did you do with the original?"

"What do you think I did with it?" Gabe sounded offended now, which was astonishing to Ethan.

"How the hell do I know?" Ethan shouted, and when he heard himself he made a valiant effort to lower his voice. "I didn't think you'd take our heritage out of the safe and make a copy, so for all I know, you sold the original on eBay!"

"Don't be ridiculous." Gabe went to the safe, hit the dial lock, spun it a few times, then swung the door open. "There's the recipe. Right where it belongs. Do you really think I'd risk everything we are to prove a point?"

"Isn't that exactly what you did?" Ethan shouted again.

Sadie squeezed his hand once more, but this time he barely felt it. This was over the top. He felt betrayed by his own damn brother. He and Gabe had argued a lot over the years, but this was something he hadn't expected.

"Hell no!" Gabe went toe to toe with his brother, and met him glare for glare. "I used the recipe, but the chef involved already works for us. I trust him as you should, too, since he's one of our top guys."

Ethan gritted his teeth so hard he should have had a mouthful of powder. "Jeff isn't the issue here."

He heard the man's sigh of relief.

"Fine." Gabe threw both hands out in supplication. "I'm a traitor. Have me drawn and quartered tomorrow. But today, try the damn chocolates."

Stunned, Ethan could only stare at him. Gabe was still pretending this was no big deal. "Seriously? You expect me to go along with this when you went behind my back?"

"You didn't give me a choice, Ethan." Gabe pushed

both hands through his hair, looked over at Pam, then back to his brother. "I wanted to do this with your approval. Hell, your involvement. But you're so damn stubborn. So resistant to change—"

"So really it's all my fault," Ethan said wryly.

"Well, I wouldn't have put it that way, but since you did…"

"You're something else, Gabe."

"Is it so hard to see my point of view, Ethan?" Gabe's voice was low and tight, filled with frustration that Ethan could sympathize with, since he was feeling it, too. "I'm not trying to wreck the company. I'm trying to make a difference and fighting you every damn day to do it."

"But you don't see it from my side, either. I don't want to change with the times," Ethan said. "Forever trying to figure out which way the wind's blowing in this business. It doesn't pay to chase trends."

"It doesn't pay to ignore advancements, either," Gabe argued.

"You guys…" Sadie tried to intervene, but neither of them acknowledged her.

"I'm not ignoring anything," Ethan said. "And I won't risk everything we are, either."

"I wanted him to use a chef I know," Pam said, speaking up for the first time. "But Gabe refused. He wouldn't risk that recipe. Instead, he insisted on using a Heart chef to protect it."

She still looked familiar to him and it was irritating to not be able to identify why. Still, she was emphasizing the point Gabe had made earlier. Mollified a bit, Ethan nodded and took a deep breath. He folded his hand around Sadie's and didn't even question why he was using her as a touchstone of sorts.

Gabe seemed to sense that the worst was over. He gave a signal to Jeff, who cautiously moved closer to the desk. Deftly, the man opened up the boxes, displaying the candies he'd personally created the night before.

"They're beautiful," Sadie whispered.

That they were, Ethan admitted silently. The variety of chocolates were artistically presented—everything from cocoa powder to the white chocolate bonbons decorated with a rainbow of colors.

"Thank you." Jeff grinned, pleased at the response.

"They're not just pretty," Gabe said, with satisfaction. "They're delicious."

Ethan scowled at him and Gabe grinned. "Admit it. You want to know what they taste like."

As angry as he was, Ethan also felt a ripple of pride in Gabe. He had his own vision and wasn't afraid to follow it. His brother had believed in something and found a way to make it happen. Not that stealing the family recipe was the way to do it, but Ethan admired that his brother believed in his own vision enough to risk everything.

"What if I don't like them?"

Gabe grinned even wider. "That won't be an issue."

"He seems sure of himself," Sadie said, with a wink for Gabe.

"Always has been," Ethan muttered.

Gabe walked to Pam and dropped one arm around her shoulders. He watched as Jeff laid out a white cloth napkin on the desk, then stepped back to wait. And watch.

"All right. Moment of truth." Ethan looked at Sadie. "I want you to try them, too. I trust your opinion."

She gave him a smile that lit up her eyes and Ethan's breath caught in his chest. Then he turned to the candy. He took one of the rainbow-decorated, glossy white chocolates.

"That's a lavender truffle," Jeff provided, then looked at Sadie as she chose another piece. "And you have a dark chocolate raspberry coconut bark drizzled with white chocolate."

"Interesting," Ethan murmured, and carefully broke the white chocolate piece in half. Satisfied at the sharp snap of the chocolate coating, he then inhaled the scent, approving of the precise blend of spice and sweet. But the proof was in the flavor.

He bit into it and let the ganache melt on his tongue while flavor exploded in his mouth. He really hated that his brother had been right. The candy was perfect.

He shifted a look at his brother and saw the triumphant gleam in Gabe's eyes. "It's great, right?"

Chewing, Ethan nodded. "It is. Better than I would have thought."

Again, Jeff heaved a sigh of relief and Ethan couldn't really blame him. The chef had risked a hell of a lot, too. He'd worked his way up at Heart and he'd gambled his job on these samples.

"Sadie?"

She swallowed the bite she'd taken and shook her head in amazement. "This bark is terrific. The raspberry is sweet but not overpowering the chocolate, and the coconut gives it a slightly salty, savory flavor. Really amazing."

Jeff smiled and Gabe looked proud enough to burst.

Ethan couldn't blame him. They went through the other chocolates one by one, with both Jeff and Gabe explaining the process and how they'd chosen the different flavors they'd blended into the ganache.

"This last one is a Sumatran coffee, orange liqueur blend," Gabe said slyly.

"Clever," Ethan murmured. "Hit me with a flavor I love."

"I'll pass," Sadie said, and took one of the lemon blackberry bonbons instead.

Pam was strangely silent, but Ethan assumed it was because this wasn't really her business. She had nothing riding on this gathering; she was simply there to support Gabe.

"You did a hell of a job, here," Ethan ruefully admitted when the tasting was completed.

He'd been backed into a corner so neatly the only way out was Gabe's way. Ethan hated change, but he'd been dealing with nothing *but* change over the last couple weeks and it hadn't killed him. And really, the damn chocolate was *good.* Maybe Gabe had a point, after all, and it was time to branch out. To test new waters, before he—and his company—became so comfortable, neither of them could grow.

"That means what, exactly?" Gabe asked warily.

Ethan looked from the candy to Sadie to Gabe. "It means we should talk privately. Pam, would you and Jeff mind stepping out of the office for a few moments?"

"She doesn't have to go," Gabe argued.

"It's okay," Pam said with a weak smile. "I'll wait outside."

When they were gone, Ethan perched on the edge of

his desk and said, "You made your point, Gabe. I don't like how you did it, but you were right about the candy."

Gabe clutched his heart. "Hold on a second. I might need an ambulance."

"Keep it up," Ethan promised with a quirk of a smile, "and you will."

Suddenly all business, Gabe asked, "So we'll go forward with the new line?"

"That depends," Ethan said, drawing Sadie over to his side and taking her hand in his.

Gabe's eyebrows lifted and a quick smile came and went. "Depends on what?"

"I don't want to start another line with only five or six offerings," Ethan said. "Can you and Jeff come up with a full dozen new flavors?"

"Oh, hell yes. Jeff's got a million ideas and—" He broke off. "You're making Jeff head chef on this project?"

"He earned it, don't you think?"

"I do. Between us, we'll come up with flavors that'll blow away the competition." Gabe was excited now, his eyes shining and a wide smile curving his mouth.

"Then go," Ethan said. "Be brilliant. But we decide together which flavors we're going to push."

"Agreed, Ethan. Thanks." Gabe went to pick up the candy boxes.

"Leave the candy," Ethan said, making his brother laugh.

Gabe walked out to tell Pam and Jeff the good news, leaving Ethan and Sadie alone in the office.

"That was well-done," Sadie said, and cupped his cheek to turn his face to hers.

"He pushes every button I've got, but he came up

with some great new tastes, textures." Shaking his head, he sighed and said, "He went about it the wrong way, but I guess he was right about something else, too. I didn't really give him any other choice."

"Wow, self-realization," Sadie mused, smiling. "I think we're having a moment here."

He caught her hand in his again. "It happens."

"You didn't have to put him and Jeff in charge," she said. "That was well-done, too."

He gave her a quick smile. "Are you kidding? He wanted this new line—now he can be in charge of making it happen. Seems fair."

Sadie laughed. "So you give him what he wants and punish him for it all at once. You're devious."

"Yeah, I know." He pulled her in close. "I missed you last night."

"I missed you, too."

"I didn't want to," he said.

"I know." She smiled wistfully.

He looked into her eyes and found himself drowning in that deep, cool blue. "I can't be who you want me to be, Sadie. But do we have to leave each other before we leave each other?"

She tipped her head to one side, those blond curls of hers sliding across her skin. "No, Ethan. Let's be together while we can."

"Good call," he said, then he kissed her.

Gabe left the meeting ready to take on the world.

Hell, if he could convince Ethan to make changes to the company chocolate line, he could do anything. He expected to find Pam outside the office waiting for him, but he spotted her with Jeff by the elevators. And it looked like they were having a conversation spiked by hand gestures and angry expressions.

Frowning, he hurried toward them, ignoring the phones ringing, the clack of keyboards and the low, muttered conversations rising and falling all around him.

"I told you I can't do it," Jeff was telling Pam as Gabe walked up. "That's proprietary information."

Pam looked desperate, furious. "For God's sake, it's not like it's a secret. You saw it last night. I'm just asking you to tell me—"

"What's going on?" Gabe looked to Pam for the answer, but shifted his gaze to Jeff when the chef spoke.

"Pam wanted me to give her the Heart chocolate recipe."

"What?" Gabe looked at her, shocked. That made zero sense. She knew that recipe was the best-kept secret in the company. Hell, she'd just been present when his own brother had reamed him for copying it. "Why would you do that?"

She took a breath and blew it out. Her gaze shifted from side to side before finally meeting Gabe's. "Because I need it for my father's company."

"What the hell, Pam?" He kept his voice low, to prevent anyone else from listening in. Jeff slipped away and Gabe barely noticed. Suddenly, a lot of things were making sense. How eager Pam had been to make up those samples. How quickly she'd suggested using her own chef to make the candy. How furious she'd been when Gabe had used Jeff for the project instead of the chef she'd suggested.

God. He felt like an idiot for trusting her.

The elevator arrived with a loud ding and Pam turned for it, but Gabe grabbed her upper arm and held her in place. "You owe me, Pam. What the hell were you doing? Was any of this real to you? Was I just a means to the recipe?" He snorted a harsh laugh as reality crashed down onto his head. She'd never been into him. It was all about Heart chocolate. "Damn, I've got to admire you. You went all out for what you wanted. Pretending to love me just to make sure your plan worked. Must have been a bitch when I didn't use your guy."

She yanked her arm free and shot him a hard look through flashing brown eyes. "Yes, it was hard. My brother's a chocolate chef. He could have made your candy and then kept the recipe for us to use against you."

Infuriated, confused, Gabe demanded, "Why? What have you got against the Hart family?"

The elevator started to close and she slapped one hand out to hold the doors open. "Because my last name isn't Cassini, Gabe. It's *Donatello*."

"What?" Everything Gabe thought he knew went right out the window. Stunned, he thought back to all the times he'd discussed business with her. How he'd told her about the Donatello buyout and how his brother was eager to take over the shop in Laguna and introduce a new venue for Heart Chocolates.

Hell, he'd *trusted* her.

Gabe looked at her as if seeing her for the first time. And still he didn't know who he was looking at. The woman he loved? Or an industrial spy? "You lied to me this whole time?"

"It wasn't all a lie," she countered, voice breaking as the first tears filled her eyes. "Cassini is my mother's maiden name."

"Oh, well then. That's okay." Shaking his head, Gabe

fought down the fury clawing at his throat as he looked at the woman he loved. The woman he'd thought was with him. A partner. "Are you even really in PR?"

"No. I make chocolate. With my family. Just like you."

"Of course you do," he muttered thickly. No wonder she'd known so much about the chocolate industry. "And you wanted to ruin Heart Chocolates as what? Payback for us buying your father out?"

"Your brother is ruining my father's life," she said, her voice urgent, desperate. "Dad can't stand up against a company the size of Heart. He has no choice, he *has* to sell because the great and powerful Ethan has decided he needs a street location and he's focused on my dad's." A hot rush of tears spilled from her eyes and streamed down her cheeks unchecked. "The Donatellos have been running that shop for forty-five years, Gabe. It's just as important to us as your company is to you. My brother and I grew up in that shop. It means everything to us."

Her tears shook him to the bone. He wanted to reach out to hold her, tell her everything would be okay, but he wasn't sure it would be. Hell, he didn't even know what he was feeling at the moment.

He loved Pam Cassini. But did that woman even really exist?

"I do love you, Gabe," she confessed. "I didn't mean to, but I do. I wasn't pretending about that. But this is about my *father*. I had to do whatever I could to help." She jumped into the elevator and kept her gaze on him as the doors slid shut. "I love you…"

"Damn it, Pam…" He lunged for her, but the doors shut him out. Then she was gone.

* * *

A few hours later, Sadie sat in the front passenger seat of Ethan's car while Gabe leaned forward from the back, still talking. They'd *been* talking for hours. Ever since Pam had dropped her bomb on Gabe.

"It's her father, Ethan," he was saying, not for the first time. "We can understand family loyalty."

"Agreed," Ethan said, giving his brother a quick look before shifting his gaze back to Pacific Coast Highway. He was just as shocked as Gabe by Pam's revelation. But at least now he knew why the woman had seemed so familiar. Ethan had met personally with Richard Donatello, and his daughter resembled him quite a bit. "She went about all of this the wrong way, but at least you two have something in common."

Sadie said, "Ethan, that's not really fair. Yes, Pam lied, and okay, I guess Gabe did, too…"

"Hey."

"Well, it's true," she said, and patted his hand. "But you both had good reasons for it."

That was surely true. From the moment he'd charged back into the office to tell Ethan exactly who Pam Cassini really was, Gabe had been like a man possessed. He couldn't stop talking about the woman. Ethan glanced at Sadie and didn't miss her wistful expression. Was she envious of what Gabe felt for Pam?

"I didn't expect you to take it this well," Gabe admitted. "I thought you'd be supremely pissed that Pam had used me to get to the recipe."

"I have to admit, I'm with Gabe. You surprised me, too, Ethan." Sadie was watching him, and even with his gaze on the road, Ethan felt the power of her stare.

He understood why the people closest to him were

shocked at his reaction. As little as a month ago, he'd have been furious, with Gabe *and* Pam. But it was impossible to be too angry with Gabe when Ethan himself had been allowing his emotions to guide his actions the past couple weeks.

"Let's just say that there have been a lot of changes lately and maybe I'm still responding to them." Ethan shot her a quick look and saw the smile that curved her mouth. "I'm not happy," he admitted, "but I can understand what she did."

He made a turn onto a side street in Laguna and pulled up outside a Craftsman-style bungalow. The house had a big tree out front, a wide porch boasting twin rockers and a small table between them. The winter flowers in the pot by the front door were a cheerful spot of color on a gray day. He turned off the engine and half turned to look at Gabe. "That's why we're here. I want to talk to Pam's father—her family—about this."

"Right." Gabe scraped one hand across his jaw. "What did he say when you called?"

"Richard already knew before I could tell him. Apparently," Ethan said, "she'd confessed the whole thing to her parents when she left you at the office. Richard's eager to talk it all out."

"That's good, right?" Gabe scrambled out of the car and stood in the street, staring at the house as if he could see past the walls to the woman he loved.

Ethan climbed out, too, and looked at his brother. He hoped this was going to end well, but he didn't have a clue what would happen when both families talked. As Sadie got out of the car, Ethan's gaze naturally drifted to her. It felt good to have her with him. Too good, really, because he was depending on her now even more than he had when she was simply his assistant. But that was a problem for later.

Ethan took Sadie's hand and she held on, glad that he automatically reached for her. She wondered if he even realized how often he did it. And she wondered how she would get along without his casual touch.

Richard Donatello opened the door for them and welcomed them inside. His daughter looked a lot like him, which was why Ethan had thought Pam seemed familiar, Sadie figured. The house itself was cozy and a lot bigger than it looked from the outside.

Richard led them through the house to the dining room, where his wife, son and Pam were waiting for them.

"Thanks for seeing us," Ethan said.

"No problem. Please. Sit." Richard took the chair at the head of the table and waited until they were seated before speaking. "Thanks for not having Pam arrested."

"Dad!"

"You could have been," her father said, his features stern.

The woman winced and gave Gabe a furtive look.

"This is my wife, Marianna, and my son, Tony." Richard paused and said sadly, "Pam told me what's been going on and I'm offering you my apology."

"Dad—" Pam interrupted, but her father shut her down with a single look.

Sadie sympathized. She knew Pam loved Gabe. And she could guess at how Pam had felt, torn between two loyalties. But of course she'd stood for her family. What wouldn't a person do for family?

"Your apology isn't necessary," Ethan said, and gave Sadie's hand a squeeze. "My brother and I were just saying that if there's one thing we understand, it's family loyalty."

"Thank you." Richard nodded, then looked at Gabe before turning to his daughter. "You were wrong to do it, Pam. And Tony, you shouldn't have gone along."

His son nodded. "Yeah, I know, Pop. We were only trying to help," he said. "To save the shop."

Sadie watched the people around the table, waiting to see where this would go. There was tension in the room, but over it all were threads of love so thick and interwoven she half expected to actually *see* them, like golden strands linking the Donatello family together.

"This isn't a hostile takeover," Ethan put in, but before he could say more, Pam interrupted.

"Of course it is. You're Heart Chocolates. Donatello's doesn't stand a chance in a fight against you."

"Pam," her mother said softly. "It's not a fight. Ethan came to us a couple of months ago with an offer to buy the shop. We talked about it—" she sent her husband a smile "—and after more negotiations, we decided together to accept."

"But why?" Pam asked, looking from one parent to the other. "Because you couldn't afford to fight back. That's why I wanted the recipe. I thought maybe we could barter for it. They get it back and we keep the shop."

"So blackmail?" Richard asked, dumbfounded. "You would do something like that?"

"To help the family, yes. I'm not proud of it, Dad," she said, and looked straight at Gabe. "I didn't want to. Didn't want to lie. But I didn't know how else to help you save the business."

"We don't want the shop," her father said, loudly enough to get everyone's attention.

Sadie was startled by that and it appeared everyone but Ethan was, too. Silence dropped onto the table in the wake of that announcement until Richard's son spoke.

"What do you mean?" Tony asked, obviously stunned. "It's ours. We've been working it together my whole life."

"And enough's enough," their mother said, smiling at her husband.

"I'm confused," Gabe muttered.

"You're not alone," Pam said, and gave him a sheepish smile.

Sadie squeezed Ethan's hand in solidarity. He looked at her and smiled, apparently knowing exactly where the rest of this story was going. He leaned in closer and said, "Remember when you suggested I talk to Richard myself instead of sending the lawyers?"

"Yes…"

"Well, I did." He winked at her and Sadie was more confused than ever. "Just listen," he said, and they both turned back to the others gathered around the table.

"I'm retiring," Richard said, letting his gaze slide around the table. "Your mom and I want to do a little living while we still can."

"But you're not old enough to retire!" Pam was clearly shocked.

"That's what makes it even better," Marianna said with a smile for her husband. "Why wait until we need someone to push us around in wheelchairs? No. We want to enjoy ourselves, Pam. It's past time for your dad to stop working so hard."

Richard nodded, smiling at his family. "Your mother's right."

"But the shop…" Pam simply stared at her father.

Richard shrugged that aside. "It's been good for us. Made us a decent living. Put you two through school and I enjoyed it, too. We both did. Working together, side by side, to build something special."

Marianna and her husband shared a secret smile that Sadie envied. This couple had what she dreamed of having. A real partnership. They'd worked and lived and loved together for decades.

"With the money Heart Chocolates is paying us for the location and our customer list and website, well…" Richard winked at his wife. "I can take your mother on all the trips she's wanted to take for years. We're going on a cruise, in May. First-class. To Europe. For our thirtieth anniversary."

"Europe?" Tony was astonished.

Sadie sighed at the romance of it all. How wonderful must it be to still love so fiercely that you wanted *more* time together, even after all those years.

"That's right," his mother said with a bright smile. "We're going to have some fun for a change. And stay up late every night, since your dad won't have to get up at three o'clock in the morning…"

"Looking forward to that," Richard said, grinning at Ethan.

"So this was all for nothing," Pam whispered.

This was such a private moment, if not for Ethan's tight grip on her hand Sadie would have felt like an intruder. But for now, anyway, she and Ethan were united. He wanted her there and that meant everything to her.

"I feel like an idiot." Pam looked at Gabe. "I'm so sorry. I didn't mean to betray you. Or lie to you."

"I know," he said, pushing up from his chair to walk

around the table and pull her to her feet. "I love you, Pam Cassini Donatello."

She gave him a watery smile and leaned into his chest, sighing when his arms came around her. "I love you, too, Gabe."

"Isn't that lovely?" her mother said. "Maybe we'll get a wedding to plan, too."

"Mom!" Mortified, Pam turned her face into Gabe's chest as he laughed.

Ethan shook his head at his younger brother and Sadie could almost hear him thinking *Not love, Gabe. Anything but that.* And her heart hurt as she realized there was no happy ending in this story for her. She and Ethan would part ways and all she'd have were the memories she'd made over the last weeks. That sounded unbearably sad.

Ethan turned to Richard. "So the deal's still in place? No more negotiating?"

"It better be in place," Marianna said. "I just made reservations for the cruise today."

"We have a deal," Richard said, and held out one hand. "I know better than to disappoint my wife. But if you don't mind my saying, you should hire my son, Tony, there. He's a hell of a chocolate chef."

"Dad!"

"Done," Ethan promised, as the two men shook hands.

A half hour later, Ethan and Sadie left the house together. Gabe stayed with Pam and Sadie had a feeling that Marianna was going to get the wedding she was hoping for. Sadie felt a pang of envy she tried to bury. Just because she wouldn't end up with her hero didn't mean she couldn't be happy for someone else.

"I'm glad that all worked out," she said, as Ethan held the car door open for her.

"Yeah." Ethan glanced back at the house. "Me, too. Gabe's in love. Never thought I'd see that."

Sadie took a breath and held it. She could let this go, but what would be the point? "It can happen to anyone, Ethan."

He looked down at her and shook his head slowly. "No, it can't. What you and I have is different, Sadie. I don't want to hurt you."

God, she felt cold. "Then don't."

Pulling her into the circle of his arms, Ethan held her close for a long minute. Sadie inhaled the scent of him, wrapping it around her like a cloak. She held on to him, luxuriating in his strength, his warmth, for as long as she could, because she felt like this was already a goodbye. He was letting go of what they had. Even if she wasn't leaving yet, a part of Ethan already had.

When he stepped back suddenly, his eyes were shadowed, like a forest in twilight. "Sadie, it's not that easy."

"I wonder why you're looking for the easy way, Ethan," she said softly. "Nothing worth having comes easy."

She couldn't keep looking into his eyes, watching as the shutters came down and the walls went up. So she slid into the car and he slammed the door after her. A couple seconds later he was in the driver's seat, turning to fix a hard stare on her.

"I'm not looking for easy. None of this is easy." It was a demand that she understand, and she'd heard that tone so many times over the last five years, Sadie didn't even blink in the face of it.

"It is," she said flatly, and watched a flash burst in

his eyes. "It's much easier to walk away than to stay and work for what you want."

"I'm doing this for you," he said, clearly angry and just as obviously trying to control it.

"Doing what, Ethan? Turning away? Shutting me out? Thanks, but I didn't ask you to."

"You didn't have to," he countered. "You think I don't see what's happening between us? What you're hoping for? I already know I make lousy husband material, Sadie. I made Marcy miserable. I don't want that for you."

Under her breath, a short, sharp laugh escaped her. "And it's all about you, is that it?"

"In this, yes." He snapped his seat belt, fired up the engine and pulled away from the curb with a squeal of tires. "You should be thanking me," he muttered.

"Right." Sadie turned in her seat and glared at him. "I should thank you for breaking my heart."

"Damn it, don't you get it yet? That's what I'm trying to avoid."

"Well you're too late," she snapped. "See, I already love you, you idiot."

Ten

Ethan swung the car to the side of the road, turned the engine off and said tightly, "Don't. Just… Don't."

"You don't tell me what to do, Ethan," Sadie said. "FYI."

"Damn it, Sadie. What're you thinking? I didn't want you to love me."

"You don't get a vote in everything," she said, shaking her head in complete amazement. Of course this was how he would take being told she loved him. Most men might feel a little surge of panic and then be happy about it. But not the man *she* loved. Oh, no. He fought like a caged wolverine.

"This is exactly what I was trying to avoid with you, Sadie." His voice was so low, she almost missed the words, and she really wished she had.

"Contrary to your own belief system, Ethan, you don't actually control the universe."

He turned his head to look at her. "You're making jokes about this?"

"Would you rather I cry?"

"God, no."

"Then laugh it up. I intend to." Eventually. At the moment it was taking everything she had not to give in to the tightness in her chest, the burning in her eyes. But damned if she'd cry in front of him. That really would be a cherry on top of the humiliation sundae.

"Really." It wasn't a question, but that's how she took it.

"Yes, Ethan." Sadie tipped her head to one side to stare at him. "I'm going to laugh at the absurdity of me loving a man for five years and he never noticed."

"Five…" His shocked expression would have been funny if it hadn't been so damn sad.

"Or how about the fun of telling that man I love him and having him order me to stop."

"Sadie—"

"I'm going to laugh because it's ridiculous." Her heart hurt, but damned if she'd let him see it. Whatever tears she would shed, she'd cry them in private. And maybe she wouldn't cry at all.

She'd known going in that loving Ethan was futile. She hadn't been able to help herself, so she was willing to accept the pain that was the inevitable result of being a damn fool. Sadie had seen today that it wasn't *all* Hart men who were incapable of loving. Just the one she wanted. And maybe it was time she simply accepted that and moved on.

"Look, Ethan, we've already agreed that I'll be leaving when we find the right nanny." She took a deep breath. "So let's just find her fast and pretend we didn't have this humiliating conversation, okay?"

"Damn it, Sadie…"

"Seriously, Ethan," Sadie said, giving him a hard, steady look. "I'm so done with this. I don't want to hear you're sorry or you're angry or whatever, okay? These are *my* feelings and I don't need you to tell me what to do with them."

"Fine." His jaw was tight and his green eyes were on fire, so situation normal.

"Good." She turned in her seat, faced the front and said, "Now, let's get back to the house. I want to see Emma."

That tiny girl wouldn't be in her life much longer. As hard as it was, Sadie was going to make finding a nanny her top priority. She couldn't stay with Ethan now that he knew she loved him. Because the one thing she *never* wanted from Ethan was his pity.

She loved him.

Ethan felt twin jolts of differing emotions—both pleasure and panic, with a little guilt tossed in. He shrugged his shoulders, trying to drop the burden. Hell, he hadn't asked her to love him. This wasn't his fault. Yes, she was wounded now and that pained him more than he wanted to admit. But her pain was far less than she would have felt if he'd tried to make a relationship work.

Ethan nodded, silently reassuring himself that he was doing the right thing as he stared out the office window at the steely sea. Sunlight pierced the clouds and slashed at the surface of the water like a golden sword. And the beauty of it all should have been enough to clear his head. But it wasn't.

It had been two days since her confession. Two days

since they'd solved the Gabe and Pam problem, only to fall into one of their own. They'd lived like polite strangers ever since and the tension in the house was so thick Ethan could hardly breathe.

Emma was the only bright spot in his life and he didn't miss the irony in that. The baby girl was the reason all of this had happened to his once orderly life in the first place, and now that everything was turned upside down, it was Emma alone who could make him smile.

He'd interviewed four nannies in the last two days and Ethan felt the pressure to find someone fast. The sooner he did, the sooner Sadie could leave and they could try to get past this mess.

Sadie. Leaving. It was the right thing, but it didn't feel that way.

A knock at the office door had him turning. "Yes?"

Sadie stepped inside and Ethan's heart gave a hard jolt in his chest. He ignored it. That was hormones. Lust. He hadn't touched her in days and his body missed hers. Hell, the sex had been great, so why wouldn't he react to her? It had nothing to do with her big blue eyes. Or the way she sang to Emma first thing in the morning. Or how she smelled. Tasted. The sound of her laugh, the touch of her skin.

"What is it, Sadie?" He sounded gruff even to himself.

One of her blond eyebrows arched. "Rick's taking over for me this afternoon. I'm going to the house to get Emma. Take her to a doctor appointment."

He straightened at that. "What's wrong with her?"

"Nothing, Ethan," she said, tipping her head to one side, and he knew she was doing it on purpose now. "She needs a checkup."

His heartbeat settled down as he nodded. "All right. Can Rick handle your desk?"

She lifted her chin. "I've been working with him. He can do the job if you're patient with him at first."

Since Ethan and Gabe weren't at war any longer, there'd been no reason why Rick from Marketing couldn't take over for Sadie. He wasn't as good at it as she was, but then no one would be.

"I'm not going to slow walk him, Sadie," Ethan grumbled. "If he can't do the job find someone else."

"He can do it, Ethan. Just don't be a jerk and you won't scare him into paralysis."

Shaking his head, he said, "Still feeling free to say whatever you're thinking, huh?"

"Freer than ever," she said with a sharp nod. "I've got to go."

She left and Ethan was alone again. Damn it.

They found the nanny that afternoon.

The woman was impeccably qualified and Sadie was trying very hard not to resent her for it. Teresa Collins was perfect. Her résumé. Her references. She'd been trained at a world renowned nanny academy, for heaven's sake, and Emma had taken to her instantly. Not to mention that at forty plus, Teresa wouldn't be leaving to start a family of her own. In other words, the woman was everything they'd been looking for.

Standing out in the backyard, where she could be alone and think, Sadie noted the finished fence—four feet of terra-cotta-colored brick topped by another two feet of wrought iron. Emma would be safe, she told herself. And happy.

She'd grow up in this beautiful house with Julie and

her daughter, with a perfect nanny and with Ethan. The only one missing would be Sadie. And since she was so young, Emma would never know that someone else had loved her, too.

Instead, the nanny would get all Emma's smiles and hear her first words and see her first steps. At that thought, Sadie had to wonder if Ethan would stay involved with the baby. Would he back away and leave it all to the nanny because it was easier?

This was Sadie's own fault, of course. She never should have stayed the extra time. Never should have moved in here with Ethan and absolutely shouldn't have had sex with him. But that part was really hard to regret. In fact, the only thing she was sorry for was that he hadn't touched her in days.

Not since the night she'd told him she loved him and he'd reacted like a vampire to a rope of garlic.

"Sadie?"

Speak of the vampire... She turned from the ocean view to watch Ethan walk toward her, and her heart did a spin and jolt just looking at him. She really needed to go. Soon. For her own sake.

"What're you doing out here?" he asked, when he was close enough.

"Just looking at the fence." She glanced at it again. "They did a nice job."

"Yeah. The view's screwed, but the baby will be safe."

Shaking her head at that, she faced him and scooped windblown hair from her face. "What did you want, Ethan?"

"I've given Teresa the bedroom beside Emma's so she'll be close."

"That's good."

"And I asked Julie to pack your things."

She sucked in a gulp of ocean-scented air and swallowed the knot of pain lodged at the base of her throat. "Well, that's…abrupt." But not surprising. Looking into his green eyes now, she didn't see the slightest hint of the man she'd spent the last nearly three weeks with. Ethan had tucked that man away and maybe he'd never escape again. He was back to being the all-powerful, distant CEO. The man who never let emotion touch him. And it was clear to Sadie that he'd already said good-bye to her and what they'd shared.

"It's best this way."

"Your way, you mean," she said softly. "The easy way."

He tucked his hands into his slacks pockets and his expression went blank, giving away nothing of what he was feeling, thinking. "The deal was you'd stay until we found a nanny. Well, Teresa's here now, so—"

"Time to get things back to normal, is that it?" Well, she'd planned on leaving today, anyway.

"It is." His jaw was tight, the only signal to her that he wasn't completely at ease with this. Funny how it was such a small thing that could ease what she was feeling.

"You're right, Ethan. It's time for me to go."

He nodded, clearly relieved, and she laughed shortly.

"What's so funny?"

"This whole situation. I've loved you for a long time, Ethan."

He winced at the words and she couldn't help the sharp jab of pain in her heart. But she ignored it to say what she had to say. "I know you and I know you're going to try to hide from Emma like you've been hiding from me."

Scowling, he insisted, "I haven't been hiding."

She held up one hand for silence, because she wanted to finish this before she did something ridiculous and cried. "Yes, you have, but that's not what I'm worried about."

"You don't have to worry about me." The wind tossed his hair across his forehead and somehow that simple thing made him seem more approachable. More vulnerable.

"I probably will, anyway, but that's my problem, not yours." God, just looking at him made her want to cry for what they could have had together. "What I want you to do is promise me that you won't ignore Emma."

"Why would I—"

"Because it'll be easier," she said, and she knew he was remembering when they'd talked about taking the easy way before. So was she. "Easier to turn her over to Teresa and tell yourself it's better that way. But it's not, Ethan. Don't cheat Emma, and more importantly, don't cheat yourself."

"Sadie…"

She shook her head. She didn't want to hear whatever he might say, because she was certain it wouldn't be what she most wanted to hear. That he loved her. That he needed her. That he didn't care about past failures and he wanted only her.

"Good luck, Ethan," she said, and started walking. Sadie really hoped that Julie had finished packing her clothes because she needed to get out of there fast—before her heart convinced her to stay and fight for what she wanted.

* * *

For the next week, Sadie slept in late, painted the living room in her condo, bought new plants to kill and visited her nephews and new baby niece. She drank with Gina, cried on Gina's shoulder, then came home to her empty place and told herself that it would get better.

Soon, she hoped.

Because sleeping was almost impossible. She worked in her garden, moved furniture around and played with her nephews, all in an effort to exhaust herself, and still she didn't sleep. How could she when her bed was as empty as her heart?

"Okay, this is enough already," Gina said, pouring another glass of wine for each of them.

Sadie took a sip and looked through the sliding glass door to where her brother was shrouded in thick smoke from the barbecue. His sons were on the trampoline and with every jump, the springs shrieked.

"Agreed," Sadie said, chuckling as Mike waved an oven mitt, trying to dissipate the smoke. "I say we go out for tacos."

"I'm not talking about Mike's latest attempt to be Gordon Ramsay," Gina told her. "I'm talking about you and the pouting fest."

Sadie sniffed in insult. "I don't pout. I sulk. It's much classier."

"Well sure, but I'm tired of it, so I'm doing something about it."

Sadie took a sip of wine, shot her sister-in-law a sidelong glance and asked, "What did you do?"

"I fixed you up with Josh. The firefighter on Mike's squad that I told you about?"

"Right." Sadie did remember talking about the

possibilities there, but how could she be interested in someone else when her mind and heart were focused on Ethan?

"You're going to meet him for coffee tomorrow afternoon."

Dread settled in her stomach. This was not a good sign. She was in no shape for a date. She hadn't slept. She had bags under her eyes deep enough to pack for a month-long vacation and she wasn't finished sulking. "Oh, Gina, I don't think so."

Gina scowled at her. "Sadie, you've been...*sulking*—"

"Thank you."

"—for more than a week now. You're in love with Ethan, but you're not doing anything about it."

Shocked, she demanded, "What can I do?"

"I don't know, fight for what you want?"

Hadn't she said something like that to Ethan not so long ago?

"I thought you were anti-Ethan," Sadie said.

Gina waved that off. "I'm anti-you-being-hurt. But if you love him, fight for him."

Shaking her head, Sadie said, "If you can't win, what's the point in fighting?"

"If you give up before you start, what's the point of anything?" Gina stopped and said, "Sorry, sorry. I told Mike I wouldn't butt in."

"Fat chance of that," Mike shouted from outside.

"Ears like a bat," Gina muttered, then said louder, "Here's the deal. If you're not going to fight for Ethan, then it's time you let yourself see that there are a few million other men out there. I told Josh you'd meet him at CJ's Diner in Seal Beach for coffee tomorrow afternoon."

Why did everyone think they could order her around? "Did you tell him what to order for me?"

"Sure," she said. "Coffee. Weren't you listening?"

Sadie laughed. She couldn't help herself. Gina was a force of nature. "Fine. What time am I meeting him?"

"Four," Gina said. "I told him if coffee goes well, you'll have time to get dinner."

"There, or are we going somewhere else?"

"Oh, I'll leave that up to you two."

"Hah! She gave Josh a list of restaurants!" Mike shouted, and slammed the barbecue lid down, trying to smother the flames erupting from the grate.

"Just suggestions," Gina shouted back.

"I appreciate it, Gina," Sadie said, and it was true. It was nice to be loved so much. Her family was her rock. Knowing that Mike and Gina had her back made what she was going through more bearable. But in spite of her good intentions, Gina couldn't know just how far out of "dating" mode Sadie really was. "But—"

"Don't say no, sweetie." Gina leaned in and squeezed Sadie's hand. "Just give Josh a chance. Meet him for coffee. See what happens. What could it hurt?"

Ethan was fine.

No problems here. He could concentrate on work again now that his world was back in order. He didn't have the distraction of Sadie to keep him from concentrating. It was only the memory of her that haunted him now. He sensed her all over his house. Her scent lingered on the pillow she used. Her shampoo was still in his shower—he should toss it out, but he hadn't. He heard the phantom echo of her laughter and when he closed his eyes, he saw *hers.*

And the office wasn't much better. Hell, he could hardly stand to sit at his desk because of the memory they'd made *there.* Plus, as much as he tried to focus, he kept half expecting Sadie to briskly knock on his office door and poke her head inside. Instead, it was Rick manning the desk outside his office, and he wasn't nearly as good at the job as Sadie had been. In the man's defense, though, nobody would be.

Hell, two days ago, they'd lost an entire shipment of chocolates when a train derailed in Denver. Sadie would have had the whole situation taken care of in an hour. This time, it was Ethan himself who'd had to handle the crisis because Rick was out of his depth.

It was only natural that Ethan would miss her, wasn't it? She had kept his life, his office, running smoothly for five years, so it only made sense that her absence would throw everything off-kilter.

"And just who're you trying to lie to?" he muttered, and tossed his pen onto the desk. "It's not Sadie's efficiency you're missing. It's everything else about her."

"Talking to yourself is never a good sign."

Scowling, Ethan looked up at Gabe. "It's traditional to *knock* before you come into a room."

"I'm a rebel," Gabe said affably as he crossed the room and dropped into the chair opposite Ethan. "So, I'm here to let you know Jeff's come up with several more candies we'll have ready for you in another week or so."

"Good." Ethan picked up his pen again and pretended to read the papers in front of him. "Great. Goodbye."

Gabe laughed. "Nice talking to you, too. You know,

you used to be easier to get along with. Wonder why that was. Oh. Maybe it was Sadie's influence."

"You want to stop talking now." Ethan lifted his gaze and gave his brother a hard glare.

"No, I don't."

Ethan tossed the pen down again. "Damn it, Gabe, this is none of your business."

Gabe shrugged. "Yeah, but you helped me out when the Pam situation got so screwed up. Thought I'd return the favor."

"I don't need help." And even if he did, he wouldn't ask for it. He'd been fine before that insanity with Sadie and he'd be fine again. At some point.

"Pam and I are engaged."

Surprising, but not. Ethan was happy for his brother, but he really didn't want to hear about love or marriage. Didn't want anything else to remind him of Sadie. "Congratulations. Get out."

Gabe laughed and settled in for a chat. Irritated, Ethan wondered what it would take to get rid of him. Probably dynamite.

"Pam's brother, Tony, has been working with Jeff on the new line."

"I know."

"He's as good as Richard said he was. Of course, Jeff's still in charge, but Tony's really pulling his weight." Nodding, Gabe added, "And we've contracted for the rehab on the Donatello shop."

"I know that, too." They'd agreed to use Donatello's storefront in Laguna to launch their new line. Gabe and Pam were in charge and Tony and Jeff would be the chefs. It would be a good test spot and if it worked, which Ethan was sure it would, they'd think about opening up more specialty stores. He wanted to tell Sadie all about it. Hear her thoughts, ideas and suggestions. She had a sharp mind and wasn't afraid to give her opinion, and damn it, he missed that, too.

"I saw Sadie yesterday."

Ethan's head snapped up and Gabe grinned. "Got your attention with that one, didn't I?"

Yeah, he had. It felt like years since Ethan had seen her. "How is she?"

"She's doing great. Looked happy. She was out with her sister-in-law, shopping at Bella Terra. You know, the Huntington Beach mall."

"I know what it is," Ethan grumbled. So Sadie was out shopping and having fun and probably dating. Why wouldn't she? Who would she be going out with? It wasn't as if she'd had a lot of time to meet anyone. Or had she already met this mystery man before she left Ethan's life? How? When? Most importantly, *who*?

The thought of her with another man was enough to send ice through Ethan's veins. But he'd let her go, right? So he'd just have to live with that decision.

How did Sadie think that walking away was easy?

Nothing about this was easy.

"When are you going to admit you miss her?"

"When are you going to butt out of my life?"

"When you stop making a mess of it." Gabe leaned forward. "Sadie's not Marcy."

Ethan drew in a deep breath and settled the blast of anger he felt at Gabe throwing his past at him. He was right, though. Sadie was nothing like Marcy. Sadie would stand up and tell him what she was thinking. Marcy had kept her resentments to herself. Hadn't told him that she was unhappy. Not that their marriage's failure was her fault. He hadn't put the time in and he knew it. What he realized now was that a woman like Sadie wouldn't have put up with him ignoring her.

But Sadie wasn't the problem, was she? It was *him*. Ethan was the same man who'd made a mess of his marriage, so how could he know this time would be different?

"And you're not the same, either," Gabe said, as if reading Ethan's thoughts. "Sadie changed you."

Change. Used to be Ethan hated that word. Now, he could almost see the good in it. He had changed. For the better?

How was he to know?

"I'm just saying," Gabe added, as he stood up, "you might want to try to fix this before the chance gets away from you."

"I think it's too late already," Ethan murmured, remembering the look on Sadie's face before she'd left his house. Not only had he let her go, he'd practically shoved her out the door. Why would she be willing to walk back in?

"Yeah," Gabe said, "but you won't know until you try."

Eleven

Josh was nice.

At any other point in her life, Sadie would have really enjoyed him. The man was gorgeous, seriously built, and he had a great smile and a wonderful sense of humor. In short, he was everything she should have wanted. Sadly, the one thing he was not was *Ethan*.

Sitting across from him at the diner, Sadie listened while he talked about the fire station and the guys he worked with. But instead of *hearing* him, she was thinking of Ethan. Wondering what he was doing. How he was feeling. Did he miss her or was he counting his blessings to be rid of her? God, that was a horrible thought.

"Hey," Josh said, distracting her. "Are you okay?"

"I'm sorry," she said quickly. "Yes, I'm fine. I'm just...tired, I think."

Sunlight slanted through the window and lay across the bright red Formica tabletop. Just across the street was the ocean, shining in the winter sun, and the crowds on Pacific Coast Highway belied the winter cold. Nothing stopped Californians from enjoying the beach.

Sadie just wished she was in the mood to enjoy *anything*. Maybe Gina was right, she told herself. Maybe she'd done enough sulking. How long could she mourn a love that hadn't happened? Was she going to wither up and spend her life sulking? Wind up alone with a houseful of cats? The best way to forget a particular man was in seeing another one, right? Well, Josh was a good place to start. She didn't even like cats.

"We can do this another day," he said with a shrug.

"No, really. I'm okay." She shrugged off her dark thoughts, pushed Ethan completely out of her mind and focused on the man opposite her. "And I'm interested. Tell me why you decided to become a firefighter."

He grinned. "It's always dangerous asking a man to talk about himself. We could go on for hours."

Sadie laughed. "I'll risk it."

Josh started talking then, and this time she really tried to pay attention. But less than a minute later, Ethan walked into the diner, carrying Emma against his chest, and Sadie was lost.

Following her shocked gaze, Josh looked over his shoulder, then back to her. "What's going on? You look like you've seen a ghost or something."

"Or something," she said, wondering what was going on. Her heartbeat was racing and her mouth was dry. Her stomach did a quick spin and flip, and she had to fight to keep her coffee down.

Ethan strode up to their table and completely ignored Josh as he said, "Honey, don't do this."

"What?" Sadie blurted.

"I know we've had some problems," Ethan continued, as if she hadn't spoken. "But we have a *baby*. You can't just walk away. We need you."

Horrified and embarrassed, Sadie stared up at Ethan. She couldn't believe he was doing this. And how had he found her? Groaning internally, she thought *Gina.* It was the only way. But *why* was he doing this?

"What's going on?" Josh gave Sadie a hard look. "Who is this? Gina didn't say anything about you having a baby. Or a husband."

"He doesn't know about us?" Ethan looked wounded as he stared down at her. "Even if you're mad at me, you can't forget about our child. Sadie, we need you. Come back home."

"Oh, for heaven's sake." She snapped a furious look at Ethan, then shifted her gaze to Josh. "This isn't what it looks like." She choked out a strained laugh. "Really. That's not my baby—"

And right on cue, Emma crowed in delight and threw herself at Sadie. Defeated, Sadie instinctively caught her and cuddled her close. She was warm and soft and smelled so good, Sadie smiled while the baby patted her cheeks with both tiny hands. Oh, how she'd missed this baby.

"Okay," Josh said, "I don't know what's going on here, but I'm out." He slid off the bench seat, tossed a ten dollar bill on the table and said, "Good luck with whatever this is."

When he left, Sadie looked up at Ethan and scowled

at the wide grin on his face. "Why would you do that, Ethan?"

He shrugged amiably. "I needed to get rid of him and I was afraid you wouldn't let me." He dropped onto the seat opposite her.

"Well, you're right. I wouldn't have." Sadie tried to be angry, but it was hard, with Emma cuddling in as if she were right where she belonged. "Gina told you where to find me, I'm guessing?"

"Not without telling me exactly what she thought of me first," he admitted. "The woman has a creative vocabulary."

Sadie laughed helplessly. Of course Gina would tell him off and then lead him right to Sadie. Beyond all else, her sister-in-law was a hopeless romantic.

The waitress came up with a fresh cup and poured coffee for Ethan, then refilled Sadie's. She left with questions in her eyes and Sadie couldn't blame her. She had plenty of questions herself.

"Why are you here?" she asked, keeping her voice down. "Why did you bring Emma?"

"When you're going to fight, bring all of your ammunition," he said, and Sadie was more confused than ever.

"Fight for what? What do you mean?"

"It means I want you to come back."

His gaze met hers. Sadie held her breath. "Come back to what?"

"To work."

She let the breath out and felt disappointment wash over her in a wave so heavy it weighed her down. "No."

"I thought you'd say that," Ethan said, cupping both hands around the mug of coffee. "So I'm offering you twice your old salary."

Sadie's heart sank even further. The minute she'd seen him, her foolish heart had hoped that he was there to confess his love. To ask her to marry him. To live and love with him. But he only wanted her back at the office and that, she couldn't do.

"No. I don't want to work for you anymore, Ethan." She scooted off the bench seat, snatching up her purse as she moved. It was hard to give Emma back to Ethan, but she did it, in spite of the fact that the baby reached up both arms to her and screwed up her tiny face to cry. "If that's why you came, you wasted a trip."

"It's not why." He stood up, too, tossed another ten on the table and led her out of the diner. "Not completely. Come on. We're not doing this here."

"Doing what?" She came to a dead stop on the sidewalk and refused to be budged until she knew what he was up to. Traffic hummed past, the wind howled in off the ocean and she had to squint up at him because of the sun.

He glanced around and frowned at the crowds and the noise before turning back to Sadie. "This isn't the place I would have picked, but screw it. This needs saying."

Sadie couldn't take much more. Tears were threatening and her throat was so tight she could hardly breathe. She had no idea what he wanted now, but she wished he'd just get it over with so she could go home. She had more sulking to do.

"Hold the baby," he said, and held her out so Sadie's only choice was to take the tiny girl.

"Okay, I offered you double your salary and you said no."

"I did," she said, "so don't throw more money at me."

"What if I offered you something else instead?"

She sighed heavily and smoothed Emma's wispy hair back from her forehead. "Like what?"

"A side job." He reached into his pocket, pulled out a blue velvet ring box and flipped it open.

She went perfectly still. Sadie was nearly blinded by the sun glancing off the enormous diamond nestled inside. Her heart actually stopped before it jumped into a wild gallop she had no hope of easing. She looked from the ring up to him and saw light and passion and love shining so brightly in his eyes it almost dimmed that diamond's gleam.

"Marry me, Sadie," he said, and the world seemed to suddenly fade away.

She couldn't hear the traffic or the people around her; all she could hear was the man she loved saying the words she'd never thought to hear him say.

"I know I'm not a good bet," he said. "And I admit, I was too scared to tell you how I felt because I didn't want to make another mistake. But I do love you. I love you so much it's making me crazy not being with you."

Sadie took a deep breath and held it. Emma leaned her head on Sadie's shoulder as if she was watching the show and cared about the outcome.

"I realized something last night, Sadie. The only mistake I was making was in *not* marrying you. You make me laugh. You make me think. You made it impossible for me to live without you. You made me love you."

"Oh, Ethan…" Tears filled her eyes and she blinked frantically to clear her vision.

"I can say the words now," Ethan told her. "I should have said it before. But if you say yes, I'll tell you how much I love you every day until you're sick of hearing it."

"That would never happen," she whispered.

His eyes speared into hers, and it was as if he was willing her to see inside him to the truth shining there. "Marry me and take your old job back, too."

She laughed wildly.

"Seriously. Come back to work, too." He grinned at her. "That way I can kiss my assistant anytime I want to. And you'll save me from Rick. He's terrible."

Still laughing, Sadie shook her head and tossed her hair out of her eyes. She didn't want to miss a moment of this.

"Marry me, Sadie," he said. "I fired Teresa."

Surprised, she held Emma a little tighter. "What? Why? She was perfect."

"No she wasn't," he said. "She wasn't you. I only needed a nanny because I was going to be alone with Emma. If we're married we can take care of Emma and all of our other kids together. And Julie's there to help, right?"

"Right…" Together. *All of our other kids.*

"If we're married—"

"Stop," she said, and stepped into his arms. She didn't need to hear anything else. He'd already said everything that mattered. Everything she'd dreamed of hearing for so long.

When he held her, pulling her tight and close, Sadie's heart started beating again. His warmth enfolded both her and Emma, and Sadie knew that this was the absolute best moment of her life.

"Is that a yes?" he asked, smoothing her hair back and out of her eyes.

"It's a yes. To everything." Sadie went up on her toes and kissed him. "Oh, Ethan, I want you and Emma and more kids, and my job."

"Thank God."

"It won't be easy," she teased, as he slid that diamond onto her ring finger.

"Who wants easy?" He scooped Emma up, then dropped one arm around Sadie's shoulders, turning to walk toward the parking lot. "You know, when we tell our kids about how Daddy proposed, we're going to have to come up with a more romantic story."

"Oh no, we don't," she said, leaning into him as they walked through the crowded streets. "This was perfect."

He kissed the top of her head and said, "I swear I'll be a good husband and father."

"I know you will," Sadie said, smiling up at him. "Because I'll be with you every step of the way."

* * * * *

THE LAST
LITTLE SECRET

ZURI DAY

For we hopeful romantics who know love always wins,
no matter the challenges when the journey begins.

Love exposes our secrets, a new world to unfold,
while nourishing our bodies and filling our soul.

One
<hr style="width:10%"/>

"Mr. Breedlove, your two o'clock is here."

"Thanks. Send her in."

"Will do."

"Hold my calls, Anita. I don't want to be interrupted."

"Got it, boss."

Nick shut off the intercom and second-guessed his decision for the fifth or sixth time. For a decisive man like Nick Breedlove, that didn't happen often. Hands down, Samantha Price was one of the best interior designers in the business, the only one he'd put complete confidence in to get him and the company out of an impossible jam. That she had become available was nothing short of a miracle. Hiring her was no doubt a sound business decision but personally, was it wise? He heard a soft knock and braced himself. If seeing her again caused the same reaction as last time, he might lose control of the meeting before it began. It had been more than four years but the memories from that night flooded his mind as though they'd happened just yesterday. The door opened. There she was. In the flesh. More beautiful than he remembered.

He stood, with hand outstretched. "Hello, Sam. It's been a long time."

"Hey, Nick," Sam replied, her smile tight yet polite as she clasped his hand ever so briefly while maintaining a good distance between them.

Was she remembering, too? Was the attraction that threatened to tighten his groin and quicken his breathing a mutual situation?

"I appreciate you coming on such short notice," he managed, a 007 coolness hiding a set of hormones suddenly rag-

ing as if he were fifteen instead of the twenty-seven he'd
turned just a few short months ago. He willed his body
to relax, behave and not embarrass them both. *Get it together, bro!*

"CANN International is one of the largest, most successful hotel developers in the world. Plus, with the urgency
given to meeting as quickly as possible, I was curious and
couldn't resist."

"Thank you for coming."

Once again Nick willed away the untimely musings and
forced his thoughts more fully into the present. He motioned
for Sam to have a seat in one of two chairs facing his desk,
while he returned to his executive chair. A wide, paper-
strewn desk created a physical barrier between them. Nick
was appreciative of being reminded about this meeting's
intent—all business, nothing personal. His body would do
well to get the message, too.

He watched Sam place her briefcase on the floor, then sit
back with squared shoulders. Professionalism oozed from
her pores. Of course she wasn't daydreaming about that
night long ago. She'd made time for the company and a possible job, not for him. Nick mentally chastised himself for
the moment of weakness that had taken him down memory lane, and the discipline it took to rein in his body now.
No matter that her hands were softer than he remembered,
the designer suit failed to hide those dangerous curves, and
the subtle scent that tickled his nose when he'd neared her
for that handshake had made him want to pull her into an
embrace. If the interview went well and Sam joined his
team, they'd be working very closely together. Too close
for a casual sexual dalliance. He'd do well to stay focused
and remember that.

"Can I get you anything before we begin?"

"No, thank you," Sam replied. "I'm more than a little
curious about what your assistant called an urgent matter
but was unable to provide details."

"As I'd instructed," Nick said, leaning back in his chair. "I was equally intrigued with the news about you—that you were not only back in the States but here in Vegas and looking for clients."

Sam crossed her legs in one graceful, fluid motion with no idea, Nick assumed, of how utterly sexy a move it was.

"How did you hear? Probably someone from the function I recently attended," she continued before he could answer. "I did a great deal of networking to get the word out about the rebirth of Priceless Designs."

"Possibly." Nick shrugged. "It's a small town. News travels fast. Especially when your mother is Victoria Breedlove."

Sam smiled, this one genuine and relaxed. Her shoulders, tense and squared since entering his office, softened along with her face.

"How is your mother?"

"Still as nosy as she is wonderful."

"I don't know her personally, of course, but from everything I've read or heard about her she appears to have a great heart. That was evidenced at the luncheon, and the generous check presented to the Women in Business organization. I didn't see her, though. Someone else presented the check."

"Mom wasn't there. She and Dad have fallen in love with Scandinavia and since he's assured Mom his retirement is permanent, Dad has cloaked hotel location scouting missions under the guise of Nordic vacations. The girls stepped in to fill the gap left in her increasingly frequent absences."

"The girls?"

"Lauren, Ryan and Dee, my sisters-in-law, or in-love, as Mom always corrects me."

"Oh. Right."

"Their marriages were the wedding bells heard round the world. Surely you read about them."

Sam gave a slight shake of the head. "I'd heard about Christian's wedding but only learned that two more brothers had tied the knot upon returning to the States. How many brothers besides you does that leave standing single?"

"I stand alone," Nick dramatically intoned. "We have several business partners on the continent who said their nuptials made a big splash even there."

"While in Africa, I lived in a rather insular world."

"Since word on the street is you married a prince, a luxurious one, no doubt."

"Yes."

A physical wall couldn't have made Sam's intentions clearer. Whatever had happened while abroad, she didn't want to talk about it. But Nick couldn't resist.

"Yet you're back here and working. What does your husband think about that?"

"It doesn't matter. We're no longer together."

"Separated?"

"Divorced."

The tone beneath that one word closed the door on the subject of Sam's personal life better than King Tut's sealed tomb. It only made Nick even more curious, about both her failed marriage and her current love life. Now was obviously not the time to talk about it, but one day… Patience was not a virtue Nick knew well, but one he could employ when necessary. Now was definitely one of those times.

His body language remained relaxed but he adopted a businesslike tone. "Whatever brings you back to Las Vegas, your timing couldn't be better. I need the best and fastest-working designer that money can buy. Before running off to become an African princess, that was you."

A grin accompanied Sam's twinkling eyes. "I'd like to think it still is. What's going on?"

"A project that has to stay on schedule and a designer who isn't delivering on the promises she made."

"How many rooms are we talking about?"

"Not rooms…homes." Nick noted Sam's surprised expression. "This isn't a hotel design. It's a series of private island homes being advertised for vacation rental among the world's most elite."

"Wow. I had no idea you guys had expanded beyond the original hotel framework. Considering how the hospitality industry is changing, though, it sounds like a smart move."

"It's proven to be right on time with industry trends."

"Does that smirk confirm the obvious, that this was your idea?"

"Still a smart-ass, I see."

"Takes one to know one."

"Ha!"

"So I'm right."

"All of the brothers are involved but yes, it's more or less my baby. Which means failure is not an option. You feel me?"

"Tell me more."

Sam leaned forward, unconsciously revealing the slightest peek of a creamy quarter-moon of her breast. When his attention returned to her face, Sam was frowning. *Damn.* To her professional credit, however, she didn't comment on eyes determined to rove on their own. She simply adjusted her blouse and sat back, waiting, to learn why Nick had brought her here.

Nick leaned back as well, determined to take control of a meeting he'd called, ensconced in the comfort of discussing an industry he knew better than he knew himself. Business now, pleasure later, he thought as he began discussing his baby, CANN Isles. There was no way around it, even pushed to the back of his mind. The attraction for one Ms. Samantha "Sam" Price was real, intense and not going away.

Before it was mere speculation. Now she was sure. It shouldn't have mattered how much she wanted to see her old lover. Not only should Sam have not returned Anita's phone call, she shouldn't have made this appointment. She shouldn't be here with Nick. Her body was clear about it even if her mind wasn't sure. Every cell of her body had lit up, awakened by the irrefutable attraction that hadn't dimmed in all this time away. An attraction that given the sticky situation that even thinking of working with Nick presented, and the increasingly troublesome email and text exchanges with her ex, had no chance of being acted upon.

Being this close to him in proximity was TROUBLE, all caps. Just seeing him relax made her heart skip. She watched the lines on his forehead fade away as he broke into a spiel he'd probably recited a hundred times. Clearly, speaking about the company was his forte, his stomping grounds, his zone. But that brief look of desire she'd glimpsed before Nick realized he'd been caught staring at her cleavage suggested something impossible. That he still felt the attraction, too. Surely after all this time it was something she must have imagined. While the night she shared with Nick was seared into her conscience, and intimacy with her husband had been fleeting at best, she imagined there'd been a constant stream of women in and out of Nick's bedroom to make him forget all about it.

She wasn't quite sure when her attention went from what Nick was saying to the lips forming the words that came out of his mouth. But somewhere within his glib delivery about CANN International's latest expansion beyond casino hotels and spas into the lucrative and growing industry of offering private rental vacation homes, she was struck by the perfectly formed Cupid lips enunciating goals and intentions and reminding her of how skillfully they'd brought her to and over the orgasmic edge and changed her life forever. If her body was a violin, Nick's tongue was the bow that had played a melody etched in her soul, stamped into her mind and burned inside her heart. That night just over four years and nine short months ago when her world was rocked and shifted on its axis, was one she had no idea would be the catalyst for an adventure that took her from America to Africa and from fairy tale to nightmare, in less than five years.

"...Djibouti. Have you been there?"

Uh-oh. The uptick of his voice suggested to Sam that she'd just been asked a question. She had no idea what about.

"Um, not sure."

Wrong answer. Nick's frown told it all.

"Djibouti isn't the most popular of tourist destinations, but it is certainly memorable. Yet you're not sure?"

"No, I'm sure. I've never been there. Sorry, I got distracted. I silenced my phone but it's still vibrating." Sam reached into her purse. "I'll shut it off."

"Back less than a month and already in demand?"

"Something like that."

She quickly checked her text messages. It wasn't a slew of potential clients trying to reach her, but the very reason why she shouldn't be sitting there. Why as much as she wanted to, needed to, was desperate to, even, she couldn't take this job. No matter the pay, which she knew would be top-shelf.

Shooting off a quick reply, she then turned off the vibrating notifier and dropped the phone in the tote on the floor. "Sorry."

"No worries."

"You mentioned Djibouti. One of the islands CANN International owns is located there?"

Nick nodded. "Just off the coast on the Gulf of Aden. The first property built there is one of our smaller hotels, only eighty-nine rooms. All suites, though, with living and dining spaces, and spectacular ocean or mountain views. The casino is the building's jewel, of course, boasting a Michelin-star restaurant and world-class spa."

"I believe you guys are onto something. From all I've seen and understand, Africa's the next great economic frontier."

"That's what we believe, with Djibouti becoming the next Dubai. It's why we're building more hotels all over the continent and have either purchased or designed a number of islands to house our luxury home rentals."

"So...you contacted me because you need someone based in Africa?"

"No. The projects needing immediate attention are mostly here in the US, along the eastern seaboard. But there are a couple in Hawaii and one in the Bahamas as well."

"All of this sounds amazing, Nick, but I don't yet understand the urgency or why I'm here."

"Because the designer we hired walked out. Last week. Couldn't keep pace with CANN's lofty vision, or take the pressures of a somewhat demanding boss—" Nick paused, Sam smiled "—and an increasingly tight deadline."

"What's happened to shrink the timeline?"

"Demand. The PR and marketing have been minimal but extremely targeted. Christian's wife, Lauren, designed the brochures and the job she did was outstanding. We knew they'd attract interest, but the response was far beyond what we'd planned. Instead of a slow rollout with an expected thirty to forty-five percent vacancy, almost eighty percent of the properties have already been booked. Including the ones that are not yet finished."

"That's impressive."

"And with the abrupt departure of our designer, problematic as well."

"So what you're saying is...the work she started on these homes needs to be finished?"

"Her work wasn't entirely up to our standards. You may be able to work your magic and salvage a few of the properties. Others will most likely need to be stripped and totally redone. Still more you'll have the pleasure of designing from the ground up. The homes were completed to the point of being an interior designer's blank canvas."

"Sounds major. How many homes are we talking?"

"Counting the properties in Hawaii and the Bahamas, twenty-three total."

Sam took a deep breath. That was a lot of designing, even for her. "And what's the desired completion date?"

Nick looked at his watch. "As of this morning…less than twelve weeks."

"Whoa!"

"Exactly. That's the urgency and why I called you."

"And why you didn't want your assistant to get into it."

"I didn't want you to get scared off before the entire scenario could be laid out. Because we know what a massive undertaking this is, and the immense pressure that will come from pulling it off, we're willing to compensate the designer who can handle the impossible with an equally unique offer."

Nick then laid out the compensation package, one so lucrative that not to accept would be stupid, insane, not even an option.

Still, she hesitated. "Can I think about it?"

"The employment package I've designed has never been offered to anyone," Nick responded. "Anywhere. Ever." Barely veiled frustration crept into his voice.

"No question the opportunity is amazing, but…"

A raised brow was Nick's only response.

"There are personal matters I'd need to consider, logistics that would have to be thought out."

"It's a phenomenal offer," Nick said, a slight frown marring his handsome face as he eyed her intently. "What's there to think about?"

"I have a son."

Crap! Did I say that out loud?

Nick's expression, subdued as it was, suggested that she had. The one thing she hadn't planned to share with Nick had just tumbled out before she could stop it.

"You have a child yet divorced the father? It's none of my business, but that had to be tough."

Sam nodded. It's all she could do.

"How old is he?"

"He's four," Sam replied, wishing the floor beneath her would turn to quicksand and swallow her whole.

"A boy, huh? I had no idea. Given all of the travel that's required, that adds a bit of a wrinkle that I didn't expect."

His eyes narrowed as he thoughtfully rubbed his chin. Sam could almost see his mind turning.

"We can add a childcare allowance to the package, work out an acceptable live-in arrangement so that your son's life isn't disrupted."

"That's an expensive suggestion and only a partial solution. Trey's life has already been upended with the move from Africa to America. I'm not sure how comfortable I'd be either leaving him with a virtual stranger or dragging him all over the States. I'd planned to put him in preschool for a bit of routine, stability. I don't know, Nick…"

"Given what I've just learned, I agree, Sam. It's a big ask. But I can't think of anyone who can do what needs to be done in the time that's required. Someone I trust. An award-winning, formerly sought-after designer whose skills I've seen firsthand.

"Listen, a large part of the charity my mom runs is geared toward helping children. Her network is filled with the best au pairs, teachers, tutors, childcare professionals, you name it. If you'd like, I can give you her number or have her call you. She can help you work something out, something beneficial for both you and… Trey, is it?" Sam nodded. "She can help with an arrangement in the best interest of both you and Trey. Don't let single motherhood be the reason you don't take the job."

Sam asked for a day to think about it, then left—translated, "escaped"—Nick's office. Accepting this meeting was a very bad idea, even worse than she imagined. Nick thought her having a child was the biggest challenge to working with him? No, the gargantuan one was that Nick was Trey's father…and didn't know it.

Two

"I didn't know Sam had a kid."

That was Nick's greeting later that day after walking into his twin brother Noah's house unannounced.

"Good afternoon to you, too, bro."

"You knew and didn't tell me?" Nick eyed Noah as he crossed the living room and plopped on the couch.

Noah shook his head. "No idea. How'd you find out?"

"During her interview for the design job."

"So you called her, huh? How'd that go?"

"Not as I'd planned. Because we need her like last week, I offered an employee package too generous for anyone to refuse. She asked for a day to think about it."

Nick laid out the package details.

Noah sat back, his look one of amazement. "What's there to think about?"

A lazy grin crept onto Nick's face. "That was my question exactly. And how I found out she'd become a mom."

Noah's phone pinged. He picked it up, tapped the face, then returned a quick text. He looked over at Nick. His expression changed. "How'd she look?"

"Sam? Better than the last time I saw her."

"The costume party, right?"

"Catwoman," Nick replied with a slow nod, allowing his mind for the briefest of moments to return to that night. Him, as a *GQ* Superman in a tight-fitting royal blue tux, red muscle shirt, and black-and-red mask. He'd been at the party for about an hour when he felt an energetic shift in the room. Samantha Price. The award-winning interior designer who'd flitted on the outskirts of his social circle for years. He flirted. She teased. As they'd always done. This time, though, he asked her to dance. After three minutes of slow dancing they left for CANN Casino Hotel and Spa, North America's only seven-star hotel and the jewel of Las Vegas. For the next twelve hours they stirred up enough electricity to light up the Strip. It was an unforgettable, mind-blowing night, when one sexy Catwoman became that Superman's kryptonite.

His twin, with whom he shared everything, was the only one he'd told.

Noah reached for his phone, viewed the lit-up screen. "You never saw her after that, right?"

"We were supposed to get together. But she left town, remember?"

"Vaguely."

"She met a prince and obviously started a family. Her body still looks amazing. I couldn't believe it when she told me she'd had a child."

"So the royal family is moving to America?"

Nick shook his head. "They're divorced."

"Sorry to hear that."

Nick nodded. That was an institution the Breedloves didn't believe in. He probably should have felt sorry, too. But he didn't.

"How old is the kid?"

"Four."

"Boy or girl?"

"Boy. His name's Trey."

"What type of father would let his kid, especially a son, move to the other side of the world, divorce or no?"

"I thought the same thing. She clearly didn't want to talk about her personal life so I dropped the subject." Nick thoughtfully rubbed his five o'clock shadow, remembering the encounter. "She was different though, no doubt. Distant. Guarded. Not at all the carefree woman I remember."

"Having had to deal with whatever was bad enough to end her marriage, that can be understood. Maybe she was hoping they could have worked it out. Stayed together for the child's sake at least."

Noah's words reverberated. *Worked it out. Stayed together for the child's sake.* Nick didn't know how he felt about that.

"That design job is a beast with a time schedule from hell. I don't see her being able to do it. Not with a child."

"That definitely complicated the situation. Where there's a will, there's a way."

The room fell silent. Nick looked up to see Noah's speculative gaze.

"What?"

"Are you sure this is about getting the homes completed before summer?"

"Absolutely."

"It has nothing to do with Sam and the fact that she's single again?"

"Nothing."

"Liar."

They both laughed. "I'm focused on work, bro."

"I can understand that," Noah replied. "Plus, those Anderson twins are probably giving you all that you can handle."

"A gentleman never kisses and tells." Nick stood and headed toward the door.

Noah got up and walked toward him. "Where are you going?"

"I have a meeting."

"With whom?"

"The only person who can help me with the childcare dilemma." The brothers looked at each other and both said, "Mom."

Nick climbed into his flashy McLaren, sped down the road and spun into the circular driveway of his parents' estate in nothing flat.

"Mom!"

Helen, the housekeeper who after all of the decades she'd been employed there was more like an aunt, greeted him in the hallway. "Hello, Nick." The two shared a hug. "She's in her new favorite place."

"The solarium. Thanks, love."

Nick walked to the back of the home toward the newly added indoor/outdoor paradise that spanned a great length of the home. He walked over to where Victoria was engrossed in weeding a bed of vibrant plants. He sneaked up behind her and kissed her cheek.

"Oh!" Victoria swatted him. "You scared me!"

"Good thing I wasn't a burglar," he teased. "Did you have a chance to work on what I asked you or have you been here all morning, communing with nature?"

Victoria pulled off her gloves and set them on the rim of the wooden box before crossing over to a canvas-covered divan. "Your multitasking mother managed to do both." She poured a glass of lemon water and held up the pitcher.

"Please." She filled a glass for Nick and handed it to him. "Thanks."

"I ran across a picture of Sam online."

By "run across" Nick knew Victoria had scoured the internet to the edges of the earth to find out what she could about her.

"She's gorgeous, son. Those deep brown eyes. That flawless skin. Stunning."

"Yes, she's attractive."

"And married to a prince. Why is she back here and working, with a child to care for?"

"Those details aren't our business, Mom."

"I was just curious. I'd imagine her child is equally beautiful. Does he look like her?"

"How would I know?"

"She didn't show you a picture?"

"It was an interview, Mom, not a social visit."

"Still, son, it's a rare mother who doesn't offer up pictures of her children at the slightest opportunity."

It would be even rarer if one such mother didn't begin another round of internet sleuthing to find one.

"Any success on finding contacts I can pass on to Sam?"

"I've asked Hazel to pull together a list of possibilities."

"Your new assistant?" Victoria nodded. "How is she working out?"

"No one will ever top Lauren's skills, but Hazel is a close second. She'll compile a list of names and agencies and forward them to you by end of day."

"You're amazing."

"I try."

Nick stood. Victoria followed suit.

"I've got more work to do." He kissed her forehead and pulled her in for a hug. "You're a lifesaver, Mom. Thanks."

"Keep me posted on how it all goes."

"I will. Love you, Mom."

"Love you more."

Nick returned to his car and immediately called Sam. It would have made more sense to wait until he'd received the list, but he wanted to hear her voice now.

"Hello?" Sam sounded breathless, liked she'd rushed to the phone. A thought flashed about another time when heavy breathing occurred, but he immediately shut it down.

"Sam. Nick."

"Hey, Nick."

"Good news. I'm about to solve all your problems."

"You know them all?"

Nick laughed. "You have that many?"

"A few." No laughter. "Is this about the job? You said I had until tomorrow, right? I still haven't made up my mind."

"If part of the indecision is about childcare, a solution is on the way."

"It is?"

"Yep."

"So…let me guess. In addition to being a vice president in a multibillion-dollar corporation, you own a childcare center?"

"No, but I know…hey. What are you doing?"

"Right now?"

"Yes, right now."

"On the computer, research stuff. There's a lot to do to get settled."

"I bet. Where are you staying?"

"South Vegas, temporarily."

"I'm headed that way. Let's discuss the childcare solution I've come up with over dinner."

"I can't do that. I need to get dinner for…for my son."

"That's no problem. Bring the little guy, too. I know a kid-friendly spot not far from our hotel. You and Trey can meet me there." Silence fell as Noah exited the freeway and headed toward CANN Casino Hotel and Spa, a towering landmark anchoring one end of the Las Vegas Strip. "Sam, you there?"

"Yeah, um, I'm here. Thanks, but no. I'm going to run us through a drive-through and get right back online. What's the name of the daycare center? I'll check out their website."

"All of your options are being compiled. I'll have them later today. With the long hours and frequent travel, the list will most likely include au pairs or child assistants with degrees in child education. That way if Trey travels with you, he'll still stay on course with his preschool studies. I think the best candidate would be someone who can look after Trey and whatever temporary households you establish wherever you're at."

"Sounds awesome, Nick, but even with your company's amazing offer, I'm not sure I could afford an arrangement like that. Her salary, airfare, extra lodging, food. It would be a huge expense."

"You're right. I thought about that, which is why her employment would be a part of your package. She'll be employed by the company and, like you, would be given a company card for travel and other expenses."

"Wow. This is… I'm speechless. Where would you find such a person? How…"

"Mom. Plain and simple. She's a better problem-solver and negotiator than a top corporate exec, including my father. Including me. The people on the list have been pre-vetted and most likely were recommended by someone Mom personally knows."

"I… I don't know what to say."

"That's easy. Say you'll be by my office tomorrow to complete the paperwork. You can meet the au pair, sit with our real estate executive to help you with housing and get ready for a trip to New York next week."

"Whoa, Nick, slow down. You're throwing a lot at me. It's almost too much."

"You can handle it."

"I appreciate your confidence but with all of the amazing designers out there, why are you doing all of this to get me?"

"That's simple, Sam. Because you're the best."

"How can I argue with that?"

"You can't."

Why did Sam's laughter make Nick feel like beating his chest and unable to wipe the grin off his face?

"I don't know, Nick. This is a lot to think about."

"You still have a few hours. Why don't you stop by the office tomorrow, say three o'clock?"

"Okay."

"See you then. And Sam?"

"Yes?"

"Just so you know. When I see you tomorrow, the only acceptable answer to my job offer is yes."

Three

Sam reached the hall at one end of the living room, turned and retraced her steps back to the fireplace on the opposite wall. She'd paced this way for the past fifteen minutes. Talking with her cousin, the one who'd graciously taken in her and Trey after their abrupt stateside return. Making her case.

"I can't take this job, Danni. There's no way!"

"There's no way you cannot take it. That job is everything you need right now. With childcare included? Girl, please."

"This isn't about the money. It's about…" Sam looked toward the hallway where her son shared a room with his cousin. She went to sit by Danielle and lowered her voice. "This is about Trey. I can't imagine what would happen if Nick ever found out."

"He's Trey's father, Sam." Danni's voice was a whisper as well. "He shouldn't have to find out. He should be told. The sooner the better."

Sam understood what was behind that last statement. Her ex, Oba, what he knew and how he could use the information if things turned ugly.

Danielle reached out and placed a hand on Sam's arm. "As much as you wanted to deny it, cousin, you knew this day would come. I told you it would."

Sam stared at the fireplace, feeling tears threaten. She watched flames dance and felt a personal inferno.

"It all happened so fast. I was so scared back then. Your friend Joi called. We talked. She gave her brother my number. Oba reached out, then flew over. The next thing I knew I was saying I do. An admittedly hasty arrangement that at the time seemed to solve both his and my problems. I thought leaving without telling Nick was best for everyone. I planned to keep the secret for the rest of my life."

"I know. I'm not blaming or judging you for your choices. If anything, I feel partly responsible. I hate that I shared what Joi told me about her brother looking for a marriage of convenience to beat their egotistical brother to the throne."

"Don't blame yourself. I jumped at the chance. Knowing how Nick felt about marriage, let alone children, made Oba's proposal seem like a magical solution. That I was pregnant gave me an advantage over the other possible candidates. At the time it seemed like a win-win for everyone."

Sam thought back to the morning after she and Nick had been together. How he'd questioned her about birth control, asked if she was protected. She told him yes because she'd been absolutely sure at that time that she could not get pregnant. A problem with fibroids that she'd had for years. He'd worn condoms from then on, two more rounds before leaving the suite that afternoon. All except for that wild, hedonistic, incredible first romp when Trey was created.

"You did the best that you could at the time. But when we know better, we do better."

Now it was Danielle who stood and began walking a hole in the rug. "This is all my fault, really."

Sam looked up. "Did you not hear a word of what I just said?"

"I heard you, Sam. If I'd never heard about the prince or told Joi you were pregnant…"

"As a wise person just told me, you did what you thought was best at the time. When we know better, we do better."

Danielle returned to the sofa. "What's the best decision now? Not just for you but for Trey, even Nick? It doesn't seem right that your ex-husband knows he's not Trey's father but Nick doesn't know that he is. I know that's advice you didn't ask for but…"

"No, you're right. I can't keep the secret forever. Nick deserves to know that he is a father and Trey needs to grow up with his dad."

"Does Trey ask about Oba?"

Sam shook her head. "Trey was always a means to an end for him. He wasn't harsh or anything—they had playful interactions. But Oba isn't overly affectionate and was never hands-on. He also felt child-rearing was 'the woman's job.'" Sam used air quotes, and made a face. "Plus, he was always gone, handling royal business, or jet-setting all over the world."

"From everything you've told me about Nick's offer, sounds like you'll be the one jet-setting now."

"For sure. Designing luxury homes on beautiful islands with an unlimited budget would be a job beyond my wildest dreams." Sam sighed, rested her head on the back of the couch. "But how can I work with Nick and not tell him about Trey? And once that happens, how could he hire me or, if I've taken the job, keep me on?"

"All good questions," Danielle said, as she stood to leave the room. "And only one way to find out."

Sam had just gone to bed when her phone pinged. She checked the text. Oba. Again. Danielle was right. She needed to tell Nick about Trey. But with her mother's cancer battle draining Sam's savings, and the rest used to flee Africa for the safety of home, she also desperately needed the job.

Sam got little sleep that night. She was grateful that Danielle had made arrangements for Trey to join his cousins at day care again. Her husband, Scott, left just before Danielle and the kids. Sam found a yoga video online, one that focused on specific postures and deep breathing. For an hour she worked to think about nothing at all and was mostly successful. As soon as the last chime on the video sounded, however, it was like all of the thoughts and questions she'd held at bay during the workout rushed in at once.

Would Nick be angry?

Would he consider giving a job to someone who lied by omission, one he'd almost surely not trust?

Would the powerful Breedloves fight to take her child? Could she support her son financially without them?

Sam took a shower, then walked to her closet to dress for success. From the time she was young her mother told her, "When you look good, you feel good." It was a lesson Sam never forgot. She flipped through the meager wardrobe she'd packed and considered a well-fitting yet respectable red dress with long sleeves and a scoop neck. She remembered yesterday's meeting, and how Nick's eyes had slid to her legs when she crossed them, his surreptitious glance when she'd shifted in the chair and her blouse played peek-aboo. It had taken everything to act as though she hadn't noticed. Or that muscle memory from their single rendezvous hadn't kicked in, and caused her to clench and harden in places that should he become her boss would be totally off-limits. His charm drove her crazy and he was still as fine as forbidden fruit. But the only thing more out of the question than whether or not she should work with Nick was whether to sleep with him. That answer was a big fat irrefutable *no*.

When she pulled into CANN Casino Hotel and Spa's valet parking, Sam still hadn't made up her mind. Time had run out before the right answer revealed itself. She entered the building, retraced her steps from the day before and decided to go with the flow. While walking through the opulent lobby, with its contemporary motif of marble, stainless steel and crystal chandeliers, her phone rang. She almost didn't answer it. But it could be about Trey.

"Sam Price."

"Hey, it's Nick."

"Am I late? I'm in the lobby and—"

"No, you're not late. I'm hungry. I hope you don't mind that I've moved our meeting to Zest, one of our restaurants. Just get on one of the upper-floor elevators. It's got its own button."

"Oh, okay. I'm on my way." Before having time to process this change of events, the sleek, fast elevator had whisked her far above the bustling metropolis below and landed her into the kind of luxury she came to enjoy as the princess of Kabata, the province her ex-husband Oba and his family had ruled for several generations. Her heartbeat quickened in anticipation.

"Good afternoon. Welcome to Zest."

"Hi, I'm Sam. Samantha Price. I'm here to meet—"

"We've been expecting you, Ms. Price," the hostess said, with sparkling blue eyes and a genuine smile. "Please, come right this way."

Sam took in the floor-to-ceiling paneless glass that blended the clear blue sky with the room's similarly painted ceilings and expected to be escorted into the dining area. Instead, they went along the outer hall of the smartly appointed main dining room to a series of doors along the dimly lit corridor. The hostess stopped in front of the first door on the left, tapped lightly and opened it.

"Mr. Breedlove, Ms. Price has arrived." She stepped back to allow Sam to enter the room. "Enjoy your meal."

Sam thought she'd do better at seeing Nick this time, since she'd just seen him hours before. But his handsomeness still unnerved her. His gentlemanly action of standing as she entered warmed her insides. What guy did that these days? The way his eyes swept her body touched her to the core, brought back feelings from that one single night as though it had just happened. Which was why in that moment she knew their one-night stand was the first thing they needed to discuss.

"Hello, Nick," she said, holding out a stiff arm. A firm handshake was all of this man's touch she could handle.

"Sam, good to see you." He motioned to a chair. "Please, have a seat. I hope you don't mind that I moved our meeting. I've been here working since before seven this morning. It wasn't until Anita reminded me of our meeting that I realized I hadn't eaten all day."

"It's no problem at all."

"Are you sure?"

Sam knew why he asked. She was acting strangely, not like herself. If she was going to work with him, a possibility that was not yet decided, she'd have to pull it together.

"Positive," she managed, trying to relax as she spoke.

"Are you hungry?"

"I'm fine."

"I know that," Nick said with a mischievous grin. "You're still as beautiful as ever. But would you like something to eat?"

Sam refused to be distracted by Nick's limitless charisma. "I'm not hungry, thanks."

"I hope that wasn't offensive."

Sam looked away from his unflinching gaze, deep chocolate orbs framed by curly black lashes. That's how the dance that started at the party all those years ago had ended up in a luxury suite. She'd gotten lost in those eyes.

Nick continued. "In this post-#MeToo world, we male execs have to be extra careful. But given our past friendship, well, I hope complimenting you wasn't uncomfortable. I meant no disrespect."

"No worries."

A second later, there was a knock at the door. A white-haired server entered with a rolling tray containing glasses and a pitcher filled with pomegranate iced tea.

"May I recommend the chateaubriand today, sir? It is exceptional."

Nick looked across the table. "Sam?"

"Nothing for me, thanks."

The server looked at Nick. "I'll take the chateau, Fredrich," he said, resting against the high-backed leather chair.

"Excellent choice," Fredrich replied as he poured two

glasses of tea. "The tenderloin comes from an award-winning ranch not far from here." Fredrich winked at Nick, then looked at Sam.

"If I may," Fredrich began with a benevolent smile. "May I have the pleasure of choosing something for you, something light, or a smaller dish if you prefer?"

"The beef is from my brother Adam's ranch," Nick added. "It's some of the best in the country. Plus, I'm buying, and this place has a Michelin star."

When Sam hesitated, Nick continued. "Come on, woman. It's not wise to turn down a fancy free meal."

The server looked so hopeful Sam couldn't refuse. "Sure," she said, blessing him with a smile. "Thanks."

Fredrich gave a short bow and left.

"Good choice. You won't be sorry." Nick raised a glass. "To a productive meeting."

Sam wasn't so sure about how productive it would be. But she raised a delicately chiseled crystal goblet, clinked it against Nick's and said, "Cheers."

"I know twenty-four hours wasn't a long time to make this decision, but I hope you've had time to think about the benefits of accepting our offer."

"It's all I've thought about," Sam honestly responded. "But before we talk about the job offer, there's something else we need to address."

Nick reached for his glass and sat back. "Oh?"

"That night the last time we saw each other. I don't know about you but for me, it's the elephant in the room."

"If memory serves me correctly, I believe it was a cat."

Nick smiled. Sam didn't.

"I need to make sure that what happened years ago has no bearing on our potential relationship now. If I decide to work for CANN International, the interaction between you and me must be strictly professional. Nothing else."

Nick gave her a look. "Of course."

It was the exact answer Sam wanted, but did he have to reply so quickly? As if the thought of a rekindled affair, even briefly, had not even crossed his mind?

Four

Nick was taken aback by Sam's statement but like the great amateur poker player he was, he didn't let that fact show on his face. Sam had just laid out in no uncertain terms the boundaries of their relationship. Hers was a wise choice, the only one really, especially given the time crunch they'd be under. What else was there to say?

"I didn't mean to imply that you… I just didn't want to assume anything. I wanted to be very clear that this is a business relationship."

"A business relationship? Does that mean you're giving serious consideration to the job offer?"

"I'd be crazy not to," Sam admitted. "Especially since you offered to assist with childcare, which was a major concern, and probably the number one challenge to me accepting the offer."

Number two, she inwardly corrected herself. Her secret about Trey was numero uno.

"If that issue is resolved, you'll take the job?"

"You've made it a very difficult offer to turn down. If it was just me to consider, the decision would be easier. But I have to think of my son. As I said yesterday, he's had what was a very stable world turned upside down. He's been relocated across continents and removed from almost all of the people he knows."

"I can't imagine." Nick's eyes conveyed the compassion he felt. "You a newly single mom. His dad now so far away."

Or not, Sam thought, but said nothing.

"Listen, Sam. CANN International, this project, means a great deal to me, but family is everything. I wouldn't want to do anything to compromise the well-being of your son.

It's why throwing in the benefits of an au pair plus was a no-brainer. Both Christian and Adam swear that their assistants are invaluable, like part of the family."

"That's who helped compile the list of childcare options you sent over, your brothers?"

"I talked to them, but Mom and her assistant Hazel made the list. She thinks live-in help who can also provide tutoring would be the best type of aide for your situation. Isabella and Kirtu, the young women who work for my brothers, are very important components in the smooth running of their households. Given what you've just told me about Trey, I know that familiarity and routine are extremely important right now."

Sam nodded. Was it her imagination or did a softness enter Nick's voice when he said his son's name?

"I think Trey having another constant in his life, someone who'd be there no matter where you're working or what the hours, would be a good thing."

"What happens when the job is over?"

"Good question, though one you might not have to confront right away. CANN International is a huge corporation. Lots of properties to decorate and stage. I could see you being a part of it for the long haul."

"That's what I thought about my marriage," Sam mumbled.

Nick rarely squirmed. At this comment, however, he shifted in his seat. "I'm sorry."

"No, it's not you. It's me. There's a lot going on. I would like to explore working with CANN but honestly, Nick, I'm in no shape to make long-term decisions right now."

"Fair enough. We could bring you on as a contractor and if it works out, look at something more permanent later on. Would that work?"

Sam hesitated before nodding her head. "It sounds like a great opportunity. I'd love to take you up on it."

Nick felt his shoulders relax. Until that moment of relief,

he hadn't realized how badly he wanted to hear some type of yes in her response.

"Good answer." The door opened. Nick looked up as Fredrich entered behind a rolling tray. "And perfect timing."

Fredrich placed a bread basket in the center of the table, along with a carousel of butters and jams. Nick reached for the butter knife with one hand and a biscuit with the other.

"These are legendary," he began, spreading a lavish amount of herbed butter on the still-warm bun. "Made fresh daily, as are all of the bakery items. Come on, you've got to try one."

"I have to admit that the smell coming from beneath that cloth is amazing." She lifted the linen, perused the assortment of mini-treats and picked up a roll. She sniffed. "Parmesan."

Nick paused to watch her. She closed her eyes and took a bite. Despite his determination to keep their relationship professional, the look of pure bliss on her face reminded him of a different type of nibbling they'd enjoyed one other time.

"These should be illegal," she said after finishing the roll.

"I told you," Nick said, with a laugh. "Bon appétit."

They spent the next several minutes discussing specifics of the contract. Fredrich returned with a medium-rare delight for Nick and an exquisite chopped salad topped with velvety slices of chateaubriand for Sam. Conversation was momentarily paused as Nick dug into his roasted vegetables and Sam poured a tangy vinaigrette over her fare.

After a few bites, she put down her fork and picked up her napkin. "I had some amazing meals while living in the palace. But I never knew a simple salad could taste like this."

"I wouldn't use that word in front of the chef. He'd probably say there's nothing simple about it."

Sam took another bite of the delectable combination of brussels sprouts, kale, sweet onion and beef, drizzled with the sweet tangy dressing and sprinkled with a finely grated cheese. She closed her eyes, chewed slowly and moaned.

Nick's dick jumped. *Down, boy.* Memories best forgotten threatened to derail his thought process again.

Sam opened her eyes. "You're right. It looks that way. So few ingredients. But the depth of flavor..."

"Sounds like you know your way around a kitchen."

"Not at all. My cousin does, though. Cooking shows are her obsession."

"The cousin you were with at the party that night?"

"Yes. Wow. I'm surprised you remembered."

It was a memorable night. "What's her name?"

"Danielle. We call her Danni."

Nick nodded, thinking back to the pillow talk they'd enjoyed in between sexual romps. Sam and Danni. Boy names for the bad-boy toys. Those had been her words that night. He kept that memory to himself. When Sam quickly changed the subject, he followed her lead.

"How did your family get into the vacation home rental business?"

Nick finished a bite of food. "By accident."

"And now you've got houses all over the world? Some accident."

"It's the truth." Nick shrugged. "At least the short version."

"What's the longer one?"

Nick finished his plate and sat back with his drink. "It started with my oldest brother, Christian, who built the hotel off the coast in Djibouti. Around that same time, I had business on an island off the coast of New York."

"The property you now own?"

"Yes. It is close to the city yet completely private and already had what we needed in place—utilities, roads. It's small, not large enough for a hotel but perfect for smaller homes. After securing that property, and as research continued, we purchased islands off the coasts of North and South Carolina, Georgia, California and Maine. All of this information will be in your sign-on packet and goes into deeper detail. Next week, you'll see it firsthand."

"Hotels, homes and islands, too? CANN International is bigger than I thought."

"Which is why coming on board to work with us is the best decision you could have ever made."

"With your biased opinion I think it best that I be the judge of that."

"Ha! Touché."

The conversation continued, becoming lighter and more organic as Sam continued to loosen up. By the time Fredrich removed the dessert dishes and poured the black coffee he'd suggested as their digestif, the easy camaraderie from that past casual encounter had returned. Nick felt even better about his decision to reach out to Sam. Not only was she the best woman for a job of this magnitude, she could be a lot of fun.

"Thanks for talking me into eating," Sam said as they stood. "I didn't think I was hungry until I took the first bite."

"Breedloves take food seriously," Nick joked. "We put as much thought into hiring chefs as we do floor designs."

They stepped out of the private dining room and continued down the hall that ran alongside the main dining area. Workers scurried from table to table, making each a perfect presentation for the dinner crowd. Nick acknowledged a few of them as they passed by, left the restaurant and headed toward the elevator.

Nick pressed the button and stepped back. "I'll have paperwork drawn up and faxed over ASAP. You have a passport, obviously, so we don't have to worry about that."

"Passport? Aren't all of the builds for this project happening stateside?"

"The last home we'll renovate is in the Bahamas. Other than that, international travel will most likely not be required. We make sure everyone working for us has the paperwork required to travel to any number of our CANN properties, just in case."

The elevator arrived. They stepped inside, both quiet during the ride down one hundred floors.

Once in the lobby, Nick held out his hand. "Welcome aboard, Ms. Price."

"Those papers aren't signed yet, Mr. Breedlove." Sam teased. "But I don't foresee any problems."

She accepted his handshake. Her skin was warm, velvety soft to the touch. Their eyes met. Something happened between them. Faint, but perceptible. A current of erotic energy sparkled in their midst. Sam pulled her hand from Nick's grasp. The spell was broken. But Nick had definitely felt it and was 99.9 percent sure that Sam had felt it, too.

They said goodbye and went their separate ways. Yet long after their meeting and into the night, Nick wondered about the elephant that Sam had brought up. It wasn't that lone, torrid night of the past that he was worried about. It was the undeniable chemistry still sizzling between them, and how long it could be successfully ignored.

Five

There were a few showers when April arrived, but for most Nevadians the warmer breezes were a welcome change from the previous month's unseasonably cold temperatures. Sam barely noticed. After signing the project-specific contract and faxing it back to CANN International, the next eight days passed in a whirlwind—a flurry of house hunting and childcare interviews. She ignored Nick's suggestion to move to Breedlove, an unincorporated area not far from Las Vegas, but accepted the born-and-bred native's advice on the best areas in Las Vegas to rent. She also politely declined the company's offer to assist with her search for a nanny. Telling Nick the truth about Trey was inevitable. But until she was ready and the time was right, Sam planned to keep the Breedloves and CANN International far away from her child. After last night's conversation with Oba, she was thankful that an ocean separated them, too. She couldn't believe he'd had the nerve to call.

"Oba?"

"You forget my voice already, baby?"

Sam didn't have to work to give her ex the silent treatment. She literally had nothing to say.

"How is life in America?"

Really? He was treating this as a social call? After how their relationship ended, and all that had happened since then?

"Oba, I'm busy, on my way to begin a very important project. I can't talk now."

"A working woman? Oh, no, *masoyina*! That is not the life for you."

"I am no longer your love, your wife or your responsibility. I thought we agreed a clean, complete break was best. Why are you calling me?"

"I miss you, baby. I miss my son."

The endearment was spoken with a low and heartfelt intonation, an emphasis on the second syllable, as was his way. The same voice she at one time appreciated now brought knots to her stomach. Oba had given Trey only a passing interest. What was this really about? That the marriage was one of convenience had been something they'd both willingly entered and ended. He needed to let it go.

"Last week, my father delivered very bad news, baby. He is still very angry at our deception."

Our deception?

"That he welcomed Trey into the family with a ceremonial tribute reserved for only those with tribal blood."

And this is my business because...

"I'm sorry that your father is unhappy, Oba. But his learning about Trey not being your son isn't my fault. That was your brother's doing. We've both suffered because of the decision Isaac made. I lost a lot, including the little money I'd been able to save while living there. I'm doing what I have to do to rebuild my life and am not sure how what is happening within your family involves me."

"My father has severely limited my royal responsibilities and by extension, my allowance."

"At least you have one."

"It is not how I am accustomed to living. He has banished me to the apartment in Lagos, a place I've only stayed in sporadically and not for several years!"

Sam visited that apartment once. It was a two-story unit with four bedrooms, five bathrooms, a tennis court and a pool. Poor baby.

"Oba, what do you want from me?"

"I need to make some moves, Sam. Maybe come to America."

"You've got Joi here. Ask her for help."

"She doesn't have any money."

"I don't either," Sam quickly retorted.

"But you can get it." Oba's tone changed, became firmer and a little less friendly. "Ask Nick to give it to you."

"What?" Sam's voice rose several octaves. That after several shocked seconds before she could actually speak, the nerve and unmitigated gall of his suggestion rendering her paralyzed and dang near mute.

She sat straight up in bed. "Are you freaking kidding me? Are you out of your mind? I don't have any money to give you and asking Nick or anyone else for help is out of the question."

"Does he know about Trey?"

"Keep Trey out of this."

"That sounds like a no."

"I don't give a damn how it sounds or what you think you know about Trey's relationship with his biological father."

Sam hoped that sentence was enough of a dam to stop the potential flood of truth hinted at by Oba's veiled threat.

"Trey is the innocent party in all of this and totally off-limits. As for what's happened because of your brother, well, we've both suffered from his actions. If anyone can and should help you it's Isaac, not me. And definitely not Nick."

"You know I'm the last person with whom Isaac would share his wealth. I helped you out when you were in trouble. Now you need to return the favor."

"How many ways do I have to say it? I don't have any money."

"According to my sister, that's about to change. She sent me a link to a press release. You're working with CANN International."

Sam hadn't given a thought to making news, would not have believed the hiring of a contractor warranted a public announcement. Damn the company and their PR efficiency, and damn Joi for not minding her business.

"It's a temporary contract," she replied, then quickly searched the web for the announcement, and hoped the verbiage didn't go into detail.

It didn't, thank God. But Oba already knew too much.

"My getting work doesn't change the answer. There is nothing I can do to help you."

"Listen, Sam—"

"No, you listen. I'm done talking." Sam stopped, took a breath, removed the crease from between her brows and calmed down. Offending Oba right now would do her no good. "I wish you the best, Oba, and hold nothing against you. But because of Isaac, we are out of each other's lives. Let's continue to move on, going separate ways. We're both doing our best under the circumstances. Please don't call me again."

Sam arrived at the airport in Las Vegas for a flight to New York. She reached the gate and looked for Nick. He wasn't there. The boarding announcement sounded over the speakers. Still, no Nick. She pulled out her cell to call him but changed her mind. He wasn't her responsibility. Maybe he'd decided not to accompany her. No big deal. She was an accomplished designer who didn't require hand-holding. That he'd planned to come at all had been a surprise in the first place. Sam had a first-class ticket but waited until several had boarded before getting on the plane. After accepting an orange juice from the attendant, she settled in for the flight, convinced she'd hear from Nick after landing in New York. Instead, just before the doors closed, he rushed in and took the aisle seat beside her.

"Hey," he said, passing off his briefcase and buckling his seat belt in a rush.

"Cutting it a bit close, aren't we?"

"Didn't mean to. Saw a buddy of mine in the lounge and got to talking. Lost track of time."

"It's all good. You made it. Considering the success of

the company you work for I'm surprised you fly commercial at all."

"I don't often," Nick admitted.

"I hope you didn't lower your standards on my account." Sam smiled to show she was joking. She was. In a way.

"I'd hardly call spending time with you in any way lowering my standards," Nick easily replied, his voice lower than usual and sexier than Sam would have liked. "Plus, with it being so long since we've seen each other I thought the long nonstop flight would be a perfect chance to catch up.

"So…" he continued, after casually chatting while the plane reached its cruising altitude. "Tell me about living the life of a princess."

It was a fair question, one Sam might have asked were the situation reversed. She shifted in her seat. "Well, as Meghan Markle would probably attest, it's not always all it's cracked up to be. But it wasn't all bad."

"How'd you meet Oba Usman, the grand prince of Kabata and rumored heir to the throne?"

"Someone's been busy online, I see." Said as Sam prided the exterior she managed, one that masked the angst she felt just beneath the surface. Given what had happened that caused Oba to lose his right to the throne, the less Nick knew about her ex, the better.

"A little background research on our latest corporate partner. This would have normally been all done beforehand had I not been under the gun to hire someone so quickly."

Sam couldn't fault him for researching her via web. She'd done the same to him after meeting that night at the party. It's where she first learned he was a successful confirmed bachelor who didn't want kids.

"Danni, who you remember from the party, was friends with his sister. Shortly after meeting me she talked to him. Thought we might make a good match. We were introduced via a video chat and it went from there."

"Interesting. Things must have moved fast. I mean, one

minute we're hanging out at a costume party and the next you're married and living on the other side of the world."

"Yes, everything happened quickly." For reasons that remained unsaid. "I admit to moving forward with stars in my eyes. Every little girl dreams of being a princess, and fantasizes about knights in shining armor once we reach our teens."

"And Oba seemed to be that?"

"I thought so, in the beginning."

"What changed?"

Sam took a deep breath and spoke thoughtfully. "I've come to realize that even under the most normal of circumstances, marriage is hard. That mine was high-profile and involved a royal family added to the challenge."

Nick whistled. "Going through that had to be tough. One of the main reasons I'm in no hurry to do it."

"Smart move."

"Why'd you marry so quickly?"

"Oba was under pressure to find a wife. Being married and producing an heir was a requirement for him to be considered as a successor to the throne, something his younger brother who'd become engaged the year prior was in a race to do. When… I became pregnant…we married right away."

"Was it what you wanted?"

Sam avoided looking into Nick's penetrating gaze. "It's what I felt best for Trey."

"And for you?"

"At the time I thought the decision best for the both of us."

"Hmm. How is the little guy? Did you find a suitable nanny?"

"I think so. For now, Danni is graciously handling everything between Gloria, the nanny, and Trey. I'll fly them up later, probably next week."

As the flight attendant began the first-class meal service, Sam and Nick retreated to their individual thoughts.

Sam was relieved for the reprieve, a time to recover from the stress felt during that conversation. She replayed and mentally tucked away what had been said, in order to make sure that the story she told now, in this moment, was one she'd remember if ever asked again.

"What about you? I know you're in no hurry but with all of your brothers married, you're not feeling the slightest pressure to walk down the aisle, have a kid or two, and contribute to the Breedlove legacy?"

Nick stretched his long, lean legs in front of him. "Not at all."

Sam couldn't help but laugh at the hasty response, even as Nick not being ready to have children made her heart skitter around in her chest.

Nick positioned his chair to lean back. "For now, these island homes are my only babies. It's the biggest company project I've taken on to date, and while the family hasn't applied any pressure, I have my own point to prove.

"In the past few years," he continued, counting on his fingers, "Christian's build in Djibouti opened up the entire African continent. Adam's Wagyu beef is the best in America, and with his land research and development gem finds he's contributed greatly to the company's bottom line. Last year Noah did the impossible by opening up a casino in what is arguably the country's most conservative state. While paralyzed."

Sam gasped. "Oh no! What happened?"

"Horrific ski accident. You didn't hear?" Sam shook her head. "Wow, you really were isolated."

"Mostly by choice. Before, my phone and the internet were like an extension of my physical self. It was nice to step away from all that and live in the real world, such as it was."

"I can't imagine, but I hear you."

"How is Noah now?"

"Much better, thanks for asking."

"Sounds like the past few years have been very productive for the family. Now it's your turn?"

"Yes."

"Do they have kids, your brothers?"

Nick nodded. "Christian has a daughter, Christina, and a son, Larenz. Both Adam's and Noah's wives, Ryan and Dee, are expecting. They conceived three months apart."

"Wow! Sounds like Uncle Nick is going to be busy."

"Yeah, being the uncle is great. I can be the fun adult, spoil them and then send them home."

They laughed, and the conversation paused as the flight attendant returned with menus. She'd been flirting with Nick since he sat on the plane and now was no exception.

"Mr. Breedlove, may I recommend the salmon." She paused, batting long lashes and flashing flawless pearly whites as she refreshed his drink. "It's really good and healthy, too. You seem the type who likes to stay in shape."

"You're right about that." He handed back the menu. "I'll have that with asparagus and rice."

"Great choice." She looked at Sam. "And for you?" Asked with no sparkling eyes, a mere hint of a smile and no move to freshen her drink.

Sam almost laughed out loud. "I'll have the Cajun chicken salad, please. And a glass of cabernet."

Both of them watched the attendant walk away.

Sam nodded in her direction. "Looks like you have an admirer."

"She's just doing her job."

"Seriously, Nick, you can't be that naive. Your modesty, though, is appreciated."

He took a sip of water. "Tell me about your family. Do you have siblings?"

"A brother from my mom's first marriage. He's seven years older than me, a techie who lives in Seattle. My dad lives in LA."

"Is that where you grew up?"

"Born and raised."

"And your mom?"

Sam quieted, swallowed past the sudden lump in her throat. "She passed away right before I moved to Africa. Breast cancer."

"I'm sorry."

"Thank you. I miss her every day."

"How is it that you were at the costume party?"

Sam knew exactly which party he was talking about, the one where they slept together and her life was forever changed.

"Danni moved here years ago, a professional dancer with stars in her eyes. Got hired for a few shows. Then she met Scott, got married and started a family. Her mom, my aunt, was my mom's sister. They were very close, always together, which led to Danni and I being more like sisters than cousins."

"What did she think about your quick wedding?"

Back to that again? Sam wondered why Nick was so fixated on a marriage that was over. She chose to answer rather than ask the question; figured the more open she was about that part of her life the less he'd feel the need to pry further.

"She's always wanted what was best for me. Since I was happy, she was happy."

"And now that you're divorced?"

Sam tried not to let her chagrin show but she had tired of this line of questioning. "Again, she supports whatever is best for me, and is happy I'm back stateside."

"Please forgive my insensitivity for asking. I imagine that ending a marriage is never easy, no matter the reason, and that talking about it could be painful."

"You're right. It's not easy. But in the end, it was for the best. Enough about me. Let's talk about your love life."

"I already told you. The only love affair I'm having right now is with the CANN Isles project."

"If that's your story you can stick to it. But an architect's art renderings can't keep you warm at night."

"Ha! True that. I go out here and there but mostly I've been too busy to date."

Sam found that hard to believe but didn't push. The conversation wound its way back to business and the cluster of island homes in New York, the first that Sam would be stamping with her designs. Were circumstances different she'd definitely date Nick. Smart and confident with a wicked sense of humor, he wasn't hard to like. That he was easy on the eyes didn't hurt, either. Being far and away the best lover she'd ever experienced would be the cherry on top of the sundae. If things were different. But they weren't. Sam needed to keep that in mind and stay focused on doing her job.

The flight attendant returned. The flirting continued. Sam put on a brave smile and hid the anguish in her heart. The best thing that could happen was for Nick to fall madly in love, thereby erasing any perceived chance of a future between them. She, Trey and Nick would not ride off into the sunset as one big happy family. Whatever feelings that were trying to resurface were best quashed before having a chance to blossom.

No doubt someone as good-looking as Nick had scores of women, one in every town. Except for the time-sensitive project and the secret she kept, Sam wouldn't have minded being one of them.

Six

Clients staying at a CANN Isles property were ferried from a port or marina in each city to the island by private yachts either purchased or leased by the company. Less than an hour after arriving in New York City, Nick and Sam had been driven by limo to the marina in Brooklyn where the boat was docked and waiting.

"Impressive," Sam said, as the two settled at the end of circular seating that could double as a sunbathing pad on the right type of day. "CANN International most definitely does everything first class."

"Nothing you're not used to, right? The life of a princess had to have been at least this upscale. Given Nigeria is Africa's richest nation, even more so, I'd imagine."

"It was very opulent living," Sam admitted, looking out over the water.

She offered nothing more, but Nick pressed the issue. The more he interacted with Sam, the more he realized how little he knew about her. Being hesitant about getting into her personal life was understandable, but Nick was determined to get past the superficial or work conversations they had mostly had to this point.

He sat against the couch, stretched his arms across its back. "I've been to several countries in Africa, but never Nigeria. We hear so many stories. How was it living there?"

"Not like most residents, I'd suppose. Most of my life happened on the grounds of the palace, which were massive. Almost everything one could imagine for living was on the premises—pools, tennis courts, parks and spas. If something wasn't readily available, it was obtained by the staff. If it was something that I or other household members needed to personally approve, wardrobe, furniture, stuff like that, it was either handled online or personally brought in."

"That sounds super restrictive. Was it because of security concerns?"

Sam didn't answer immediately. Nick wondered if he'd overstepped.

"My ex-husband's family were very protective of not only family members but also their brand." Again, she paused, as if choosing her words carefully. "They went to great lengths to protect their privacy. However, I don't believe their actions or attention to safety went beyond that of other royals. As I said, their land holdings are massive, about an hour from Lagos, a sprawling complex that's completely secure. Life was somewhat scripted but not as rigid as it sounds."

"You loved a good party back in the day. I know you were a married woman with a child but there were no fun times on the beach or wild nights at the club?"

Sam sighed, frowned slightly. "The homes of the wealthy are gated playgrounds. There wasn't really a need to go other places."

Nick quickly and keenly felt her mental retreat. He changed course. "Did you visit other countries?"

"Several."

"Do you have a favorite?"

"Each had its own beauty. I could live on the island of Madagascar."

"Madagascar's a sweet spot for sure. What about Maasai Mara?"

Sam shook her head. "Never heard of it. What's there?"

"Lions, cheetahs, zebras."

"A safari?"

"The best country to go on one, or so we were told. I have to admit they were right, based on the experience I had."

"What about the country where the CANN hotel is built?"

"Djibouti? Beautiful."

"How'd your brother find it?"

"You know what? Good question. You need to ask him the next time we meet."

Both slipped into silence as the boat skimmed the dark blue waters, taking them farther from the city into the deep part of the sea. Sam excused herself to call Danni and check in on Trey. Nick used the time to call the office, read his emails and return a call to his mom. Thirty minutes later, he stood and stretched as land came into view.

He walked over, opened the cabin door and yelled below. "Sam!"

"Yes?"

"We're here."

"Okay. Coming right up."

The boat docked. Within minutes, Nick and Sam were in an ATV, their luggage behind them, traveling over the bumpy terrain at a high rate of speed.

"Slow down!" Sam yelled.

Nick laughed. "Hang on. I've got this!"

As the vehicle rounded a curve and the house came into view, Sam's jaw dropped. An architectural masterpiece of glass-fiber-reinforced concrete, gleaming steel and pane-less windows was far and away the most beautiful home she'd ever seen.

"This place is amazing." She spoke in a hushed, awe-inspired tone, just barely above a whisper.

"That's exactly the type of reaction we want from our guests."

Adam leaped out of the ATV, then went on the other side to let Sam out. A house employee appeared as if by magic to handle their luggage and fulfill any requests from the boss.

"The inside isn't as finished as the outside," Nick warned. "But don't let that scare you as it did the designer before you."

"Thanks for the warning," Sam replied, her heartbeat slightly quickening as they walked through an atrium filled with lush tropical plants, angel statues and an impressive waterfall. "For the inside to come anywhere close to this home's exterior is a very tall order."

Adam reached the door, then stepped back for Sam to enter. "I believe in you."

Sam stopped just inside the door. "Oh. My. Goodness." She turned to Nick. "When you said the interiors needed designing, I didn't think that meant from the studs up."

"This is one of the least finished models. Others aren't quite this bad."

"This job is way bigger than I imagined. Large crews will be needed if there's any hope of finishing these homes in eight to twelve weeks. Have workers been lined up and contracted?"

Nick shook his head.

"No carpenters, painters, installers, nothing?"

"Again, some of the other homes are a bit further along than this but basically, many of the jobs are from the ground up."

Nick watched as Sam reached into her tote, pulled out a tablet and began jotting down notes as she walked room to room.

"I'd be lying to not admit that this feels overwhelming. Where was my luggage taken? It contains some of what I'll need to get this ball rolling. I need to get started right away."

Nick made quick work of finishing the tour, ending on the third floor of the massive mix of contemporary and bungalow styles.

"Here are the two remaining master suites," Nick pointed out, having shown her five in all. I had the maids prepare these two for our stay."

"You're staying?"

Nick worked to hide a smile. That Sam seemed concerned about the close proximity of their bedrooms pleased him more than he could let on. "Don't sound so alarmed.

It's just for the night. I have an appointment in New York tomorrow morning."

"Oh, okay."

"I've got work to catch up on while you do your thing, but what say we take a break around seven for dinner tonight?"

"Thanks, but that's not really necessary. I'd rather grab something quick and continue working."

"No problem. A panel similar to the one I showed you just beyond the foyer is also in your room and can be used to summon the chef or any of the other employees to help you. If there is anything at all that you need done, don't hesitate to ask."

"Okay, thanks, Nick. I'll see you later."

Nick retired to his room but with Sam consuming his thoughts, there was no work getting done. After basically doodling and checking social media accounts for over an hour, he donned a pair of swim trunks to douse his heated bod in the Atlantic's cold waves. Knowing Sam was down the hall would make it a challenge, but he purposely wore himself out swimming in hopes of a good night's sleep. Back at the house, he took a hot shower. Noah called just as he finished drying off. Having passed Sam downstairs hard at work on her tablet, he strode naked from his suite to the hall linen closet, looking for a particular robe he was told had been placed there, a simple terry number to replace the heavier one left in the room.

"Are you flying up or no?" he asked his twin, entering the walk-in hall closet and bypassing several robe choices before finding the one he preferred and slinging it over his shoulder. "Cool. Then let's meet at the restaurant in the office tower lobby and go over the plans before sitting down with their group."

Nick stepped out of the closet just as Sam rounded the corner.

"Oh!" she yelped, her eyes appearing to take him in like

a tall glass of water in an arid desert before remembering to be professional.

"Sorry." Nick kept his eyes squarely focused on Sam as he casually slipped on the robe. "Your room is on the other side."

Sam said nothing, just wheeled around and headed in the opposite direction.

"Call you back, twin." Nick hurriedly ended the call. "Sam!"

The only response he heard was the sound of her door closing, and the lock being firmly latched behind her.

Seven

Shit! Sam reached her room, closed the door and repeated the expletive. About a dozen times. Why hadn't she paid more attention to her surroundings before leaving the room? She'd commented on the matching masters and what a good selling point that would be for potential renters. Why hadn't she focused on where she was going? And why the hello fantasy island did he have to be naked when she entered? At the thought, his image sprang into her mind. Hot. Hard. The appendage that had brought her both instant and lasting pleasure still amazingly impressive, even in its languid state. Only now did Sam think about how long it had been since she'd had sex. Too long to be on an island alone with a gorgeous man. *Shit!*

Sam jumped as her phone pinged. She picked it up. Nick.

Sorry that happened. U ok?

In her mind, sarcastic responses stumbled over each other. But her response was short and sweet.

I'm ok. ☺.

Liar. What happened wasn't okay at all. So much so that a short time later she sent Nick a second text feigning exhaustion and asked if they could meet first thing the next day. Cross-country trips and changing time zones could be tiresome, but fighting the attraction to Nick is what zapped Sam's energy. After making contact with a few of her old suppliers and surfing CANN International's website to study hotel room pics, she took a shower and slid between

designer Egyptian cotton sheets. The material felt soft and
seductive against her skin. The memory-foam mattress caressed her body. The pillows smelled faintly of lavender,
a scent known to relax the body and quiet the mind. The
combination worked wonders. Soon, Sam was fast asleep.

It seemed only moments later when the door to her room
opened. Sam looked up. Nick, once again in all of his practically naked glory. He seemed ethereal, almost otherworldly,
his partially clad body backlit by subdued hallway lighting.
His steps were slow, measured, as he boldly approached her.
He reached the foot of her bed and silently waited for an invitation to join her. Sam sat up, letting the sheet fall to reveal
her bareness. Her exposed nipples pebbled quickly. Goose
bumps broke out all over her ebony skin, and not just from
the cool breeze through the open balcony doors. He shook
the robe he wore from his shoulders, let it puddle at his feet,
then crawled onto the bed like a panther, stalking its prey.

He stared deep into her eyes. Not a word had been spoken.

Sam watched as though mesmerized as Nick pulled down
the sheet and exposed every inch of her body. He took a
finger and slid it lazily from the heel of her foot to the insides of her thighs, flicking it along the folds of her paradise before branding her with his touch on the way back
down, then sexily licking his finger. Without warning, he
bent over and sucked a toe in his mouth. So delicious was
his touch, so amazing, so forceful, that Sam almost had an
orgasm right there!

But she didn't.

Instead, she lay back against the fluffy pillows, writhing
as Nick's tongue bath continued over her ankles and shin.
He kissed a sensitive spot behind her knee before trailing
kisses up the insides of her thighs, gently parting her legs
wider until she was fully exposed. Only seconds passed before she felt his lips touch her nether ones, before his tongue
swiped the dew from between her folds, until he feasted on

her feminine flower. Sam felt short of breath and tried to get away lest she die from pleasure. But Nick wasn't having it. He held her firmly by her thighs—licking, sucking, biting, kissing—until an orgasm that began at the core of her being burst forth on the waves of a scream that reverberated around the room. She lay back spent, finished.

Nick was just getting started.

He positioned himself just beyond her shoulders, his thick, stiff manhood dangling precariously close to her face. Obviously, he figured that turnabout was fair play. Who was Sam to argue? She wrapped her hands around his massive sex weapon, kissed the tip and then sucked him into her mouth. His gasp of breath let her know that she was onto something. She continued the assault, breathing him in, pulling him out, setting up a rhythm to match the pace of his hips as she ran a hand over his hard cheeks and outlined his mushroom tip with her tongue. One last thrust to her face and apparently Nick couldn't take it any longer. He pulled her up, turned her over and in one long, glorious plunge, entered her from behind.

Ah!

Sam relaxed to take in all of him before rocking back and forth in their dance of love. She moaned when he massaged her breasts and twiddled her nipples, never missing a beat as he drove himself deeper and deeper inside her, until he touched the very core. She came once, twice, but still Nick wasn't finished. He climbed off the bed, took her into his arms and walked through the open balcony doors. There, under the light of a full springtime moon, he sat on one of the lounge chairs that dotted the large balcony and directed her to sit on his still-engorged shaft. She felt like a sex goddess, watching his eyes flutter closed, feeling the wind on her sensitive buds, throwing back her hair and enjoying the ride. She rose up until only his tip was inside her, then slid down his pole like a trained firewoman. Back and forth. In and out. They made love for minutes. Or was it for hours? Or days? Finally, she felt Nick's pace quicken, heard him mumble unintelligibly until he, too, let himself go and went over the edge. The orgasm was so climactic it made her ears buzz. The sound began as if in the distance, then got louder and louder until...

She woke up.

Sam looked around the room, disoriented to find herself back in bed and not on the lounge outside. The bedsheets had been tousled and were now wrapped around her. Nick wasn't in her room. Unfortunately, she was very alone.

That had been a dream?

The buzzing she'd heard earlier sounded again. She looked to see a light coming from the phone on the table beside her. Taking a deep breath, she picked up the receiver.

"Hello?"

"Good morning, beautiful."

"Hey, Nick."

Sam fell back against the headboard. On one hand she was glad that their making love had not happened in real time. On the other, she was sorely disappointed.

"Meeting in Manhattan got changed from lunch to breakfast but I wanted to touch base with you before leaving the island."

"You're leaving right now?"

"In about five or ten minutes. In addition to the meeting change there's a storm coming in. The captain suggested we get an early start. It sounds like I may have awakened you, though, so go ahead and finish your sleep. I imagine you have a long day ahead. We can catch up next week, when you're back home."

"Sure. I'll plan and sketch today and will forward the 3-D renderings. Perhaps we can chat by phone before I schedule contractors from the names you sent over. Thanks for those."

"No worries at all. I look forward to the sketches."

Sam heard a beep.

"Ah, I have to take this. Call me if you need me."

"Will do."

"Bye, Sam."

Just as she was about to put down her phone, a text came in. She tapped the screen. Oba. Well, wasn't that just the wake-up she needed. It was a warning to not get caught up in the feelings of her exotic dream. Because in her waking world, unless she was very careful, life could turn into a nightmare—snap—just like that.

Eight

For the next couple weeks, Nick and Sam didn't see each other but were in almost constant communication. In the mornings he'd receive detailed 3-D images of each room's design plan, sometimes updates from plans sent before. Nick appreciated that unlike the previous designer, Sam kept him apprised of the progress without being prompted. He wasn't usually a micromanager, but with the challenging timeline and the millions of dollars at stake, rest came easier knowing of any potential challenges with contractors or material deliveries and having an overview of what was happening overall. At night they'd communicate by phone, text or email, and not always about work. Nick encouraged Sam to get off the island and take advantage of being in the city that never sleeps. Sam teased at Nick that she'd do that as soon as a certain taskmaster stopped cracking the whip. While working in New York, Sam was also viewing the floor plans of the homes off the coast of Georgia and the Carolinas, which were next on the schedule. Every idea was well-thought-out and top-notch, homes to fulfill every whim of the wealthy, just as he'd envisioned.

On the professional front, all seemed to run smoothly. Yet his thought often returned to the day after he arrived in New York, and the conversation he'd had with Sam just before leaving. Nick wondered if it was his imagination, or had he heard a bit of trepidation in Sam's voice? Had she tossed and turned half the night, had trouble sleeping as had been the case with him? There was a lot on his corporate plate but Nick didn't try to fool himself. Sam being just down the hall was the reason he'd found it hard to rest that night. That more than anything is why he'd left early.

The stress of another night in the same house but different beds with that woman would have taken years off his life.

Nick clicked on the 3-D image that showcased Sam's plans from an aerial perspective. He projected it from the computer to the eighty-inch wall-mounted screen, then walked over to take a more in-depth look.

A soft tap sounded behind him. Nick turned around.

It was Noah. "Got a minute?"

"For you, I do. Come over and take a look at this."

Noah stopped a few feet away to fully examine the life-like rendering, before stepping up for a closer look. He pointed to an area near the screen's left side. "Is all of this part of the atrium?"

Nick nodded. "It's already finished. And absolutely gorgeous, bro. It definitely makes an immediate statement to our guests. Sam suggested putting at least a modified version on as many homes as possible. What do you think about that?"

"What does the team think?"

"I'll find out in the meeting on Friday. Didn't you get the memo?"

"Probably. I've been tied up with Bionics all week. I'm sure Essie placed it on my calendar."

Noah's attention returned to the screen. "Do you have real photos of that?"

"I sure do. Hang on." Nick walked to his desk and reached for the mouse. His cell phone rang. A frown accompanied his greeting. "Breedlove."

"Hello?" A few seconds and then, "Who is this?" Nick sighed as he ended the call and slid the phone back to the desk.

"What was that about?" Noah asked.

"I don't know. It's been happening for a couple days now."

"Someone probably has the wrong number and keeps

calling hoping that whoever they're trying to reach will answer the phone."

"You're probably right." He clicked a remote to begin the slide presentation. "Check this out."

Nick showed Noah the New York renderings and what he had so far on the other homes.

"What about Hawaii and the Bahamas?"

"Navigating the world of contractors in both locations is a bit tricky. If necessary, I'm hoping to be able to fly in the manpower we need while employing as many of the townsfolk as possible. Doing that often makes it easier for the officials to be more agreeable in other areas."

"If Sam can duplicate what's happened in New York everywhere else, she'll indeed be a miracle worker. But I don't know, man. We're into April, about ten weeks away from the first reservations. It's going to be tight."

"It's going to be amazing."

Anita interrupted via intercom. "Gentlemen, your mom is on line two."

"Who does she want to speak to?" Noah asked.

Nick picked up the phone. "Who did she call?" He pushed the blinking extension and placed the call on speakerphone. "Hey, Mom."

"Hi, Mother." Noah gave a wave as he turned and walked out the door.

"Is that Noah?"

"It was. He just left."

"Oh, dear. I hope I didn't interrupt anything."

"Just discussing trying to finish a project valued in the hundreds of millions is all."

"Oh, good. Then of course you've got time to talk with me about next month's carnival."

Nick suppressed a groan as he sat and swirled his executive chair. He knew where this conversation was heading. "All the time in the world, Mother. What's up?"

"We're finalizing the carnival's special guest list. Have you spoken with Samantha about bringing her son?"

"First of all, why are you talking about her as though she's someone you know? No one calls her Samantha, Mom. She goes by Sam."

"Duly noted. Have you asked her?"

"Honestly all I've talked about with her are the island homes."

"How are those coming along, son?"

"I'm happy to report that so far, so good. I just showed Noah the slides from what was just completed in New York, and the 3-D pictures of the next focus, which are our islands in the Southeast. Her plans look amazing."

"So did the other designer's, as I recall."

"The difference is that Sam has the reputation and with what we've seen in New York, the experience to back up that vision."

"Sounds like this Sam is quite a woman."

"Quite the interior designer," Nick gently corrected. "That's the part of her that plays a part in my life."

Victoria chided right back. "Oh, come now, Nick. Those working alongside us have never been mere employees. Every time someone joins the corporation, our family expands."

Nick's lips went into a straight line. His grandma Jewel taught him that when one didn't have something good to say, they need say nothing at all.

"Is it possible to get Sam's email address so that I can send her a proper invitation?"

"She's really busy, Mom. I don't think—"

"Good. You don't have to. Just send over the address so that our amazing interior designer can decide for herself whether she'd want her child to attend the carnival of any child's dream."

"Send over the invitation to my cell phone, Mom. I'll forward it."

"Excellent! As soon as possible, sweetie. Have a beautiful rest of day, now. Bye-bye!"

Classic Victoria. Light a bomb, then scatter before the flame reaches the end of the wick. Being around Sam in a playful atmosphere was probably not the wisest move, but he'd do as requested and forward the invite to her. To further balk or outright refuse would only serve to make his mom that much more curious and determined. Given the pace she'd kept up for almost two weeks, Sam would probably want to spend the weekend doing something much more productive than petting animals or watching her kid's face get painted. Like sleeping.

I wouldn't mind spending the weekend sleeping in, too... with her.

The thought popped into his head before he could stop it. He was mostly successful at keeping it at bay, especially since Sam had made it clear that she didn't want to mix business with pleasure. Now with his mom's interest pricked, he definitely wanted to keep things platonic. If Victoria connected with Sam, felt she was a possible Breedlove bride and got the slightest whiff of romance, she'd start searching for suitable wedding venues and order the cake.

His phone dinged. The invite from Victoria. He clicked on it and downloaded the attachment but finished viewing Sam's latest renderings and making notes before placing the call. By then he'd mentally placed her back in the work safe zone and convinced himself that he was making too big a deal of the carnival invite. She and Trey would be two of over a thousand people his mother expected to descend on the estate next weekend.

Noah texted the invite to Sam, then got up to take in the all-encompassing Las Vegas view from his high-rise corner office. "Sam, good morning."

"Almost afternoon on the East Coast. You're calling about the Southeast island designs?"

"Yes, and something else. I just texted you an invite."

"An invite? For what?"

"Did you get it?"

"Hold on." Nick watched a plane descend toward the nearby airport. "A CANN Kind of Carnival?"

"Yes, that's it, forwarded at the specific request of my mother."

"Please join us for…" Sam's voice diminished as he imagined her quickly scanning the invitation.

"Um, yeah, this is very kind of Victoria, but I'm going to have to decline."

"About that feeling like you have an option? You don't. It's why I called."

"Let me make sure I've got this straight. My first weekend off and I'm required to attend a carnival?"

"One hosted by the CANN Foundation, which my mother heads up? Yes. It's going to be an amazing event with the proceeds benefiting children in hospitals, foster care and at-risk situations. My mom has dreamed up a ton of creative efforts over the years, but this literal fair on the grounds of the estate is a first."

"And you're saying this is mandatory?"

"I'm saying it would be in your best interest."

"Why? I don't remember attending CANN charity events being in my agreement."

"Mom knows you're new to town and a single mother. She feels an outing like this would be a great way for you and Trey to meet other moms and young kids in the community."

"That's very thoughtful of her, but honestly, I was looking forward to a simple weekend, a movies-and-pizza kind of affair. Especially with the Carolinas on the schedule next week and a few potential material availability fires already cropping up. Since you're such an ace business negotiator, why don't you decline the RSVP on my behalf."

"Because Victoria is a partner possessing debate skills that make winning arguments darn near impossible. I believe the invitation allows you to include a friend or two. Perhaps your cousin or another mother would like to join you? As much as I appreciate your focus, a short break from the stress might do you good. You'll enjoy yourself and your son will love it."

After a pause, Sam responded. "I'm sure he'd have fun. I could probably find an hour or two to hang out there."

"Good."

She chuckled. "Is that relief I hear in your voice?"

"Ha! Picked up on that, did you? If you knew Mom, you'd be relieved, too."

"I don't understand."

"Victoria Breedlove lives life on a chessboard. She never makes one move without having thought three or four moves ahead. I've played on this board all my life and know for sure that it would be better to say yes to this invitation and have whatever conversation she obviously wants to have with you, than to decline and make her even more determined to make a connection."

"Does she know about us, I mean, our one-night stand?"

"No."

"Does she usually meet with or invite all new employees to charitable functions?"

"I can't say that she does. Look, I don't want to frighten you. But you might as well know that you'll be under the V-radar. Mom looked you up online. She saw your picture, thinks you're gorgeous, is familiar with your work and is an incurable matchmaker. She'll more than likely want to get all up in your business and has the uncanny knack to be halfway through your personal secrets chest before you realize the lid has been opened. Be cordial, but know that you are under no obligation whatsoever to share anything outside of casual pleasantries. I'll introduce you to the girls, who between the three of them can share a bevy of appropriate diversionary comebacks."

"The girls...your in-laws."

"My in-loves—Lauren, Ryan and Dee."

"Ah, right."

Nick heard the sound of a beep and a whispered expletive on the other end of the line.

"Nick, I've got to go."

"Everything all right?"

"It will be."

The line went dead.

In the world of construction, delays, snags, errors and snafus came with the territory. The angst heard in Sam's voice was not uncommon, especially given the scope and scale of what they were building. Yet it bothered him to hear it, to think that something was dimming the light in those gorgeous brown eyes.

A few minutes later, his cell phone rang. Unknown caller. Again.

"Breedlove." A slight rustling was heard on the otherwise silent line. "Hello? Who is this? Look, whoever you're looking for is not at this number. Do not call it again."

Nick ended the call more than a bit chagrined. The calls were increasing to the point of becoming a nuisance. An unknown number could not be blocked. Much like the errant erotic thoughts that kept springing up about Sam.

He couldn't block them. That bothered him, too.

Nine

Every part of Sam's mind was exhausted. With the unexpected delays and back-ordered materials, her stay on the idyllic island was by no means a vacation. But she'd gotten the job done. Except for the furnishings that had been ordered but not yet delivered, CANN Isle-New York was finished, enough so that Sam felt confident moving on to the Carolinas next week. After speaking with Danni about the woman she'd hired to look after Trey, and watching the nanny's interaction with her son, she also felt very good about hiring Gloria Monroe.

"Come on, little man. I've got him, Gloria, thanks."

Sam reached into the car seat and pulled the sleeping tyke from the car seat, then followed an equally tired live-in nanny into the condo. The driver pulled their luggage from the trunk and deposited it at the entrance.

"Would you like me to take these inside, ma'am?"

"No, that's okay. We can get it from here." She reached inside her purse and pulled out a bill. "Thank you."

"I appreciate it, ma'am. Have a good night."

While Gloria handled the luggage, Sam continued on to Trey's room. She set down her purse and undressed her son. She'd just pushed his last extremity into his favorite Black Panther superhero pajamas when her phone rang.

She fished it out of her bag, placed it on Trey's bed and pushed the speaker button. "Hey, cuz, can I call you right back? I just got home and am putting Trey to bed."

"Okay. Call ASAP."

Sam's brow creased. Danielle didn't sound happy. Sam tucked Trey into bed, proceeded to her room and even though she wanted nothing more than a quick hot shower and her soft, warm bed, she had a brief chat with Gloria, giving her the weekend off, then retreated to the master.

She hit Redial. "I've got a date with a pillow, cousin, so make it quick. What's up?"

"I'm not sure you want to know, but you need to."

The cryptic answer pushed a bit of Sam's exhaustion away. She sat straighter on the bed. "You don't sound good, Danni. What's going on?"

Sam heard a deep sigh on the other end of the line.

"I recently met up with a few girlfriends. One of them had heard talk." A beat and then, "About you."

"Me? I barely even live here. Who can say what about me?"

"Not as much you as Trey."

Sam's blood cooled. When she spoke her tone was low, deadly. "What is being said about my son?"

"The word is out that Oba is not Trey's biological dad, and a few nosy Nancys are speculating on the father."

"Why don't they speculate on minding their business?"

"You working with one of the town's most eligible bachelors makes you their business. Especially Joi, who's obviously been running her big mouth."

"Dammit."

"I know, girl. I almost called you the night I found out but I know how busy this job has got you—figured tonight would be soon enough."

"You know what? I'm not totally surprised. Oba's been calling."

"No way. For how long?"

"Off and on since I've been here. But they really ramped up a few weeks ago when his dad kicked him out of the palace. Said he needed help maintaining his lifestyle."

"And he thought you, a single, working mother, was the one to give it to him?"

"When I told him I didn't have any money, he suggested I ask Nick. There was a barely veiled threat with the request but honestly I thought he was bluffing. Now, with what you're telling me, and especially at the mention of his sister, the recent conversations make even more sense."

"There always was something about that girl. Don't get me wrong, she has a kind side. We've always been cool and used to hang out all the time before the kids came along. It's how she gossiped and talked about others that used to bug me, and the way she treated those she considered subpar. I guess because her messiness was never directed toward me, I ignored it. I shouldn't have. Asking Nick for the money may have even been her idea."

"Probably. She's how he found out we were working together."

"And the only other person who knew that Oba wasn't Trey's father."

"Until Isaac sneaked a piece of Trey's hair, had a DNA test done and ensured their whole family knew the truth."

"I think it was Joi. Like I said, she's got a messy side."

Sam flopped back on her bed. "I've got to tell Nick, now, at the worst possible time."

"While the two of you are working so closely together."

"That's not all." Sam told Danielle about the carnival happening that weekend. "I can invite a guest. Will you go? Please?"

"Absolutely, I'll go. Jaylen and Trey will have a ball. You'll be fine, too. It may feel like the end of the world, Sam. But it's not."

The next morning, Sam slept in and enjoyed a light breakfast with just her and Trey before getting them dressed for their outing.

Once in the car, Trey asked, "Where are we going, Mama?"

"First, to pick up Danni and Jaylen and then to a town called Breedlove."

"What's in Bead Love?"

"It's BREED-love, honey, and it's a surprise."

Less than forty-five minutes later, Sam bypassed the stately wrought iron privacy gates to the Breedlove Estate and continued via the texted instructions to a tree-lined side road about a half a mile down from the family mansion. Signs had been erected welcoming guests to the CANN CARNIVAL, with directions to parking lots and the main entrance. Rounding the corner, Sam couldn't believe her eyes. A fairground rivaling any town, big or small, had been erected on Breedlove land. The boys squealed, their heads pressed to the glass as they chatted excitedly.

"A carnival!"

"With rides and everything!"

Upon reaching the entrance and receiving a map to the grounds and armbands allowing free rides and other niceties for special guests, Sam sent Nick a text.

I'm here, FYI. Wow. Amazing!

The women had their hands full with two wide-eyed boys and put them on the first available ride simply to catch their breath.

The ride finished. Nick texted back. Where are you?

Near entrance. Boys on the first ride they saw.

☺ There will be a raffle in the casino in an hour. Meet me there.

Sam referenced the map as the group made their way around the carefully planned scene. There was a Ferris wheel, merry-go-rounds, carnival games and a petting zoo. There were bumper cars and a video arcade, along with more adventuresome rides for teens. The adults hadn't been left out, either. Towering zip lines and soaring rock-climbing walls had been erected aside more traditional rides like the

Kamikaze and Tilt-A-Whirl. A large tent housed the mini-CANN casino described on the back of the map, complete with slot machines and poker, blackjack and roulette tables. Music and other sounds filled the air. Dotted throughout were food trucks and sweets stands. In short, Nick's mom had organized a child's best dream. The meticulously manicured lawns had been carefully turned into a Memorial Day wonderland for both the young and the young at heart.

An hour later and Sam still wasn't ready to face Nick. She was sure that meant meeting his mom and possibly other members of his family.

"Why don't I take the boys to the petting zoo?" Danielle offered.

Sam could have kissed her. "That's a perfect idea. Keep your phone handy. I'll text you when I'm done."

She watched her cousin and the boys walk away, then crossed over to and stepped inside the casino. After pausing for her eyes to adjust to the dimmed lighting, she looked around and spotted Nick almost immediately. He looked up to catch her staring, smiled and waved her over. Sam gave herself a pep talk, remembering Danielle's parting words before she left with the boys. *They don't know anything until you tell them. Remember that.*

"Hey, Nick."

"There she is. The miracle worker!" Nick pulled Sam into an enthusiastic hug. "Congrats on a bang-up job out there. Our New York guests are in for a treat."

Sam was embarrassed at the show of affection but appreciative of the praise. She was also über-aware of other eyes on her. "One down, twenty-plus to go. Let's not pop the cork yet."

"Just a matter of time," Nick responded, full of confidence. "I picked the one person in the world who could get the job done."

At this, an older woman standing near him, who even

in casual slacks and an oversize top oozed refinement and class, smiled and held out her hand.

"You must be Samantha. I'm Victoria, Nick's mom."

"It's a pleasure to meet you, Victoria. Please, call me Sam. Thank you so much for the special invitation to attend this spectacular event. My son is already over the moon. He won't want to leave."

Victoria looked to both sides of Sam. "Where is your son?"

"With his cousin visiting the petting zoo."

"Always a child favorite. I'm glad he's having a good time."

A young woman walked up. "Excuse me, Victoria, but it's time for the raffle."

"Of course. We'll talk more later, Sam, all right?"

No, it was not all right. "Sure."

During the raffle, Sam met Noah, Adam and Christian. Their wives and several others assisted Victoria on stage. The guys were fun and easygoing. Sam was happy to know she'd overreacted. What could go wrong at a carnival, where folk walked around with big smiles on their faces? Even after the raffle, when Nick insisted on walking with her to meet back up with Danielle, Sam only felt the slightest of flutters. Nick didn't yet know what she hadn't told him. There's no way he'd have an inkling that Trey was his. Nick had a light complexion. Trey had inherited his mom's richly melanated skin. Trey was tall for his age but he was still only four, bearing hardly a hint of resemblance to the six-feet-plus of deliciousness his father carried around.

"Danni, you remember Nick?" she said, once she and Danielle reunited.

Danielle smiled. "Of course. Nice to see you again."

"Likewise." Nick shook her hand.

"Trey, Jaylen, this is Nick. I work with him building houses."

Nick knelt to their level and held out his hand. "Hello, Trey. Hello, Jaylen. Are you boys having a good time?"

"Yes!" They sang in duet.

"Uncle Nick!" A high-pitched yell rose over the din of noises before a little girl wearing pink overalls and a straw hat burst through the crowd.

As soon as she reached him, he scooped her up. "Hey, Angel!"

"My name's not Angel, it's Christina!"

"But you look like an angel."

Curls bounced as the four-year old shook her head from side to side. "I don't look like an angel. I don't have wings!"

Christian strolled up to them. "Another debate within seconds? You two never see the world the same."

"Which is what makes life so exciting," Nick said, easing Christina to the ground. "The world opens up wider when viewed through the eyes of a child."

Christian turned to Sam. "Do you believe that?"

"Sometimes."

Nick put an arm around Sam. "Good answer. Where's Lar?"

Nick looked around for Christina's little brother, Larenz, and saw Christian's wife Lauren pushing a stroller. Sam quietly watched the family's interactions. The adults, thoroughly enjoying each other, the kids clearly loved. This was the life her secret kept from Trey. It wasn't fair and considering the rumblings, it wasn't wise, either.

"You know what, Nick. I need to speak with you about something."

"Okay."

"Uncle Nick!" Christina interrupted. "Can you take me to ride the horses?"

"We can ride them?" Trey asked wide-eyed.

Danielle looked toward the large white tent where she'd taken the boys. "I didn't see horses at the petting zoo."

"They're not a part of the carnival. They're on Adam's ranch."

"Horses," Trey cried. "I want to ride horses!"

Sam took the arm of a child on his way out of control. "Trey! Come on, honey. The horses aren't here. Let's go ride the merry-go-round or Ferris wheel."

"Those horses are fake," he announced, spitting out the last word as if it were vile, before doing something he rarely did. Began to throw a fit. "Horses! I want to ride the horses!" Screaming and crying, with Sam looking at him as she would a stranger.

Whose child is this?

"Hey, hey, hey." Nick knelt until they were face-to-face. "Trey, look at me. Only big boys can ride the horses. With you crying like that, and screaming and stomping, you'll scare them away. Trey, do you hear me?"

Somewhere in his wall of hollers Nick's words sank through. The crying stopped as quickly as it started.

"Yes," he answered, throwing in a sniffle for good measure.

Sam watched, amazed and more than a little touched. Their first father-son interaction and neither of them knew it.

"Mom, can I go ride the horses? I'm not crying now."

Sam looked at Nick, who only now realized his error.

"You said it."

"I did, didn't I." He lifted Trey into the crook of his arm. "Tell you what. The horse I have in mind for you to ride doesn't like crowds. But if you act like the little man that I believe you can be for the rest of the day, I'll ask Mommy to bring you back in the morning, and we'll go riding then. But you have to be good. Your mom will tell me if you're not. Deal?"

Trey nodded in reluctant agreement.

"Is that okay with you?" Nick asked Sam.

"Well, since you've just made a huge promise to a four-year-old," she said under her voice before announcing, "I guess...yes."

"Sorry." Nick talked softly as well so that only Sam could hear. "I guess I shouldn't have done that. In my effort to come off as the savior, I've committed you to another day at the fair, or back here to ride horses at least."

"Worse could happen."

"Indeed."

The group split up soon after the convo ended. Sam and Danielle ended up staying much longer than they'd planned and enjoyed the goings-on possibly more than adults should. For Sam, it was the first time since accepting the contract that she allowed herself to unwind, to forget about materials and drawings and deadlines and simply have a good time. By the time moms and sons left the fairgrounds, both Sam and Danielle were glad they'd brought strollers. The kids were knocked out.

"How did it feel to see—" Danielle tilted her head toward the back seat "—with his father."

"It's hard to describe." Sam caught a mental image of Nick picking up Trey. "I didn't know there was that much love in my heart."

"For the son...or the daddy?"

"I can't help but love Nick. He's the father of my child. But that and my temporary boss is all that he is."

Danielle let it go and changed the subject. Sam was glad that she did. The truth of the matter was that she wanted Trey to get to know Nick better and looked forward to tomorrow. Hopefully the more Nick felt an affinity with Trey, the easier it would be to accept that he was his son, too.

That night she lay in bed thinking. *It's coming together. I may be able to rebuild my life after all.* The good feeling lasted a full fifteen minutes, until her phone buzzed and she read the text that had just come in from overseas. Without checking the name, she knew who it was.

No more asking. No more waiting. Wire 500K to my bank account before the end of the month. Or I tell Nick everything.

Ten

Nick took a seat at the long patio table on his parents' back porch, then waved away his twin, who'd prepared to sit beside him.

Noah's brow raised. "Are we expecting someone?"

"I invited Sam over. Yesterday Christina mentioned riding horses in front of her son and suddenly the Merry-Go-Round became a poor second choice."

Noah walked around to sit across from Nick. "So Sam's bringing him over to go riding?"

"Yep. You're welcome to join us."

"Thanks, bro, but I'm going to stay close to sweet lady. She's had a couple premature contractions and chose to stay home."

"Makes sense. Then why are you here?"

"To pick up the cinnamon rolls she craves. And now that I know Sam is joining us…to stick around a little while for the show."

Nick knew Noah was talking about the creative ways their mother tended to question any female she deemed clan-suitable. While his mother had only spoken casually with Sam yesterday, that she'd done online research was enough for him to know his designer was on her radar.

Brunch was in full swing when one of the housekeepers brought Sam, Trey and another woman around to the back. Nick took in her unsure expression and met her at the patio's edge to make her welcome.

"There they are! Hey guys." He noticed a dip in conversation as the duo approached.

Nick knelt down. "How are you, little man?"

"Fine."

"Ready to ride horses?"

"Yes!"

He turned to Sam. "Hello."

"Hi." She looked at the woman beside her. "I hope you don't mind that I brought my nanny, Gloria. She was so excited by what I shared yesterday that I felt bad at not inviting her."

"No worries. She can join Chris's au pair Kirtu in the other room with Christina and Lars."

He looked beyond her. "No Danni today?"

"Like me, she's never ridden a horse. Unlike me, she'd like to keep it that way." After brief instructions to Trey on how to behave, he and Gloria headed toward the kids' room.

"You've never taken a ride before?" Nick asked, leading them toward the buffet line. He noticed Sam's eyes flicker just enough to confirm she'd caught the double entendre. "No, I've never before ridden a horse, though I once caravanned on a camel."

"I thought you'd never gone on a safari?"

"I haven't. That ride occurred during a tour of the Egyptian pyramids."

"There you go! You'll be fine."

After walking through the buffet line and loading up their plates, they took their seats at the table.

"Everybody, you remember Sam from yesterday? Those who weren't there, this is Sam Price, the extraordinary interior designer who's ensuring our island guests are properly blown away by their surroundings."

A variety of greetings rang out from the dozen or so gathered around the table. Small talk ensued, mostly about the success of the CANN Carnival, raising millions of dollars for children needing assistance in Nevada and beyond.

During a lull in the conversation, Victoria spoke. "Samantha, I understand you recently moved back from being an expat in Africa. Do you miss that beautiful continent or were you happy to return home?"

"You're right, Victoria, there are areas of Africa that are absolutely stunning, some of the most beautiful scenery I've seen. But I'm very glad to be back in the States."

"Well, I can tell you that Nick for one is glad you're back as well. He sings your praises as a designer."

Sam smiled at Nick. "Thank you." Then to Victoria, "CANN is an excellent company. I am thankful to have gotten such a wonderful opportunity so soon after arriving."

"You two seem to get along very well. Did you know each other prior to coming on board for the island project?"

"Aren't these crepes delicious?" Noah asked, a question so unlike what he'd normally ask that everyone knew its purpose and laughed at the blatant subject change to bail out his twin.

Nick stuffed a bite in his mouth and talked while chewing. "Ah, bro, they're delish!"

"For sure," Adam added. "With these sweet potato crepes Gabe has outdone himself!"

The conversation was successfully diverted long enough for Nick and Sam to finish their dishes and make a graceful exit. They stopped next door where the kids were playing board games. With Gloria and a very excited Trey in tow, they headed toward Adam's ranch and the stable of horses he kept there.

Nick introduced Sam to the ranch manager, Rusty, who walked them over to where Adam's growing collection of prized horses was housed. He picked an apple from a barrel near the barn's entrance and gave it to Nick.

"For when the little one meets Queen."

"Ah, good choice," Nick said, about the gentle mare. "Little man and I will be riding together." Rusty nodded. "We'll want someone equally gentle for Sam here. It's her first time riding."

"No worries, pretty lady," Rusty said. "We'll get you fixed right up." He gave them apples, too.

Sam turned to Gloria. "Am I the only one on a maiden voyage, or have you not ridden before either?"

"It's been a long time ago, back in Oklahoma on my grandpa's farm."

"It's like riding a bike," Rusty assured her. "Sit the saddle properly and it's all downhill from there."

When they reached Queen, Nick handed Trey the apple. "One of these always helps to make a proper introduction."

Trey took the apple and was properly awed as Nick guided his hand for the horse to softly remove it, then picked him up to pet Queen's mane.

Nick winked at Sam. "He's a natural, same as Noah and I were when we were his age."

The four got saddled up—Nick and Trey on Poker, Gloria on an Appaloosa named Lucy, and Sam on Queen. Gloria's was an easy mount, but Sam needed help. Nick was happy to oblige. Any excuse to caress her glorious backside would do. Queen began to prance. Sam tensed up right away.

"Just relax," Nick said, his tone low and soothing. "Animals can smell fear. Hold the reins with confidence. She needs to know you're in control."

"That's still up for debate."

Nick helped Sam until she felt more comfortable, walking them around in a circle near the gate.

"You ready?"

Sam nodded. "I think so."

With that, they took off across the glorious countryside at a comfortable pace. Even after spending his entire life on the land, Nick was still moved by its beauty. After about ten minutes, when he felt Sam had a handle on Queen, Nick gave his horse his head and sped up a bit. Trey squealed with delight. Nick focused on Trey, even as he himself enjoyed the chance to get out in nature and feel the wind on his face. All the brothers had grown up in the saddle, but he and Christian rode far less often than Noah and Adam. Today reminded Nick he needed to change that.

"Let's go fast again, Nick!"

"Okay, buddy." Nick secured Trey in his grip, then lightly touched the horse's flank.

"Nick!"

"Don't worry, Sam! I've got him."

"It's Sam, Nick!"

Nick turned toward the sound of Gloria's voice in time to observe Queen's trot increasing to a gallop at a quick pace. Sam must have unknowingly directed the horse to run. Without thought, he wheeled Poker around and headed toward Sam.

"Relax, Sam! Don't pull so hard on the reins!"

Nick quickly eased alongside Sam and grabbed the horse's reins. Within seconds, the horse slowed down. Nick made a few sounds and talked to Queen until the horse came to a stop.

"You all right?" He'd been so busy getting the horse under control that only now did he see the tears in Sam's eyes, or that an ashy sheen to her deep chocolate skin alluded to how frightened she was, as did the shaky hand that had grabbed him once he was close with nails now almost piercing his cotton shirt.

Nick didn't need to hear her answer. She was not okay.

By the time the horse stopped, Gloria had rounded back to where they all were. "Can you ride with Trey?" he asked her.

She nodded. "I think so."

"Good. Because Sam's going to ride with me." Nick glanced at his watch. "The carnival opens in an hour. We'd planned to go to the house to freshen up anyway. We'll just do that now."

Nick helped Sam into the saddle, then mounted behind her. Immediately, he knew he was in trouble. Sam's body, warm, curvaceous and shaking, folded into his embrace. For the woman he'd always seen as strong and confident, the vulnerability was foreign. The need to protect her sprang up with force in his chest. He felt capable and needed, feelings that opened up a space for Sam in his heart. Instinctively, a protective arm went around her. He tilted his hips back in an effort to hide an oncoming arousal, but Sam followed his body with her own, as if his touch alone reassured her. It made him powerful; his testosterone surged. He grew heady from the scent of her cologne, the feel of her soft locs brushing against his neck and chest and her body folded into his own. By the time they reached his home, he was on fire with desire, felt almost drunk with need. He helped her down, then took the horse around back and dismounted in private, until his own privates were under control.

She was standing by the window when he entered, seemingly still as shaken in his living room as she'd been outside.

Gloria stood near her, a concerned look on her face. Trey hid behind Gloria's legs. "Is there anything I can do for you?"

"I'll be okay."

Nick watched Sam attempt a reassuring smile for her observant son. He guessed she was trying to assure herself as well.

Nick's doorbell rang. He frowned slightly at the unexpected intrusion. "Who could that be?" he murmured.

"It's probably Kirtu," Gloria offered. "We talked about meeting up so that the children could continue playing together. I'll tell her we'll meet later on."

Sam shook her head. "No, please, you guys go on to the carnival and text your location. I'll be along shortly."

Nick opened the door. Indeed it was Christina's nanny. She spoke to everyone.

"Where's Christina?" Gloria asked.

"With Lauren. They're spending a bit of time together before she goes off with Christian. We're supposed to meet them at the food court."

Gloria turned to Sam once again. "Are you sure?"

"Absolutely, Gloria." Sam looked at Trey. "Are you ready for more rides and games, Trey?"

Trey reached for Gloria's hand and vigorously nodded.

"Good. I'll meet you there in a little bit. If you leave that area, Gloria, just text me where you are. All right?"

"Sure."

As soon as Trey was gone, Sam collapsed against the wall. "Crap! That was scary!"

Nick was immediately by her side. "I'm sorry, babe. I've ridden Queen many times and seen others ride her. You must have unknowingly given her the signal to run. Doing so on her own would be very uncharacteristic.

"How about some hot chamomile tea. Or something stronger if you'd like."

Sam managed a smile. "Tea is fine. Thanks again, Nick," she whispered, flinging her arms around his neck, pressing her body against him. "I don't know what I would have done without your help earlier. I'm so glad you were there."

Nick was glad he was there, too, and that Sam was in his arms. It felt good, too good. He gently gripped her arms and meant to set her away from him. But just then she turned her face so that their lips were parallel, then pressed those soft cushions of sexy goodness against his eager lips. Whatever control he had went out the window. He placed his hands beneath her butt and lifted her up against the wall, his lips never leaving hers as he secured himself between her legs.

"Nick."

Sam's voice was light, shaky, caught up in ecstasy. He watched, mesmerized, as she reached for the hem of her top and pulled it over her head. Then to the back of her bra, snapping the clasp from the back. Everything she did was everything he'd imagined. The switch had happened so quickly he felt it almost surreal, as though he were an observer instead of a participant, needing to be prodded to play along.

"Nick, please…"

Her soft entreaty was all the encouragement he needed. He pulled a soft nipple into his mouth, unzipping his jeans while he feasted. They kissed every part of exposed flesh available, and quickly realized that was not enough. They needed more, much more. They needed all of each other.

Sam slid from the wall and reached for her pants. They quickly joined Nick's in a pile on the floor. He lifted her once again and placed her on the living room's oversize ottoman. The bedroom was too far away, would take too long to consummate a reunion more than four years in the making. Dropping down in front of her, Nick gently spread her legs apart. He slid a finger along the folds of her thong and after pushing it aside, buried his head in her heat. She squealed and squirmed but he gave no quarter. He lapped and lavished her pearl, feasted on her nectar. Her soft thighs rested on his shoulders, gripping him hard as she reached and then went over the edge. Her whimpers sent his dick rock hard. He retrieved a condom from his pants pocket, positioned his shaft where his tongue had been and deepened the dance.

"Nick, Nick," she purred, in beat with this rhythm. He thrust and plunged himself into her core, grabbed the juicy cheeks that drove him wild and ground deeply some more. Their bodies came together like two long-lost pals who'd known each other forever, who'd always loved this way. They ended up in the bedroom, where Sam performed oral feats that left Nick shaken to the bone, that made him forget about every other woman who in the throes of passion had ever called his name. When he felt Sam ready to burst again, he increased his thrusts to join her going over the edge. There was one woman on his mind, one name on his lips. He whispered it as he shuddered.

"Sam."

Eleven

Sam's orgasm had barely ended before regret set in. Not that she and Nick had sex. In retrospect, the act seemed a foregone conclusion from the time she'd stepped in his office on that first interview. An ending they both saw coming but tried to ignore. No, Sam's regret was about what had been unleashed inside her. Rekindled. Reawakened. It was the feeling she'd had the first time she saw Nick. A palpable hunger. An undeniable connection. But leading to what? Even now, as Nick stood behind her, held her, kissed her neck and nibbled her ear as the shower water washed over them, Sam felt a longing in her heart for something she feared Nick could not fulfill, or wasn't interested in fulfilling.

"We need to hurry," she whispered, stepped away from him and reaching for a loofah on one of the shelves. She quickly unwrapped it, performed her ablutions and left the bathroom. By the time Nick came out she was dressed and on her phone, texting Gloria as to her and Trey's whereabouts. She went to the kitchen and reheated the tea that had earlier been poured and forgotten, added cream and sugar, then took small sips to calm her nerves. This helped her put the tiger of desire back in its cage, regain control of her body and rid her mind of happily ever after fantasies that only came true in romance novels.

He walked straight toward her. "That was amazing, babe."

She dodged his intended embrace and put distance between them. "We need to talk about what just happened."

A smile slid onto Nick's face, as slow as molasses and Sam knew, equally sweet. "I hope you're not expecting that talk to include an apology, because I am not at all sorry about being with you. In fact, I want to do it again. Soon. And often."

Sam worked to stay focused on what needed to be said and not how good Nick looked in the white tee, low-slung black jeans and sandals that now covered the body that had so pleasured her just moments ago. Hard to do. Every movement reminded her of something he'd done. How the fingers fastening his belt buckle had played her body like an instrument, had trailed from the back of her neck to her thighs and left goose bumps in their wake. How his soft, thick lips had touched, branded, almost every inch of her body, and how his tongue had—for those few intimate seconds, or hours, who's counting—wiped away every worry about Oba, Trey's parentage, the projects and everything else. She turned away as he looked up, convinced that the desire dredged up by those too-recent memories were written all over her face.

She took a breath and began again, her back toward him as she walked to an abstract painting hung on the wall. "No regrets, it's not about that. Or the attraction," she continued, boldly turning to face not only her fears, but him as well. "Which especially after what just happened, I won't try to deny. This is about you being my boss. And me having a job to do. A physical relationship might get in the way of that."

He smiled in obvious agreement.

The grip on her mug of tea tightened. "It would definitely get in the way."

"You're probably right." His eyes never left hers while raising a bottle of water to his lips.

Both sipped in silence.

"That's it?" Sam finally asked.

Nick shrugged. "What else can there be? I don't agree with your position but your message is clear."

"I don't want this to create an awkward vibe between us."

"We're both adults. I don't foresee a problem if you don't."

Although I don't think tamping down what's flowing between us will be as easy as you think. I mean, damn. What happens when we're together, the way our bodies fit like perfect puzzle pieces, the way you mold around me like a custom-made glove…"

Damn if hearing that sexy voice and seeing that lethal tongue didn't make her want to do it again. "Nick, stop. I'm serious."

"So am I. Look, beautiful, may I suggest something?" *Not in the voice that makes my panties wet.* "What?"

"Why don't we relax around what's happening, not make any rules or resist what is abundantly clear. I'm not dating anyone right now, are you?"

"No, but…"

"No buts. I get that you want to focus on business. I respect that and will be a total gentleman. I won't do anything you don't want to do. I'm just saying that if the situation arises, as it did just now, let's deal with it then, in the moment, and see what happens."

"Okay." Sam's phone buzzed. She checked it. "That's Gloria. She and Kirtu are with the kids in the Fun Zone."

"Do you want to get your face painted, too?" Nick teased.

"No, but I might accept one of the clown's animal balloons…since I feel like an ass," she finished, mumbling under her breath.

"What was that?"

"Nothing."

Sam was determined to try Nick's approach. She tried to act casual, as if it were just another day. But as they neared the crowded fairgrounds, she felt that the fact she'd just been screwed to within an inch of her life and loved every second of it was readily apparent. If so, however, Gloria didn't let on. She relaxed even more and instead of feeling paranoid with Nick beside her allowed herself to enjoy his company. He really was amazing with children. Clearly his niece adored him.

"Hi, Uncle Nick!"

"Come here, Angel." He easily lifted Christina into his arms.

Trey, feeling left out, whined to also be held in Nick's arms. "Pick me up! Pick me up, too!"

Sam prepared to admonish him, but Nick complied. He reached down, easily balancing a child in each arm. They laughed at the kids' obvious attempts to garner the most attention from a man both children clearly liked. So caught up was she in the joy of the moment that danger sidled up beside her undetected.

"Nick, or Noah?"

Sam turned to see a beautiful woman with flawless skin and long black hair peering carefully between the kids and Nick. The smile Nick put on Sam's face with his lovemaking and charming personality slid off faster than she'd slid off Queen earlier. The last person on earth that she wanted to see appeared like an apparition before her.

Joi.

Nick looked at her. "I'm sorry. Do I know you?"

"Not really." Joi smiled at him while looking every inch of amazing, and seductive. "We've met socially a couple times. A few years ago, we were at the same costume party, in fact."

She slid a quick glance at Sam. Sam stopped breathing.

"My name's Joi." Nodding toward the children Nick was placing back on the ground, she said with hand outstretched, "Which one is yours?"

Nick uncoiled back to his full height. "Nick."

Joi shook Nick's hand, then looked at Trey standing close by Nick's side and tried to shake his, too. Trey pulled it back. Sam stopped herself from stepping between them.

"Hello, little one! Is this your son, Nick?"

"No. Trey belongs to this beautiful lady, Sam Price."

Joi turned, eyes wide in feigned surprise. "Sam!"

Sam had the distinct feeling her presence was not a surprise to her former sister-in-law. She worked to keep a WTF look off her face.

"Oh my goodness, I was so focused on Nick and those cute little kids I didn't see you!"

"A woman you've known for years?" *And a child who's your nephew?* Sam so wanted to add that line, but now wasn't the time. "I find that hard to believe but…okay."

Joi leaned into Sam for a hug. It was like embracing a board. "Don't play me," Joi quietly hissed. "Or you'll get played."

Not a hint of meanness showed when she stepped back, all smiles and bright, wide eyes. Joi was a beautiful girl, Sam decided, whose performance could have easily won an Oscar.

What an actress. It was incredible that the same woman who appeared as an angel years ago could behave so much like the devil right now. Her threat answered one question. Joi may not have suggested that Oba blackmail her for money, but Sam was convinced that Joi was somehow involved. Their knowing what Nick didn't was a very real threat to Sam getting back on her feet. But she'd be damned if she let Joi think they held an advantage. When pressed, Sam could be an actor, too.

"I heard the news about your getting a job with CANN International."

"I heard you've been spreading quite a bit of news about me and you need to stop." Said as quietly as Joi's warning, and as sweetly as though honey had been poured over the words. But the glint in Sam's eyes conveyed "don't start none, won't be none."

A slight narrowing of Joi's eyes was the only hint that Sam's words had hit a mark.

"You two obviously know each other," Nick said, as tension crackled.

"We're family," Joi replied, with a fake laugh that made

Sam's skin crawl. Her mind whirled with possible motives for Joi being here. None of them were good.

Sam turned to Nick. "Not anymore. Joi is my ex-husband's sister. She's how he and I met."

"Ah, I see." Nick looked at Joi with renewed interest and an unreadable expression. Sam imagined that information caused him to look at this overly friendly interruption in a new light. "Yet you didn't recognize Trey?"

Good question, Sam thought. Would-be actress Joi didn't miss a beat.

"It's been a couple years since I've seen him. He was just a baby when a myriad of business opportunities brought me back to live full-time in the States. He's gotten so big!"

She looked pointedly at Sam. "Wonder where he gets his height? My brother is average height, as are most men on that side of the family."

"My brother's tall," Sam said before reaching for Trey's hand. "So is my dad. It's understandable you'd be confused since you never met my side of the family, and since the few interactions we had at the palace were too brief and infrequent to develop a bond."

"Since we're both back in America, maybe we can change that. You and Oba are divorced. But I'm still Trey's aunt, right?"

In light of no good answer, Sam remained mum.

Sam didn't want to leave Joi alone with Nick, but she couldn't stay and watch the Oscar-worthy performance one moment longer. There would come a moment when Sam could tell Joi just what she thought of this messy charade. But not today.

"We've got a date with a puppet or two," Sam finally said, forcing a casualness into her voice that she didn't feel.

"Hang on," Nick said. "I'll bring Christina."

"Enjoy the fair," Nick said, already turning to walk away from Joi.

"Goodbye, Joi!" Sam kept her voice light, tried to hide

how much she'd been affected by the exchange. She was only partly successful. The smile in Sam's voice did not reach her eyes.

When they neared the tent where the puppet theater was housed, Sam sent Trey in with Gloria. Nick followed suit with Christina and her au pair. Once alone, Nick's concern was immediate.

"You okay?"

"Why wouldn't I be?" Sam snapped back. It was enough that Joi had come and effectively ruined what in spite of her roiling, disjointed emotions and unplanned romp in the sack with her boss had been a pretty awesome day. Had Nick picked up on it?

"That was a pretty tense situation back there."

Yes, he had.

Sam shrugged. "Joi's known for starting trouble. I don't care much for folk like that."

"Yet she's the one who introduced you to your ex."

"I rest my case."

Nick chuckled. "I don't remember ever meeting her. Then again, I meet a lot of people so it's entirely possible that she and I traveled in the same circles. As I always say, this town is small."

"Speaking of small, I'm going in." She nodded toward the theater tent. "Are you coming?"

"No. I think I've met my kid-stuff quota for today. I was going to suggest we become kids ourselves and enjoy some of the adult rides."

"Thanks, Nick, but I'm going to have to pass. I head to South Carolina first thing tomorrow and have quite a bit to get done. After this show, I'm going to take Trey home."

"Come here." Before Sam could react, she'd been pulled into Nick's arms. "Today was amazing," he whispered, his voice wet and hot against her ear. "Thank you."

"Sure. See you later." Sam hurriedly ducked inside the tent, her body thrumming from his embrace, her mind whirling from seeing Joi and reliving conversations with Oba.

That night, she sent him a text.

I saw your sister today, which you probably know. I didn't appreciate your threats about Trey. I don't appreciate your sister's, either. Back off, Oba. Let me rebuild my life.

His response? A smiley face.

Seriously?

Sam didn't bother trying to interpret what that meant. She forced her focus from what had happened at the fair-grounds to the three homes on the Carolina islands and what she needed to accomplish next week. Hopefully her text was enough to throw off Oba or anyone else from thinking Nick was Trey's dad. Either way, she needed to tell Nick the truth. Time was running out.

Twelve

Nick had planned to fly over to the Carolinas the day after Sam arrived. But other CANN business demanded his focus the first part of the week. It wasn't until Thursday afternoon that he boarded Christian's private jet and headed to the other side of the country. He told himself it was to see in person the 3-D images and photos Sam had sent over. The truth was, he wanted to see her. Just moments from landing in Charleston, he texted Sam of his whereabouts and invited her to dinner.

Dinner?

Yes. Landing in Charleston.

Charleston, SC?

Nick smiled. A slightly confused Sam was adorable. Yes, beautiful. I have impossible-to-get reservations at a quaint spot with only ten tables. Highly recommended.

A minute passed. Then five. Ten.

Nick began to get nervous. That never happened.

Can't. She finally texted back. Contractors on the island. Problems. Call after landing.

We'll talk tomorrow. I'll be there at 8.

Nick was disappointed but of course he understood. He also realized he'd been highly presumptuous to think that someone with the type of deadlines Sam had could drop everything to skedaddle over to the mainland for a ridiculously expensive candlelight meal personally prepared by an award-winning chef. As for problems with construction, they were as common as dust. He'd worry about those tomorrow.

Knowing from Sam's photos that furniture had yet to be delivered, Nick had Anita arrange a room at a hotel, and set up one of the chefs who'd responded to their targeted ad for personal service on the islands to be at the house the next morning. He planned for Sam's day to start with a delicious, satisfying breakfast. No matter how busy the day was, she had to eat. Once those plans had been made, he forwarded them to Sam so she wouldn't wake up to a stranger knocking on her door.

"What are you doing here?" was her greeting the next day.

Not quite the warm welcome he expected but again, he understood.

"Good morning."

"That's debatable."

Sam looked haggard, as though she'd hardly slept. "Come here."

She gave him the briefest of hugs. "I know this is your baby, Nick, but there's a ton happening today. I can't believe that you'd arrive unannounced."

"It's good I did from the looks of things. Did you get any sleep last night?"

"Very little and thanks, but I've got this. I know how to call in reinforcements if needed."

"I wouldn't have hired you had I not thought you capable. I wanted to see you, okay? As Nick, not your boss."

Those words seemed to break through the wall of frustration around her. When he again invited her into his arms, she stepped in and squeezed back when he wrapped his arms around her. He kissed her cheek, eyes, forehead.

"Did the chef arrive?"

"In the kitchen."

"Hungry?"

"I could eat."

Nick looked around at the empty rooms.

"There's a railing outside on the patio where we could sit," she said.

Someone behind them cleared their throat.

"Excuse me, good morning, sir."

Nick turned to the chef in a signature white coat, his long locs neatly wrapped into a bun at the nape of his neck.

"Hi, I'm Nick."

"Gregory, sir. Nice to meet you. I've set up a bit of a beverage station in the other room. My instructions were to forgo taking personal orders and fix something amazing."

"That sounds like Anita," Nick said, smiling. "Thanks, Gregory. We'll help ourselves to the drinks and be waiting outside."

"I've taken the liberty of preparing a spot out back, sir. There was a picnic table and benches set up. I hope you don't mind."

"Not at all." Nick looked at Sam.

"It's where the construction crew eats. Let's get our drinks and head out there."

They walked into the other room where Gregory had set up a table with coffees, teas and juices.

Sam filled a tall mug with coffee. Nick poured tea. Both grabbed glasses of orange juice, then walked outside to a beautiful, slightly humid day in the Palmetto State. The dusty construction area had been transformed into an idyllic scene. The area around the table had been swept of debris. White linen covered the table where a vase of wildflowers sat in the center of the table.

"Hope you're hungry."

"A private chef, Nick. I appreciate the gesture but seriously... I would have been fine with a breakfast sandwich."

"Each vacation home comes with a staff, including a

chef. The guy fixing breakfast is on an audition of sorts for one of three positions on this island that will need to be filled."

"These magnificent homes and a private chef, too. I'm almost afraid to know the nightly rate."

"The smaller homes go for just under 10K, nightly. The price and amenities go up from there."

"Crazy that some people can spend in one night what could pay somebody else's rent for a year."

"Rich people are going to spend money, babe. Might as well be with us."

Sam held up her orange juice. "Touché."

While waiting for Gregory, they engaged in small talk about the weather, Nick's family and the kids.

"Speaking of, where is the young equestrian?"

"Back in Vegas with Gloria so that he can attend his cousin's birthday party."

"Sounds like she's working out for you."

"She's a godsend, and very good with Trey."

Once the food had been brought to the table, Nick returned to business. "I'm very pleased with the progress I see so far. Tell me about the problems you're having."

Over a superb breakfast that included crispy spiced chicken over fluffy pecan waffles, truffle-infused egg whites and mouthwatering crab cakes, Sam shared the challenge with suspending the bridge as her drawings had rendered, over a sizable koi pond. Later, they met with the contractor and with Nick's insightful suggestions, came up with a workable alternative. Sam loosened up. Nick spent the night. With Sam obviously having forgotten about them not repeating their sex romp, they christened the shower with their lovemaking, then cuddled in a twin-size futon, the home's lone piece of temporary furniture until the main shipment arrived next week. He returned to Breedlove spent and satiated, able to once again focus on work.

The day after returning back home and having put in almost ten hours at the office, he called his brother to hopefully shoot some hoops.

"Twin, let's ball," he said, once Noah answered.

"You're back?"

"Yeah, where were you today?"

"Working from home."

"How's Dee?"

"Better. The premature contractions stopped and there's been no bleeding."

"Whoa, TMI, dude!"

"Hey, it's all part of bringing another being into the world."

"I'm happy to leave that up to my brothers and be the best Uncle Nick in the world." Noah didn't respond. "That was a joke."

"When are you coming over?"

The seriousness in Noah's voice could not be missed. Had he caught attitude because of Nick's joking comment? Nick chalked it up to Noah being concerned about his wife and the health of his child. Damaris "Dee" Glen Breedlove helped save his brother's life once. Nick knew Noah would do all he could to return the favor.

Nick stopped by his place, changed clothes, then continued down the road, around the bend and toward the mountains to his brother's new home. Noah and Dee had designed it together, a combination of the styles Dee grew up seeing in Utah and the rustic yet modern touches Noah enjoyed. There were cows for fresh milk and chickens that provided Dee's preferred organic eggs, a pet pig named Rosy, two dogs, and a cat. Dee had changed his twin brother, no doubt about that. It made him wonder what kind of changes someone special would bring into his life. An image of Sam floated into his mind. Remembering there was no time in his life for that kind of special, he pushed it away.

He knocked on the door. Dee answered. "He's out back," she said, her hands dusty with flour.

"What are you making?"

"Pies, and yes, I have one for you."

Nick gave her a thumbs-up, then jogged around to where Noah was putting up free throws on the combination basketball and tennis court located several yards beyond Dee's garden. Anyone else would see a guy loose and relaxed, casually playing a sport. But Nick knew his twin almost better than himself. Something was going on.

"What's up, bro?"

"You got it." They exchanged a fist bump. "How was the Carolinas?"

"Hot. Humid."

Noah jogged for a layup. Nick jumped up to block it. Noah faked left, rolled around and easily laid it against the board.

"How's Sam?"

Nick couldn't help smiling. "She's good."

Noah stopped bouncing the ball. "What does that mean?"

"There are a few challenges but so far we think this build can stay on schedule."

"I meant the smile."

"Oh. That."

"Are you sleeping with her?"

"Wow, kind of blunt, don't you think?"

"Well, are you? I have my reasons for asking."

"Which are?"

Noah began bouncing the ball again but made no move toward the hoop. "Really, Nick, I don't even want to respond. It's all gossip, and you know how much I hate being a part of something like that."

Nick stole the ball and rested it on his hip. "What's the rumor?"

"It's about Sam."

Nick's heartbeat increased. Was she getting back with her ex? Was there another man?

"What about Sam?"

"And Trey," Noah said.

"Spit it out, twin."

Noah sighed. "I guess that's best. There's talk going around that the dude in Nigeria, the African prince, isn't Trey's biological father."

Nick began breathing again. Was that all? Since the two were divorced that didn't seem so important; may have even been why they broke up.

"Doesn't sound like any of my business," Nick said, pausing to shoot three from the top of the key.

He headed over to retrieve the ball. Noah intercepted him and grabbed it instead.

"Word is the father lives here, in Vegas."

Nick shrugged. "I still don't see what that has to do with us. I hate gossip as much as you do. Someone obviously has too much time on their hands. Wait a minute. Where'd you hear this?"

"Lauren. She has a client who's opening a high-end boutique and travels in certain societal circles, the bougie crowd and whatnot. Said Sam's son didn't belong to the prince."

"Was the person who put this bug in her ear named Joi by any chance?"

Noah's brow creased. "Who's Joi?"

"Oba's sister. Sam's ex-sister-in-law. I met her last weekend at the carnival. Sam was with me and it was clear that there was no lost love between them."

Nick swiped the ball from Noah. "I wouldn't put too much stock into that kind of gossip, man. Come on. Twenty-one. Let's go."

"Normally, I'd say you're right. I wouldn't give those kinds of rumors the time of day. But this one is different, bro."

"Why?"

"Because of who they're claiming is Trey's father."

"Who?"

"You."

Thirteen

Sam woke up with a bad feeling, a complete paradox given she was working in what looked like a swampy paradise. She got up, made coffee and tried to shake it off. She called Gloria, texted Danni and her dad. Everyone was fine, yet the feeling persisted. She finally allowed herself to consider that the continuing angst was from the incident with Joi at the fair. The text she'd sent her ex and the reply she'd gotten. And how he'd gone radio silent since then.

What an impossible situation. It seemed that every major decision she'd made since that heavenly night she initially spent in Nick's arms had been less than smart. Not telling Nick that she was pregnant. Moving to Africa. Marrying Oba. Returning stateside to Las Vegas instead of LA. Taking the contract for CANN Isles. Not telling Nick about Trey after they began working together. Underestimating Oba's greed. Not telling Nick the moment Oba threatened to do so, then sleeping with her child's bio dad more than once. Thinking that any of this would be easy, that Nick would somehow understand her betrayal. How could she think he'd be understanding when she was finding it increasingly difficult to justify her actions? At the end of the day, Sam had to face the hard truth. There was only one person to blame for what was happening right now.

Her.

Sam's mind settled enough for her to start the workday. Admitting her role in this mess, acknowledging that what she was experiencing was something that she in large part had created, was strangely liberating. In taking responsibility Sam felt some of her power being restored. She'd felt vulnerable after the confrontation with Joi, as though someone else had the ability to call the shots on her life. That was an illusion. It wasn't true. She'd made mistakes, but it wasn't the end of the world. Most importantly, the end result of that night hadn't been all bad. It had produced that which she treasured most in life. Her son.

For the next few hours, Sam focused on the home's furnishings—double-checking that shipments were still on schedule; confirming contractor appointments and speaking with the landscaping crew. Finally, she took a long shower and rather than heating up one of the meals left by the chef, decided to take the yacht into Charleston for a proper meal.

Thirty minutes later, she was at the boat's stern, watching the Atlantic churn beneath the sleek yacht's powerful motor. People often dreamed of a rich, carefree life where having a job or not was an option. Sam had lived that life, and until now didn't realize how much she'd missed her career. She was thankful for the tight timeline, and the plethora of problems to solve it presented. Doing so gave her less time to think about her own. And just like that, the sense of foreboding came back.

She knew just the person to help lighten her mood, reached over and picked up her phone. "Hey, Danni."

"Cousin! I was just thinking about you. It's about time you called. How's it going?"

"Okay, for the most part."

"I hope you're calling to say you told Nick about Trey."

"I'm going to. Soon. How was the birthday party?"

"Loud. Scott bought Jaylen a drum set. I wanted to take those sticks and beat him with them!"

Sam laughed. "I bet Trey was happy. I miss him."

"Hmm, I see. Do you miss his father?"

"Next question."

Danielle laughed. "Where are you?"

"Off the coast of South Carolina, heading into Charleston."

"From the island?"

"Yes, the island where the homes are located. They're super secure, super private and available only by boat."

There was a slight pause, and then, "How do you do it?"

"Do what?"

"Land these dream situations in your life. First, the marriage to a prince—"

"You had a hand in that."

"And now designing island homes for a rich guy? I'm doing something wrong."

"You're doing everything right. You've got a good man, a great kid and an amazing nephew."

"Ha! I can't argue with that. Hey, speaking of my nephew, he just ran down the hall. You want to speak with him?"

"In a minute. How are you?"

"Rested. That angel named Gloria who calls herself a childcare specialist is just the type of person I need in my life. She volunteered to help with the party and a few times since then, and made me wonder how I worked and ran this household without her."

"Frankly, I don't know either. Working full-time, taking care of a family and helping with Trey? I swear there's an S on your chest."

"Ha! I'm not your superwoman," Danielle sang. "Seriously, the workers at the day care are like family and my boss is a gem. As a single mother, she's well aware of the struggle in balancing family and work."

Sam looked out over the water, rippling and glowing in the sunny afternoon. Her cousin was right. She was blessed. Even with the design problems she'd encountered and her recent divorce, all the trouble she'd left behind in Africa and the secret she kept, life was good. She was on a yacht sailing in the Atlantic, having scored a contract any designer would want, one that would boost her résumé to the point she could be picky about clients and name her price. Her son was healthy and her dad was glad she was back on his side of the world. There was no room for complaints. At least, that should have been the case. But…that feeling.

"Sam."

"Hmm?"

"You got quiet all of a sudden. What's going on?"

"I don't know. I woke up with an eerie feeling that I've had all day."

"Was it a dream about Oba?"

"No. But something happened over the weekend that I didn't tell you about." Sam told Danielle about the run-in with Joi.

"And you're just telling me now?"

"I didn't want to even think about it, much less talk about what happened."

"Sam, you need to tell Nick about Trey. Today. The last thing you want is for him to find out about it from someone other than you."

"You're right. I know. I almost did that this weekend, too, right before Joi walked up and interrupted. And something else happened that day."

"What?"

"Nick and I slept together."

Danielle sucked in a breath. "No!"

"Yes." She painted the picture of them out riding, the spooked horse, sharing the saddle with Nick, and the inevitable conclusion from such close proximity.

"It was just that one time?"

"No."

"Twice?"

Sam sighed.

"You guys are working and dating?"

"Not officially dating, no."

"Friends with benefits?"

"You might say he's now a part of my compensation package." Sam's attempt to lighten the mood was an epic fail.

"You've got Nick hanging out with a child he doesn't

know is his, and sleeping with him, too? Sam. You've got to tell that man the truth."

Sam's screen lit up. Her stomach flopped. "Well, Danni, looks like we talked him up."

"Who, Nick?"

"He's calling. I've got to take it. Look, I'll call you back."

"Tell him!" Sam heard Danni yell before disconnecting the call.

"Hey, Nick."

"Sam."

Uh-oh. Was it paranoia about her secret or was there an ominous tone in Nick's voice? It had to be her freaking out. There was no way that he knew.

"The one and only," she said with a forced cheerfulness. "If you're calling about the drawings, that'll have to wait until I get back to the island. I'm on my way into Charleston. Wish you were here to join me for dinner."

"In a way, I wish I were there, too. But I'm not sure I'd have much of an appetite."

"Why? What's the matter?"

"Earlier today I hung out with my brother, who'd heard a crazy rumor, that your ex is not Trey's father."

Sam felt nauseous and she wasn't seasick.

"Who told him that?"

"Lauren heard it last weekend, from a client she met."

Sam sighed. "That is not a rumor. Trey is not Oba's biological child."

"Whose child is it? Do I know the father?"

Sam closed her eyes, unaware of how tightly she squeezed the phone. "You don't want kids," she said, in what hopefully sounded like a teasing tone. "Why this sudden interest in Trey's dad?"

Nick paused for so long Sam thought they may have gotten disconnected. She glimpsed her phone's face. He was still on the line.

"Nick?"

"Am I Trey's father?"

There was a lump as big as the future in her throat. She swallowed past it. "Yes."

Silence.

"Nick? Hello?"

She looked at the phone again. Nick was no longer on the line. Danni's words had proven prophetic. The secret was out and pierced her like an arrow. Straight through the heart.

Fourteen

Nick didn't think it possible to feel so many different emotions at once—shock, anger, bewilderment, confusion. He was Trey's father? Impossible. He went through all of the reasons that could not have been true. All but a sliver in the back of his brain was convinced that there was no way. But that 1 percent chance kept him from sleeping. The next morning, the sun had barely announced its presence when he walked through the front doors of the estate. Helen the housekeeper greeted him. She whispered, a nod to the early hour.

"Nick, is everything okay?"

"No, Helen, it's not. I need to see my parents."

"They're sleeping."

"I figured as much. They won't be for long."

Something in his voice must have warned her against making a fuss. Instead she asked, "Can I get you something? Coffee or tea?"

A shot of whiskey, Nick thought, but shook his head. One shot wouldn't be enough. This situation called for an entire bottle.

He reached his parents' suite and tapped on the door. "Mom. Dad. It's Nick."

"Nick?"

He heard the grogginess of his mother's voice, accompanied by shuffling noises, and felt a twinge of guilt, but only for a second. There were times when even a grown man still needed parental counsel. Now was one of those times.

"Just a moment, son."

Victoria opened the door wearing a floral lavender robe

with a matching silk cap and heeled house shoes, the epitome of style even in sleepwear.

"Good morning, darling." She touched his face. "What's the matter, son?"

Nick hugged her and walked into the room, past the sitting area and into where his dad was leaning up against the headboard.

"Son?"

Victoria came in behind him and joined her husband on his side of the bed. "Nick, what's wrong? You've got me very concerned."

"You know Sam, the woman who's working with me?"

"Of course. You don't forget a woman like her."

Nick snorted. "You don't know how right that statement might be. After confronting her about a rumor, she blindsided me with the news that Trey is my son."

He watched his parents exchange a look.

"What do you have to say about that?" Victoria asked.

Nick began to pace. "I say it's impossible!"

His father, Nicholas, raised a brow. "Is it?"

Nick turned to look at him. "Yes!"

"You two have never been intimate?"

"A long time ago but—"

"How long ago, son?" Victoria asked.

Nick frowned as he did the mental calculations. Around the time Sam got pregnant, a thought he didn't share.

"He's not my kid."

Victoria moved from the bed to sit on the antique bench beyond it. "You're sure? You always used protection?"

"There's no doubt about that," Nicholas interrupted, confidently crossing his arms. "That's how I taught all my boys. To use protection every single time."

"And you did?" Victoria pushed.

Nick ran a frustrated hand through his curls. "There may have been one time…"

"Then there's only one thing to do. Have a paternity test taken and then go from there."

"Go where from there? I don't have time to be a father. I told her that these island homes are my babies right now."

"So you two have discussed this?"

"No. We talked about kids once and I let her know then as I've told every woman before her that having a child wasn't a part of my plans and still isn't...not for at least another ten years."

Nicholas eased out of bed, straightening his pin-striped designer pajamas. "Was that before or after the unprotected sex, son?"

"How old is her son?" Victoria asked.

"Four."

"Yet you're only now learning that he might be your child? Why?"

"I don't know!"

"Well, you need to find out. If the child is yours, you've lost four formative years of his life. He's missed out on being a Breedlove and we may have someone with our DNA that we don't know. All of that is reason enough for a conversation with Samantha. That girl's got some explaining to do."

The conversation moved from his parents' master suite to the breakfast nook where over coffee they talked for more than an hour. Victoria worked her mother magic. Nick left the house feeling infinitely better than when he arrived. He was angry with Sam, beyond disappointed in her actions, but because of the people who raised him, he would try to follow their advice and not judge her too harshly or prematurely. A hard ask, but he'd try.

Nick was in no shape to go to work. He called Anita and rearranged his schedule to work from home. Once there, he retreated to his home office but still couldn't work very much. His thoughts kept drifting to the possibility that he was a father. He could close his eyes and see's Trey's face, searched his memory for any sign of himself in it. He went back to the day that he met him, how he'd actually told Sam the adventurous child reminded him of himself at that age. He went over every detail of the day they went horseback riding. He replayed the showdown between Sam and Joi. Sam's behavior now made much more sense, as did Joi's comment.

Which one is yours?

She knew. Sam knew. Yet kept him in the dark.

And there was one more thing. Those anonymous calls he'd been getting from the blocked number and the person who never spoke. Did that have something to do with the secret that Sam had been keeping?

Nick spun around angrily, determined to focus on work. He fired up his laptop, gritted his teeth against the myriad of emotions and opened his email. His eyes were instantly drawn to one from Sam. Something about the build, he thought.

But it wasn't.

Nick,
I'm sorry. I wanted to tell you. I should have told you. I was afraid of your reaction. I didn't know how. Please give me the chance to explain why at the time I thought what I did was best for everyone. I'm not saying it was right. In hindsight, I realize it was a horrible decision, one not fair to you, Trey or me. Please forgive me. For everything.
Sam.

Nick didn't respond right away. He didn't trust himself to write an appropriate answer. Later that morning, his reply was succinct.

The only thing we need to talk about, besides work, is a paternity test. I'll schedule it and forward the details. N.

To say they talked that week would have been generous. While she was in the Carolinas Nick communicated through email and text. Dr. Lucas, a longtime family friend who could be trusted to operate in confidence, orchestrated the testing. It was he, not Nick, who contacted Sam, who swabbed herself and Trey in the privacy of her condo when they returned from the Carolinas. After swabbing Nick, Dr. Lucas personally delivered the tests to the lab and ordered the results be rushed.

Twenty-four hours later, all doubt was removed. Nick was a father. Trey was his child.

Fifteen

Sam had never been this nervous. Even while pregnant, while facing an uncertain future with a man she'd just met and carrying the child of another, her nerves had been less traumatized. Nick had agreed to come over to the condo so that they could speak in private. Trey was with Danielle. It was what needed to happen, and what she wanted. But that didn't stop another part of her from being scared to death.

She'd gone through her closet and changed several times. Finally, already mentally exhausted with frayed nerves, she pulled on a pair of jeans and a cropped tee. Her locs were pulled to the top of her head. She wore no makeup. She expected him. But when the doorbell rang she jumped from the couch, then paused for a deep breath. Was he angry? Hurt? Shocked? Resigned? The only way to find out which Nick was on the other side of the door was to open it.

"Hi, Nick."

"Sam."

The look on his face made her mouth dry. A combination of anger and sadness, disappointment and fear. That handsome face that was usually smiling was now almost ashen in its somberness.

She stepped back. "Please, come in."

He took a couple steps inside and stopped, his back to her.

"Let's, um, sit…at the table." Sam walked into the dining room and took a seat. Nick silently complied, barely meeting her eyes.

"Can I get you anything—"

"Let's get one thing straight. This is not a social visit. This is the opportunity you asked for, a chance to explain why almost five years later I'm finding out about someone out there with my blood in his veins."

He hadn't raised his voice, but Sam felt the restraint it had taken to not do so, could almost feel the heat on his words. Tears burned the back of her eyes. She dug fingernails into palms and dared herself to cry. She was not the victim here. She'd perpetrated a problem that now needed to be fixed.

"When getting dressed to go out that night, I had no idea how that party would change my life. Like you I was single and loving it, living life like it was golden, totally carefree. I think that's one of the reasons we gravitated to each other. We had the same energy, the same thought about living our lives.

"Discovering that I was pregnant sent me straight into shock, and panic. I'd recently ended a relationship with a guy in LA, had come here to get him out of my system. Boy, did you ever help me do that! As soon as the home test I took came back positive, I knew it was you. But I didn't know you—I mean, we'd seen each other in passing what, maybe five or six times? Then I followed up with a doctor's visit and his timeline further confirmed it."

"But you still didn't tell me, Sam."

"I couldn't."

"Why not?"

"You didn't want kids! I'd gone online to find out more about you and the first article I read was about how dedicated you were to your family's business, how you were happily single with no time for a family of your own. Then, as fate would have it, shortly after that Danni got talking with Joi and found out about Oba's dilemma."

Nick's head shot up. "What dilemma?"

"Oba's elderly grandfather was pressuring his grandsons to get married and produce heirs. Oba was determined to beat Isaac having a child."

"Isaac?"

"His brother."

Nick's frown deepened.

"I know. It's complicated, the same as Oba and his brother's relationship. They were born less than a year apart. Their grandfather cultivated a fierce competition between them and upped the ante when he said the first one to marry and provide an heir would get the throne."

"How'd you get involved?"

"In a moment of frustration, Joi shared the stress of watching her brothers' ongoing fights with Danni, and how if given a choice she thought Oba would be the better king. Danni knew how freaked out I was at the prospect of being a single mother. She told Joi I was pregnant. Joi told him about me. Danni told me about Oba and..." Sam heaved a sigh. "The next thing I knew I was an African princess."

"That is totally crazy."

"In repeating the story out loud it sounds like pure insanity, but back then, in my mind, getting married solved everything. You wanted nothing to do with children, yet here was a guy where a child was not only what he wanted, but what he needed as well. I envisioned my son growing up royal and privileged, who'd lack for nothing he wanted in life."

"Nothing except the truth."

"There is no excuse for what I did. There's no way to make it right, only to make it better. For almost five years, I've deprived my son of his birthright. I will regret that decision for the rest of my life."

"I think your ex has been calling me."

Sam's head shot up. Her eyes registered fear.

"It was just a few times and I can't be sure. It was a blocked number. They never said anything. But since it's never happened before and considering what I've learned..."

Sam sighed and ran weary fingers over her eyes. "It was probably Oba. He's been trying to blackmail me."

"What the hell?" Nick had never been a violent man but

he was glad Sam's ex wasn't anywhere close to him right now. "Why?"

"It's a long story, but don't worry. If it's him, they'll stop. Now that the secret is out he has nothing to use against me."

"Even with what you've told me, I still don't get it. How you could justify not telling me that you were pregnant? I don't know if I can ever get over that type of betrayal, the lack of trust, the anger. You watched me play with the kid, teach him how to ride a horse, and stayed silent while knowing I was interacting with my own son. That's fucked up, Sam!"

Nick stood and walked away from the table, as if just being near her was too much to handle.

Sam steepled her hands and worked to remain calm. "You're 100 percent correct. I effed up, in what may very well be the biggest mistake of my life. I don't expect you to understand something that no longer makes sense to me. I only hope that there can be some type of relationship between you and Trey and that one day...you'll forgive me."

"Of course there'll be a relationship. What kind of man do you think I am? Oh, that's right. You didn't think I was man enough to even want to know I had a child. So scratch that question. I don't give a damn what you think about me.

"I'm sure you know that if there was any possible way to pull you off the island project, I'd do it today. But given the time constraints and what has already been designed, it wouldn't be economically or logically prudent. That said, I can't be around you right now. Noah is familiar with much of what I'm doing. I'll bring him in as a go-between. All exchanges between us need to be electronic. In just over three weeks, the necessary homes will be completed. It'll be difficult, but I think I can handle the interaction for that long."

"What about Trey? I understand that you hate me right now, but I'm his mom and a necessary bridge between the two of you. Is there a way that we can at least work together to ensure as smooth as possible a transition for him, from considering Oba as his father to knowing you're his dad?"

Nick's eyes remained fixed on the window, though Sam doubted he saw anything beyond the mess she'd made.

"What do you suggest?" he finally asked.

"Maybe bring him over to the estate. He already loves going there. He really likes you, too."

Nick winced. The hole in Sam's heart tore wider.

"Maybe Christina can be a part of easing him into your family. I don't know what they think about all of this but…

"I'm so sorry, Nick." Instinctively, she took a step toward him.

"Don't." His jaw rippled with the force it took to not say more. Words Sam doubted she wanted to hear anyway.

"What about his nanny, what's her name?"

"Gloria?"

"Yes. She's friends with Christina's nanny Kirtu. I think it would be better if Trey came with her."

Ouch. "Okay."

"My family is understandably upset. They need time to absorb all of what's happened, as do I."

That night, Sam told Gloria about Nick being Trey's father, the conversation they'd had and Nick's request. The next morning Sam woke up Trey and helped him get dressed. That she wasn't going to be there for this first father-son interaction where Nick knew the truth literally hurt her heart. Still, she was grateful that Nick wanted to get to know his son. For that reason alone, she found a smile to put on for her child.

"Where are we going, Mommy?"

Sam looked at her heartbeat, melting as she always did when she heard Trey's voice. "You and Gloria are going someplace to have lots of fun."

"Where"

"Do you remember Nick, the man I work with, the one who taught you to ride the horse?"

"Yes. I'm going over there?" Trey's eyes were wide and bright with anticipation. In that moment, to her mind, he looked like Nick's chocolate-covered mini-me. "I like horses, Mommy."

"I know you do."

"I want a horse, Mommy."

"That would be fun, huh?"

Trey nodded. "I would ride it every day."

"But horses are a lot of work, Trey. They require a lot of care, to feed them and house them and give them exercise."

"I'll do it!"

"Who'll watch the horse while you're at school?"

Trey's brows scrunched together as he pondered this question. Studying his face, Sam was taken aback. Why hadn't she noticed Nick's features before on Trey's face? Was it only in the truth being revealed she could see them?

"Are you going, Mama?"

"No, Mama's been working really long hours so while you and Gloria are riding horses, I'm going to get some rest. Is that okay?"

"Okay."

Sam would have liked there to have been a little push-back, to feel that her son needed her to tag along. But Trey had always been adventuresome, with an independent streak. Just like his father.

Sam heard a tap on Trey's bedroom door before it opened slightly.

"Good morning!"

Said a little too forced and a little too brightly. Sam could only imagine how awkward this had to be for her childcare specialist.

"Good morning, Gloria." She walked closer and lowered her voice. "Are you sure you'll be okay?"

"I still think it should be you who takes him over."

"Maybe next time. Right now, it's better this way."

"Should I fix him breakfast?"

"Knowing Nick and his family, any kind of gathering will likely involve food. I'll get him a Pop-Tart to tide him over."

Sam kept up the casual chatter until Gloria and Trey left the house and she locked the door behind them. She made it all the way back to her bedroom before the tears came, and then allowed herself a good cry. Trey would get to spend time with his father, even as Sam's days were numbered. She tried to find comfort in that.

For the next three weeks, a routine was established. Gloria took Trey to the Breedloves' on weekends. During the week they traveled with Sam, who buried herself in work. The good news was that for the most part she stayed on schedule, finishing the last home mere days before the occupants were set to arrive. The more challenging news was that she'd done all of this while consumed with a myriad of feelings about Nick and Trey. Delight that they were getting to know each other. Sorrow that things between her and Nick would never be the same.

The ice had thawed somewhat. The texts and emails had graduated to a call here and there, focused strictly on work or questions about Trey. She still wasn't sure how she felt about his reaction, that he'd been less than enthused about claiming the smartest, cutest, brightest most intelligent kid on the planet as his own. But in the end, as Danielle had so aptly pointed out, it would have been less than responsible for him to react any other way. His disappointment in missing out on Trey's first four years overshadowed the joy Sam was sure that Nick also felt. Whether he knew it, acknowledged it or ever owned up to it or not, Nick was a perfect father for her son. And thanks to the contract they'd negotiated, she would be fine financially and otherwise, whether or not Nick chose to be in her son's life.

She was in Maine preparing to catch a flight back to Vegas when her phone rang. Nick.

"Hey."

"Hi, Sam. You're headed back tonight, right?"

"Yes, headed to the airport now."

"What time do you land?"

"Seven forty-five."

"We need to talk. Can you meet me for dinner?"

Could it be that Nick was finally coming around to the two of them at least being friends for their son's sake? Sam's heart leaped.

"Sure. Should I bring Trey?"

"This needs to be just the two of us."

"Okay, text me the address and I'll meet you there. And, Nick?"

"Yes?"

"Thanks."

Once home she swapped jeans for a flowy jumpsuit and headed to Breedlove. Her phone rang. Thinking it was Danielle, she clicked the Bluetooth immediately.

"Hello, Sam Price," she fairly sang, her heart lighter than it had been in ages.

"Is that you, baby?"

Hearing the accent almost made her run off the road. Before Oba had only texted. Now he was calling. The nerve of his actions caused a rage to form in the pit of Sam's gut. That with all she was going through, he'd put her through more. But what could he do now? He'd lost his power. The thought calmed her anger. She almost smiled.

"Oba, we've been through this already. It's over. We've no need to talk."

"Oh, really? Then maybe you'd like me to talk to your baby's real daddy."

"Oba Usman, I don't give a damn what you do. There's nothing you can tell Nick that he doesn't already know. I told him, all right? He knows that Trey is his son. Call again threatening blackmail or anything else and you will hear from my lawyer. Think I'm playing? Try me. Now go off and have a nice life."

Sixteen

Having grown up in a nurturing, supportive environment filled with love, Nick wasn't used to being nervous. Yet as he pulled into the parking lot of BBs, his brother's popular hamburger joint, he felt wisps of discomfort, uncertainty, even a little despair. He'd always been the master of his own destiny, in total control of his life. Yet in the span of a few pivotal weeks that had all changed. He was a father. He had a son named Trey. Life was no longer all about him and while he'd already developed true feelings for what his brother Christian called Nick's "mini-me," he didn't quite know how he felt about that. Or about Sam.

He entered the restaurant, aware of the desirous eyes from female patrons that followed him only because the hostess pointed it out. After taking a seat near the window he pulled out his phone to check messages and texts until Sam arrived about fifteen minutes later.

"Sorry I'm late," she began, with a flustered demeanor. "There was an accident and…"

He put a hand on her arm and gently squeezed it. "Relax. It's fine. This isn't an interview."

Sam blessed him with a smile that lit up those warm brown eyes. "I guess you're right. Thanks for the reminder."

She sat down and threw her purse strap over the chair back. "This is your brother's place?" she asked, looking around.

"His pride and joy, except for the ranch and the cows he raises."

"I like its no-nonsense casual atmosphere. A contrast to what I imagined it would be."

"Adam wanted a place that would feel comfortable for

everybody. Non-pretentious, as it should be when scarfing down burgers and fries. And speaking of, don't you dare say you're not hungry. I'd put these burgers up against anybody, and bet my vacation homes that they'd win."

"Wow, lofty bet."

"Confident brother."

They spoke casually until the server delivered their drinks and took their orders.

"A premium champagne would have been more appropriate, but such is not on BBs menu. This is all I have." Nick held up his frosty mug of beer. "A toast is in order."

With a slight frown, Sam held up her iced tea. "To what?"

"You. Congratulations on a job well done."

"Oh. That."

"I know the team congratulated you on managing the impossible. Noah, and my brothers. I think even my dad. I realized that no matter what was happening personally between us, not giving props where they were due made me a total jerk."

"It means a lot to hear that, Nick. It was the most difficult job I've ever tackled, and the most rewarding."

"To the only woman who could have pulled it off."

Sam lifted her tea. The glasses clinked. Each sipped from their glass as they drank in each other.

"We're having a dinner at CANN to celebrate the project's completion. I'd love for you to join me."

"As your date?"

"As one who deserves to be officially recognized."

"Are you sure? At our last physical interaction you hated me, Nick. This change, it's…welcomed, but uncomfortable."

"You're right. All I wanted was you out of my sight. Not telling me about my son was cruel and unthinkable. I thought I'd never forgive you."

Sam's head dipped. "I totally understand that, because I'll never forgive myself."

"Then I talked with Grandma Jewel, my dad's mother.

She told me that the unforgiveness in my heart wouldn't hurt you or myself as much as it would Trey. That kids are closest to spirit and could feel words that remained unspoken. My son has already been through enough. I don't want to be the cause of more pain.

"One more thing," he continued, before Sam could speak. "Since I've done the impossible and forgiven you, you might as well forgive yourself."

Nick watched as Sam's head dipped lower, and she brought a hand to her face. He was out of his chair in an instant and sitting beside her.

"Come on, none of that," he said as he reached for a napkin and blotted her tears. "This is a celebration, remember?"

Sam pulled herself together, her expression über-serious as she turned to face him. "There's only one thing left to do."

Nick's heart skipped a beat. What had he missed? "Go ahead," he said. "I'm listening."

"We've got to tell Trey that you're his real father. He doesn't know that he's your son."

For the rest of the evening conversation swung between CANN Isles and Trey, mostly. The celebratory dinner took place a couple weeks later. Sam looked delectable in a designer original. Her good looks and effervescent personality endeared her to everyone in the room. Pics of her achievements were leaked to the media. In several issues of local and national newspapers and websites, she was the focus of both the business and society pages. No one was more impressed with her than his family. As though the person she was had overridden what she'd done. When Trey asked him if his mom was joining them for Thanksgiving dinner at the estate, Nick told him he'd like nothing better. The day marked for giving thanks seemed infinitely appropriate to being the one where his son learned the truth about their relationship.

Thanksgiving at the Breedlove estate was its usual grand

affair. Nick and Sam, however, excused themselves shortly after the Christmas tree lighting, for a talk before Trey went to bed. He was excited from the day's festive activities but after Sam had given him a bath, he slid into his Black Panther pj's more than ready for sleep. Nick and Sam followed him into the massive guest room that had been renovated into a little boy's dreamland. Trey crawled onto the bed shaped like a race car. Nick sat down beside him. Sam, in the nearby chair.

Trey looked from one parent to the other. "You're both going to read me a bedtime story?"

"Not from one of your superhero books," Sam offered. "But Mama does have a story to tell."

Nick watched Sam take a deep breath as a myriad of emotions played across her face. "I know you think Prince Oba is your father, baby. But he is not your real dad."

Trey's look of confusion was understandable to both Nick and Sam. "He's not my father?"

Sam slowly shook her head. "No, baby. When I married him, you were already in my tummy."

Trey thought on this a moment and then asked his mom, "Do I have a father?"

"Absolutely," Nick interrupted, pride underscoring the word. "I'm your father, Trey. I only found out when you guys returned to America that I am your real dad."

He held his breath and watched Trey's young mind try to process adult information. "For real?"

Nick nodded.

"Like Christian is Christina's dad and Scott is Jaylen's dad?"

"Yes," Sam told him. "Exactly like that."

"Is that okay with you?" Nick asked him, unaware that he was no longer breathing.

"I love it!" Trey finally screamed, shooting like a missile into Nick's arms.

Trey's arms around his neck felt better than he could

imagine. Nick finally exhaled. Sam didn't go home that night. The love shared between them was better than bliss. The work done. No more secrets between them. The next morning, she fixed them breakfast. Then Nick and Trey went riding with Adam and Noah. Family life continued when they returned and watched a movie.

The time felt so right, so natural, that Nick did the unthinkable when just before Sam and Trey prepared to leave that Saturday, he asked her, "Would you like to live here, to move in with me? Trey loves being here. There's plenty of room."

And other reasons, which Nick had yet to admit to himself.

Sam was understandably taken aback and didn't answer immediately. Nick understood. When it came to relationships, she'd gone through a lot. Yet his emotions surprised him as he awaited her answer, and at how lonely his home felt when he was the only one there. As he continued about his routine and enjoyed the rest of the holiday weekend, he knew one thing for sure. Even though the project with Sam Price was finished, the business between them wasn't over. Not by a long shot.

Seventeen

"Hey, cousin!" The front door had barely opened before Sam pulled Danielle in for a hearty hug.

Danielle stepped back. "What was that for?"

"Can't your cousin be happy to see you?" Sam entered the home.

"You're a little too happy. Where's Trey?"

"With Nick."

Danielle stopped and turned.

"For real? Even though it's not his weekend?"

"All the cousins were over playing in the pool. He begged to stay and hang out with them. With all I have to do trying to restart my business, I couldn't say no."

They continued down the hallway. Danielle glanced back a time or two.

"Somebody's holiday must have gone very well."

"Better than I could have thought possible."

Sam entered the living room and walked over to where her young cousin sat engrossed in a game.

"Hey, Jaylen!"

"Hi, Sam." Said with eyes still glued to the screen, his hand quickly shifting the control to combat and destroy enemies far and wide.

"Jaylen, take that warfare into your room. Mommy and Sam have some grown-up talking to do."

"Wait! I've almost vanquished the leader!"

"Vanquished?" Sam asked. "Good word."

"Boy, I'm going to vanquish your behind if you don't move!"

To prove she meant business Danielle walked over, picked up her son and began blowing smoochies—loud, air-

filled kisses that tickled the skin. Jaylen's laughter floated
down the hallway. Sam smiled, reminded of the rough-
housing that Sam witnessed between Trey and his uncles.
It seemed they were experts in everything from Adam and
bucking broncos to Christian and any sport. Noah's collection of robotic toys had dropped Trey's jaw. Hers, too, actually. She'd never seen her son more impressed.

"Whew!" Danielle joined Sam on the chenille-covered
sofa. "I'm too old to have a six-year-old."

Sam gave her a look. "You're thirty."

"Tell that to my body." Danielle shifted with a hand to
her back. "That boy is getting too big to pick up. Now my
back is killing me."

"That's because you need to work out."

"I need Gloria to find a twin to come help run my household, that's what I need."

"I hear that. She's been such a blessing to me and Trey,
like part of the family."

"I'm teasing. That kind of help is above my pay grade."

Danielle shifted to a more comfortable position. "Enough
about our angel assistant. It's time for you to spill the tea on
all that happened in Breedlove. I want the turkey tales with
all of the trimmings, thank you very much."

"Wow." Sam grabbed a pillow and leaned back, too. "So
much happened. Where do I begin?"

"How about the beginning?"

Sam chuckled. "Good idea. You remember how incredible their place is, right?"

"They held a frickin' carnival on the most beautiful spot
in all of Nevada, land that went on forever. How could I
forget?"

"The holiday decor is even more spectacular."

"That's hard to imagine."

"Hopefully you and Jaylen will get a chance to see it.
There were games and live music and incredible food. The
night ended with a lighting ceremony that rivaled any I've

seen, officially beginning the Christmas season. But I'm getting ahead of myself. The fun started with my meeting the true Breedlove matriarch, Nick's grandmother Miss Jewel…"

Sam recounted the unparalleled Breedlove Estate experience that for the past four days had been her enchanted life.

"You know I don't get along with just anybody. I can spot a fake real quick and don't suffer them lightly. But I have to tell you, Danni, the Breedloves aren't like most bougie folk. And I've seen one or two. Can we say 'royalty'?" Sam used air quotes.

"We could but we won't."

"Agreed. Nick and his family are different. They can hold their own with the caviar crowd but are down-to-earth, too. They're the real deal. I like them. The brother's wives were open, friendly, made me feel like family."

"Sounds like a family you want to join."

"Slow your roll, chick. That's unlikely to happen. Nick is warming up to being a father. The same doesn't necessarily apply to his taking a wife."

"I know you have to act as though it's not something that matters."

"For now I'm just happy we're getting along."

"That's all? No sex?"

"Well…"

"Girl, quit playing. Don't make me have to drag words out by consonant and vowel."

"I spent the night."

Danielle squealed. "That's good, right?"

Sam shrugged.

"Nick is one fine brother. You could do far worse than him."

"Look, I'm perfectly fine being sin—"

"Really? Then perhaps you should let your face know. Now back to the story before your nose starts to grow."

Sam burst out laughing. "I hate you."

"Thanks, hon."

Sam shifted the conversation out of the bedroom and back to the variety of activities that the estate offered, and how comfortable it was hanging out with members of Nick's family she knew already while meeting others for the first time.

"The brothers all have a natural affinity for socializing, comfortable mingling with others regardless of social status. The staff was treated more like family than employees. But I thought the family gathering, especially Thanksgiving dinner, would be different somehow. Haughtier, buttoned-up. I envisioned a dining room straight out of a castle with bone china, pristine manners and a servant behind each chair."

"What? No servants?" Danielle feigned indignation.

"Yes, but only behind every other chair," Sam deadpanned. "I'm kidding." Added a beat later.

Danielle bopped her with a throw pillow.

Sam's plan for a quick visit with Danielle turned into a chat-athon lasting all afternoon. After speaking with Nick, Jaylen joined Trey in Breedlove so that Sam and Danielle could take a rare spin on the Strip. Vegas residents seldom ventured to the areas that made their state famous, but Danielle felt lucky and Sam wanted to shop. When they returned to the estate that evening, the holiday theme was on full display. Danielle was as blown away as Sam thought she'd be. It was the perfect ending to her four-day weekend, and probably Sam's last bit of downtime before Christmas. There was work to do. Decisions to make. After a particularly wonderful evening involving the three of them, Nick had invited her and Trey to move in with him. Tempting offer. But he'd focused on Trey, not her or their relationship. She'd be the first to define herself as a modern woman, one leery of vows with a failed marriage under her belt. Still, she loved the security of commitment and knew few successes topped that of a good marriage. Seeing Scott and Danielle together was proof of that. Then there was her old-school grandmother's most popular saying that after being with Nick sometimes played in her head.

Doesn't make sense for a man to buy a cow when he gets the milk for free.

On their way home from Nick's after his offer, those words had played on a loop in her head. By the time she'd pulled into her garage, she'd made a decision. Sam and Trey would continue to call the condo home. Grandma, 1. Modern woman, 0.

On Monday, Sam rose early. She'd created a to-do list the night before and was ready to tackle each project. She showered and dressed as if she were headed to an office. Sometimes a suit produced better results than yoga pants and a tee. Five minutes after sitting down with a mug of peppermint tea, her phone rang.

"Sam Price."

"Good morning."

"Hi Nick." *Breathe.* "What's going on?"

"Thinking about you. Thought I'd call."

"You're not working today?"

"Not for another hour."

"Oh."

Sam fell quiet, conflicted, as she'd been off and on all weekend. No doubt she was very attracted to Nick and loved being with him. Maybe a little too much for a casual affair. She'd played it off when Danielle teased her, but the deeper she'd examined her feelings about Nick and the more honest she'd been about the probability that they'd deepen further the longer they dated, the more she realized that continuing the casual affair might not be a good idea.

"Are you working? Did I interrupt something?"

Yes. You interrupted the lie I've been telling myself.

"Yes, I am working. There's only three short weeks until the world shuts down for Christmas. I have a lot to do before now and next year."

"Okay, cool. No worries. We can talk later today."

"Goodbye." Sam hung up and turned back to the to-do list on her computer. She tried to focus but her mind kept returning to her unresolved feelings about Nick. Getting up from the couch, she set down her tablet and walked to the window, her life over the past four-plus years playing like a video across a mental screen. The party. The pregnancy. Oba. Africa. CANN. Trey. The actions that had shaped her past. Her vision for the future. What did she want it to look like?

Determined to complete at least some of the tasks on her list, Sam picked up her phone and called Danielle.

"Hey, Sam!"

"Hey, cousin. Do you think the day care would mind watching Trey this afternoon? Gloria isn't here. I need to focus and right now home is too distracting."

"Probably not, but I can call and find out."

"Jaylen's there?"

"Yep. Scott will pick him up on the way home. He can get Trey, too, if you're not done with what you're working on by then. You can pick him up here later."

"Perfect. Let me know."

"Okay."

Minutes later, Danielle texted that the day care would watch him, but at the full-day rate even though it was almost one o'clock. Sam would have gladly paid them double. She was out of the house in less than thirty minutes and another half hour after that had dropped off Trey and was seated in a local library's private room with her tablet on and cell phone off.

The change of scenery helped but didn't squelch the thoughts completely. She managed to check off a few items and make the most time-sensitive calls. But three hours later, thoughts of Nick and their situation were still all-consuming. Her shoulders were tense with stress. Rotating her neck to try to remove the kinks, she remembered a conversation with Adam's wife Ryan, who co-owned a

spa and suggested she should come for a visit. Maybe a
little pampering was just what she needed to ease her body
as well as her mind. After making an appointment online,
Sam called Danielle to have Scott pick up Trey. She left
the library and soon after arrived at the Integrative Heal-
ing Group, located in a nondescript mall about fifteen minutes from the Strip. The place didn't look like much from
the outside, but one step inside the red door that marked
Ryan's business and Sam was transformed.

A soothing shade of blue covered the waiting room walls,
with a backlit fountain as the room's showpiece. The water
flowed into the vase of a tall, vibrant plant. More plants were
set in floor urns and on tabletops. Notes from the instru-
mental music—something spiritual, earthy and from the
East—seemed to wrap themselves around her, while the
scent of lavender added to the paradise-like atmosphere.
Sam looked around for the button that would announce
her arrival and pushed it, as the confirmation email had instructed. It wasn't long before she heard the sound of bells,
these tinkling as the door to the inner rooms opened and
Ryan appeared.

"Sam, hi." Ryan stepped forward and offered a quick
embrace. "I was so excited to see your name come up on
our scheduler and actually moved a client over to another
specialist so that I could personally attend you."

"Thank you, Ryan." Out of the three Breedlove sisters-
in-love, Sam had most connected with Ryan, who never
seemed to judge her after learning of Trey. She was effortlessly attractive yet genuine and kind. Her heartfelt gesture
made Sam like her even more.

"I didn't know what to expect when I pulled up outside,
but your place is truly beautiful."

"Yeah, the outside is pretty deceiving. But we put our
heart and soul into the designing that went on inside, wanting to effect a certain mood and vibration that would immediately put the client at ease."

"You designed this?"

Ryan nodded. "My and my partner Brooklyn's souls are in every room."

They entered a massage room. Here the shade of blue was darker, contrasted against a stark white ceiling flecked with gold. Abstract paintings, angel statues and renderings of spiritual masters brought in an ethereal effect. "Ryan, I love everything about what I've seen so far. You guys did an amazing job."

"Oh my gosh, Sam, I appreciate your saying that. Nick brags that you're the best designer money can buy, so coming from you that's high praise."

So much for getting away from thinking about Nick. Then again, she'd made an appointment at the business of one of his family members. What did she expect?

As soon as Sam was ready and the massage began, so too did the questions.

"You're really tense, Sam. Working a lot of hours?"

Sam nodded. "Now that my contract with CANN is over I'm focused on rebuilding my company, Priceless Designs."

"That can be stressful."

"Yes."

"Because of Adam, I know that CANN's business is booming right now. I'm surprised Nick didn't have you stay on for other builds."

"It was discussed early on but a contract worked best. The last few years have been a whirlwind. I need time to regroup, focus on Trey and decide how best to move forward."

"I don't know much about what happened, but divorce is never easy."

"No."

"Nick seems to care a lot about you."

"Sorry, Ryan, I know he's your brother, but I'd rather not discuss Nick right now."

Ryan graciously changed the subject without missing a beat before ending conversation all together to focus on her work. She was skilled and thorough. When finished, Sam's body was as limp as a noodle. Ryan gave a short tour and explained other services. Sam scheduled another appointment for the works—facial, body wrap and float tank session—the latter of which she'd heard of but never tried. When they reached the outer door, Sam turned and hugged Ryan.

"Thanks for inviting me to your spa. I feel so much better and can't wait to come back."

"I can't wait for your visit, which doesn't have to be limited to the spa, by the way. If you're ever in need of some girl time or want to bring Trey and hang out at the ranch, you're always welcome. Just give me a call. The business card you picked up has my cell number."

"Okay. Thanks again."

They stepped outside.

"Sam?"

She turned around.

"I know it's not my business and you don't want to talk but if I may offer a bit of advice about Breedlove men?" Ryan waited and when Sam didn't speak or turn to leave, continued. "They are fierce companions who love as hard as they work. If you grab their attention, even fleeting, it's pretty amazing. If you're lucky enough to capture their heart, though, don't release it. You won't find a better man."

For the rest of the night, Sam's feelings remained scattered. She woke up to them cemented behind the strength of her truth. The desire at the core of her heart that until now she'd dared not think about, let alone speak. She was precariously close to falling in love with Nick and wanting more than the man was willing to give. She wanted a real relationship. She wanted love. Commitment. A forever man. Happily ever after was sometimes hard to come by, but it was possible. She believed she deserved to have the life that she wanted. And that true love was worth the wait.

Showering and preparing breakfast, Sam felt more grounded and sure of herself than since leaving Africa.

The insecurities that had dogged her since the divorce were replaced by feelings of a woman who remembered who she really was—worthy enough for a man to want to put his name behind hers. It might be a while before she was ready to jump back into the dating waters. There was still baggage from the marriage of convenience left to unpack. But one thing was for sure. Whenever she was ready and open to look, she'd be highly unlikely to find him while rolling around in Nick's bed.

Later that day, after crossing off 75 percent of what was on her schedule, she didn't wait for Nick to call her. She called him. She needed to set things straight before losing her nerve or, after seeing that hard, toned body again, her will.

He answered quickly, his voice low and sexy. "I was just thinking about you. Again."

"I've been thinking about you, too, all day off and on."

"All good thoughts, I hope."

"It probably depends on how you look at it. Either way, I've come to a decision."

"Uh-oh. This sounds serious."

"I think we should cut out the intimacy between us and focus on co-parenting Trey."

"Okay." The word had only two syllables but the way Nick dragged it out made it seem to have more. "May I ask why you feel that way?"

Sam sighed. "I'm still figuring that all out myself. What I do know, what I recently discovered or acknowledged about myself, is that I'm past the whole casual dating thing. While Oba's and my marriage didn't work out and I'm not looking to blindly jump into another, I am looking for more than someone just to spend time with."

"Such as?"

"Feeling connected more than physically. Feeling that I'm not alone in the world, that someone has my back and will be there for me. I don't want to use the word *claim*, that sounds so draconian, but there's a part of being a woman that wants to be wanted, needed, loved, who wants to be valued enough by someone willing to acknowledge that she's enough for him, that she's all he wants."

"That sounds like the marriage thing you're not wanting to jump back into."

"Mine was mostly a marriage in name only, and I said blindly jump."

"Y'all didn't have sex?"

"We had sex. We never made love."

"And that's what you want. Love, not sex."

"Yes. That's what I want."

As she talked, revelations continued to pour into Sam's soul. Fear diminished. She was emboldened to stand in her truth. She wanted a real father for Trey and real love for herself. To have both was possible. She now knew that for sure. If she couldn't get the love she wanted from the father of her child, she'd get it somewhere else.

Eighteen

Nick tossed a stack of papers on his desk and punched the office intercom button with more force than necessary.

"Yes, Mr. Breedlove?"

He didn't answer her because he'd jumped out of his chair and stormed out of his office.

"What in the hell is this?" he yelled before reaching his destination. He tossed the report on Anita's desk. Files, pens and sticky pads went flying. "The revisions I requested are not on that doc."

"Oh no, Mr. Breedlove!" Anita hurriedly straightened the messy report papers, then scrambled to retrieve the items off the floor. "I absolutely made the changes and must have forwarded the uncorrected document."

"Find it. Send it," Nick growled, punching the air with a finger for emphasis. "Now!" Instead of waiting for an answer he marched back into his office and but for the hydraulics would have slammed the door. He continued to the window, his brow creased in a perfect bad-boy scowl as he shoved his hands in his pockets and tried to calm down. He wasn't angry about the report. He was upset at the restrictions Sam had placed on their relationship. Wait, there wasn't a relationship. That was the problem.

The intercom sounded. "Mr. Breedlove, I just emailed the corrected version. I thought I'd deleted the first one after it was revised. My apologies for—"

"None needed, Anita." He walked over and plopped into his chair, then spun around to face the phone. "I'm the one who needs to apologize."

"It's okay, Nick. There's a lot going on."

She had no idea. Then again, Nick suspected she'd had

an inkling. Victoria called it Mother Wit. Plus, Anita had been with CANN for over twenty years, back in the days when Nick and Noah played Nerf ball in the halls and stole candy from the vending machines. It's the main reason he corrected her when she first called him by his surname.

"Call me Nick," he'd said.

She refused, wanting to give him the respect due an executive and, if his hunch was correct, boost the confidence of a twenty-two-year-old who was wet behind the ears. But when a bit of chiding or support was needed, she reverted to being the mother she was, with sons and daughters almost Nick's age.

"That's no excuse," he said after the long pause.

"Well, I know you're busy and want those letters to sign before end of day. So I'll get back to work. But if there's anything else you need or ways I can help relieve any stress, just let me know. Okay, kiddo?"

Nick smiled. "Yes, ma'am." He reached over to disconnect the call. "Hey, Anita. Got a question."

"Yes, Mr. Breedlove?"

"So we're back to that, are we?"

She chuckled. "Absolutely. Sir."

"Cut that out."

"What's your question?"

"I'm seeking your opinion as a woman, not my assistant."

"I think I can handle that."

"Is it true that no matter how independent a woman acts, she secretly wants companionship and…you know…to get married?"

"Are we speaking…generally?"

"Yes."

"Then generally speaking, yes, I believe that's true. Much has changed, with the women's movement, the rise of feminism and such, and some women are able to remain single and be happy. But I personally believe that deep inside most women, most people in fact, want to love and be loved, to have a partner in life. You're still young, Nick, and driven. But one day I believe that you, too, will grow tired of dating, and want something more substantial, more grounding in your life. Until then, have fun!"

"Good advice. Thanks, Anita."

"Anytime."

Nick went back to work. He perused the report Anita had corrected. Went to the meeting he'd mentioned to Sam. The hardest work he did all day was trying to forget about her and the decision she'd made. His fingers itched to tap her name on his phone, but he didn't. Until now he hadn't realized the easy flow they'd fallen into of talking almost every day. Mostly about Trey, sometimes with design or architectural questions. He'd grown used to regularly hearing her voice, and missed it. Then on Thursday night, as he left the office early to prepare for one of his mother's many social functions, his phone rang. Sam. Coming to her senses about her sex ban, he hoped. He'd had his share of women but when it came to his child's mother, he had to admit that their connection was different from those others. Special. At another level. He was a passionate brother. She was the first to match him stroke for stroke.

"Breedlove."

"Nick, it's Sam."

"I know. What's up?"

"It's about Trey."

So the call wasn't about sex, or him. He ignored a pang of disappointment.

"He's okay, right?"

"He's fine."

"Then what is it?"

"Is it possible that he can stay with you this weekend? Gloria is off for the holidays. As soon as my lease is up, I'm moving back to LA. I want to fly over there tomorrow, do some house hunting, speak with a few potential clients, stuff like that."

Nick's bad week just got worse.

"What's wrong with Vegas?"

There was a slight pause before Sam answered. "Nothing. However, the bulk of clients requesting my assistance are in metro LA. It makes sense for that to be my home base."

"What about Trey?"

"What about him?"

"Will he be staying here, on the estate?"

"Most definitely not."

"It's not definite at all, babe. I don't want my son growing up amid smog, gang violence, police misconduct, the celebrity culture. He needs to be here in Breedlove, where he can run, play, breathe fresh air and be a worry-free kid."

"He's my son, Nick. There's no way I'm going to be separated from him."

"Me, either."

"There's got to be a way we can come to a mutual agreement that will allow me to grow my business and for us to continue to co-parent Trey. You've got the plane, and money is no object. You can visit on the weekends and spend time together, just like now. There's tons of father-son adventures that you can have there."

"That wouldn't work."

"Why not?"

Because that would leave little to no time to work on us. The thought startled Nick. The truth unnerved him. Did he really want an "us" with Sam? The past couple months had been amazing. What about six months from now? A year? Five? He'd had his pick of women since the age of sixteen. Variety had always been the spice of his dating life. All of his brothers were married and seemed happy. Nick thought he was fine living single. He enjoyed the bachelor life.

"Because I don't want to be a long-distance dad. I won't let you take him out of state."

"You won't let me? You can't stop me. You may be his

biological father but that's where it ends. Your name is not on his birth certificate. You have no legal rights."

"That can be changed."

"Where is this coming from? You've never seemed concerned about it before."

"You never before suggested moving Trey out of town!"

"You have all of the resources in the world and can see him whenever you want!"

"How about I set up an account to cover your flight expenses so that you can come here and see our son. Whenever, as you said."

"If you start a joint custody battle, believe me, you'll lose. There's no way a judge would grant that to a man who's known his son for less than six months."

"Whose fault is that?"

"Doesn't matter. The court will rule in the child's best interest."

"And you think that's away from an estate with over a thousand acres, with trees to climb and lakes to fish in? You think the judge will look unkindly upon an extended family that is successful in business and pillars of the community in a town that bears the child's grandfather's name? Don't bet on how a judge will handle this, Sam. Or on how hard I'll fight."

He heard a sigh and could imagine her pacing, running a frustrated hand through those gorgeous locs as she often did.

"Look, Nick. I don't want to argue. So far, you've shown yourself to be an amazing dad. I don't want to take away from Trey the opportunity for you to be a big part of his life. I also need to rebuild my business in a city that will provide an almost unlimited amount of potential clients. We should be able to make a decision that will work for all of us."

"There's an unlimited amount of work for you at CANN. You should come back to work here."

"I think that given the circumstances it's best that we keep our lives separate, except for Trey."

"I'm fine with that." Not. "As long as you remain here, where I can see my son as often as I like, and where he can grow up as part of our clan."

"You're being unreasonable, Nick. Are you using this as a way to get back at me for not having sex with you?"

"Do I look like a brother who can't get sex?" He instantly regretted the words and hurried on in an effort to clean them up. "This isn't about us. It's about Trey. The best place for a young, growing boy like him is in Breedlove, Nevada. I'll understand it if you decide to relocate. But Trey stays here."

Sam hung up without saying goodbye. She was pissed, no doubt. Nick didn't blame her. He'd be upset, too. But he meant every word he said. So much so that he reached for his phone, tapped the face and then a number. "Hey, Chris. Quick question."

"Shoot."

"Didn't Barry's divorce involve a custody battle?" Barry Hammel was an up-and-coming architect CANN had snagged from a competing firm.

"A straight-out war, brother. The wife used the poor kids as pawns. Brainwashed them into thinking Barry didn't love them. Insinuated that there'd been sexual abuse. It was ugly. But he won in the end."

"He got the kids?"

"Joint custody, and a ruling that without his knowledge and permission, she could not take the kids out of state."

"Do you know his attorney's name?"

"No, but I can get it. Why?"

"Sam's thinking about moving to LA. But Trey's not going anywhere."

Nick exited the highway as he ended the call, feeling sure about what he planned to do. He couldn't control what had happened in Trey's life before finding out he was the boy's father. But he'd have a hand in everything that took place from here. That was for damn sure.

Nineteen

An hour later and Sam was still so hot from the conversation with Nick that she probably could have flown over there on her own steam, with Trey tucked under an arm. He was beside her in the passenger seat gabbing away, excited to see his father. And the horses. And birds. For that reason, she played nice. From the answer to the text she sent, Nick wasn't calm either. His response to the fact she was on her way over? One letter. K. She reached the estate and waved at the guard who opened the gate for her to drive through. She'd been impressed with these lands since her first arrival. Nick's words wafted like rings of smoke in her ears.

It's about Trey.

It surely was, which was why Nick shouldn't have a problem flying to California. A child belonged with his mother, and this mother was about to be in LA.

The best place for a young, growing boy is in Breedlove, Nevada.

She slowed around a curve and took in the landscape. Breathtaking, with lush green grass, sparkling lakes, animals dotting the countryside and majestic mountains beyond. Straight out of a storybook. Did she have the right to deprive Trey of growing up here? Maybe not, but she couldn't imagine not having a daily presence in his life. Was it right to request it of Nick?

I'll understand it if you decide to relocate. But Trey stays here.

The obvious solution was for her to accept Noah's offer and stay in Las Vegas. But could she survive regular contact with a man she wanted for the long term but would most likely never have?

She pulled into Nick's driveway. Memories assailed her. The Thanksgiving holiday. His master suite. The night they'd spent under the stars making love. Sam jerked the door open. There was no time for a trip down memory lane. She had a plane to catch. Trey got out of the car and ran to the door. Sam had hoped Nick would be outside. Easy hand-off with little talk. He wasn't. She caught up with Trey and grabbed his hand as they mounted the twenty-plus steps to Nick's front door. The landscaping made for mind-blowing curb appeal, with its majestic waterfalls and towering trees that hid the five-thousand-square-foot man cave that Nick called home. A thought assailed her that was so unnerving she almost tripped.

Trey loves it here.

The door opened just as they reached the last step. Security system cameras, Sam surmised. He was at his home and could do what he wanted, but did he have to be shirtless, showing off the abs she loved to tickle with her fingernails? His hair was damp as though just out of the shower. He clutched a red towel hanging from his neck. He looked tempting. Devilish. Perfect for all sorts of sins. More images assailed her. She hadn't shared the details of that night with anyone, but she'd never look at a shower stall or marble bench the same.

Nick crouched to look Trey in the eye. "Hey, buddy. You ready to have fun?"

"Are we riding the horses again?"

"If you want."

"With Christina and Jaylen?"

"Sure."

"Yes!" Trey pushed past him and ran into the house.

"Trey!" Sam stepped around Nick. "Are you going to leave without giving me a hug?"

Trey spun around and trudged back toward Sam. "I forgot." The hug was brief and noncommittal. "Daddy, can I play video games?"

Nick nodded.

"Bye, Mama!"

They watched Trey race down the hall. Nick turned to her. "Hey."

"Hey."

The air pulsated with words neither dared say. Nick kept his feelings behind a hooded gaze.

"You coming in?"

Sam shook her head. "I need to get to the airport."

"Still going to LA?" He leaned on the doorjamb, cocked a brow, looked like a centerfold.

"Yep." Sam pulled the carry-on holding Trey's clothing and toys toward Nick. He reached for the handle. Their hands touched. Something akin to an electrical shock ran up her arm. It took everything within her not to jerk away. She played it cool, stepped back and headed down the stairs. She took a couple, then turned. "I'll be back Sunday night. Will text you on the way from the airport."

A short nod was his only response before stepping back into the house and closing the door. An uncomfortable feeling swirled in Sam's gut. She reached her car and hesitated before starting the engine and driving away. One of the clients she was scheduled to meet the next day interrupted her thoughts. By the time she arrived at the airport, the exchange with Nick had been forgotten. She boarded the plane and lost herself in 3-D designs.

Forty-five minutes later, the plane descended over the massive metropolis known as the City of Angels. Sam looked out at the imagery of the place she'd called home since the age of five, when her family left their Tennessee roots and chased her mother's acting dreams to Hollywood. It was a place she'd found a little scary but immediately exciting. Her family had settled in the San Fernando Valley. Sam flourished there. Her dad Marcus preferred country living. She'd always loved the city. Yet as the plane touched down and taxied on the runway, she felt strangely disconnected.

After securing a rental, she plugged into Bluetooth and tapped a number on her screen.

"Hey, Dad!"

"Hey there, babe. How you are you doing?"

"Good. But I'd be doing even better if you say you're not busy tonight and agree to meet me for dinner."

"You're here in LA?"

"Yep."

"For good?"

"Maybe. I'm meeting with two new clients and have an appointment with a Realtor."

"Is Trey with you?"

"No. He's with his dad."

"The prince is over here, in the States?"

The feeling of discomfort Sam had shaken during the plane ride returned and rumbled in the pit of her gut. Moving back to California wasn't the only thing she needed to share with her dad.

Marcus spoke into the silence. "It's a shame that child barely knows his grandfather."

"We need to change that. I'll bring him with me next time, promise. Where do you want to meet?"

"Hmm, there's a Mediterranean spot that opened up not far from here. I've been meaning to try it out."

"Text me the address. I'll meet you there."

Sam pulled into the parking lot of a restaurant anchoring a small strip mall. She spotted her dad's pickup and parked beside it. Inside, she saw Marcus right away.

"Hi, Daddy."

He stood to greet her. She melted into his embrace and was surprised to find herself fighting tears.

"You all right, baby girl?" Marcus asked after the hug.

Sam sat in the chair Marcus pulled out for her. "Life's a little crazy, but overall I'm good."

The first few minutes were spent perusing the menu while talking about family and mutual acquaintances. After they'd placed their orders and received their drinks, Sam felt her father's eyes boring into her.

"Why are you staring? Has it been so long you'd forgotten what I looked like?"

"Damn near." He shook his head. "Hard to keep up with that fast lane you're living in. I still don't know what happened with you and the prince."

"Just didn't work out, Dad."

"Was he violent? Did he hit you?"

"No."

"Was he a good father?"

"A great deal of his time was spent on royal duties. I don't doubt that he loves Trey, but he wasn't hands-on."

"I never understood why you married him in the first place. If you ask me, everything happened too fast. At least your mom got to see you wed."

Sam nodded. That her mom got to see her walk down the aisle was the best that could have happened.

"You came back from Africa, had barely unpacked your bags before moving to Nevada and now you're coming back here? Sam, what's going on?"

It was a dicey question. As far as her parents knew, Sam and Oba had met, fallen in love and enjoyed a whirlwind romance before her "unexpected" pregnancy led to a grandiose albeit hasty wedding. It was time to tell her dad about Nick.

"You remember why I moved to Las Vegas, to work on a specific project?"

"With the casino hotels."

"Specifically CANN International. It's owned by the Breedlove family. I worked on the project with one of the sons, a guy named Nick, whom I'd briefly dated in the past."

"Oh, Lord. Don't tell me y'all got into it and you lost a good job."

"No, the contract for what I worked on is over. But not me and Nick."

"You just got out of a marriage, honey. Now, I'm not one to tell you what to do but you might want to let your heart heal."

"Nick is Trey's father. He's my son's biological dad."

"Something tells me that for this story I might need something stronger than that cola I ordered." Marcus flagged down a server. "Miss!"

Sam gave her father the condensed version of what happened. Even with her father's questions, she wrapped up the story before the entrées arrived.

"What about getting more work down there, close to his father? It can't be healthy moving Trey around so much."

"There's more work here. Nick can visit often. It's a short flight. Plus, we'd be closer to you. Kids are fairly resilient. Trey seems to adapt easily. I think he'll be fine and you said it yourself, he needs to know his grandpa."

"He needs to know his daddy, too. The one he just met."

Sam thought her father would be thrilled about her move back to LA. Instead, having dinner with him brought up questions she'd thought resolved. When she boarded the plane Sunday night, however, her decision to move back to Los Angeles and reclaim her life held firm.

Sam arrived back in Vegas to a text from Nick to pick up Trey after Monday's preschool. She quickly unpacked her luggage and placed an order with her favorite Chinese restaurant for delivery an hour later. She turned on the water to fill the jetted tub, then walked back into the bedroom to undress. The zipper of her jeans was only halfway down when her doorbell rang. Sam looked at the clock and frowned. Surely that wasn't the delivery guy already. She'd just placed the order.

After rezipping her pants, she strode to the door and looked out the peephole. The man on the other side looked like a delivery guy. She opened the door.

"Yes?"

"Sam Price?"

"That's me. But I just placed my order five minutes ago."

The man reached into what she now realized was a pouch containing several types of mail. He pulled out a large manila envelope and held it out.

She took it. "What's this?"

"Those are papers that required a personal delivery. You've been served."

The man hurriedly turned and began walking away.

"Wait, who are you? What?"

"Have a nice evening, Ms. Price!" he yelled over his shoulder.

Puzzled, Sam watched the man until he'd reached the end of the short hallway that led to her unit and turned the corner. She eased back inside her house, closed and locked the door. She surveyed the envelope the man had delivered, then walked over to her desk, pulled the mail opener from a cup holding pens, markers and other office items, and slit it open. Inside was a stapled document of several pages. She didn't have to go past the first one for her world to tilt. The bold, black letters at the top stole the joy from the weekend—the new client, housing prospects, reconnecting with old friends, starting life anew again.

Nick had petitioned the court for primary custody of her son. What would she do now?

Twenty

Nick walked into work Monday morning carrying a bag of guilt. He could only imagine how Sam had reacted when she got served papers from him seeking primary custody of Trey. He wasn't sorry for filing them. He had every right to be a part of Trey's life, to share an equal role in raising and shaping his young, spongelike mind. He hadn't wanted to do it. His mother had suggested doing so from the time she learned she had another grandchild. He hadn't. There was no need. The arrangements he and Sam had agreed to worked for both of them. The less involvement the judicial system had in his life, the better. The conversation on Friday changed everything. Trey's living in California was not an option. Going from one home to another in the same town was hard enough. He would not subject Trey to commuting between states.

He'd barely fired up the Keurig in his office when Anita beeped in. "Mr. Breedlove, someone is here to see you."

Nick sighed. "Send her in."

He didn't have to ask who. Today there was only one person who would arrive at his office first thing unannounced. Sam. She swirled into his office, a look of anger mixed with determination on her face, and threw the order at him.

"You have some kind of nerve."

"I had to do it."

"You did not have to do this. We could have worked something out!"

"We tried that on Friday. You want to move to California. I want to keep Trey here. It's an impasse I didn't see us getting past without third-party intervention."

"You will not get my child, Nick Breedlove. I will do whatever it takes to keep him with me."

"There's no place you can run to with him that I won't find."

"I'll fight you tooth and nail, and I'll win. You didn't even know Trey six months ago. Do you really think there's a judge in any state in America who would assign a virtual stranger as the custodial parent?"

"Any judge would once they heard the details of how I was purposely kept out of being a part of my child's life. And for the record, I'm no stranger to Trey. I'm his father!"

"I never should have told you."

"You should have told me from day one."

"We've already been down that road. You know why I didn't."

"I know what you told me. It doesn't change the fact that it was wrong to outright lie to both me and Trey, presenting another man as the father of the child you claim to love so much."

Sam's gasp should have been a warning that Nick was going too far. But the horse was already out of the barn and running at a full-speed gallop.

"If that's true, prove it. Stop making it so difficult for me to be a part of his life. Stop thinking only of yourself and think of what's best for him."

"How dare you!"

"The best place for him is here, in Breedlove. If you want to continue having equal access to him I suggest you rethink your relocation plans."

"I hate you right now."

"You'll get over it. Or not." Nick strolled over to where the cup of coffee that was now lukewarm still sat in its holder. He felt Sam's eyes boring into his back and considering her state of mind right now, thought he'd be better off not turning said back.

He walked to his desk. "You're the one making this difficult. Not me. I offered a solution. You weren't interested."

"Moving into your home so that we could play family? So that you could have the life of an adult while still acting like a kid who'd not yet put his toys away? How was our living together supposed to look, Nick? How would the whole revolving-door dating situation work out? And once I found happiness, which I am ready to do, where would he and I hang out? Oh, but wait. Your home is pretty roomy. Or we could expand it. Each have our own wing to do our own thing."

"Ha! I wish you would try to bring another man into my house."

"I'd do so the minute you brought in another woman."

The intercom sounded. "Excuse me, Mr. Breedlove?"

"Yes, Anita. My nine o'clock meeting. I haven't forgotten."

"Just checking. Thank you."

Nick reached for a folder on his desk, opened it as he leaned back in his chair. "This conversation isn't going anywhere. Neither is Trey. You need to decide what's more important. Your career or your son. It's as simple as that."

Sam said nothing for several seconds, just stared, eyes narrowed, hands clutched into fists. She took a deep breath, walked calmly over to where Nick sat, and slapped him squarely across the face. Then with head high and back straight, she walked out of the room.

Nick watched her exit, slowly rubbing the area she'd smacked. "You're forgetting something," he said as she reached the door.

She paused, then continued out. Nick's eyes returned to the court papers she'd left behind. If someone tried to take his child he'd have them taken out. Given that consideration, that all she'd given him was one slap in the face, he'd gotten off easy.

Nick finished the nine o'clock meeting. He returned to his office, packed his briefcase and stopped by Anita's desk.

"I'm going to be out for a while. If anything urgent happens, hit me up. Tell everyone else I'll return their calls tomorrow."

"Will do. Are you all right, Nick? When that woman left she seemed extremely angry."

"Her name is Sam. She's Trey's mom."

"Oh."

"We're having a bit of a disagreement. But I'm okay. Hold down the fort."

Nick got into his Bentley Azure convertible, popped the top and sped down the highway. He was headed to the one person he could depend on in times like this. Someone whose advice was always spot-on, who gave it to him straight no chaser and suffered no fools.

Victoria Breedlove.

When he pulled into the circular driveway, he saw his father Nicholas just back from walking Ace, the newest family member. The long-haired Komondor with locs like Bob Marley, only blond, was a bit too friendly for Nick's taste and sure enough, the moment he saw him came bounding over, tail wagging, tongue hanging, ready for love.

"Hey, son."

Nick sidestepped the dog. "Hi, Dad."

"What brings you by in the middle of a workday?"

"Needed to talk with Mom real quick. Is she here?"

"No, son. She and Lauren left early this morning for an impromptu shopping trip."

"When will she back?"

"Day after tomorrow. They're shopping on the Champs-Élysées."

Victoria would choose this crucial time in his life for a Parisian jaunt. Exasperated, he let out a short huff.

"Something I can help you with, Nick?"

"I was hoping for a woman's perspective, but I guess you'll do."

"Ha! Come in. Let's have a cigar."

They walked through the spotless mansion and entered Nicholas's office. The stately room, with its high ceiling, dark woods and a lingering scent of premium tobacco, had a calming effect. Nick felt his shoulders relax as he walked over and took a seat in one of two high-backed chairs that had been imported from France and were purported to have once been in the royal palace. He watched Nicholas pull down a box from the shelf, almost reverently, his eyes sparkling as he sat and opened the lid.

"New brand?"

"More than a brand, son. This is a happening."

Nick wasn't that into cigars but even he was impressed with the story his father told while carefully preparing the cigar to be lit. Learning about pre-banned Cuban and Dominican leaf-wrapped tobacco that had been soaked in the most expensive cognac created, and that only one hundred boxes of the exclusive brand were sold each year, made Nick eager to taste it. Once he did, he was even more impressed. People didn't spend five hundred a pop without blinking for one cigar for no reason.

The next few minutes were consumed in the ritual of cigar smoking, of enjoying the first puffs of the exclusive smoke in the silence it commanded. Nick knew his dad took his cigars seriously and waited for him to break the silence.

He blew out a puff and smiled at Nick. "Now, for sure, I've lived."

"It's amazing," Nick agreed.

"Okay, son, tell me why you're here."

"It's about Sam."

"I figured as much."

"And Trey."

A slight frown marred Nicholas's handsome face, an

older, slightly more rugged version of Nick's. "What about my grandson?"

"Sam plans to move to LA and take him with her."

A slightly raised brow was Nicholas's only reaction. "What do you have to say about that?"

"I said hell no. Trey belongs in Breedlove. I tried to tell Sam that but she wouldn't listen. So I hired a lawyer. She got served papers last night. I'm going for primary custody."

Nicholas nodded. "Good for you." He tapped the cigar against a tray before placing it there. "What is your question for me?"

"Sam flew into my office first thing this morning, angrier than I've ever seen her."

"Can you blame her?"

"No. She was so upset that she slapped me."

"Is that all? Had I done something like that to Victoria I imagine she'd have come after me with something that held bullets."

"Mom wouldn't let anyone take us from her, which is why I feel bad for where Sam and I are now. The attorney and I discussed joint custody first. But that would involve an immense amount of travel for Trey, a disruptive school schedule, that every-other-holiday mess that would be painful as hell. I couldn't bear to put him through that and I will not live without being a part of his life. I didn't see any other way around it."

"You did what you had to do, son. I would have done the same."

"Seriously?"

"Without a doubt."

Nicholas's words were comforting and should have made Nick feel better than he did. He left the estate and headed to Adam's and a horse ride to further clear his head. He believed that filing for custody of Trey was the right thing to do. Then why did it feel so wrong?

Twenty-One

Sam stayed pissed for three days. She canceled a couple appointments. Didn't take calls. Except for texts to Danielle and her dad, calls from potential clients, and Trey of course, she didn't speak with anyone. The situation between her and Nick was too personal. She imagined that those close to her would be on her side, just as she assumed Nick's family had affirmed his position. In this instance, she'd seek her own counsel. After what felt like thousands of hours of thought, she made a decision and placed a call.

"Breedlove."

"Hi, it's me."

"Sam, if this is about Trey, I've been advised not to speak with you. Communication has to go through my lawyer."

"I've decided to stay." Silence. "Nick, did you hear me? I'm not moving to California. I'm staying here."

"What made you change your mind?"

"Trey. Not anything he said, but the decision became clear when I focused on him. I'd never deny Trey the chance of knowing and being close with his father. You were right. Breedlove is the best place for him to grow up. I'm not sure there are any affordable options for me out there, but it's worth finding out."

"I wish you wouldn't do that."

"What, move to Breedlove?"

"No, spend unnecessary money. I know you don't want to live with me, but there are guest homes available on the estate."

"I appreciate that, Nick, but that would be too close for my comfort. I care about you," she continued, voicing a truth she hadn't planned to share. "Not just as Trey's father, but as someone for whom I have a deep attraction. But you've made it clear that there's no chance for a real relationship. So I need to put myself in the position to attract the love I want. It's the most beautiful place I've ever set eyes on, but your family estate is not that place."

"I can understand that."

A major declaration and that's all he could say? Sam wasn't sure he understood at all. In fact, she'd place a CANN casino bet that he hadn't a clue she'd fallen in love with him.

"What are you doing later? Perhaps we can get together over dinner and discuss how to do what's in Trey's best interest from here on out."

"I can do that."

"What about seven? I'll book one of the private rooms and—"

"I'd rather we meet in a neutral location."

"Fair enough," Nick replied without hesitation. "You choose the spot."

"I'll text it."

"See you then."

After making arrangements to drop off Trey at Danielle's house, she texted Nick the address to her favorite Indian restaurant, walked into her closet and began the search for the perfect negotiation-wear. There was no mistaking the mission. This would be a negotiation. Sam needed to convince Nick to withdraw the papers requesting primary custody of Trey. She'd also like to increase the amount of time Trey and Nick had together; to work out something more regular than every other weekend and "whenever he was available or felt like it" they'd established just after Nick learned he was a dad. She wanted them to come to a place where if not being friends, they could at least be friendly. Sam didn't want Trey to grow up with them fighting, with him in the middle feeling that he had to choose. Sam wanted a lot.

She aimed to dress for success in this meeting with Nick. It was an interview of sorts, the most important one to date in her life. Jeans were out, as was a casual maxi or anything too sexy. Nick would perceive that as a ploy for favor or worse, a mixed signal of what she wanted. Her bed became littered with unacceptable choices. Her hand finally touched the perfect item—a grape-colored knee-length number that complemented her curves without squeezing too tightly. She pulled her locs into a loose topknot and left a few tendrils to hang around her face and neck. Swarovski crystal earrings and necklace were her only jewelry pieces. They matched the blinged-out slingbacks she chose to finish off the look. Makeup was minimal but the grape-colored matte MAC made her lips pop. A spritz of cologne and she was ready for her close-up.

There was little traffic. Sam arrived at the restaurant with ten minutes to spare. She parked, went inside and sat at the bar. Maybe a glass of chilled chardonnay would help calm her nerves.

A young bartender with a shock of red hair ambled over, slowly wiping the bar as he neared. "What can I get for you, pretty lady?"

"A glass of white wine, please."

The bartender rattled off a list of options. Sam settled on one and ordered the drink. Seconds later the door to the establishment opened again and all Sam could think was that a god had strolled in. Nick, looking incredible. Literally, good enough to eat. He wore black. Black suit, black shirt beneath it, black shoes. His face was clean-shaven, his hair newly cut. A diamond stud sparkled in one ear. Sam didn't even bemoan her body's reaction. The way her nipples pebbled and her inner walls clenched. For a woman not to react to a brother that fine she'd have to be blind. Or dead.

He approached her with a leisurely stroll and a hint of wariness in his eyes. "Good evening."

Sam gave a cool nod warmed by a soft smile. "Nick. How are you?"

"I'm okay." She felt him relax. "You look nice."

"Thank you." He looked better than nice, greater than amazing and finer than wine. Sam kept that opinion to herself.

The waiter returned. "Your chardonnay, ma'am." He looked at Nick. "What can I get for you, sir?"

"I'll order from the table." Then to Sam. "Shall we?"

The server led them to a corner booth of a spacious dining room. The stark linen, dark carpet and dim lighting made for a romantic ambiance. The smell of Nick's cologne that wafted past Sam's nose as she walked beside him made her work to remember that this was basically a business meeting. Definitely not a date. She wished it were. After they'd ordered and the server had gone, Sam spoke up.

"I'd like to start this conversation off with an apology. I can't remember ever being as angry as I was that day in your office but it doesn't excuse my behavior. I should not have slapped you. I'm sorry."

"I think both of us could have said or done things differently. I accept your apology and offer mine as well. There has never been any doubt in my mind that Trey comes first in your life. For me to suggest otherwise may have warranted a slap. And for the record, woman, you pack a mean palm."

"I've never hit anyone in my life. Losing my temper like that was not cool. The suggestion that I would put work before Trey cut deeply. But hearing that caused me to take a step back as well. It made me become unflinchingly honest with myself and the real reasons behind my decision to move back to LA."

"Something besides it being a bigger, better market with more potential for work?" Nick reached for his water glass.

"Yes." Sam's chin lifted a bit as she said, "I was relocating to get away from you."

Nick almost spewed out his drink. "Whoa!"

"Too honest for you?" Sam shrugged. "It's all I've got. I figure being as honest as possible is the only way to move forward, the only way we can develop an authentic relationship where we get along. Again, for Trey's sake."

"How was I responsible for you wanting to move?"

Sam gave him a look. "You have no idea?"

Were men really that stupid?

"You want to get married but… I'm not ready for that."

"I know. That's the problem. It's difficult for me to be around you and not…want to be with you. Yet it's hurtful to be with you intimately and know that's all it is."

"That's all it was the night we met. We were practically strangers."

"Which is why it was easy. My heart wasn't involved."

Nick eased back against the booth, sipped his water. No response. Sam figured it was just as well. Since he wanted to continue to sow his opulent oats, what was there to say? She decided it was time to stop talking about the "we" that wasn't and focus on why they were there.

"About Trey…"

He leaned forward, steepled his hands, engaged again. "Yes."

"I'd like you to withdraw your case for primary custody."

"Done."

Sam didn't try to hide her surprise. "Really? That simply? What's the catch?"

"No catch. I'll no longer seek primary custody. However…"

"Ah, here we go."

"Wait. Hear me out. I'm not a fan of the judicial system involving themselves in family matters unless absolutely necessary. We're intelligent people who both love Trey and want the best for him. I think we should be able to work out a mutually agreeable joint custody arrangement, one that will be drawn up by my attorney—"

"So much for no judicial involvement."

"This is legal involvement, an officially written position on what we both decide is best for Trey. It holds us accountable and in the case of another major disagreement would prevent either party from doing something crazy."

"Oh, so you're calling me crazy?" The twinkle in Sam's eye let Nick know she was teasing. The atmosphere lightened, a little.

"Not at all, though you did marry a prince you barely knew and move to the other side of the world. It's not a stretch to believe you could change your identity and appearance and go on the run with my kid."

Sam put a finger to her chin. "Hmm. Ideas."

"Woman, don't you dare."

"I wouldn't."

"There's not a place on earth you could hide with Trey. I can't imagine him not being in my life."

"Me either. Drawing up a legal document is reasonable, I guess. That way neither could change our mind and go off on a tangent."

"There's one more thing."

"What?"

"I want my name on Trey's birth certificate."

"Done, and we can change his last name."

"Really? That simply?"

"Stop mocking me."

"Hard to do. You're so pretty with a chagrined face."

"A chagrined face? Is that supposed to be a compliment? You'd better be glad your looks get you women because your flirt game needs work!"

Dinner was served. Nick and Sam fell back into the easy camaraderie that marked their being together when not fighting like cats and dogs. Over the next ninety minutes they worked out a schedule that suited them both. Because he was often busy weekdays, Sam agreed for Nick to have Trey every weekend, with wiggle room for special events or celebrations when Sam would want Trey with her. During the week, with advance notice, he could stop by and visit Trey, or take him out for dinner or to the estate. Nick understood how important it was for Trey to bond with Sam's father, and would give up a weekend or two if Sam was scheduled to be in LA. They discussed a few more particulars such as schooling, doctor appointments and male bonding during haircuts.

"One last thing."

Sam's fork stopped in midair. "You said that about the birth certificate."

"Okay, this is the last of the last thing." He paused to finish his bite. "I want you to move to Breedlove."

"If things were different it would be a dream come true. The place is like paradise. But we've already discussed this, Nick. I don't want to live on the estate."

"I know. You've made that painfully clear. So I called up a buddy of mine and asked about properties around town. Turns out there's a three-bed, two-bath place near the town center that just became available. It's small, less than two thousand square feet, and is a bit unfinished. I told him you were a designer and not to worry about that. It might be better that there's work to be done. You can put your own stamp on it."

"What's the asking price?"

"Don't worry about it. I'm buying it for Trey. I'm doing what I wasn't able to for the first four years of his life—be financially responsible. Take care of him."

It was a position Sam couldn't argue.

"So how does that work? The house would be in his name?"

"He's not old enough to own it legally until he's eighteen. I've established a trust for him. If you both like it and want to move, the home will be bought in his name through the trust."

"Good to know I get some say in it," Sam teased.

"Of course. He sent me a picture of the outside. Would you like to see it?"

"Sure."

Nick tapped his screen, scrolled a bit and then handed his phone to Sam. The home was nothing like the simple abode she imagined. On the outside at least it was stunning, a contemporary Craftsman, with what looked to be sweeping city and mountain views, and large windows across two-story ceilings that she imagined let in lots of natural light.

"If you'd like I can give you his number. You two could take it from there, let me know what you think."

Sam nodded. "Okay. This doesn't mean that for sure I'll move there but it's worth checking out."

Dinner ended. Nick and Sam went their separate ways. Her mind reeled with the implications of Nick buying the home where she and Trey would reside. She didn't know how she felt about that but damn if it didn't feel good hanging out with him again.

Twenty-Two

Nick bopped up the stairs and tapped a tune on his twin's doorbell before opening the door and walking inside.

"Yo, No!"

He continued past the impressive foyer and down the hall in Noah's new home. "Noah!"

Noah's expecting wife Damaris rounded the corner. "Wow, you're up early."

"A lot to do. Where's Noah?"

"Swimming."

Since facing health challenges the year before, Noah had taken to daily swims to keep his body toned and his back muscles limber. He and Damaris had built a stunning home near the estate's mountain range and included an indoor pool with a retracting roof for an outdoor feel in the summer months. It was a stunning construction, a clever mix of the English Tudor style popular in Damaris's home state of Utah and the clean, simplistic yet ultramodern look common in the Scandinavian country of Denmark, where Noah and Damaris traveled several times a year.

Nick bent his face to Damaris's stomach. "Hello, nephew!" He held the greeting as an echo.

Damaris laughed. "You mean niece."

"You'll have a son, trust me. Ask my mom," Nick threw over his shoulder as he proceeded toward the home's north wing that along with the pool contained a full-size exercise room, sauna and game room. "It's the Breedlove way."

He reached the pool. It was empty. "Twin!"

Noah came out of the shower, wiping off with a fluffy white towel. "It must have worked." He pulled on a pair of long shorts.

"What?"

Noah's lips eased into a smile. "Yeah, it worked. Sam's moving into the house."

"I'm pretty sure of it. Larry called last night. She made an appointment for a walk-through first thing today."

"I think you're on the hook, twin."

Nick turned to Noah. "What do you mean?"

"You know what. I think Sam has caught a big fish. You look like a man in love."

"I'm a father who wants a secure life for his son."

"And the son's mother. Don't even try to lie. That smile is too big for one little boy, even one with your DNA."

Nick didn't answer. The twin thing. When one of their hearts beat the other could feel it. No doubt Noah could feel the seeds of love for Sam that had been steadily growing in Nick's heart since before he even realized.

Noah began walking toward the main part of the house. Nick fell into step beside him.

"You're feeling pretty good about yourself, aren't you? By the way, you're welcome."

Nick gave Noah a playful punch. "I'll give credit where it's due. Sam would have never accepted a home I purchased for her outright.

"Going from the Trey angle worked perfectly. What mother would deny their son a beautiful place to live?"

"Not a smart one."

"Sam's very smart." Nick winked.

"Beautiful, too."

"Man, don't remind me. She showed up last night with a dress that hugged her body the way I wanted to do. Locs caressing her neck. Skin showing, eyes glowing. Damn!"

They reached the kitchen. Damaris had prepared a smoothie and handed it to Noah.

"Thank you, baby." Noah gave his wife a quick kiss.

"You want one, Nick?"

"No, I'm good."

"We'll be in the office, baby."

"Remember, love, the doula comes at ten. Will you join us?"

"Yes, Dee. I'll be there to learn all I need to know about helping bring my son into the world."

Damaris chuckled as she shook her head. "You two."

The men continued down the hall into Noah's office.

"You not going to work today?"

Noah shook his head. "Working from home, bro. That's the good thing about Utah being virtual. I can monitor everything from the central control center."

Noah referred to a layout in the next room that gave him the ability to see everything happening in CANN's Mountain Valley, Utah location, where Noah had done the impossible and brought gambling to the state.

"All right then, man. I'd better let you get to it." Nick walked over and gave his twin a shoulder bump and fist tap.

"You heading to the office, or over to your lady's new home in Breedlove?"

"She's not my lady."

"Not yet, but from the look in your eye when you talk about her...she will be."

Nick didn't answer his brother, but long after he'd left the house, slid into his fancy ride and headed toward the Strip, what Noah said stayed on his mind. Did he want Sam to be his lady under the terms she presented? Truth of the matter was he hadn't been with another woman since he and Sam reconnected. But he was only twenty-seven. Was he ready to commit to being a one-woman man for the rest of his life?

Once in the office his mind was quickly pulled elsewhere. A private island in the Seychelles that Christian and Nick had their eyes on for over a year had just come on the market. It was one of less than half a dozen large enough to hold the type of opulent casino hotel they wanted to construct, one that included individual tiki-type houses that would sit directly over the water. Both knew they had to act fast to secure the deal.

Anita buzzed him. "Boss, Silver State Bank is on line one."

"Thanks, Anita." Nick tapped the line. "Breedlove."

"Nick, good morning. It's Harold. How are you doing?"

"Any day is good that starts out with a call from the bank president."

The two men conversed about the hundreds of millions needed for the Seychelles project, and how they would go about positioning funds that would be used by a variety of parties across continents. They scheduled a meeting among all necessary players for later that week. Afterward, the chat turned more social. Updates on family, plans to play golf. Nick's phone pinged with a text from Larry. He wrapped up the call.

"Harold, I have to run. Nice talking to you, buddy. See you soon." He hung up the landline and returned the call to the real estate agent from his cell. "Larry, talk to me."

"Sold!"

"Ha! She liked it, huh?"

"Are you kidding? She loved it."

Nick stood and walked to the window. The smile on his face could have replaced the sun. Having worked with Sam on the CANN Isles projects, he'd gained valuable insight into her tastes and design aesthetics. He knew she'd love the high ceilings, the myriad of windows and the open layout. Everything installed was high-end, yet there was enough left unfinished for Sam to stamp it with her signature style. He couldn't wait to see what she did with the place. Not that he felt she'd invite him over. But he'd have to go there to pick up Trey. The child that he never thought he wanted was becoming ever more intertwined in his life, and either directly or indirectly leading him toward a certain destiny. And though he wasn't quite ready to admit it, even to himself, Sam's stock was rising, too.

Later that night, as he was thinking about her, Sam called.

"Are you sure you didn't have anything to do with selecting that house?" she asked.

"Why would you think that?"

"The backyard is a boy's paradise."

"I heard there was a rock-climbing wall," was Nick's noncommittal answer. "I think Larry also mentioned that it was open concept as well."

"We… Trey loves the house."

"Great. I'll put in an offer tomorrow."

The home had already been purchased but Nick had to follow the charade all the way through.

"I'm still grappling with the fact that you're buying the house."

"I understand. But it's an investment for Trey. When he becomes an adult he'll have a place to stay, or an investment opportunity. If the market continues to move in a favorable direction and the city expands outward, the price of that home could double or triple in the coming years."

"It's an amazing gift for him, Nick. Having a home and with it financial stability at such a young age. Thank you."

"You're welcome."

Nick got the impression she wanted to say more. But she didn't.

"Like I said, I'll get with Larry tomorrow to put in an offer. When is the lease up on your condo?"

"Month after next."

"Will that be enough time for you to get the home ready?"

"I think so, if I can get the right help."

"CANN has a healthy Rolodex of contacts—electrical, flooring, installation, landscaping. We have established accounts within all of construction. I'll give you a card to get whatever you need."

Again. Silence.

"For Trey."

"Yeah, okay."

"I'll be speaking with my attorney later this week, to have him draw up the papers we discussed."

"You mean that you demanded?"

"Demanded is a rather harsh way of putting it, don't you think?"

"Do I have a choice in whether or not to participate?" Nick didn't have a comeback. "As I thought. I believe demand is perfect."

"Sam…"

"It's okay. I'm sorry. It's been a long day."

"Do you want to talk about it?"

"No."

"Listen, I don't want the legalities of my involvement in Trey's life to become a problem between us."

"It won't. I understand why you're doing what you're doing."

"But you don't agree with it."

"I wish it wasn't necessary but considering the circumstances and not knowing what tomorrow will bring, I guess it is."

Nick stretched out on the couch, feeling a strange yet definite comfort having Sam's voice in his ear.

"The document will only outline what we previously discussed. I want you to feel comfortable with what you're signing. So I'll have a draft version sent over to you before we lock in the wording. If you find a problem, let me know. We'll work it out. The attorney drafting this is Coleman Hughes. I can send his number as well, so you can ask any questions you have directly."

"I appreciate that."

"See how easy life is when we get along?"

"Bye, Nick."

Said sternly yet softly, in a way that made Nick feel all warm and sticky inside.

"Bye, Sam."

Nick watched a bit of television before retiring to bed. He lay awake for a long time, thinking about his dating life, trying to recall the women who'd most affected his life. There'd been more than a few but for the life of him Sam's was the only face that came to mind.

Twenty-Three

Sam's professional life was in chaos but thanks to Nick, the personal side was easy breezy. Diving into Trey's home's renovation brought the joy she felt these days. As for her son, she'd never seen Trey so happy. Every afternoon after preschool when they went to the home, he was out of his seat almost before the wheels stopped turning. The back-yard was already his unspoken domain. The construction team had surprised both of them with a customized wood-and-steel fort-styled playground with holes for play shoot-outs and an enclosure to take cover. There was a slide and swings and beyond those, a sandbox. Behind it was a mini-trampoline. Sam was sure that Trey could live out there until he was a teenager and except for meals and bathroom breaks be perfectly fine.

"Sam!"

Danielle's voice bounced throughout the largely empty rooms.

"In the bedroom!"

"Which one?" Danielle said, with a laugh.

"Master."

Danielle stepped into Sam's favorite space. "Ohmygood-ness! Look at your chandelier and ceiling fan combo. Just like you wanted. Where did you find it?"

"What I envisioned wasn't out there. I had it designed."

"Looks like it cost a fortune. Are the blades glass?"

"It's the next level up from PC, polycarbonate plastic. It's lighter and more durable than glass."

"I love the shape, like a sexy octopus."

"Now that you mention it, there is a resemblance."

"The way the crystals sparkle and play off the shiny

stainless steel is just stunning. It's like magic. Every time I come over there's something beautiful and new."

Sam slid her hands into her jeans back pockets and looked around. "I have to admit, it's all coming together nicely."

"Nicely is an understatement. Sam, this place is amazing. It's perfect for you and Trey. Does it have a dimmer?" Sam nodded. "For those oh-so-romantic nights."

"With who, the hero from my latest Reese Ryan?"

"No." Danielle laughed at Sam's recent fixation with romance novels and her new favorite author. "Your baby daddy. I don't know when you're going to stop acting like a virgin and holding this all-or-nothing position. You love him."

"I never said that."

"Don't have to." Danielle spread her arms to take in the room. "Obviously he feels some kind of way about you. He's not just buying any woman a house like this."

"This house belongs to Trey."

"Son might own it but the mama runs it. Come on, Sam. Stop splitting hairs with the fact. Nick bought this place for you. He may not be ready for a relationship on your terms but love is a verb. The verbiage here is pretty awesome. Keep being stubborn and somebody else might snatch up that beautiful black king. Take a chance with your heart and let life flow!"

Sam kept the chain around her heart firmly in place by ignoring everything Danielle said. Easy for her to think life clear cut. She and Scott had dated off and on for years before tying the knot. Danielle had no idea what it was like to have your mind blown and body scorched by a lover like Nick, to be in the company of someone brilliant and witty and sexy and strong, and know that at any moment it could be over. That someone he felt was more beautiful or exciting could come along and take away his breath.

After the Thanksgiving holiday, when she didn't hear

from him for a week and then the talk, when he made his preference for the single life abundantly clear, Sam tried to cut Nick from her heart. The longer she went without him, the deeper her feelings grew. It felt that if she ever again allowed herself a taste of him without promise, it would be like gambling with air.

Later that evening back at the condo, Sam was in the middle of a rare act—cooking. Trey had requested tacos, the one dish she'd mastered. He preferred hers to those from a drive-through. The day Trey shared this observation Sam had felt like a Michelin chef.

"Alexa, play nineties hip-hop."

Though Sam hadn't been alive when these songs were released, Sam's father Marcus was a die-hard nineties hip-hop head. It was the soundtrack of her life through high school and beyond, along with today's popular pop, neo-soul and a little R&B. While bobbing her head to the beat, Sam poured oil into a stainless-steel skillet. She crumbled up a couple pounds of ground beef, added it to the oil, then began chopping onions and peppers to add to the mix. She'd just reached for a jar of diced garlic when the doorbell rang. No one ever came to her house uninvited. Who in the heck could it be?

She quickly grabbed a towel and wiped her hands as she walked to the door. *Nick? What's he doing here? And what's he brought with him?* She opened the door and verbalized those thoughts directly.

"There is an explanation. Can I come in?"

"Sure. You probably texted me but I was in the kitchen and didn't have my phone with me."

"No, I didn't, but I couldn't help it. I got so excited about what I brought over that I headed out of the door without thinking to call."

"What could be that impor—"

"Daddy!" Trey bounded out of his bedroom and into the

arm that Nick had free. He placed down the large box he carried and scooped up his son. "What'd you bring me?"

"Who said what I have is for you?"

"It's mine, Daddy!" Trey said, laughing. "You never bring Mommy anything."

"Trey, Nick brings you goodies because you're his son."

"So? You're my mom!"

Sam locked eyes with Nick. "Kids."

"Gotta love them." Nick pulled the bag open. "Actually, son, this is for your mom."

"Really?" Nick had thought to bring a gift for her? Sam's heart fluttered.

"Well...in a way."

Nick reached inside the large bag and pulled out an equally sizable box.

"What is it, Dad?"

Nick's eyes warmed as he looked at Trey's cherubic up-turned face, his expression one of wonder and awe.

"Something pretty amazing."

All eyes were on the box as Nick pulled a cutter from his slacks pocket and cut the box top. He tossed protective bubble wrap to the floor, then lifted out a silver-colored head and torso with a childlike face.

Sam squinted her eyes. "Is that an r-o-b-o-t?"

Trey gasped. "It's a robot!"

Her eyes widened. Had his spelling capabilities grown that much?

"R. O. B. O. T!"

Yes, they had.

"The Academy is one of the best preschools in the nation," Nick said. "I thought you knew."

He pulled the bottom portion of the machine out of the box and now connected several wires before attaching the two parts together.

"Is it a robot, Dad?"

"Yes, but more specifically this..." He pulled a remote

from the box and tapped a button. Lights began to flicker. The eyes of the robot lit up a bright blue.

"It's Ven." He tapped another button. "Ven, say hello to Trey."

There was a short pause before the robot turned to where Trey stood wide-eyed. "Hello, Trey."

The voice was not the electronic, robotic monotone Sam expected, but that of a boy who sounded about Trey's age.

If possible, Trey would have jumped out of his skin. "Mom! He said my name! He talks! He said my name!" He took a step to approach him, then stopped, a bit unsure.

"It's okay, Trey. Ven is very friendly. In fact, in Danish, *ven* means friend."

"Can I touch him?"

"Sure, come on over." Trey walked up to the machine that stood slightly higher than the taller-than-average four-year-old. "Hold out your hand and say hey." Nick sniffed the air. "Is something burning?"

"Oh, shoot! The meat." Sam ran from the room.

Nick hollered after her. "Did I interrupt dinner?"

Trey tugged Nick's hand. "Dad, we were talking to Ven!"

"Hang on, son." Nick walked into the kitchen in time to see Sam scraping the contents of a skillet into the sink.

"What's that?"

"Before the doorbell, it was ground beef. Now it's burnt garbage." Sam flicked the garbage disposal switch. "Dang it! The one dinner Trey likes that I know how to fix and I mess it up."

"What were you making?"

"Tacos."

"It's my fault. I'm sorry."

"Daddy!"

Sam looked over the bar counter at Trey's impatient face. "It's okay. You'd better finish assembling Trey's gift."

Nick pulled out his phone and sent a quick text. "Okay,"

he said, walking back to where Trey stood next to the robot with remote in hand.

He nodded toward the robot but spoke to Trey. "Talk to him."

"What do I say?"

"What do you normally say when you meet someone new?"

"Nice to meet you?"

"Okay. Try that."

Trey looked at Ven. "Nice to meet you."

The robotic arm began to move. Trey gasped, then giggled with delight as the arm slowly raised until the rubberized steel hand was perpendicular to his waist. The mouth moved rhythmically. "Nice to meet you."

"Wow!" Trey threw his arms around Nick's legs. "Thank you, Daddy!"

Sam looked at Nick, as impressed as her son. "Where on earth did you get this?"

"Denmark. It's the next frontier of Breedlove Bionics."

"When did the company get into bionics?"

"They didn't. Noah and I did." He shared how similar technology had helped Noah through a health crisis. The twins had been so impressed that they started their own bionics company and hired personnel to design cutting-edge products.

"Last year, when the world changed and America found millions of children home from school and largely isolated, the group began toying with the idea of robots to replace the schoolmates they could no longer interact with physically. Video games are great, but nothing beats one-on-one interaction."

"I'd say. It's almost human."

"The wonders of AI."

"Daddy, can Ven and I go play?"

"No, honey. We need to run out and get you something to eat. Or I can have something—" The doorbell rang. Sam looked at Nick. "Delivered."

He began walking toward the door. "Mind if I get that?"

Sam simply crossed her arms. Nick opened the door, had a brief conversation with whoever was on the other side of it and returned with a large bag of something smelling delicious.

"What's that, Daddy?"

"Tacos." He winked at Sam. "Your favorite."

"Yippee! Mama, can Daddy stay for dinner?"

Two pairs of identical eyes fixed on Sam. There was only one right answer, yet it took several seconds to push it through her lips.

"Sure."

Trey grabbed Nick's hand and began pulling him toward the dining table. "Let's eat." He reached his seat and turned. "Ven!"

"Coming!" The robot rolled across the hardwood floor. It stopped beside Trey.

"Sit down!"

The robot did, except there was no chair. It toppled over. Everyone laughed.

"It's a prototype," Nick offered. "Needs more work."

"If you pull out the food, I'll grab dishes and pour drinks."

"You got it."

Sam entered the kitchen feelings all sorts of ways. The scene was too comfortable, too homey, too much of what she wanted but knew could never be. She gritted her teeth, ready to pull and lock emotional bars around her heart. Then she heard Danielle.

Take a chance with your heart and let life flow.

Might as well, Sam decided. Life was heaven whenever he was around and close to hell without him. Right then she determined to stop living in the future and enjoy what happened now. An image of what could happen flashed into her mind and caused her walls to constrict. Nick had brought Trey a playmate. She was in love. Maybe it was time to let Nick be her boy toy again.

Twenty-Four

Something shifted after the night filled with tacos, laughter and Ven. Nick and Sam settled into a comfortable co-parenting flow, centered on their shared love and adoration for Trey. They began spending more time together, the three of them, at least once a week. The two who'd started out as lovers now began getting to know each other and becoming friends. Sam invited Nick to check out the ongoing new home renovation. Nick invited Sam out for horseback riding. Sam invited him to the condo for tacos she'd cooked. That night, Nick helped her stack the dishwasher before settling on the couch to watch an animated feature. Trey fell asleep before the movie ended. Nick and Sam watched it until the end. Afterward it felt totally natural to carry Trey into his room and tuck him into bed and when he turned, having Sam leaned casually against the wall watching them was the perfect portrait.

He'd almost kissed her that night.

That was a month ago and since then, his desire to do so had only deepened, along with his feelings for her. Watching Sam with Trey made his heart sing. She was an incredible mom. She was an intelligent, business-savvy, beautiful woman. She was the best interior designer in the game. And she wanted him. He could feel it, could see it in her eyes. There was only one thing in the way of their reconnecting on a deeper, more intimate level. Her terms.

Tonight, Sam had invited him to what she'd termed a "small gathering" in her new home. She and Trey had moved in the week before. He'd been in the Seychelles finalizing the island purchase and couldn't wait to get home. Tonight, he'd have two things to celebrate with Sam. His new island. Her new home. The invitation had listed dress as business casual. It had been an unusually cold winter. As Nick walked into his dressing room, he was definitely feeling the fresh newness of spring. He walked past rows of signature black and stopped at a group of clothing recently sent over by A-list fashion designer Ace Montgomery, items tailored for him from his spring collection. His hands caressed the expensive fabric as he checked out each piece, bypassing a baby blue suit of finely spun wool and a deep gold number that gave a nod to the seventies leisure suit. He paused at a pair of ivory-colored slightly baggy trousers, a sophisticated mix of sporty elegance with a fitted waist, flared pant leg and 18-karat-gold threads running throughout. Since it was still a bit cool in the evenings, a light gold turtleneck was the perfect complement to the slacks. Nick finished the look with his new favorite timepiece—appropriately called the Billionaire—and his signature three-carat diamond stud. A splash of cologne, a cigar to enjoy later and he was out the door. On the way over, he ruminated on his decision for a housewarming present. To think what he'd chosen was a good idea may prove to have been presumptive. Time would tell.

Pulling up curbside, Nick couldn't help but feel proud of Sam's handiwork. He'd purchased the house but she'd made it a home. The landscaping was impeccable, lush and commanding without being showy. Carefully placed outdoor lighting highlighted the slate siding, the redbrick walkway and the front door's stained glass. He tried the knob. The door opened. Softly playing neo-soul greeted him amid a din of cheery-sounding voices. He glimpsed himself as he passed a mirror in the foyer and noted how the five-foot floral arrangement anchored the hall just as he thought it would.

He reached the living room and stopped to look around. The first person he recognized was Sam's cousin Danielle, who spotted him at the same time, waved and walked over.

"Hey, Nick!" They exchanged a light hug. "Well, don't you look like a breath of spring!"

"Thanks, Danielle."

"Call me Danni. The other is only used if I'm in trouble or in court."

Nick chuckled. "Got it."

As they briefly exchanged chitchat his eyes scanned the room. He wasn't surprised to see faces he didn't recognize. Noah was there with Adam and Ryan, along with Larry and his girlfriend. Their eyes met, followed by a head nod as Larry held up a drink in greeting. His perusal continued beyond the L-shaped living room into the dining room, where Sam, looking like the queen that she was, sat chatting animatedly with a handsome older man.

"That's her father," Danielle offered, having followed his eyes.

"Really? He came down from LA, huh. Nice."

"Sam was very excited to show this place off." Danielle leaned in. "She may never tell you but she has never treasured anything more than she does this home. She always corrects me when I say her house—" she used air quotes "—by telling me that you bought it for Trey. That may be true legally. But a part of me says you bought it for the both of them. Am I right?"

Nick missed the last of what Danielle was saying and didn't hear her question at all. In the middle of it, Sam had looked up and seen him. Her eyes widened slightly. She said something to her father, who looked over, before rising to come toward him. She looked like an ebony goddess, draped in an ivory jumpsuit that made Nick jealous because it hugged her body the way his arms longed to do. The simple elegance of the one-piece, one-shoulder design was complemented by gold jewelry. As she grew closer, he noticed thin strands of gold beading wrapped around an errant loc. No adjective was strong or accurate enough to describe the perfection before him. His body reacted on its own. Arms reached out and pulled her into a light yet firm embrace.

"You look incredible," Nick murmured huskily into Sam's ear before releasing her. "I see you got the ivory dress code memo."

Sam smiled. Nick's penis pulsated. If his hormones continued raging, this was going to be a long night.

Sam appreciated Nick's hug and teasing comment. It gave her time to catch her breath, gather her composure and recover from seeing the man she had fallen head over heels in love with walk into the room and outshine everyone present.

She couldn't deny it now if she tried. Not after seeing this six-foot-two-inch bundle of *GQ*-sexy stroll confidently into the room. She. Was. In. Love. With a capital *L*.

"You look good, too. I can't believe you're not wearing black!"

"It's springtime, according to the calendar at least. Thought I'd switch it up a little bit. It seems that great minds think alike."

"Indeed."

Danielle loudly cleared her throat. "Um, clearly I've been dismissed."

"My apologies, Danni," Nick began, a hand to his chest.

"Save it. I'm just teasing." Danielle reached into her purse. "You guys belong on a magazine cover. Let me take your picture. By the fireplace." She adjusted her screen. "All right, here we go."

All eyes turned and conversation stilled as Nick and Sam struck a pose.

"Give me a couple more."

They offered another angle, then Nick surprised Sam by twirling her around and dipping her down.

Danielle squealed. "Perfect!"

The room broke out in applause. Sam was completely embarrassed. But damn, that man smelled good.

Nick looked around. "The place looks incredible, babe. Perfect for entertaining."

"It's exactly what I wanted. There's not one thing I would change. Come with me. There're a few people I want you to meet, starting with my dad. And while he's probably not as…curious…as your mother, there may be more than one question from him that you won't want to, nor are obligated to answer."

"Thanks for the warning."

"Ha! Anytime."

Sam was surprised at how nervous she was for her dad to meet Nick, and how much she wanted him to be impressed by the man walking confidently beside her.

"Dad, I'd like you to meet my former business partner and Trey's dad, Nick. Nick, this is my dad, Marcus Price."

"A pleasure to meet you, sir."

Sam watched her father measuring Nick up. "Likewise."

"Considering we just met I might be speaking prematurely," Nick said. "But would you by any chance like a good cigar?"

"Why? Do you have one?"

Nick nodded. "Have you heard of the Cubano Rare?"

Marcus looked from Nick to his daughter and back. "You have one of those?"

Sam couldn't guarantee it but was pretty sure she heard reverence in her dad's voice.

"In my car. It'll blow your mind."

Marcus slapped Nick on the back and gleamed at Sam. "I like this guy already."

Sam's smile reflected how happy and relieved she was that Nick and her dad seemed like they'd get along. Because the truth of the matter was not only was she in love with her child's father, but she really liked him, too. The next time the opportunity presented itself, she intended to let him know how much.

Twenty-Five

A month after Sam's housewarming, she was on a CANN private plane headed to the Bahamas. Nick was beside her, but the trip wasn't about work. It was about their burgeoning ongoing attraction. And what they were going to do about it.

During the flight over they kept the conversation light, mostly about Trey, now truly a Breedlove, having had Nick's name added to the birth certificate and his last name officially changed. They talked about the home on a small island not far from Nassau that because of legal and other logistics had only recently been completed, and even flirted a bit. The plane's landing was smooth and once outside, they were welcomed with hugs from the balmy Bahamian wind. After a short helicopter ride from the capitol of Nassau to CANN Isle-Bahamas—the home that would be their private paradise for the next several days—the couple were minutes from their final destination. With everything about Sam having driven him wild for the past few hours, Nick couldn't get there soon enough. He and Sam hadn't yet moved out of the friendship zone back into that of lovers, but he hoped this trip would change that.

They reached the home that in luxury and originality rivaled the New York villa that was Sam's first assignment. They were met by the house staff, conferred with the chef, and went to change for an agreed-upon swim before dinner. Nick went to one of two matching master suites. He donned swim trunks, grabbed a towel and slipped into a pair of sandals. Stepping into a living room shared between the two suites, he encountered a sight that stopped him in his tracks. Sam's juicy booty, a work of perfection that was just right for squeezing, swayed rhythmically from side to side as she walked toward a patio on the other side of the room. She wore a gold-colored wrap over a bikini bottom almost powerless to fully encase her lusciousness. Its luster made her ebony skin appear all the more radiant, wrapped in a way that highlighted curves deadlier than those found in Tail of the Dragon, one of the most scenic roads in Tennessee. He'd gripped the handlebars of a rented Harley while navigating its 318 curves in eleven miles, but it didn't compare to the ride he experienced whenever he journeyed to paradise with Sam in his arms.

Sam turned, her brow arching when she discovered Nick in the room, watching her. "You coming?"

Nick's long strides quickly ate up the distance between them. "I'll come later," he whispered once beside her.

"One-track mind."

He grabbed her hand and squeezed it. "The best kind."

The two accepted refreshing adult drinks from Colin, their thoughtful chef, then made their way to a stretch of soft, white sand, miles away from eyes that might be attempted to pry. After a brief splash in the water, they settled into a sturdy hammock erected under a tree by the shore.

"Hold my drink, please?" Sam handed her drink to Nick and then shifted her body to remove the wrap and settle into a comfortable position beside him. "There, that's better."

"If we're to keep this relationship platonic, I don't know about that."

He handed Sam back her drink.

"To us and a lifetime of adventures with our son."

"Eighteen years, anyway." Sam lifted her glass to clink it against the one Nick held.

"What, after Trey graduates from high school you're running away?"

"One never knows what the future holds."

Nick took a long sip of his beverage and pondered Sam's comment. He had plans for this vacation, felt fairly sure of how they'd go. But Sam was right. In life, nothing was guaranteed.

"How's your drink?"

"Delicious. I can't believe that here where they have the best rum in the world, you chose to drink beer."

Nick shrugged. "Obviously Colin got the memo. He knows what I like." He placed his arms more securely around Sam's shoulders. "When I find something I like, I usually stick with it."

"Hmm."

Sam said nothing more but the way she moved her butt so that it brushed his manhood made Nick believe his double entendre had been received.

"I like your stick."

"Now who's bringing it up?" He lifted his head to look her in the eye.

"Must be the rum."

"Hmm." His hands began a lazy journey up and down Sam's thigh. Goose bumps sprang up almost immediately, as did his python. He kissed her temple, shoulder, cheek. "I'm glad we did this."

"Me, too. So much has happened."

"I know."

They slipped into a companionable silence. Nick placed his foot in the sand to push the hammock into a gentle rocking.

"Did you ever think we'd get here?"

"I didn't even know there was a here here," he replied. "If someone had told me a year ago that I had a son and was about to be…"

"About to be what?"

"…in a serious relationship, I would have thought them way off. I thought life was perfect. Business going great. All the girls I wanted. I didn't know my life was empty until you came back into it. And brought Trey."

"Life is crazy."

"Right."

"Want to know something?"

"Hmm."

"I almost didn't go to that party."

"What party?"

"The costume party where we met. I'm not big on those types of functions."

"Then who do I owe the million dollars to for talking you into coming? Danni?"

"It was Danni, but I'd say you owe her at least two million."

"Naw, probably more like five or ten."

Sam shifted, turned up her face. "Kiss me."

He did. Leisurely. Lovingly. Sam gave as good as she got, even outlined his mouth with her tongue when they finished the sultry exchange.

"Damn."

"Uh-huh," Sam murmured, again grazing his dick with her behind in the way that he loved.

"Okay, baby, after that and on second thought, I'll just give your cousin a blank check."

They finished their drinks and swam in the ocean. The sun began to set, splashing vibrant colors along the sand and cooling the air. They went inside.

"The next time over, we'll have to bring Trey."

"He'd love that."

"Know what I'd love?"

"Another beer?"

"Another kiss." Nick pulled Sam to the couch and plundered her mouth. She had other plans, shimmied out from beneath him and turned her body so that her mouth faced his crotch. Without fanfare or permission she slid her tongue down the length of his penis, while softly fondling the family jewels. Nick had always appreciated a take-charge woman, especially one whose treasure hovered just beneath his nose. He placed a hand on each cheek, brought her heat to his mouth and slid his tongue between the fleshy folds.

Yum.

They took their time. Sam lavished Nick's dick from base to tip, using her fingers and tongue to make his slack member steel. Nick nibbled her pearl, sampled her star, feasted on her dewy kitty until she fairly meowed. Until the dew became a fountain of ecstasy, and she screamed his name. Nick could have easily joined her in going over the edge.

But this dance wasn't over. It was just getting started. He led them into the bedroom.

He removed their clothes. They lay down, flesh against flesh from head to toe. He eased his hand between her thighs, slid his fingers into her sweet spot and began to play. They kissed, the essence of love on their tongues—swirling, dancing, flicking across the cavernous warmth until he reached such depth of passion Nick thought he might drown.

"Who does this belong to?" His breath was hot, branding, as he whispered into her ear.

"Me."

"After all that good loving?" Nick said. "Wrong answer."

Sam chuckled, her hand lazily running over six-pack abs. "Oh, really?"

Nick slid off the bed. "Get on your knees."

Sam traced a finger along his jaw. "What if I don't want to?"

Nick smiled. "Oh, you'll want to."

She chuckled and rose to her knees as instructed.

"Turn around."

She complied, her round, plump booty in the air and fully exposed. Just right and ripe for...plucking.

With a hand on each hip he eased her body to the edge of the mattress. The king-size four-poster was the perfect height for the takeover he had in mind. He watched Sam wiggle her backside. Impatient. Anticipating. But Nick wasn't in a hurry. They had all night.

Nick reached over for the glass of water on the nightstand. He took a drink, held a cube in his mouth, then quietly dropped to his knees. Instead of the warm, hard shaft she was expecting, a cold sword of delectation slid into her womanly folds.

A harsh intake of breath followed. Goose bumps appeared. She pulled her body away. But not far enough. With Nick's hands still securely on her hips, he held her body in place and continued his relentless assault. Sam swirled her hips against his tongue. He bathed every inch of intimate areas, kissed and massaged her smooth, dark skin. After she'd cried out for the second time he stood, placed his dick at her core, then slowly, oh...so...slowly, eased himself inside her. His manhood pulsed with pleasure at her tightness, even after having a kid. He pulled out to the tip, then slid in again. In. Out. Thrust. Sway. He went at this pace for as long as he could, then settled into a rhythm he could have danced to all night. On the bed. Against the wall. Out on their private balcony, where the breeze was as hot as the sex. Back in the room on a chaise, he covered her and entered her completely.

"Whose is this?" His voice was harsh, labored, as his body rumbled. He scorched her insides with passion, pressed himself deeply into her core. Over and over he loved her. Their bodies shone with the evidence of the hearty endeavor.

"Who. Does. This. Belong to?" A thrust punctuated each word that was growled.

He felt her body grip him, heard the familiar sounds that began at the base of her throat, felt her grinding faster against him.

"Ah! Oh my God!" Sam screamed with pleasure.

Nick quickened the pace, joined her in cascading over the edge. Spent, satiated, they crawled into bed.

Sam kissed him lightly, snuggling her backside against him. "You," she whispered, and fell asleep.

The deep sleep lasted just a few hours. Awakened by the

hazy Bahamian sun, Nick stretched amid a yawn. He rolled over slowly so as not to awaken the sleeping beauty. Perched on an elbow, he took in her serene expression. It shouldn't make someone this happy watching somebody else sleep. A few minutes is all he lasted until he kissed her. Softly, just at the edge of her eye.

Her lids fluttered before her eyes opened fully. The look in her deep brown orbs was mesmerizing as her lips slowly morphed into a smile.

"Good morning, beautiful."

"Good morning. I can't believe you're awake already."

He nodded toward the open balcony door. "The sun."

Sam perched on her elbow and looked over her shoulder. "This view is to die for, truly paradise."

She threw her arm over Nick's body, resting her hand on his shoulder. "I think I kinda love you."

Nick kissed the top of her head. "Really?"

Sam fixed him with a look. "And?"

"You aiiight."

She reached behind her for a pillow to smack him. "Just all right?"

"Okay. Better than all right."

Sam turned her body to face him directly, adopting her sexiest tone. "How much better?"

Nick licked his lips. "Damn. A lot more. So much so that…wait a minute. I can show you better than I can tell you."

He bounded out of bed.

"Nick, where are you going?"

"Be right back!" There was the sound of rumbling before Nick spoke again. "Okay, now close your eyes."

"Why?"

"Must you always engage that beautiful brain? Just do it, woman!"

"Okay."

Nick peeked around the corner before walking back over to the bed. "Okay, hold out your hands."

"Why? Okay, never mind." Sam lifted her hands. The sheet floated away from her body. Her nipples pebbled against the early-morning breeze. Nick almost forgot what he was about to do. Change both of their lives. After which, there would be plenty of time for lovemaking.

Still, he kissed the exposed nipples before covering her up.

"You're making it hard to keep my eyes closed."

"Yeah, you're making me hard, too. You've made me a lot of things. An executive with rental properties sold out worldwide. A father to the most adorable boy on the planet. A man who's ready to stop playing around and make a real commitment."

Sam's eyes flew open.

"What did I tell you?"

"I can't keep them closed when you're talking like this! What are you saying?"

Nick reached for her hand, began stroking her finger. "I'm saying that I love you, and that I'm in love with you."

He brought the hand from behind his back and slipped a ring on her finger.

Sam was shocked speechless, her eyes tearing up as she gazed into his.

"I'm saying, Samantha Price, that I can't imagine spending my life without you and Trey, and maybe a few brothers and sisters for him to play with."

"Nick…"

"I'm asking if you'll do me the honor of becoming my wife. And that the only acceptable answer is yes."

Sam's eyes sparkled. She remembered. It's the same thing he'd said when she got offered the job.

"Are you sure that's the only acceptable answer?"

"Unless or until I hear it, we're not leaving this island."

"Well, in that case…yes, Nick Breedlove. I'd love nothing better than to become your wife."

"Good answer."

Without another word he reached over, slid the sheet away from her body and began covering it with soft, wet kisses. There were no more secrets, big or little. Tonight, there was only love…

* * * * *

UNDER HIS OBSESSION

CATHRYN FOX

For my dear friend Claudine Laforce.
You are kind, generous and supportive and
I'm lucky to have you in my life!

CHAPTER ONE

Khloe

"THERE'S THE DOOR. Feel free to use it."

Stomach in knots, I stare wide-eyed at my boss, hardly able to believe what I'm hearing. Then again, is it really so inconceivable that he's canning my ass? Disobedience comes with a price, and like all other men in power, Benjamin R. Murray, owner of *Starlight Magazine*, can do what he wants and say what he likes. Privileged men like him think the world is theirs for the taking and will walk on, or over, anyone who gets in their way.

"You're really firing me?" I ask, as Manhattan's midday sun shines in through the floor-to-ceiling windows, warming the blood zinging through my veins and stirring the nausea in my stomach. My skin begins to moisten, but no way will I let this man see me sweat. I don't want him to think he holds all the cards. Even though he does. But I'm not a girl to go down without a fight.

"That depends." Benjamin drops the chicken leg he's been gnawing on and wipes greasy, sausage-thick fingers on the stack of paper napkins before him. His chair groans under his impressive weight as he pushes away from his desk and stands to square off against me. The situation is clearly dire if he's abandoning his beloved bucket of chicken. "Are you going to do the exposé on Will Carson or not?" he asks. His deep voice is hard and unwavering, letting me know my future at the magazine depends on what I say next.

Though I can't afford to lose this job, I refuse to dig up dirt on Will Carson, a brilliant software developer—aka, the Millionaire Rocket Scientist of Wall Street. Partly because the exposé done on him a few years back by one of *Starlight*'s reporters ruined his life and partly because my father used to work for Will's grandfather, James Carson.

James isn't like other powerful men—he treats those who work for him fairly, respectfully. He was always generous and kind to my late father, going above and beyond to make sure a single father and his daughter were looked after. I have no doubt those care boxes containing food and clothes came from him—he knew my love for M&M's and somehow my size—even though he vehemently denied his involvement.

The man owns half of Manhattan, and after I graduated with a journalism degree, he offered me a job at the *Grub*, a magazine that reviews restaurants.

I politely declined, since I live off frozen food and know nothing about fine dining. Although it might have been a better jumping-off point than *Starlight*.

I want to write meaningful articles, to earn my place in the cutthroat news business and to get there on my own merit. From watching my father, I learned to work hard and to never take handouts—he didn't like it when those care boxes materialized on our doorstep. And I won't abandon my principles by twisting information for a headline like I'm some damn bottom-feeder.

Then why are you working at Starlight*?*

Because I can't get hired at a reputable magazine without experience, and I can't get experience without getting hired. So, *Starlight* it is. Or was…

"Well, are you?" he asks again, pulling my focus back to the matter at hand.

I cross my arms and plant my feet. "No," I say through gritted teeth. It's not a smart answer, considering rent is due next week, and my groceries consist of a single sleeve of stale crackers and a half-eaten box of pizza pockets.

"It's my way or the highway, Khloe," he says, his beady blue eyes arctic cold.

"Why me, Benjamin?" He doesn't tolerate anyone saying no to him, but what do I care? He can't fire me twice. "Why take me off sensationalized crime stories and put me on celebrity gossip, especially when you know I have a connection to the Carson family?"

His grin is sardonic. "That's your answer right there. You have an in, and any good journalist would use that connection to get information."

"You already ruined Will's life. Why twist the knife?" I ask, even though I already know the answer. Money. That's the answer to everything in a rich man's world.

"The public is interested in the famous Carson family. It's time we told them what Will has been up to since his fiancée left him."

Starlight's front-page spread on Will had never sat well with me. I've never met him, but from the stories James told, Will didn't seem like someone who'd get drunk and jump into bed with another woman at his bachelor party.

The pictures splashed across the front cover, however, painted a different story. Money and power. They mess with people. In the end, Will proved to be no different from any man with millions and authority—and because of the spread, he lost his supermodel fiancée. But I still refused to do the exposé. My father would turn over in his grave if I suddenly sank to slimeball level.

"I guess this is goodbye, then." I turn and see a flurry of activity in the hall. Great, my colleagues were eavesdropping. At least they'll have something to talk about at the watercooler. "I'll clear my desk."

"If you change your mind…"

"I won't," I say. Heads duck and eyes are averted as I walk down the hall. Despite the storm going on in my stomach, I straighten my back and calmly walk to my four-by-four pod.

I reach my desk and stare at the papers strewn across it. Nothing truly belongs to me, but I spitefully shove the stapler into my purse. I'm about to walk away but can't. Dammit, I'm not a thief. I put the stapler back and go still when a pair of heels tap rapidly on the floor, growing louder as they approach.

Breathless, Steph skids to a stop. "I just heard." My only real friend at the magazine—all the others would slice and dice anyone who got in their way— Steph takes my hand. Thick painted lashes blink rapidly over caramel eyes. "What happened?"

I lower my voice and explain, even though I'm sure everyone knows—around here, rumors spread faster than a Sean Mendes You Tube video.

"He's such a worm," she says.

"Hey, don't insult worms. They have their purpose."

"Wait, I got it." Hope fills her eyes. "Just say you couldn't find anything on Will. I mean, he might be a grade A asshole—"

"Will's an asshole?"

"Yeah, that's what every reporter who tried to get a story on him says."

"They do?"

"Oh, yeah." She holds her hand out and starts tapping one finger after another as she says, "Opinionated, arrogant, bossy, patronizing."

"What you're saying is he's no different from any other Wall Street millionaire."

She nods. "I also heard he doesn't keep any of his assistants around for long. They're fired for the smallest of mistakes."

"I guess I haven't been paying close enough attention to the Carson family drama."

"Well, anyway, he's become a bit of a recluse, taking privacy to the extreme. You could just say you didn't find anything."

I give her a look that suggests she's insane. "Steph, come on. If I don't bring the story Benjamin wants or twist it to his liking, I'll be fired anyway."

"But I don't want you to go." She pouts. "You can't leave me here with all the two-faced piranhas."

"You have that interview with the *Cut* next week, right?" While it's Steph's dream to write about trends and designs, I'm more interested in politics and current events. My ultimate dream is to write for the *New Yorker* magazine, and in my spare time, pen a novel.

"Yes, but—"

"No buts. You got this. And something will come my way," I say. I hike my purse up higher and lift my chin, showcasing confidence I don't currently feel.

Steph steps to the side to let me pass. "If he offers it to me, I'll tell him to shove it up his—"

"Thanks, Steph, but I don't want you to lose your job, too."

"The *Cut*, remember." She jabs her thumb into her chest. "It's mine."

"Good girl," I say, and give her a hug. "I'll text you later."

"Wait, Khloe." Her gaze moves over my face. "Are you sure you're okay? You look a little pale."

"I'm fine."

Her eyes narrow. "You need some sun."

I run my tongue over one of my molars. "A piece of filling chipped off this morning." There had been something strangely hard in the sausage on the left-over pizza I had for breakfast. "Maybe if I put it under my pillow, the tooth fairy will leave enough money for us both to go on a vacation."

Steph laughs. "Your sense of humor is still intact. I guess that means you're all right."

"I'll be okay," I assure her with false bravado.

I make my way to the elevator and realize that while I refused to do the exposé, the next person likely won't. Dammit. I hurry downstairs, step outside and hail a cab. But instead of going to my small apartment in Brooklyn, I give the driver directions to James's mansion on Sixty-Fourth. I have no idea if he's home, but he's well into his nineties, so I doubt he'll be out for long.

When we arrive, I pay the fare and step out, lifting my eyes to take in the looming building before me. I haven't been here since I was a teen. The first time I ever saw James's mansion was when I was five. I'd had the chicken pox, and the after-school day care teacher had sent me home. Dad had put me in the back seat, and I'd sat quietly as he'd driven James to wherever he needed to go. We'd picked up one of his grandsons from swimming lessons— apparently, he'd already had the pox, so it was safe to sit him in back with me. For all I know, it could have been Will beside me that day. I was quiet and shy, and other than answer a few questions James directed my way, I stayed silent.

Until I vomited all over the back seat.

I take a deep breath and step up to the front door of the mansion. Unease presses down on my shoulders as I jab the bell. I haven't seen James in years, and part of me worries he might think I was behind the last exposé. I wasn't, of course. I'd had no idea Avery Roberts was working on an article that would ruin a man's life.

Behind me, people rush by, always in a hurry. One of these days I'd like to go somewhere with a slower pace. Maybe write that book. But with the meager funds in my pocket, the farthest I could trek is to Starbucks, two streets over. When I got there, I'd have to order a water, no straw. I snort at that thought and pray that the tooth fairy comes through. But I'm quick to pull myself together when the door creaks open.

I expect to be greeted by a servant. Instead, James Carson himself is standing in the foyer, his hazy blue eyes moving over my face. I wait for recognition to hit, and I can tell the second awareness creeps in by the way his eyes widen.

"Mr. Carson," I begin, and place my hand over my uneasy stomach. "I don't mean to bother you—"

"Bother me. Of course you're not bothering me, child. Come in, Khloe. Come in, and please call me James."

"It's been a while. I wasn't sure if you'd remember me."

"You haven't changed a bit."

I can't say the same for him. Over the last decade, his winter-white hair has thinned, and the lines bracketing his milky eyes and pale lips have deepened. He's a little shorter, his body much frailer than it was when I last saw him.

"Come along," he says. Gnarled fingers tighten around a cane, and his gait is slow as he guides me down the hall.

"Maybe I changed a little," I say for lack of anything better. "It's been quite a few years."

"Ten, to be exact," he answers. While his body is deteriorating, it doesn't appear that his mind is following suit. I shadow him into his den and admire his extensive library as the vanilla smell of old books fills my senses. James turns and offers me a warm, grandfatherly smile, and my heart squeezes. He was like the grandfather I never had and always wanted. It was only Dad and me growing up. We lost Mom to cancer when I was just a child. I only have a few fleeting memories of her.

He winks at me. "Have you decided to take the job at the *Grub*?"

"The only thing I know about food is how to eat it, and even then, I make a mess of it. Believe me, I'm not cut out to cover restaurants and do reviews. I'd be a detriment, not an asset, to your company. But thank you for the offer."

"I always loved your honesty." He taps his cane on the wooden floor. "Max did a great job raising you."

Warmth fills me at the mention of my father. "You were always so good to us. My dad talked fondly about you."

"He used to tell me your dream was to write for the *New Yorker*."

"Still is," I say.

A beat of silence takes up space between us as we both get lost in our thoughts. A moment later, James breaks the quiet. "Then to what do I owe the pleasure of your company?" he asks, his voice gravelly as he smooths his hands over an imaginary tie and nods at the ebony leather chair.

I lower myself and sink into the soft cushion. It's heavenly, and if I weren't so anxious, my stomach roiling, I'd love to curl up and have a nap. Although I'm not sure why I'm so tired. I get enough sleep most nights, and it's not like I could be pregnant—unless it was immaculate conception.

"There is something I think you should know."

He walks up to his bar and picks up a brandy decanter. "Drink?"

After the morning I've had, I sure could use one, or two, but I politely decline. I'm not sure I'd be able to keep it down. He pours a generous amount into a crystal snifter, swallows it in one smooth motion, and refills his glass.

I wait as he slowly makes his way to the sofa across from my chair. I take stock of the room, my gaze going from the colossal desk in front of the window to the Polaroid camera on the side table. I note the stack of what looks like wedding photos beside it. I cringe, knowing they're not happy photos of Will's wedding, considering he never had one. While a part of me is mortified about the terrible invasion of privacy, I can't help but think his fiancée had a right to know what was going on. I sure as hell would have wanted to know. But I'd have to have a fiancé before he could cheat on me. Aren't I a real catch now? Jobless, penniless and soon to be homeless. I can't understand why men aren't lining up.

"You still work for *Starlight*?" James asks, like he's reading my mind.

I fold my hands in my lap. "As of today, no."

He straightens. "You quit?"

"Fired, actually. That's why I'm here."

The lines around his eyes deepen as he squints at me. "What is it you want me to know, Khloe?"

"First, I'd like you to know I had nothing to do with the exposé on Will. I had only just started at the magazine and had no idea they were doing a story on him."

"Never thought you were involved, child," he says quickly, and my shoulders relax slightly.

I lean forward and put my hands on my knees. "I was asked to do a follow-up today because I had connections."

He nods slowly and takes another swig. "And you were fired because you refused?"

"That's right." Yeah, the man is still sharp. "But I wanted to warn you and Will. I might have said no, but the next reporter won't."

"I appreciate you coming to tell me this." He sets his glass down, and his curled fingers adjust the gray cardigan around his shoulders. His eyes shut, and at first I think he's deep in thought, but he goes quiet for so long, I fear he's fallen asleep.

I'm about to rise and tiptoe to the door so I don't disturb him when his lids open and his blue eyes pin me in place.

"Do you have work lined up?" he asks.

"No, it just happened, but I'm about to start pounding the pavement."

"I have a job for you."

I shake my head fast. "While I appreciate your kindness, I—"

"As stubborn as your father." His chuckle is deep and raspy. "But you see, Khloe, you'd be doing me a favor."

"What kind of favor?" I ask, settling back in my seat.

"Will needs an assistant for his upcoming trip to Saint Thomas."

Oh God, a trip to Saint Thomas sounds heavenly right now. A Caribbean beach, sand, water… But I suppose if I'm in some boardroom taking notes for Will Carson, I'll see none of the island. Still, getting out of New York for a while does sound nice.

"It's a temporary job, until you find something in your field, of course."

I consider my meager savings. I'm adamant about making my own way in life, but a paying job until I can find something else, well, that would cover next week's rent and put food in my belly—once it stops churning. Plus, James did say I'd be helping him out.

"What would I have to do?" I ask.

"You can write, can't you?"

"Of course."

"I must warn you. He's not always an easy man to work for."

"I've dealt with worse, I'm sure."

James chuckles. "I'm sure you have. Will, however, is very regimented and has high expectations of those who work for him."

"I have high expectations of myself," I assure him. After Steph telling me Will was pretty much an ogre, I'm not sure why I'm working so hard to sell myself. Oh, right… I like having a roof over my head.

"He also has a strict dress code."

"A dress code? Really?" From what I know about software developers, they go to work in jeans and wear T-shirts with sayings like Cereal Killer or I Paused My Game to Be Here. Then again, people think all reporters are heartless sharks. I'm not heartless, and for all I know Will is a suit-and-tie kind of guy, like James used to be. But a dress code means I'd need to go shopping. I consider my budget and there is very little room for new clothes. Maybe I won't be able to take this job after all.

James finishes the brandy in his glass and sets it on the table. "An assistant is an extension of Will and is expected to act and dress a certain way. Is that a problem for you?"

"I...uh...what does he expect his assistant to wear?"

"No worries, your clothing will be supplied."

"Oh, okay." A measure of relief washes through me.

"You'll find a new wardrobe in your closet when you reach your destination." He glances the length of me, like he's trying to determine my size. I debate whether I should outright tell him, but in the end, I don't want to say the number out loud. Honest to God, from the little amount I eat, I should be thinner than I am. But no, my body likes to store every damn calorie I take in. While I've come to terms with it, that's one of the many things my ex-fiancé, Liam, wanted to change about me. Apparently, I didn't fit in with what was expected of his affluent family. Douchebags. Every last one of them.

"Anything else I should know?"

"You'll have to sign a nondisclosure agreement. Anything you see or hear cannot be repeated."

Jeez, the more he talks about Will, the more intrigued I am about the secretive, regimented asshole who provides clothing to his assistants. The same man caught in bed with another woman during his bachelor party. The more I think about it, a man like him getting caught seems rather contradictory to his character. If I hadn't seen the pictures with my own eyes, I might not have believed it. Will flat on his back, some random girl riding him like he was her own personal pony. It's rather disgusting that Avery sneaked in and took the pictures.

James sits back in his chair and lifts his head. He riffles through the Polaroids beside him, finds what he's looking for and hands it to me.

"That's Will," he says, but he doesn't need to tell me. Nor does he need to tell me I'm looking at the hottest guy on the planet. One who can't keep it in his pants, even when he has a beautiful fiancée.

"Whose wedding?"

"Will's brother Alec and his beautiful bride, Megan. Married in Saint Moritz near my resort." Under his breath he says, "Now there's only one left."

"I'm sorry, what?"

There's a new spark in his eyes when he says, "You're perfect for Will."

Perfect for Will?

Something feels a little off in the way he phrased that. Then again, he is in his nineties, and perhaps he's not as sharp as I thought. "You mean I'm the perfect *assistant* for Will, right?"

"That's right. Isn't that what I said?" That spark is back in his eyes, and before I can answer he continues with, "You'll do it then?"

"I'd never say no to a favor for you, but can I ask how it *is* a favor for you?"

"Will is a very private man. He hires a new assistant for every trip. He's not so trustful, you see. Doesn't let anyone get too close or hang around too long. There is no room for complacency in his world."

"I can understand that."

"Every assistant is vetted through my agency, and I'm their last stamp of approval. Unfortunately, no one quite fits what he needs."

"You think I do?"

"I think you're perfect. But there is one more thing, Khloe." He leans toward me. "It's very important."

I eye him carefully, not at all sure I like the sound of this. "Okay…"

"I realize you don't put articles out in your own name at *Starlight*, but please don't mention you're a journalist, or anything about the magazine."

I'm about to question him on that, but quickly realize why it's important to keep that information private. Will, undoubtedly, has a deep hatred and distrust for reporters after the exposé done on him. "I don't like to lie."

"It's not a lie. It's just not something he needs to know."

"Why hire me if he hates reporters? I'm sure there must be at least one temp at the agency who could give him what he needs."

"Not the way you can. Now you'd better get a move on—his plane leaves in a couple hours."

When I catch what looks like mischief in his cloudy eyes, unease trickles through me. While I'm certain James would never steer me wrong, I can't shake the feeling that I'm about to go down the rabbit hole and not come out the same.

CHAPTER TWO

Will

AT THE SOUND of hurried footsteps on the metal stairs of Granddad's Learjet, I lift my eyes and say, "You're late."

"Excuse me?"

I take in the breathless woman glaring at me. Damn, if looks could kill…

I sit up a little straighter, fold the newspaper I'd been reading and carefully set it on my lap.

"I said, you're late."

One hand planted on her hip and one foot tapping restlessly, she says, "I do apologize," her dark brown eyes flaring hot. "I'm usually punctual, but not only did I have little time to prepare for this trip, traffic was horrible, and my driver was a maniac. I'm lucky I made it here alive."

"You didn't use Granddad's driver?"

"No. I left from home and didn't see the need for him to backtrack to pick me up."

I raise my brows. "That's what his service is for."

"I just didn't want to put anyone out," she says, and it surprises me, considering most temps love to ride in Granddad's limo.

She rakes agitated fingers through a mess of wavy chestnut hair, her chest rising and falling as if she's been running. Her tight yoga pants hug her curvy hips like a second skin, and the relaxed V-neck T-shirt she's wearing showcases an abundance of creamy cleavage. Something inside me twitches at the sexy sight and reminds me I haven't been with a woman in far too long.

Nevertheless, despite the fact that the mere sight of this woman rouses something primal in me— reminds me I'm a man with needs—I'm not about to get involved with her. My traitorous dick might be showing interest, but I never mix business and pleasure. It's one of my many hard rules. After the exposé done on me, I don't let anyone get too close. Which means, while I can acknowledge my desire for her, I'm not about to act on it.

"I thought I'd be taking this trip solo until Grandfather called and said he found someone suitable last-minute."

"Yes," she says, her breasts jutting out a little more as she squares her shoulders. "I'm Khloe."

"Khloe," I say, trying the name out on my tongue. "Have you signed the nondisclosure agreement, Khloe?"

Her eyes drop to my mouth when I repeat her

name. Is she, too, wondering how it would sound on my lips if she were in my bed, beneath me?

Cool it, Will. She's an employee, and that makes her hands-off.

"Yes, at James's house," she says quickly. "He has a copy. We both do." She taps the big bag slung over her slender shoulders.

I eye her for a moment, and with a lift of her chin, she stares back unflinchingly. There's no denying that she's different from the women who normally travel as my assistant. Most don't look me in the eye, and are all fidgety and nervous around me. It's rather irritating. This woman, however, has a confidence about her and doesn't look like she'd put up with any kind of bullshit, especially from me. Which begs the question—why did Granddad hire her? It's not that I'm a complete asshole, although I've been called that and worse a time or two. It's just that I'm careful and private, a guy who likes things done in a certain way, and most importantly, a guy who trusts no one.

"I don't tolerate tardiness, and I certainly expect my employees to dress in a certain way. There are rules."

Her teeth clench with an audible click, and I can almost hear her brain spinning as a violent streak of pink colors her cheeks. If I had to guess, she's about to tell me where to shove my rules. Either that or she's contemplating which foot to use to kick me in the nuts. It's rather odd how I find her reactions amusing. But I can't give that any more consideration. No, not when she's smoothing her hand over her mess of hair and arousing my dick all over again.

"I'm well aware you have rules, and while your grandfather mentioned that you expect those in your employment to dress a certain way, I assumed for travel…" She pauses and runs her hands down the length of her body, and my eyes follow in appreciation. "I assumed that this would be more comfortable for the long flight." She takes a breath, lets it out slowly, and I grin as she works fervently to tamp down a flash of temper. I'm pretty good at reading people, and my gut tells me those weren't the words she wanted to throw my way. This woman is becoming more intriguing by the moment. "When we reach our destination, I'll be sure to dress appropriately."

"Very well. You should settle yourself in for take-off, and once we're in the air, I'd like a brandy."

Her head rears back at my request, and instead of sitting, she stares at me, mouth dropped open, like I've grown a second head.

"Wait, what?" she asks, then glances around the private jet.

I'm not sure who or what she's looking for, but her attention returns to me when I say, "A brandy. Is that a problem?"

"No… I just…"

I take in her narrowing eyes and tightening mouth and can't shake the feeling that something about her is…off. Granddad is pretty particular when it comes to my assistants. Then again, he's not getting any younger, and I do worry about him. Can I still trust his judgment?

"My grandfather explained your duties, did he not?"

"I…" She briefly looks down, her dark eyes stormy. A second later, her head lifts and she shakes her wavy hair back, her composure returning. "Yes, of course."

"Then you know you'll be running errands, cooking, cleaning, taking care of my needs while in the air and at my beach house."

"Yes. Right. Exactly. Your needs. I'll get you a brandy as soon as we're in the air."

"Please, have a seat so we can take off." I gesture to the leather recliner across from me, and she quickly lowers herself and buckles in.

The copilot secures the cabin door, and I give him the all-clear nod before he disappears into the cockpit. My attention travels back to Khloe. Her gaze flits to the window, then to the magazines and newspapers flared out on the round table between us. Brows angrily squashed together, her hand goes to her stomach, and her fingers splay.

"Are you a nervous flyer?"

"No, I've just never flown in a private jet before." She smiles, but it's forced. "It's nice."

"Help yourself to something to read," I say. She shakes her head and pulls what looks like a hard-covered journal from her bag. I go back to reading my paper, but every few seconds I glance over the top, curious about the woman my grandfather hired. She's young and fresh-faced, but there's a light of intelligence and experience in her eyes—unlike the recently graduated college girls who normally sign up at the agency.

I never delve into the personal, and I'm about to ask her what she does, or rather did, for a living, and why she is no longer employed, but my buzzing cell phone draws my attention. I tug it from my suit jacket and slide my finger across the screen.

"Hey, Jules," I say, and don't miss the way Khloe's eyes lift and travel to mine. They latch on briefly, hold for a second too long, then she goes back to the pages of her journal as if uninterested. My niece begins to talk a mile a minute. While I love and miss her, I have no idea how my cousin Tate and his wife, Summer, stay sane. "No, I can't come over tonight. I'm going to Saint Thomas. Remember I told you that the other night." She jabbers on some more, and I can't help but smile when I hear Summer in the background, telling her to slow down. "Of course I'll be back for your birthday party, and no, I'm not telling you what I got for you. You're really going to like it, though."

Summer takes the phone. "You tease."

I laugh at that, but it's true. I am a tease. I've been known to push buttons as well.

"Hey, be nice." I steal another glance at Khloe, who's looking out the window and feigning disinterest in my conversation. How would she react if I pushed her buttons? She didn't like it when I reprimanded her for her tardiness or her clothes, and I can't deny that I enjoyed that quick flash of anger in her eyes. What would she do or say if I fueled that fury?

"You promise you'll be back for her party?" Summer asks.

"I wouldn't miss it for the world." I love hanging out with Jules and spoiling her. I used to want kids of my own, thought I'd have them with Naomi, until I fucked everything up between us. Jesus, I have no idea how I got so drunk at my party and found myself in bed with another woman. What kind of guy pulls a shitty stunt like that, anyway? Not one worth marrying, that's for sure. I thought I was different from the generation of men who'd come before me. All of them had been unfaithful. I prided myself on my ability to engage in monogamous relationships, but I guess after a few drinks, my true colors had come through. I'd never meant to hurt Naomi—I'd loved her, for Christ's sake. But at the end of the day, she's better off without a bastard like me in her life.

I talk to Summer for a few more minutes, and hint at Granddad's old age. I am worried about the man's judgement. As a doctor and Granddad's former aide, Summer assures me he's well and fine. We're well into the air by the time I end the call. I catch Khloe's eye, take in the pallor of her skin. Perhaps she's lying about being a nervous flyer. If that's the case, she never should have agreed to this job. Then again, it pays well, and she might have circumstances I don't know about. But I'm not about to ask. Her business is hers, mine is mine.

"Seat belt sign is off," I say. When she nods, I arch my brow at her, and she looks puzzled for a second.

"Right, your drink." She's quick. Damned if I don't like that about her.

She unbuckles and turns to set her journal down on her seat. When she gives me an up close, unobstructed view of her curvy ass, it captivates my cock. Goddammit. It's all I can do to swallow the groan rising in my throat.

Jesus.

She turns to me, and I scrub my hand over my chin. "How would you like your drink? With ice, cola, water?" she asks.

"Brandy on the rocks," I say.

She gives a curt nod and makes her way to the small kitchen area at the rear of the plane. My gaze is latched onto her backside as she walks away, and I shake my head to pull myself together. I've been working so goddamn hard lately, long into the nights, developing a new algorithm platform for Carson Management Investments, the hedge fund company I run for Granddad. I've forgotten what it was like to crawl into bed with a soft, curvy woman who smells like sweet vanilla.

I turn back to the newspaper, and while my focus is usually laser sharp, the clanging at the back of the plane pulls my attention. What the hell is she doing back there, busting the place up? Something falls and smashes, followed by a round of muted curses. I unbuckle to see what the hell is going on. Khloe has her back to me as I walk toward her, and I'm about to look over her shoulder when I reach her. But she turns at that exact moment, and the large glass of brandy in her hand hits my chest, soaking us both.

"Dammit," she says, and tries to jump away, but with the counter digging into her back she has nowhere to go. I, on the other hand, have plenty of room behind me. So why aren't I distancing myself, putting a measure of space between our vibrating bodies?

My dick twitches.

Ah yes, and therein lies the answer.

"I'm so sorry, Mr. Carson," Khloe says.

"It's Will," I grumble.

Back arched, she fishes a cloth off the counter and dabs it to my chest. Tension arcs between us, sizzling down the length of our too-close bodies. I haven't felt this kind of arousal in a long time. It's definitely not something that comes along every day.

I slip off my suit jacket and work the buttons on my shirt.

"What are you doing?"

"Getting changed. I'd rather not spend the next four hours in a wet shirt."

"Oh, right. Of course."

"Do you have a change of clothes?" I ask.

"Someone on the ground put my luggage in the outside baggage compartment."

With only a breath of distance between us, I peel

my shirt off and take the cloth from her. I mop the brandy from my chest, and a strange little squeaking sound rises in Khloe's throat.

"You okay?"

She blinks twice, rips her focus from my chest and straight-up asks, "I suppose you're firing me for this?"

My attention drifts from her eyes to her mouth as she drives her teeth into her bottom lip. "You think I'd fire you for something as trivial as this?"

"I heard things about you."

I let loose a laugh and shake my head. "What's the latest I'm being called, Khloe? Asshole?"

A grin flirts with her lips as her eyes cut to me. "Well, maybe."

"Don't believe everything you hear," I say.

I hand the cloth back to her and step away to grab a clean shirt from my bag. I pull my case from the overhead bin and take out a dress shirt and T-shirt. Khloe still hasn't moved from her spot.

"Which would you prefer?" I ask.

"Both will probably float on me." She shrugs. "But I guess I can tie the dress shirt at the waist."

"Dress shirt it is," I say, and tug on the T-shirt as I move to the back of the plane to hand the button-down over. Her fingers curl around it, and she glares at me as I stand there.

"Do you mind?" she finally blurts out.

"Mind what?"

"I'm not about to get half-naked in front of you. I don't even know you."

"Are you saying if you knew me, you'd get half-naked?" I ask, and keep the smile from my face as her cheeks flame red. Look at that. I guess now I do know how she'll react when I push her buttons. Truthfully though, I shouldn't be teasing her.

"Either turn around or point to the bathroom so I can change."

I jerk my head to the left. "Bathroom's right there."

She slides past me, her warm body brushing mine, and her sweet vanilla scent reaches my nostrils.

"What do you like to drink?" I ask, switching focus.

She turns back to me. "I'm easy."

That makes me smile, because I don't get the sense that anything about her is easy.

"But leave it. It's my job. I'll fix us both a drink after I change."

"And I can fix us both one while you change."

She eyes me like she doesn't know what to make of that. "Fine, I'll just have what you're having then."

"Brandy on the shirt?" Her eyes widen at the joke. "See, not always an asshole," I say, and turn my attention to making the drinks. I reach for two tumblers and add a splash of brandy to both. I take a sip of mine as I head back to my seat. Newspaper back in hand, I begin to read again. My mind drifts to the real reason I'm headed to Saint Thomas. While I have a home there and plan to work on my algorithms, I need to check on Granddad's luxury hotel. It was destroyed by hurricanes, and a lot of people

were out of work because of it. It's back up and running now, and I want to make sure everything is pro-
ceeding smoothly. I also need to work on staffing
for Leonard Elementary, the school we're building
to replace the old moldy one. As I consider that, I
realize Khloe hasn't returned to her seat. What the
hell is she doing in that bathroom? I check my watch.
Christ, she's been in there for a good twenty minutes.

Pushing from my seat, I go to the door and knock.
"Khloe, is everything okay?"

"Uh, just not sure about this shirt."

"You'd prefer the T-shirt?" I ask, and reach over
my shoulder, about to peel it off.

"No, that won't help either."

"Come out here. Tell me what's going on," I demand. A second passes, and the sign on the door finally changes from Occupied to Vacant. Her damp
T-shirt is balled up in her hands, and she's pressing it
hard against her chest as she steps from the lavatory.

"I had to remove my bra," she says, "and this
shirt is white."

"All my shirts are white. So are my T-shirts."

"That's why I said nothing you have will help."

"Help with what?" I ask, and when her chest
heaves, understanding dawns. She's worried her nipples are going to be visible. But now that I'm thinking
about her nipples… Shit, that's a distraction I don't
need. "Hang on." I open the overhead compartment
again and pull out a blue blanket. "This should help."

For the first time since she boarded the plane, a

smile makes an appearance, and something inside me twists. "Thanks, Will." She adjusts the blanket over her shoulders, and my gaze drops to take in a hint of pink brushing against the fabric before it's hidden from my view.

Jesus.

Her body is ripe and lush, and my hands itch to slide down her back and grab a fistful of her sweet ass. Not only is she different from the young, fresh-out-of-college girls who do temp work for me, she's the opposite of the rail-thin women in my social circle. I loved Naomi, but she needed to eat more than a salad. No matter how much I encouraged it, she always refused.

I clear my throat. "When we land, I'll get your bag, and you can change before you deplane."

I wave my hand for her to sit, and she tightens the blanket around her shoulders as she hurries to her seat. I follow, all the while admiring her curves. As she settles herself, I wonder what her story is. Married? Single? Boyfriend? Then again, it's none of my business. Still, I might ask Granddad how he found her and why he thought she was a good choice. I hand her drink over, and she takes a sip, her skin paling even more. Something buzzes in the back of my brain, something just out of reach as my gaze rakes over her white face.

"Do I know you?"

CHAPTER THREE

Khloe

"Ah, I'm not sure," I say, the cold pizza I'd eaten for breakfast threatening to rise up and make a second appearance. I thought I was nauseous from my ordeal at *Starlight* this morning. Now I think I might be coming down with something. Either that, or I shouldn't have eaten that leftover slice sitting on the kitchen counter all night.

Will's eyes narrow in on me. "Khloe," he says, and the way he says my name, like he's savoring it, does the weirdest things to my insides. Then again... leftover sausage pizza.

He sits forward, and I catch a hint of his aftershave. Sandalwood, beach and... Will. I inhale slowly. That scent could magically melt the panties right off a woman. I'm pretty sure mine are currently on fire. Honestly, if someone bottled it and called it Panties Be Gone they'd make a fortune.

Strength and power radiate from Will's hard body

as he inches closer, his long legs stretched out before him. I do my best not to envision them wrapped around my body.

Sometimes my best just isn't good enough.

"I think I might know you," he says.

"You...think?" I ask, trying to focus on what he's saying to me.

"Is your last name Davis?"

Oh, God, he knows. He knows I'm Khloe Davis, sensationalized crime reporter from *Starlight*. He's liable to open the deck door and toss me out midflight. But I don't think that's possible at our flying altitude. At least I hope not. I gulp, and the world spins around me.

"Yes, it is," I manage to get out as bile punches into my throat. I'm not sure if it's from his revelation or my upset stomach. Either way, this isn't good. Not good at all. James wanted to keep my identity a secret, and this man hates reporters.

"Your father used to work for my granddad, right?"

"He did," I say quickly and realize there is no way he could put it together since I use a pen name. A wave of relief hits me, but it's short-lived. I take a few deep breaths as an invisible fist grips my tightening throat.

"You were in the car that day Granddad picked me up from swimming lessons."

"That was you?"

"Yeah, and you were as pale then as you are now."

"I…I had the chicken pox."

Don't get sick, Khloe. Don't get sick.

"Right, I remember." Alarm widens his eyes. "Wait, you don't have them again, do you?"

"No, I think I have…" We hit an air bump, and before I know what's happening, Will has me by the elbow and is rushing me to the bathroom. No. No. No. I am *not* going to throw up in front of the hottest guy on the planet.

Wrong.

Two seconds later I'm on my knees bent over the toilet heaving my guts out, and Will is standing directly behind me. He pulls my hair back, and in that instant, with my head buried in the porcelain bowl, I pray to God I get sucked out into the abyss. But no, I don't have that kind of good luck.

"I'm…okay," I say. "Can you please leave and shut the door?"

My hair tumbles gently over my back as he lets it go, and I'm grateful when he leaves me to die alone. I groan, but then he's back. He's saying something, but I can't quite hear with my head in the toilet.

He drops to his knees behind me, his pelvis pressed up against my rear end as he leans over me and puts a cloth to my forehead. I moan against the damp coldness. "That feels soooo good," I say. Will's body goes rigid, and a soft hiss leaves his mouth.

Oh, wait, crap!

"I mean the cloth," I hurry on, my voice muffled

as I stick my head deeper into the bowl. "The cold cloth feels good."

"You probably shouldn't talk."

No kidding, since I'm not thinking with any sort of clarity, and my words could be construed as sexual. It's not like I was saying it felt good to have his pelvis pressed up against me.

Even though it does.

Good God, how desperate am I that I'm enjoying the feel of Will's body—well, one part in particular—while I'm losing my breakfast in his toilet? Even if I had a chance with this guy, not that I want one, my current predicament would no doubt quash any interest on his part.

"I think you have the flu," he says.

While I'd like to come back with some smart-ass comment that involves Einstein, the sarcastic retort dies on my tongue. We might have gotten off on the wrong foot, but he's trying to take care of me as I die a slow and agonizing death. I vomit again, and Will reaches past me to flush the toilet. I heave a grateful sigh and wait to get sucked into space, but no. Like I said, I don't have that kind of luck.

"Here," he says, and puts a plastic cup to my mouth. I take a drink of water, rinse my mouth and spit. Not a dainty girlie spit either, if there is such a thing. No, it sounds more like a baseball player hacking up a sunflower seed.

And this, my friends, has become my life.

I moan and lift my head from the bowl.

"Feeling better?"

"A little." I take another big drink and spill half the water over my shirt as the plane lurches. "God-dammit." A sound crawls out of Will's throat, and I glance at him over my shoulder. "Are you laughing?"

"Not even a little bit."

"This isn't funny."

"Never thought it was. But I have to say, you're handling it better than most." Concern dances in his eyes.

Okay, maybe he wasn't laughing, but I've been on the defense with him since I boarded the plane.

"Mouthwash?"

"Yes, please." He pulls a travel-size bottle from the vanity, opens it and hands it to me. I rinse repeatedly and go back on my heels, only to end up sitting in Will's lap. I'm about to apologize and slide off when his hand goes around my waist to hold me in place.

"It's okay. I got you," he says, and my heart does a ridiculous thump at his thoughtfulness. Truthfully, I'm not used to anyone taking care of me, and this is actually kind of...nice.

Nice? What the hell am I saying? I just vomited in front of Will Carson. There's nothing nice about that—for either of us.

"You don't have a parachute on this thing, do you?" I ask.

He chuckles slightly. "No, why?"

"I'd like to get off."

I'd like to get off.

"I mean…"

"I'm actually getting a complex," he says, a hint of teasing in his voice.

"What are you talking about?"

"I've met you twice now, and you vomited both times. How's a guy not to take that personally?"

I groan and reach for a paper towel. My cheeks burn from sheer mortification. "I am so embarrassed."

He puts his hand to my forehead. "You're cold and clammy and slightly warm."

"Pizza for breakfast," I say. "Wasn't my best decision."

"If it was food poisoning, it would have hit you earlier. How about some ginger ale?"

"Not a bad idea."

"Maybe some toast? It might help settle your stomach."

"I don't think I can eat anything."

"Do you think you're going to be sick again, or do you want to go lie down? The sofa opens to a bed."

"I think I'd like to lie down. I guess now I know why I was so tired when I met with James today." Worry grips my stomach, and I clutch Will's arm. "I hope I didn't give it to him."

Will holds me by my hips and repositions himself so he can stand. "I'm sure he's fine, but I'll call him just to make sure." He hauls me up with him and turns me around. With infinite tenderness, he slides a strand of damp hair from my face, and I let out a shaky breath. His arm drops, but his gaze stays locked on mine. His gorgeous blue eyes bore into my face, his gaze probing, searching.

"I'm okay," I say. "My stomach is settling."

"Yeah?"

I nod, and he slides his arm around my waist, but the damn plane hits another air pocket, and Will stumbles backward. I fall with him, until he's splayed across a table and I'm on top of him.

I yelp and unsuccessfully try to push off of him. "I can't get up."

His arms lock me in place. "Hold on," he says, his voice a degree deeper. What the hell? Why is he still holding me? Does he like me on top of him like this?

"Rough air," he explains.

Guess not.

The plane bumps again, and for a split second I'm floating over him. But then I drop, press down on his hardness, and arousal slams into me as our bodies collide.

"We need to ride it out for a second longer," he says.

Ride it out.

A strange, inappropriate giggle rises in my throat and a crinkle appears between his brows at my bizarre reaction. I swallow—hard—and pull myself together. Good Lord, this flu has me acting completely out of character.

Yeah, blame it on the flu, Khloe.

"How long do you think it will last?" I ask, and when a grin tugs at the corner of his mouth, my cheeks once again flare hot.

What is wrong with me? No matter what I say, it comes out sounding sexual. Why is that? Oh, probably because I'm flat out on top of the sexiest man alive, and even though I just finished losing my breakfast, everything about this guy reminds me I'm still a woman—one who hasn't been touched in a long time.

"Shouldn't be too much longer," he says. "The pilots will adjust flying height to get us out of the wind shears."

"I'm probably squishing you," I say, and wiggle as I try to shift to the side of the table.

"Please stop moving." His hands tighten around my body, and that innocent touch seeps beneath my skin and burns through my blood. "At least we managed to get you horizontal."

"For your sake, you'd better hope I don't get sick again."

He laughs. An honest-to-God belly laugh. "You'll give me a heads-up, right?"

"It's possible. But the words might come out too *late*." I emphasize the last word to let him know I'm still pissed off at his greeting. And seriously, James totally misled me with this assignment. I thought I'd be attending board meetings and taking notes, but no. I'll be getting this man his brandy and whatever else his assistant does for him. Why would I need writing skills for that?

"Khloe," he says, his voice a bit more serious.

I blink slowly, and when my lashes lift, I'm staring at blue eyes brimming with questions. "Yeah?"

"It's not my business, but you're different from the other girls who apply for temp work."

"I was fired recently," I say.

"Oh, shit. Sorry." He goes quiet, his mouth tight.

"It wasn't my fault." I roll my eyes and can't keep the disgust from my voice when I add, "Men in power, they're all alike."

"What's that supposed to mean?"

"My boss wanted me to do something, and when I refused, he canned me."

His expression turns angry. "Jesus, sorry."

I know what he's thinking. That my boss wanted sex, or something equally disturbing. The sudden visual of a naked Benjamin batters my uneasy stomach. I think of a naked Will instead, but that just batters another part of my body.

"Yeah, he was a real jerk, but I don't want to talk about it. I just want to move forward, okay?"

"Just so you know, I would never put you in any position you didn't want to be in."

Even though he doesn't strike me as a missionary sex kind of guy, I glance down at our vanilla position—the only one I'm familiar with, sadly—and take in the two hundred pounds of rock-solid muscles beneath me. Lord, he's everything fantasies are made of, and a thousand new ones begin to run through my brain.

"Um," I say.

He laughs. "Current position excluded. This was for your own safety. But you know what I mean, right?"

"Yeah."

"I have rules." His eyes narrow, and the muscles along his jaw ripple. "A lot of them."

"James warned me."

"Getting involved with an assistant is a hard no."

Too bad my nipples didn't get the memo.

I let out a shaky breath. "Getting involved with my boss is a hard no for me, too."

"Then we're on the same page."

And the same table.

I nod. "I think we can get up now," I say, throwing up a silent prayer that he can't feel my pebbled nipples pressing into his hard chest. "The plane has stabilized."

"Slowly," he says. "Any fast movement could turn your stomach again."

I inch up from his hardness. And my God, every movement is agonizing, like slowly tearing a bandage off—if said bandage were covering every erogenous zone in my body. Will follows me up and stays close as he guides me to my seat.

"Sit here," he commands in a soft voice, and while I'm not one to take orders, a shiver goes through me at his. "I'll open the bed."

I do as he says, noting the way his T-shirt strains against his biceps as he opens the sofa and makes me a bed. I wipe my mouth with the back of my hand and smooth my hair from my face. I glance down, and groan when I see the water stains on my shirt. In all the commotion, I left my blanket behind and now my nipples are staring straight at the man turning my way. Is the universe trying to play some cruel joke on me? I'm a good person. Kind to the elderly and animals. Yet...this.

Before I can cover up, his glance drops, and his eyes linger on my puckered nipples for a brief second.

"Khloe."

"Yeah?"

"Your blanket," he says gruffly, but I'm already reaching for it.

Get it together, girl. I might be attracted to him, but clearly I'm not his type. Not only does he date model-thin girls, he made it clear that I was hired to cook, clean and cater to his needs. Those needs don't involve sex. Which is a good thing. I'm not about to mess around with my boss. Even if he asks me to.

Okay, maybe if he asks me to...

CHAPTER FOUR

Will

I CRACK OPEN a new bottle of water, pour it into a clean glass and make my way to Khloe's room. She fell fast asleep on the plane the second her head hit the pillow and has been coming in and out of consciousness ever since. I've been giving her ibuprofen every four hours, and her temperature has come down, but this flu has definitely kicked her ass to the curb.

At first light I called Granddad, but Summer, who's been checking in on him, answered, saying he wasn't showing signs of the flu but was resting. She assured me she'd give him the message and have him call back, but I've yet to hear from him.

As I approach Khloe's door, a low, agonized groan reaches my ears. I slow my steps and walk softly. After the night she had, I'm sure her head must be killing her. I inch the door open and find her sitting up in the bed, dark circles under bloodshot eyes as she catalogs the unfamiliar room.

"Will?" she asks when her gaze lands on me.

"Welcome to the living," I say.

She smooths her hand over her wayward curls, and I can't help but grin. With bedhead hair, cheeks puffy and red from fever, and big glassy eyes, she's a hot mess, but goddammit, she's still as sexy as hell. She's off-limits, I get it, but no red-blooded male could possibly be immune to those full round curves and thighs I could really sink my teeth into. I had a handful of her lush body when I carried her from the plane to the car and then again to this bed. Not a single bone jabbed me, and I have to say I damn well liked it. Perhaps that's why all her sexy curves infiltrated my dreams a time or two last night.

How is a girl like her still single?

Not your business, Will.

She smacks her lips together, peels her tongue from the roof of her mouth and cringes as she swallows.

"Here, drink this."

I hand her the glass, and she gives me a grateful smile.

"Thank you." She swallows half the contents and sets the glass on the nightstand. "You didn't happen to get the license plate of the truck that ran me over, did you?"

"Afraid not." I lean into her and place my hand on her forehead. "How are you feeling?"

"Like the walking dead." Her eyes narrow. "How long have I been asleep?"

I give a low, slow whistle. "You've had one hell of a night, Khloe. Tossing and turning and moaning for hours on end."

"Hours?" Her gaze goes to the closed curtains, a hint of morning sun peeking in through the cracks.

"It's eight in the morning," I say.

She presses the heels of her hands into her eyes and rubs. "My God, the last thing I remember was lying down on the plane. I have no idea how I got here."

I sit down next to her on the edge of the bed, and she sways toward me as the mattress dips. "I brought you here, put you to bed and have been waking you every four hours to give you ibuprofen."

"You have?" she asks, her eyes big.

I rake my hands through my hair. "Is that so hard to believe?"

"What I can't believe is that I threw up in front of you."

"Again, you mean?" I say, hoping to coax a laugh out of her. I don't.

"Yeah, again," she groans. "I haven't been sick like that since I was—"

"In the back seat of Granddad's car?"

"Ugh."

"Projectile vomiting. I've never seen anything like it."

"Yeah, it's quite the gift." She covers her face, hides behind her hands. Suddenly she pulls them away and her gaze flies to her chest. Her shoulders drop from her ears when she finds herself still in my button-down. At least it was dry when I put her to bed, and I didn't have to suffer the visual of her gorgeous full tits, nipples poking through the dampness.

Oh, the hardship.

Seriously though, her body is, to sum it up with one word…banging.

As my blood starts to leave my brain, she tugs the sheet up to her chin.

"Ugh, I need to change into some clean clothes."

"I didn't want to put you to bed in a dirty shirt, but I wasn't about to undress you." I put my hand over my crotch. "You know…with me being fond of my nuts and all."

That brings a smile to her face, for about two seconds. "Did you get any sleep at all?"

I give a casual shrug, but her concern for me is appreciated. "I dozed."

"I…feel horrible," she says her voice so soft and sincere it tugs at something inside me. "I hope you don't get it."

"I've had my shots."

"Me too, and yet…" Her eyes widen. "Wait—"

"I called Granddad, and he's resting. No signs of flu."

She relaxes. "Thank God. At his age…" Her nose crinkles, and as I take in the sprinkle of freckles, I note the tinge of sadness in her eyes. "I really appreciate you taking care of me. You didn't have to… I mean I never expected you to…"

What, has no one ever taken care of her before?

"See, not a total asshole."

"I'll give you that."

"Mighty generous of you. How about I get you to the shower and then make us something to eat." Her stomach takes that moment to growl. "I'm starving."

I stand and hold my arm out to help her up.

"What?" she asks, looking at my hand like it might grow a snake head and bite her.

"I'll help you to the shower."

"Oh." She pushes the sheets down. "I can get up myself."

I drop my arm and shove my hands into my jeans pockets. Her gaze follows as my pants slide lower on my hips.

"Granddad used to say your dad was stubborn. I see the apple hasn't fallen far from the tree."

"I've put you out enough." She swings her feet over the edge of the bed.

"I don't mind putting out."

Jesus, Will. What the fuck are you doing?

Her feet stop seconds before hitting the wood floor, and her gaze flies to mine. Dark eyes narrow, like she's trying to figure out if I'm flirting or not.

I am, but I shouldn't be. She's an assistant, and the last girl I should be screwing around with. Yeah, sure, she signed a confidentiality clause, and Granddad vetted her. But sex with the help is wrong, and something the media would leap at and twist if they got wind of it. The last thing I want is my face splashed all over the papers again. I've brought enough shame to the Carson family as it is, and I'm sure Khloe doesn't want her history out there for all to examine and pick apart.

"Believe it or not, when someone needs help, I help," I say, getting my head back on right and redirecting the conversation. "That, and you're a friend of Granddad's. He'd kill me if I didn't treat you properly." She nods, and I continue with, "Why don't you shower, and I'll make us something to eat."

She scurries off the bed and wobbles a bit as she stands. "Whoa," she says, and puts her hand to her head.

"Let me help you." I wrap my arm around her waist and tug her against me. She's stiff at first but then relaxes into me. "You're still pretty weak."

She takes in the big room as we head to the en suite bathroom.

"This place is gorgeous." Cold air blows down from the overhead vent, and she shivers.

"I'll adjust the air-conditioning, and when you're up to it, I'll show you around the place." I slowly guide her across the room, taking short steps to match hers. "Your room has a spectacular view of the ocean."

"Really?"

"Yeah, mine is next to yours, with an equally great view." I point to the curtains. "Behind those, you'll find a patio door and a private deck, just for you. We have amazing sunsets here in Saint Thomas. Unlike anything I've ever seen."

A happy sigh catches in her throat. "Will, I think this is just what the doctor ordered."

"Good," I say, although I'm not sure why seeing her this happy has suddenly turned me into the grinning village idiot. Maybe it's because she got fired and was violently ill all on the same day and could really use a break.

"Just yesterday morning, I was thinking how much I'd love to get away," she says, and her smile is a little off-center when she adds, "Talk about fate."

"If you believe in such things."

She arches a brow. "A skeptic?"

"I believe our destiny is in our own hands, not someone else's."

"If I hadn't decided to go see James, I wouldn't be here. I believe everything happens for a reason."

"Why did you decide to go see Granddad, anyway?"

Her body tightens ever so slightly. If I wasn't holding her, I might never have noticed.

"Someone mentioned his name, actually." She gives a casual shrug. "Thought I'd pay him a visit."

I nod but get the sense that she might not be telling me everything. I think about pushing, but she's not feeling well. When Granddad calls, I'll get answers from him.

I flick the light on in the bathroom, and her eyes

widen. "This is bigger than my entire apartment." She steps away from me and makes her way to the tiled shower. She runs her fingers over the taps. "I have no idea how to use these."

"Simple." I move around her to turn on the water. "This is for the rain shower nozzle," I say as it sprays down. "This one is for the body, and this one is for the feet."

"All angles covered. Literally."

I adjust the temperature and step back. "I'll make us something to eat."

"I'm supposed to—"

"Yeah, well, not today." I tilt my head when she gives me a confused look. "It's for my own good."

"Isn't cooking part of my duties?"

"Yes, but if you were me, would you let the Ebola monkey touch your food?"

She puts one hand on her hip, and her brown eyes flare. "Did you just call me a monkey?"

I chuckle. "Get a shower, Khloe. There are towels in the cabinet, and you'll find everything you need in the vanity, even a new toothbrush."

She glares at me a moment longer, but today the fight just isn't in her. She softens and says, "You thought of everything."

"Part of the assistant's job is to stock this place for the next assistant."

She opens and closes the vanity and pulls out a few drawers to check the contents. "I heard you went through assistants fast."

That gives me pause. I don't like anyone knowing too much about me. "Who told you that?"

Her hair tumbles as she gives me a quick glance over her shoulder. "Ah, I don't remember. I think maybe your Granddad."

"There's a reason for that," is all I say.

"Okay." She shrugs. "Not my business."

I'm about to leave but turn back and say, "You should probably know you talk in your sleep."

A streak of red flares across her cheeks. "I do not."

I grin at her, and despite myself I say, "Yeah, I'm afraid you do."

She pulls in a deep breath. "What did I say?" she asks, and when her fingers grip the sink hard, I cut her some slack.

"Mostly mumbling, but I did hear you say my name a time or two."

Her eyes narrow. "You're making that up."

"I believe you said something about my cologne." I tap my finger to my chin. "What was it you called it again…?"

"I was delirious, Will. High fever, remember?"

"Then you mumbled something about bad or being bad. Wait, maybe you were saying I wasn't so bad."

"I vomited the two times I met you, or have you forgotten?" she counters, and I keep my grin hidden.

"We may have gotten off to a bad start, Khloe. With you showing up late and all." It's true, we did. But honest to God, she's like a breath of fresh air.

"I told you, I pride myself on my punctuality, but James offered me the job at the last minute, and traffic, and...and...ugh, forget it. I'm wasting my time."

Under the guise of strengthening my next point, I let my glance race the length of her. In reality, I'm simply enjoying the view of her in my button-down. "And of course, you were dressed improperly, but for what it's worth, I don't think you're so bad, either."

She pulls a big round brush from the drawer, and I step outside and close the door before she can throw it at me. It hits the door with a thud, and I laugh out loud. I shouldn't enjoy pushing her buttons so much. But goddammit I love the way she gets all fired up.

I head to the kitchen and busy myself with making the coffee, anything to keep my mind off her curvy naked body in the shower. The woman is a distraction I don't need. I'm here to work on my algorithms and check on the hotel and school. What I should not be contemplating is all the ways Khloe and I could get down and dirty.

Once the coffee is brewing, I boot up my laptop and answer a few emails. The shower turns off, and I power down my computer and grab eggs and bacon from the fridge. I'm not sure how she likes her eggs, so I decide scrambled is safest. I drop bread into the toaster and fish the jam from the fridge. Soon enough everything is ready, but Khloe is nowhere to be found.

I retrace my steps to her room. Her door is slightly ajar, the way I left it, and I catch a flash of black inside.

I knock softly. "Everything okay in there?"

"As good as it can be," she says, her words tight.

"You're not feeling sick again, are you?"

The door swings open, and I nearly swallow my tongue at the unbelievable sight before me.

Sweet mother of all that is holy.

"Is there a problem?" she asks, one hand on her hip, her expression far from amused.

"Um…no," I lie. Because yeah, there is a problem, and it's between my legs, growing thicker by the second.

She pushes past me. "I hope you made coffee. I'm going to need a gallon."

"I made coffee," I mumble as my eyes latch onto her backside, which sways sexily, spilling out of the too-tight French maid uniform. Her heels tap the floor as I steal a glance at the lacy stockings hugging her thighs. This…this is what she thought Granddad meant when he told her I had a dress code? I think the tables have turned, and now she's the one who's going to be pushing my buttons, every last one of them.

She disappears from my sight, mumbling angrily about men in power and how they're all the same, and I gulp. Cupboards open and slam closed, pulling me from my trance, and I force one foot in front of the other, rounding the corner to find her filling a mug with coffee. She plasters on a smile, but there is anger in her eyes as they bore into me.

"Coffee?" she asks, her smile saccharine sweet.

"Uh, yeah. I can get it."

"I believe that's my job." She grabs a mug, slams it onto the counter and fills it to the brim.

"Thanks," I say. She tugs on the hem of her small skirt, but it doesn't budge. She grumbles something and turns to me when a sound I can't control rumbles in my throat.

"Is there a problem, Will?"

If I were a gentleman, I'd tell her she didn't have to dress like a French maid straight out of my fantasies. Yeah, if I were a gentleman, I'd tell her that a costume is not required in my home, and that if she insists on wearing it, I might break my hard rule and tear it from her lush body. For a brief second, I lose myself in that erotic fantasy. My hands on her soft flesh, slowly sliding those stockings down, then licking a path back up her legs. Of course, in my fantasy, she's quivering and moaning my name—not cursing it under her breath and glaring at me like she'd like to fillet me with the biggest damn knife in the drawer. Yeah, if I were a goddamn gentleman, I'd yell abort, but unfortunately, it's not my brain calling the shots.

"Well, is there?" she asks.

Come on. Tell her, Will. Tell her this isn't what you meant by a dress code.

"Uh, no…no problem at all," I say.

I am so fucking dead.

D.E.A.D.

CHAPTER FIVE

Khloe

I TAKE A much-needed sip of my coffee, when what I actually want to do is throw it at Will, mug and all. What the hell? After taking care of me, holding my hair back and wiping my face when I was ill, not to mention checking on me through the night, I thought he was a decent guy, was more like his grandfather—until I looked in my closet and found a dozen French maid outfits.

I mean seriously!

This…this ridiculous costume—two sizes too small for me—is what he insists his help wear? Maybe I should have told James my size. But who in their right mind could have foreseen this insanity? Yeah, that must be it. Will Carson is insane. What other explanation can there be? I can see the headline now. *Woman dies of suffocation in a too-tight French maid outfit her rich, clearly insane employer forced her to wear.*

Okay, I might have to trim that a bit. But that's certainly the gist of it.

Anger courses through my blood, and I swear to God if I didn't need the money that came with this job, I'd toss my coffee at him—although it's possible I'd wait until the second cup, since I really need this one—and storm out the door.

"Breakfast is ready," he says. I take a breath and let it out slowly.

"I lost my appetite," I grumble through clenched teeth.

"You should eat something."

My stupid stomach takes that moment to growl. "Fine." If I catch him grinning, that's it. I'm out of here. I spin, and his expression is thoughtful and maybe even a bit confused. I'm about to ask what his problem is, but the smell of breakfast hits me. My mouth waters at the sight of two plates with toast, bacon and eggs.

He waves his hand toward a patio door. "We can eat here or on the deck."

"Deck," I say, and scoop up my plate. "Lead the way."

Will gathers his plate, and I follow him. I'm pissed off, and the last thing I should be doing is admiring the man's ass in his low-slung jeans as he heads to the patio door. He opens it, and a warm breeze washes over me. I step out into the sunshine and breathe in the briny scent as waves lap against the sandy shore below. I glance down at the infinity pool overlooking the turquoise waters. My anger instantly dissipates, and I forget all about the stupid outfit. Well, not entirely. But if the ridiculous getup is the price I have to pay for this unbelievable Caribbean view, then so be it. Cripes, I'm such an easy sellout. But the view...

"My God, this is beautiful." I glance around, the wind blowing my hair from my face, but there are no other villas close to us. Will's home is at the end of a strip of land, the ocean on all sides. "And so private."

"That's why I bought the cottage. I value my privacy."

Cottage? I think he means mansion.

"That's Magdalen Bay," he says, and I take in the strip of secluded white sand below.

"I could go skinny-dipping and no one would see me."

"I'd see you," he mumbles, his voice an octave deeper.

I turn, watch his throat work as he swallows—like he's afraid I might really get naked.

"I'm not going to go skinny-dipping," I blurt out. "I don't even know why I said that. It's just that I've never seen anything like this, and I love how private it is. I value my privacy, too, Will."

"Well, I'm glad you like it."

"Wait, how long are we here?" I ask. I was in such a rush to get ready, I never had the time to ask James.

"Granddad didn't tell you?"

"There's a lot James didn't tell me," I mutter.

"Three weeks," he says as he pulls a chair out

from a small round table and gestures for me to sit. "That's not a problem for you, is it?"

Moisture dots my forehead as the warm wind whips around my body. "You could have said six months and that wouldn't be a problem for me."

"Not in a hurry to get back?"

"No." I lower myself into the chair and set my plate down. A bird sings in the tree near the deck, and it smooths all my ruffled feathers. "Why would I ever want to leave this place?" I take in the opulence a second time and shake my head. "Why do you?"

Will drops down into the seat across from me. "My work is in New York."

"Can't you write code from here?"

"Yes, and that's what I plan to do these next few weeks, but I want to be close to my family. Granddad is…" His gaze lowers, a deep sadness in his eyes.

Without even thinking about it, I place my hand over his. "I understand that. He's the patriarch that keeps you all together." It was something my father once told me. He'd also told me all of James's sons had a penchant for younger women and had left a trail of broken homes behind them. It saddened me, although Will isn't the kind of guy who'd want anyone's pity. I can relate. I don't want pity, either. He nods, eyes locked on my hand as I give his a gentle squeeze.

"It was just you and your dad growing up, right?" he asks.

My stomach tightens, and my heart misses a beat

at the mention of my dad. He died right after I graduated from journalism school, and I miss him terribly. At least his dream of seeing me walk the stage to receive my diploma was realized before he passed away. That gives me a measure of comfort.

I slowly pull my hands back. "I was three when we lost Mom."

Sympathy lurks in his eyes when he says, "That's tough, Khloe."

"I had my dad, though. We were very close."

Will makes a strangled noise, and his lips twist painfully.

"What?"

"Dad left us when we were young."

"I'm sorry."

"I mean, he didn't die, he's still in our lives, but…"

I dig into my eggs and slide the fork into my mouth. "Delicious," I murmur, and note the way Will's attention turns to my mouth. "Sorry, go on."

He shrugs like his father's leaving was nothing, but I get that it's something. "He bailed. None of the men in our family have staying power."

My Dad pretty much said the same, but I don't believe it's a trait passed on from generation to generation. "You truly believe that?"

"Yeah, sure. So does my mother. She warned my brother Alec not to get married." He laughs, but it holds no humor. "You read the papers, don't you?"

For a secretive guy, I'm a little shocked at how open and honest he's being with me. I guess he wants to ensure that I know exactly what kind of guy he is and where the two of us stand so I don't go and get any ridiculous notions about us. With his power, money and looks, I'm sure he has women throwing themselves at him. I find none of those things appealing. Okay, maybe that's a small lie. He's drop-dead gorgeous, and fine, my traitorous body finds that appealing.

"I read the paper," I say, the eggs catching in my throat. Not only do I read them, I've written some of the articles. At least I didn't twist things to ruin a man's life.

"Right," is all he says.

I pick up the toast and nibble on the corner.

"Going down okay?" he asks, his brow quirked, and that concern does strange things to me. Blunt and demanding one minute, caring the next. He's quite the contradiction.

"Yes, thanks." I wash the toast down with my coffee. "Your brother ignored your mom and did get married, right? Those were the pictures James showed me, weren't they?"

He laughs at that. "Granddad and his damn Polaroids." Big fingers curl around his cup, and he looks at me over the rim. "Alec is married, yes."

"So how is that working out?"

His left shoulder rolls. "Time will tell, I guess."

"Wow, you are so jaded."

He looks at me long and hard, and I get the sense

he's not sure if he should ask the question dancing in his eyes.

"What?" I finally ask.

"What about you, Khloe? Why aren't you married?"

I exhale. "Damn, I should have seen that coming."

He chuckles, and the rich, deep sound sends a current of heat zinging through me, teasing every erogenous spot as it settles deep between my legs. I squeeze my thighs together, but all that does is arouse me even more. Damn, this man's charm is like a high-voltage jolt. If he harnessed it for good, he could be our next superhero. The lace on my ridiculous outfit takes that moment to itch, reminding me he's no Prince Charming. No, he's an insane millionaire who abuses his power and authority. Why can't guys like him use their assets for good instead of evil?

"I was close," is all I say. "So what are my working hours? I'm hoping to get in some sightseeing on the weekends."

"Way to change the topic, Khloe."

"You liked that, did you?" I blow on my fisted knuckles and wipe them on my shoulder. "I am a woman of many talents."

"Your weekends are yours. Monday to Friday, you're mine."

You're mine.

My pulse leaps when I catch what looks like lust in his eyes, but it disappears so quickly I'm sure

I must be hallucinating. Yeah, this warm weather is simply messing with my brain…and my libido. I need to get a leash on that right away. Because I am so *not* Will's type. Not that I want to be. I don't.

Tell that to your aching nipples.

He clears his throat, and the corners of his mouth tighten. "Your duties are written out for you in my rule book," he says.

Come again?

"You have a rule book?"

"You don't?

"Well no, that's kind of…" I want to say insane, but he doesn't look like a man who would appreciate bluntness from a subordinate, and I can't forget what Steph said. He goes through assistants in the blink of an eye. "Different," I say.

"I'm a man who lives by certain rules." His tongue slips from his mouth and brushes over the groove in his top lip, sending a shiver through me. "It's best for all of us this way."

As I study the streak of moisture on his lip, a blast of heat warms my blood, and I'm pretty damn sure it has nothing to do with our tropical location. I tamp it down and try for normal when I say, "Whatever you say, sir."

Will goes still for a second. What? Does he not like being called sir? Damned if it doesn't make me want to do it more.

He smooths his hand down his chest. "I think you should take the rest of today to rest, and make sure you're germ-free before you touch any food. My workload is light today, so I can pick up the slack."

"Sure thing. Maybe I'll go for a swim in that gorgeous pool or lounge on the beach."

"Whatever you like. You packed a suit?" he asks, like he's worried he's going to see me naked after all.

Yeah, I get it. No one wants to find a beached beluga on their private piece of paradise. My God, my ex was a jerk. If a man can't appreciate a woman with curves, then he can go to hell. Although I'm beginning to believe no man in Manhattan does. At least my battery-operated friend doesn't judge when I get naked.

"Khloe?"

"Yeah?"

"You disappeared there for a second."

"Right, I do have a bathing suit. Is wearing one in your rule book?"

That brings a half grin to his face. "Of course."

I resist the urge to roll my eyes. He goes back to his food, and I do the same, eating slowly when I really just want to scarf it down and put some much-needed distance between myself and my new boss.

He finishes and stretches his arms over his head. I try not to stare, or admire the way his muscles flex and bulge, but I do it anyway.

"Are you up for a tour of the place?" he asks when I set my fork down.

"I'd love a tour, sir." I note the tension on his face as I push away my plate and stand. We make our way into the kitchen. "How long have you owned this house?"

"A few years now. I bought it after... Let's just say, it's a secluded location that no one knows about, and the locals respect my privacy."

"So the locals know who you are, then?"

"Yes," he says. I wonder how they feel about a famous millionaire living among them, especially when there are some very poor areas, not to mention the damage done from the hurricane a few years back.

"You get along with them?"

"We get along just fine." He waves his hand. "This is the kitchen, obviously. You decide what meals you want to cook. I like breakfast at seven sharp, lunch at noon, and dinner at seven. You don't have to use local culture recipes if you don't want to, although one of my assistants left a cookbook if you're so inclined. My likes and dislikes are in the rule book."

"I bet they are," I murmur.

"What's that?"

"Nothing. Want to show me the rest of the place?"

We leave the kitchen and move through the mansion. He shows me the airy living room, a dining room that could comfortably seat eighteen, his large den with a massive desk and not much else, all the bathrooms, and all the bedrooms—most decorated in beach decor. I think there were six. I take in the opulence of the place, but it saddens me. There are no pictures, no homey touches, no stamp of a guy who entertains friends and family, a guy who welcomes love and laughter into his home. He's become quite the recluse after the exposé, and damned if I don't feel a niggling of remorse myself. I might not have written the article, but I worked for the magazine that did.

He goes on to explain more of my duties: shopping, cleaning, laundry, running errands. Our last stop on the tour is his bedroom, and he doesn't invite me in. Instead, we stand in the hall and his eyes cut to mine.

"Just remember, anything you see or overhear doesn't leave the confines of this house."

I glance into his room, take in his perfectly made bed. It doesn't even look like he slept in it. That brings a pang of guilt to my stomach. He stayed up to take care of me and probably never even got a wink of sleep. Maybe he's not such a bad guy after all.

My gaze roams to the comfy-looking soft blue bedding, and I engage my mouth before my brain. "What kind of noises are you worried I'm going to overhear?" His throat makes a sound, and I turn to him. "Oh, right. I get it. You...visitors...women."

Things would have been so much easier if I'd just been flushed out into space.

"No one is to come into this house unless they are vetted by me." He dips his head, and as he pins me with a glare, his mouth is right there. If I wanted to kiss him, all I'd have to do is go up on my toes. But I don't want to. The man is the most gorgeous specimen on the face of the earth, but clearly insane. Not to mention he can't keep it in his pants, and straight up admitted it. "Do you understand?"

"What I think you're trying to say is you're allowed 'visitors.' But I'm not."

"I never said that—" He runs his hands down his chest, a gesture that is becoming familiar, and that crinkle is back in his forehead. "Do you want visitors, Khloe?" he asks.

He's been honest so far, so I don't see the need not to return the favor. "For the record, my days of Netflix and chill are over," I admit.

His eyes narrow in on me. "Why is that?"

"They just are, okay?" I am not about to admit that men don't find me attractive, and that my ex wanted to change me, and that I've given up finding anyone because I no longer believe there is a match for me. No, it's best I keep my deepest flaws to myself.

He studies me too closely, too intently. He opens his mouth like he's going to push, but the door chimes.

"Expecting a *visitor*, sir?" I ask with a raised brow, even though it could end up in him canning my ass. But for some reason I just can't help myself.

"No," he grumbles, but I catch a hint of caution in his tone, a rigid restraint in his body as he heads to the front door. My teasing turns to concern as I follow him. He opens the door, and a gorgeous olive-skinned woman who looks to be in her early thirties stands on his steps. She gives him a sexy, come-hither smile when their eyes meet.

"Will," she says in a singsong voice, heavy with a creole accent.

His smile is back in place. "Bevey," he says, his body relaxing slightly.

"I heard you were back," the gorgeous Bevey says. "I came as soon as I could. I brought your favorite dish."

Yeah, I just bet she did. And I also bet it's called Bevey, with a cherry on top.

CHAPTER SIX

Will

"COME IN," I say to Bevey, and stand back to allow her entrance. Her dark brown eyes widen, and her smile turns a bit forced when she sees Khloe in her ridiculous uniform. "Bevey, this is Khloe, my new assistant."

Bevey shifts the plate of johnnycakes from her right hand to her left and extends her arm to greet the shorter, curvier woman beside me. "Nice to meet you, Khloe."

"Nice to meet you, too," Khloe says, and points at the dish in Bevey's hand. "Would you like me to take those for you?"

"Yes, thank you. I made them this morning. They're Will's favorite." She gives me a big toothy smile that lights up her pretty face. "He says my johnnycakes are the best."

"I bet he does," Khloe says under her breath. "I'll put these in the kitchen, sir. And if you need me, I'll be in the pool."

Sir.

Okay, she's seriously fucking with me. Maybe I should fuck back.

Maybe I should fuck *her*.

Khloe disappears, and I will my dick to behave as I turn to my dear friend. Bevey and I go way back. I came to the island with Granddad years ago, when he was first looking to buy a resort, and Bevey was the one who greeted us at the airport. She drove the shuttle bus, but after one taste of her johnnycakes I knew her talents were being wasted. Granddad bought the resort, and I promoted her to chef.

"It's so good to see you." I open my arms, and the bright yellow scarf covering her hair tickles my face. After a firm hug, we break apart. I gesture with a wave, and we walk farther into the house. "How are things? How are Samuel and Chardane?"

"We're doing so much better now, thanks to your generosity. The new housing complex is more than we ever expected, and—" she sighs and claps her hand together "—running water."

That brings a smile to my face, but it falls quickly. "The school should be completed this month. I'm back to check on progress." It kills me to think the middle school kids at Leonard Elementary, including her daughter, Chardane, are being educated in an old building that had once been waterlogged. I can't even imagine the mold and mildew they're subjected to on a daily basis.

Her big brown eyes widen, and her full lips curl. "The kids are all very excited about the new school."

I guide her through the kitchen, and the delicious scent from the johnnycakes reaches my nostrils. I'm tempted to have one, but I'm full from breakfast. Besides, Khloe might enjoy one with me later, along with a cup of coffee. I had a hard time swallowing mine this morning with her sitting across from me, her body barely clad. Wait, what am I doing? Khloe is here to work for me. I shouldn't be thinking about taking coffee breaks with her or how much she would like Bevey's johnnycakes.

Shouldn't be thinking about how hot she is in or out of that ridiculous uniform.

"Any more news on filling the positions?" I ask.

"Applications are still open for English teachers. After Jess and Mari went back to the States, we haven't been able to fill their spots."

I open the patio door and we step outside. "I'll run that by Granddad. He can check at the staffing agency." I widen my arms. "Who wouldn't want to spend their time here?"

"It is a beautiful island, yes," she says in her creole accent.

I pull the chair from the table and gesture for her to sit. "Is everyone well?"

"We are well," she says, tucking her long white dress around her knees and lowering herself into the chair that Khloe had recently occupied.

"Can I get you a coffee, tea?"

She waves her hand. "I'm fine." Her eyes narrow in thought, and her full lips pinch tighter.

"What?" I ask, worry invading my gut. She clearly has something on her mind. "Are you sure things are good at home and work?"

"It's not me I'm concerned about."

"You're worried about me?"

She leans in. "I'm worried about your new assistant. What is that silly costume she's wearing?"

That brings a laugh to my throat. "Granddad told her I had a dress code, and I guess that is what she thought she had to wear."

She grins and points a finger at me. "And I take it you aren't planning to tell her the difference anytime soon."

"Where's the fun in that?"

"Oh, Will. You are trouble, but I am glad to see you having fun." She leans in and lowers her voice even more. "She's a beautiful woman, no?"

I smirk. "That she is."

"It's time you settled down, Will. Found yourself a nice wife."

"Bevey," I warn. "You know I'm not interested in marriage." Not anymore, anyway.

"Foolishness. It's not natural to be alone. You just have to find the right woman."

I don't bother telling her I had the right woman and ruined it.

"Don't you be too hard on this one. She has potential."

Hard on her?

Yeah, I think it's the other way around, judging by my dick's response whenever she's near.

"I'll be my usual charming self."

Bevey laughs and glances around. "Has James come with you? I do miss that man."

"No, he's home. I'm actually waiting to hear from him. I'll let him know you stopped by with the johnnycakes. He'll be disappointed that he missed out."

"Before you fly back, I'll bring a fresh batch for James."

I put my hand on hers. "You're too kind."

"You're the kind one, sir."

Sir.

Jesus, when Khloe called me that earlier, a streak of anger behind the word, my dick stood up and took notice. I have no idea why I want to hear that on her lips in the bedroom.

"Things are good at Great Bay Resort?" Her husband, Samuel, had been injured in the hurricane, and after millions of dollars' worth of repairs to Granddad's resort, he's back working. But now he's out of maintenance—the lifting had aggravated his back—and working in the kitchen with Bevey and the rest of the culinary crew.

She steeples her fingers and looks at the sky. "Give me strength."

I laugh. "I take it he's underfoot."

"He needs to leave me to the cooking. The man can't boil water without burning it."

"How about I pay him a visit and see what other job he might enjoy."

"You are a savior," she says, and a big splash below catches our attention. I glance through the glass-panel decking and catch a glimpse of Khloe swimming from one end of the infinity pool to the other. A bead of sweat travels down my back when she surfaces on the other end and I glimpse her breasts barely tucked in to a too small bikini top.

"I won't take up any more of your time," Bevey says, and when I turn to her I catch a knowing grin on her face.

"Don't be silly. I enjoy spending time with you."

"Something tells me there is someone else you'd rather be spending time with."

I cock my head, a playful challenge. "Then you'd be wrong."

She laughs and stands. "You're selling, but I'm not buying," she says. I just laugh and follow her back inside the house. The cool air-conditioning dries the moisture on my flesh. "You'll be attending the Carnival in the village, yes?" I open my mouth, and she cuts me off. "You need to work less and play harder."

"Have you been talking to Granddad?"

She laughs. "He's a wise old man, Will. You should listen to him."

I glance at my watch. "I would listen to him if he'd ever call me back."

We head to the front door, and I give her a hug to see her off. Back inside, I'm about to go to my den but instead find myself wandering to the deck. I lean on the rail and look out, but Khloe is no longer in the pool. Now she's making her way down the wooden steps that lead to the ocean. A warm breeze washes over me as I enjoy the view—and I'm not talking about Magdalen Bay.

Khloe steps into the water, slowly going deeper. For a moment, she disappears in the rough waves, then she jumps to the surface a little farther out. Her squeal of delight carries in the breeze and reaches my ears. It brings a smile to my face. I tug at my T-shirt and consider joining her, but that could only lead to trouble. It's best I lock myself away in my office and get some work done. That and I should call and check on Granddad again.

I pull my phone from my back pocket, but my heart jumps into my throat when Khloe's squeals of delight turn into a cry of pain.

What the hell?

She disappears under the water, and I take off running. I bolt through the house, push open the door leading to the lower back deck and take the steps to the ocean two at a time. I tug off my shirt and toss it as I go, then kick off my shoes. I reached the edge of the water and search for Khloe, but Jesus, I can't find her. As full-blown panic burns through my blood, I splash into the surf and dive under. I swim, search, the salt water stinging my eyes. I break through the surface for air and catch a glimpse of Khloe trying to swim ashore.

"Khloe!" I call out.

"Will," she whimpers, and I hurry to her. Her lips are twisted, and tears prick her eyes, but I can't see any physical injuries. "What happened?"

"My leg. I don't know what happened."

I scoop her up and fight the tugging waves as I carry her back to the shore as quickly as possible. The second the sand goes from wet to dry, I set her down and take her leg in my hand.

"Damn," I say, and study the spreading red rash.

"Shark bite?"

"No," I assure her, but her eyes are so big and wide, so worried she was attacked by a shark in five feet of water, it's all I can do not to smirk.

"Are you laughing?"

"I'm not laughing. This isn't funny."

"You seem like you're laughing." She reaches for the red spot and winces. "It hurts." I catch her hand before she can touch the sting.

"A jellyfish sting is nothing to laugh about." I search her face. "Are your tetanus shots up to date?" She nods. "Okay good, the sting isn't too bad. You likely only brushed up against the jellyfish, but we need to treat it right away."

"No way, Will." She tries to push me away. "Get away from me. I mean it."

"What the hell, Khloe. We have to remove the tentacles. There looks to be about two. That's not many, but we have to remove what's there."

"You are *not* peeing on me. Ohmigod. Could this week get any worse? First I vomit in front of you and now you're going to pee on me." She covers her face with her hands. "And this bathing suit. I have no dignity left. None."

This time I do laugh.

She pushes me again. "See, I knew you were laughing."

"I'm not laughing. Well, I am." Only because she's so wildly sexy when she gets angry, and she was worried I was going to pee on her.

She gives me the death glare. "Stop it."

I shake my head, seriously thrown off my game by this woman. I brush her hair back and meet her wild eyes. "You're really having a bad week, aren't you?" My heart misses a beat, an imaginary band squeezing it as she curls into herself.

She softens against me, and I catch a hint of vulnerability in her. This woman is strength and independence, and I'm sure helplessness is not a trait she'd like for me to see in her. Although I must say, it does bring out the protector in me.

"I've had better," she murmurs.

"I know you have," I say in a soft voice. "And I'm going to take care of this sting, okay?"

"Will…please…"

"Don't worry, my pants aren't coming down anytime soon." I scoop her up and head back toward the house. "Peeing on a jellyfish sting will cause more pain than relief. Urine can actually aggravate the jellyfish's stinger to release more venom."

"But I thought—"

"You thought wrong." Guilt worms its way into my gut. "Goddammit, this is my fault."

"How is it your fault? Did you tell the jellyfish to sting me? Or maybe you stock the ocean to keep people away?"

Is that what she thinks of me? I know I take privacy to the extreme, but I'm not a monster who would purposely hurt anyone.

I frown at her. "I should have warned you. In the rule book, it says to wear water shoes."

"How would that have helped? The sting is in my calf."

"Yeah, true, but it could have been worse. Could have been a stingray. I was…distracted when you told me you were going swimming."

She gives a very unladylike snort. "Oh, is that what you were?"

I get the sense she thinks I'm talking about Bevey distracting me—she is a beautiful woman—and maybe it's best I let her believe that. Khloe doesn't need to know my brain has been working at half capacity since she first boarded Granddad's plane. I don't want her to get the wrong idea…or the right idea. Or any idea.

"Did you pack water shoes?" I ask.

"No."

"I'll go to town and get you a pair." I look at her feet. "Size eight?"

"So the size of my feet you know?"

I have no idea what she's talking about but come back with, "Apparently you're not the only one with special gifts."

"Shut up," she says, clearly catching my reference to her projectile vomiting skills. Her lush mouth twists into a grimace. "Maybe I'll stick to the pool and just admire the ocean from the deck."

"Jellyfish tend to come to shore on windy days. I think you'll be okay to get in again. It'd be a shame for you not to enjoy the Caribbean waters. Let's just make sure it's when the winds are down, and I'll go with you."

"I'm not going to put you out like that, and I'm supposed to be the one taking care of your needs, not the other way around."

I hold her tight and think about that as her arms wrap around my neck. "Still believe in fate, Khloe."

She snarls at me, and I must say I love her spirited nature. "I don't think getting stung by a stupid jellyfish had anything to do with fate."

Warm sand squeezes between my toes as I hurry my steps, well aware of the way my body is reacting to having her lushness pressed up against me. I shift her an inch higher in my arms before she feels all eight inches of me against her sweet ass. "Didn't you say everything happens for a reason?"

"Well, yeah, but…"

"What do you think the reason for this is?"

She opens her mouth, but it doesn't matter what she says, not when my swelling dick has come to its own conclusions.

That my pants do indeed need to come down… soon.

CHAPTER SEVEN

Khloe

MY LEG MIGHT be hurting, but that's not the only part of my body that's throbbing. Okay, so I might not really like rich guys who say and do what they like—ones who make their help wear revealing costumes—but I can appreciate his hard body and lean muscles as he runs to the house like I'm a light weight in his arms. Trust me, I'm not. And Will has been kind to me, even depriving himself of sleep to watch over me.

I press against him and breathe in the scent of his skin as he opens the door and carries me down the long hall to *his* bedroom. He sets me on his big comfy bed and steps back, studying my face. A thoughtful, concerned look backlights those gorgeous blue eyes.

"How are you feeling?"

I give an exaggerated exhale to hide my arousal. "Like I really pissed someone off in a past life."

He laughs and sinks to his knees. "No dizziness or nausea? Do you feel like you're going to be sick?"

I slap one hand to my forehead. "Please tell me that's not going to happen again."

His big fingers circle my wrist, firmly removing my hand from my face to place at my side. "No, you'll feel sick to your stomach only if you're having a severe reaction." He cocks his head. "No abdominal pain, numbness or tingling, muscle spasms, or breathing troubles?"

Well, I am having a bit of trouble breathing, but I think it's from the strong and steady way he moved my hand to my side. Would he move me around like that in bed? I'm a take-charge kind of girl, so I have no idea why the idea of surrendering my needs to Will arouses me so much.

"No, I'm good," I push past my lips.

He takes my leg in his hand to examine it, and I suck in a fast breath. His gaze shoots to mine.

"Am I hurting you?"

"I'm good," I lie, as he gently holds my thigh. Honest to God, his touch is one thing, but his current position on the floor—between my spread legs—is something else altogether.

"Don't you think I should go to a doctor?" I croak out, trying to get my focus on something other than how good his touch feels.

"If you're not experiencing any of those symptoms, I say no. For the next twenty-four hours I'm going to have to watch you for signs of a serious re-action, though."

"I'm not going to keep you up all night again, Will."

"I don't mind you keeping me up all night."

His head is dipped, and I can't see his face, can't tell if he's teasing or not. But when he says things like that, and things like he doesn't mind putting out, my thoughts go off in an inappropriate direction, and damn the flush crawling up my neck and warming me all over.

"We'll worry about that later, okay?" he says, "Right now, we have to clean this and spray it with vinegar."

I crinkle my nose. "Vinegar? Are you kidding me?"

"Do I look like the kind of guy who would kid in a situation like this?

I lift my chin an inch. "I don't really know you that well."

"Then you're just going to have to trust me on that."

"I don't trust anyone." Working at a cutthroat magazine like *Starlight* is enough to make anyone jaded. And I can't forget my ex promised to love me forever. Look how that turned out.

"Makes two of us," he says quickly. "But I do know what I'm doing?"

"You've been stung?"

He nods.

"The vinegar worked?"

"Yeah. The pain you're feeling, I can relate." His eyes hold a measure of sympathy as they meet mine. I study him for a second, debating my next move. His jaw clenches, and he finally breaks the silence. "Am I doing this, Khloe?" he asks, and even when frazzled with my obstinance, he's still so goddamn sweet and charming I think I might get a toothache.

"Has anyone ever said no to you?" I ask.

He responds with, "The vinegar works. I promise."

"Vinegar it is, then," I say.

"Stay put, okay?"

I nod and he disappears into what I assume is the master bathroom. Drawers open and close, and a minute later he comes back with a spray bottle and tweezers.

"I'll be as gentle as I can," he says, his mouth tight, like he knows this is going to hurt. "But this might sting a bit."

"It's already stinging. Besides, I can handle a little pain." As soon as the words leave my mouth and I catch a grin curving his kissable lips, I wish I could get them back, swallow them down into the depths of my stomach, never to be heard from again.

What the hell is wrong with me?

Maybe I should sleep with him, get this insane arousal out of my system so I can talk and act like a woman who isn't obsessed with sex. But he's my boss, and we both have rules about that.

"Good to know," he says, his voice an octave deeper. "Take a big breath, Khloe."

I do as he says, and his gaze drops from my mouth and moves to my expanding chest. That's when I become acutely aware that I'm in a revealing bathing suit, and my nipples are pressing hard against the thin material, making my current arousal painfully obvious. Why am I constantly in revealing clothes around this guy?

"Okay," he says gruffly. "Okay, okay," he repeats, like he's talking to himself and trying to pull it together. He mutters what sounds like a curse and turns his attention to my sting.

"Tell me what you used to do for a living," he says, and I get that he's trying to distract me as he uses the tweezers to pull the first tentacle off.

"My dream is to someday write a book," I say, hedging the question.

"Oh yeah? What kind of book?"

"Maybe a thriller. I love psychological thrillers and horror."

He casts me a quick glance. "Really? I never would have guessed."

"No?"

"I would have thought something along the line of satire."

"And why is that?" I give him a sassy look that suggests he knows nothing.

"That's why," he says with a laugh. "You've got a sharp tongue."

"You don't know anything about my tongue," I shoot back. His hand stills over my leg, trembles a tiny bit, and my mind once again goes off in an erotic direction, envisioning him getting to know my tongue better by pressing his lips to mine.

"Just one left," he mutters and steadies his hand enough to pull off the last tentacle.

"Not so bad," I say, until he sprays the open wound with whatever is in that bottle. I let out an ungodly scream, and I'm pretty sure I pierced Will's eardrums judging by the way his face is contorting.

I grab the spray bottle from him. "What is this fresh hell?" I read the label. "Sting No More. It's clearly mislabeled. It stings twice as bad."

"Give it a second," he says, a grin playing with the corner of his mouth. "The vinegar will neutralize the venom."

"My day is just getting better and better." I toss the bottle to the bed, but lo and behold the pain starts to settle.

"Good?" he asks.

"Better."

"Now we have to put your leg into very, very hot water."

"Sure, why not. It's been fun so far."

He presses his hands to my thighs, leaving a burning imprint as he pushes off me to stand up. "You really are a good sport about all this, Khloe."

"Yeah, that's me, good sport Khloe."

"I actually admire that."

I meet his eyes, and it's rather silly how that simple compliment managed to jump-start my pulse, speeding it up enough to make me breathless.

He holds his hand out to me, and I let him lift me to my feet. I'm about to put pressure on my leg, but once again find myself in his arms. Good thing, considering the muscles in my legs have dissolved. He carries me to his master bathroom, which is twice as big as the bath in his spare room, and sets me on the marble countertop. I take in the room as he fills a claw-foot tub. Steam rises, dampens the sliding glass shower doors and the mirror behind me. I don't dare turn to look at my tear-streaked face and beach hair. I had enough of a fright with the jellyfish.

"All set?" he asks.

I nod, and he lifts me from the counter and sets me on the side of the tub. I wince as I plunge my leg into the water, bracing the other on the edge of the tub. My flesh instantly turns red from the heat. "When you said hot water, what you really meant to say is water so hot you can boil an egg."

He sits on the tub beside me, his feet on the floor. "You okay?"

"I will be." I let out a sigh. "Thanks to you."

He nudges me with his shoulder. "Was there a compliment in there somewhere?"

"Probably not."

He laughs, and it comes out rough. His body rumbles, and I become acutely aware of his close proximity and what it's doing to me.

"Can you get me a towel, please?"

He grabs a towel from the cabinet and hands it to me. I drape it over my shoulders.

"Are you cold?"

"No." I'm pretty sure I'm going to spontaneously combust. "I just... I'm in my bathing suit."

"I've noticed."

My gaze cuts to his. My ex spouted some pretty harsh comments the last time I wore a suit around him. The thing is, I have no problem with my curves. I rather like them, and I'll be damned if I'm going to starve myself to fit society's expectations. But I get that men prefer waif-thin models, and Will here is no exception.

"I wasn't expecting anyone to see me in it." I shrug into myself, but my breasts only spill out more. "It's last year's, and I didn't have a chance to go shopping."

"You don't like it?"

"I never said that."

"But you did say something about it earlier. I wasn't sure what you meant."

His hand moves, brushes against mine as I grip the edge of the tub. "I wouldn't have worn it if I thought you were going to see me in it. It's just that it's a bit small."

"Yeah." A sound catches in his throat as his gaze slowly skims downward. "I noticed that, too."

I'm about to die of mortification, until I catch the heat in his eyes. And his breathing is a little more labored. Am I reading this situation right, or has the venom gotten to my brain?

"In the rule book, two-piece bathing suits are prohibited."

"Are you kidding me?"

"No," he grumbles, and scrubs his face.

"That's really in the book?"

His jaw tightens, his muscles rippling. How is it possible that he's getting better- and better-looking by the second?

"It's going to be in about two minutes," he murmurs.

The air around us charges, and my heart speeds up. "Will…" I say, his name coming out a little soft, a little husky around the edges.

He shifts closer, his breath warm on my face. "You remember my rule about not getting involved with those in my employment."

"Yeah," I say, and he touches the cotton towel, rubs his fingers over it in a way that has my thoughts sliding off track. I take a moment to envision the rough pad of his thumb touching another part of my body in much that same manner.

"You're a beautiful woman with a killer body, Khloe, and if you wear this again…" He lets out a slow breath, and it blows a tendril of hair from my face. He moves closer, breathing me in as his mouth goes to my ear. "Let's just say, I've never been tempted to break that rule. Until now."

I take a few deep breaths. Is this guy for real?

Wait, I've already established the fact that he's insane.

"My ex," I begin before I can think better of it. "He wanted me to lose weight, fit in more with what a woman is expected to look like." I turn my head slowly, and there's a mixture of heat and anger in Will's eyes.

"Your ex is obviously an idiot."

"That's why I left him."

"You shouldn't change yourself. Not for anyone."

"I don't plan on it. I like myself just fine." He smiles at that, and heat arcs between us. I take a fast breath to get my head together. "Even if you were tempted to break the rules, I'd never sleep with another woman's man."

"Bevey is an old friend," he explains.

"That's not who I'm talking about."

He stares at me, his brow furrowed. I give him a moment to process—personally I'm not thinking straight, and I suspect a lot of blood has left his brain, too. Damned if I don't want to glance down to check. A second later, his eyes widen in understanding. "You're talking about Jules."

"That's right." I lift my chin a little. "I have rules, too, you know."

His grin is slow, sexy as hell. "So you *were* listening in to my conversation."

"No... I..." Shit. Busted.

"It's okay, you signed the nondisclosure agreement."

"It was hard not to listen. You weren't trying to

be quiet. I am curious, though. What is the present you got her? Diamonds would be my guess."

"What would a four-year-old want with diamonds?"

"Four?" Okay, now that I didn't expect.

"Jules is my four-year-old niece."

A thrill I wish I wasn't feeling races through me.

"Don't you keep up with the news, Khloe? My cousin Tate and his wife, Summer, have a little girl."

"Now that you mention it."

He leans into me, his mouth grazing my shoulder. "Is that the only thing stopping you...?"

My left leg drops from the edge of the tub and plunges into the hot water. It splashes up on us, dousing the lust bubbling between us.

He pulls back, fast, and his face hardens, his eyes a blazing mess of lust and regret. "Khloe... I. Damn. I don't know what I was thinking." He inches back, putting a small measure of distance between us. It does nothing to extinguish the heat in my body. "We...ah...probably shouldn't let this happen, right?"

My brain is so fuzzy, I can't tell whether he's making a statement or asking a question. "You're right," I say. Getting involved with my boss is wrong on so many levels.

And why is that, Khloe?

Oh, because...

I rack my lust-induced brain, but can't come up with an answer. He's single. I'm single. He's made it clear he's not the settling-down type, and I'm not looking to settle down with him. I don't even like rich, entitled guys. But there is no doubt we're physically attracted to each other, and we're both consenting adults. Why can't we have a little fun if we're clear on the rules from the get-go?

"Here," he says, the deep tenor of his voice dragging me back to the present as he hands me another towel. "I'm going to lift you out, and you can drape that around your leg." He bends into me, hooks his arms under my legs and gently lifts me from the tub.

I put my hands around his neck, and he hisses quietly as I spread my fingers to touch more of his skin. I slide my hand down his back, palm his muscles. His jaw is so tight I fear something might snap as he sets me back on the counter, takes the towel from me, and with the utmost care pats my leg dry. I widen my thighs a little more to make it easier for him, and maybe to tease him a bit. Now that I know what I do to him, that he too feels the heat between us, I plan to torment. I'm not going to make things easy on Will. In fact, I'm going to make things very *hard* on him.

As a delicious, devious plan forms in my mind, I say, "I think I need to see this rule book of yours, sir."

CHAPTER EIGHT

Will

WHAT THE EVER-LOVING hell is going on in my life? It's been three days since I touched down on Saint Thomas. Three long, torturous days with Khloe prancing around in her skimpy uniforms and bending over to dust every possible low spot. At night, when she's not driving me insane, she sits on her deck, her head buried in her journal, her soft humming sounds filtering in through my bedroom window and caressing my cock.

I glance up from my laptop as she hums a tune and bends to run a feather duster over the baseboards—again. I only have so much control, and with her aiming that sweet ass my way, it's about to shatter.

"Haven't you cleaned that already?"

"Yes," she says and goes back to her humming.

"Do you think you could stop humming?" I command in a deep voice.

She blinks innocent eyes at me, although I'm beginning to believe there is nothing innocent about her. She's been reading over the rule book for the last two nights while I've been in my office working on a new Do Not list.

My phone pings, and I reach for it. It had better be Granddad. I've put a call in to him every day, and he's yet to call me back. This time it's Tate.

"How's Saint Thomas?" he asks. "Is the view still as spectacular as always?"

I lift my eyes slightly as Khloe sways her hips to an imaginary song inside her head. "More spectacular than ever," I grumble.

Tate laughs. "Sure doesn't sound it."

"Just a lot on my mind. Like how is Granddad? Why isn't he calling me back?"

"I'm not sure. I was with him earlier, and he never said anything about you calling."

"Is he okay?"

"As good as can be expected. He's midnineties, after all."

"Do you think... Do you think he might be losing his mind?" I blurt out.

"I've been thinking that for years, but why are you suddenly asking?"

Khloe leaves my office, and I lower my voice. "The woman he hired to accompany me to Saint Thomas. I'm not sure what he was thinking."

"She's not working out?"

"She broke the vacuum, a few dishes, everything she cooks she burns, and she..."

Papers rustle in the background. "She what?"

"I'm not sure you'd believe me if I told you."

"Now I really need to hear."

"She wears these French maid uniforms. Hang on, I'll send you a link of what the outfit looks like." I do a quick search, find the image on Amazon, grab the link and shoot it off to Tate.

I wait a second. As soon as a low, slow whistle followed by a hoot of laughter comes through the line, I know he's opened it.

"Lucky you," Tate says.

"No, not lucky me. You know my rules."

"Yeah, fuck the rules, Will. If she's hot, and I think Granddad said something about your new assistant being a looker, then I'd go for it. What do you have to lose?"

"Right now, I'm losing my mind."

Tate lets out another roar. "Hey, you never know. She could be the one."

"Tate, you know—" I stop when, from the kitchen, something hits the floor and smashes.

"What was that?" Tate asks.

"Lunch, I'm guessing."

"Sounds like things are in bad shape."

Khloe's not. Her shape is just perfect. My cock, however...

I lean back in my chair and look out into the hall. Pinching the bridge of my nose, I say, "Maybe I should cut this trip short."

"Nah, just don't work so hard. Put your feet up and have some fun for a change."

"Wait, you called me. Did you need something?"

"Nope, just checking in. Jules is excited about her party, and I'm just making sure her uncle Will is going to be there," he says, but I have a feeling that's not entirely true. I never get calls when I'm here in Saint Thomas. Everyone knows I come when I need solitude, and I'd assured Summer I'd be there for Jules's party. What is this really all about? Before I can ask, Tate says, "So you'll be there?"

"I'll be there. If I don't spontaneously combust first."

Tate laughs again. "Yeah, you need to get laid, man."

I'm beginning to believe he might be right.

"While that sounds about right, I haven't had a chance to check on the resort or the school's progress yet. I've been afraid to leave Khloe alone. She nearly lit the kitchen on fire the other day. I was thinking of getting Bevey to give her a few lessons."

"You're good in the kitchen. Maybe you could show her a few things."

Goddammit, the things I want to show her involve the use of a mattress, not a stove.

"I better go check on her. Can you get Granddad to call me?"

"Will do."

We say goodbye, and I push from my chair to check on the commotion in the kitchen. I don't smell smoke, which gives me a measure of relief. I step into the kitchen to find Khloe at the table, writing something in my rule book.

She closes it and flashes me a smile when she sees me.

"What are you doing?"

"I was just finishing my notes," she says.

I shove my hands into my pockets. "In *my* rule book?"

"I've given that some thought, and since I'm working for you, I believe it's *our* rule book, and I thought I should jot a few rules down, too."

Since I'm not sure I like the sound of that, I change direction. "I heard a crash."

She crinkles up her nose—her freckles are more prominent now that she's spent time in the sun. "Sorry, broke a plate. You can take it out of my pay, like the last couple I broke."

"I told you I'm not going to do that."

She puts the end of the pen in her mouth, nibbles a little and says, "I've given that some thought, too. I made notes in the book on how I could repay you, *sir.*"

Jesus, she's fucking with me. I'm sure of it.

"How's that?"

She just grins and says, "Your lunch is made. It's in the fridge. The wind has finally died down, so I thought I'd take my hour lunch break and go for a swim."

"Don't forget your water shoes," I say. I went into

town yesterday with Khloe to stock the fridge and pantry, and we picked her up a pair of shoes as well as a few new one-piece bathing suits and a couple of cover-up dresses.

"I do need to pay you back for the shoes and all the clothing. But it's all outlined in the book." She taps the leather cover, giving me a small grin that pushes all my buttons.

I make my way to the fridge, pull the door open and find a sandwich and salad. "Have you eaten?" I ask. "We could sit on the deck…"

She wipes the back of her hand across her forehead. "I'm not hungry yet. I'll grab something after my swim."

I curse the disappointment in my gut. Dammit, I shouldn't be trying to find ways to hang around her longer. I should be trying to find ways to avoid her.

"I'll just eat in my office," I grumble, and keep my head down.

"Whatever you prefer, sir."

"Khloe," I say around a thick tongue. "Call me Will."

I snatch up my lunch and make my way to my office. I toss the sandwich down and catch a glimpse of Khloe on her way to her bedroom to change. I'm pretty sure the new suits will look amazing on her killer body, and damned if I don't want to sneak a peek. Her soft humming sounds reach my ears as she makes her way to the door. It opens, closes with a soft click, and my dick urges me to head outside to enjoy the show.

I bite into my sandwich and shake my head. How the hell can anyone screw up a turkey sandwich? I peel it open to see that she used mustard instead of mayonnaise. I'm beginning to believe she didn't read the rule book at all.

I toss it aside, my appetite dissolving, as a new kind of hunger takes up residence in my body. I push my chair back, my heart thumping a little faster.

Don't do it, Will. Don't give in to temptation.

Then I remember what Tate said. I need to get laid. The man's not wrong. What *is* wrong is sleeping with the help.

Unless she wants that, too…

I jump up and make my way to the kitchen. The rule book sits on the table where Khloe left it, like she wanted me to flip through it. Who am I to disappoint? I scoop it up and run my thumb over the leather as I step out onto the deck. The warmth of the day falls over me, and I scan the beach for Khloe. Her head pops from the green water as she leisurely swims in the bay.

I pull out a chair, sit and flip the book open. I leaf through the pages with my writing and stop when the script changes. I settle myself to read, but the first line has me sitting up a little straighter, sweating a little harder.

This…this is what Khloe's been up to? I take a couple of deep breaths before I begin to read *her* rules. And from the title alone, I'm ready to blow my load.

Ten Rules for Sleeping with Your Assistant:
1. The affair is secret.
2. Sexual pleasure only.
3. No dating.
4. No overnights in the same room.
5. No kissing.
6. No gifts.
7. No getting personal.
8. Life goes back to normal when we return to the US.
9. For every plate I break or any inappropriate behavior, there should be some sort of reprimand. I should also be required to pay for the things you've purchased for me.
10. I'll leave the details up to you.

The world closes in on me, goes a little fuzzy around the edges. All this time, Khloe has been making rules of her own, rules that totally make sense. Rules I can live by. Humming sounds reach my ears. I push from my chair, look out over the ocean, and nearly bite off my tongue when I find Khloe standing on the sand, staring out at the ocean, dressed in nothing but her goddamn water shoes.

Sweet Jesus.

CHAPTER NINE

Khloe

I DON'T NEED to turn around to know his eyes are on me. I can feel them boring into my naked flesh as I admire the green waters of the bay. Every nerve in my body is alive and on fire, knowing Will is either going to send me packing or meet me on the sand and accept the rules of the game. The move is risky on my part, but from the way he looks at me to the tortured curses I hear in his throat when I bend to dust… Yeah, he wants this as much as I do.

A noise sounds on the stairs behind me, but I don't turn. This is Will's private paradise, and the only one who can be coming my way is the man I want in my bed. My heart crashes against my ribs, pounds behind my eyes. His vibrating energy, volatile heat, reaches out to me, slides over my skin as he closes the distance. Staying perfectly still, I breathe deep, catching his scent.

He steps up behind me, his harsh breath so damn

hot on my skin, I'm sure I'm going to ignite. I'm about to turn to face him when he stops me.

"Don't move."

I have no idea what it is about his strong commands that get to me. He runs his fingers from my shoulders to my elbows, and I shudder.

"I read your rules." Warm lips brush my shoulder, and erotic sensation shoots straight to my sex.

"And?" I ask, a thrill going through me. If he's kissing me, it must mean he's in agreement.

"There are a lot of them."

"Not compared to the two hundred rules you have. But enough to keep us on track. No mistakes. No misunderstandings."

"Yes, that's why rules are important."

"Very important," I agree.

His teeth graze my flesh as his hands drop to my waist, shape my curves. "New rules for sleeping with the assistant. I never would have thought of that."

"But you agree with them?" I ask, my voice coming out a breathless whisper.

Touch me already.

"Arms above your head."

My pulse leaps, and I swallow as I do as he commands. A warm breeze washes over my naked body as Will steps close enough for me to feel his hard cock pressing against the small of my back.

"I'm still trying to decide," he says, and I feel a moment of panic. Him being here, touching me, his blatant arousal…aren't they all signs that he's made up his mind?

"Decide what?" I ask, doing my best not to sound as needy as I feel.

"What the punishment for breaking my dishes should be."

I scrape my teeth over my dry bottom lip. "It's a big decision."

"Very big," he says, his fingers biting into my hips as he pulls me against his hardness. I wiggle, grind against him, and his deep groan of approval is my glorious reward. Damn, I love how I get to this man.

His big warm hands leave my hips, begin a heated journey up my stomach until he has two handfuls of my breasts.

"These," he begins, as he kneads my flesh, "have been driving me crazy for days now."

"Sorry, sir," I tease.

"Jesus, Khloe." He growls into my ear, and my body shudders. "You've been fucking with me, haven't you?"

"Who, me, sir?"

"Yeah, you." One hand leaves my breasts, and he shifts his stance to grab my ass. He squeezes, pulls his hand back and gives me a small slap. I let out a little yelp.

"What…what was that for?" I ask, a new kind of pleasure dancing on my flesh.

"For pushing my buttons." He takes my hands, puts them by my sides and steps back. He goes silent for so long, I'd think he'd retreated if not for the tortured sound of his breathing.

"Like what you see, sir?" I ask, just to get a rise out of him.

"Turn around."

Sand squishes beneath my shoes as I slowly spin, and my breath catches when the heat in his eyes burns my flesh. I have never seen that look on a man's face before. Intense, frustrated, excited... needy.

"Yes, I like what I see."

My gaze leaves his face, takes in his loose blue T-shirt, going lower to examine the bulge in his khaki shorts. My mouth waters, and my fingers itch to close around him, weigh him in my palm.

"I'm not seeing enough," I say. His body stiffens, and as he grumbles a curse, I bite back a grin. I have no idea what it is about this man that brings out the bold side in me, but I love his reactions.

"Widen your legs," he commands.

I spread my legs, and my sex moistens, my inner thighs becoming so wet, I'm sure he can see them glistening. His deep groan confirms it.

He rubs his hand over himself. "Every night in bed, I take my cock in my hands and think about burying my mouth between your legs."

Holy...

I figured this man was the opposite of vanilla, but I've never had anyone talk dirty to me before, and I have to say...I love it.

"I believe in rule number two," I say. "Sexual pleasure is on the table."

"The table, huh? How about the bed, Khloe?"

"Yes, sir," I say, and his nostrils flare as he steps up to me. He lightly runs the rough pads of his thumbs over my hard nipples, plucks at them, and once again slides his tongue over the dip in his upper lip.

"Have you been touching yourself, too?" he asks. "Thinking about me with my mouth between your legs, licking you until you explode?"

A whimper catches in my throat as my sex squeezes.

"Yes," I manage to say. "When I'm in bed at night, listening to the waves, I widen my legs and touch myself, imagining it's your fingers inside me."

His hands leave my breasts, slide down my body and slip between my spread legs. The black in his eyes bleeds into the blue as he runs a finger along the length of my pussy.

"God, you're so wet."

He slides a finger into me, and my muscles hold him tight. I take a few deep breaths and make a move to touch him. "No," he commands. "Just stand there."

"Will," I murmur as he slides another finger in and strokes me a few times.

"I can't wait to get my cock in here," he says.

"What are you waiting for?" I ask.

His grin is slow, so damn sexy when he scoops me up and hurries to the house. I hold on to him, reveling in the strength of his body, the rippling of his hard muscles. I'm pretty sure I won the man lottery with this guy.

"My room or yours?" he asks. "It wasn't in the rule book."

"Your choice," I say. "Just please…hurry."

He carries me to his room, and I slide down his body as he lets me go. We stand there for a moment, and he cups my face. His head dips, and for a second I think he's going to kiss me. I'm about to remind him of the rules when he steps back.

His gaze roams the length of me, a leisurely inspection. I'd feel self-conscious if it were my ex, but all I feel as Will looks at me is desirable. I put my hands on my stomach and slide them up until I'm cupping my breasts. His eyes never leave my hands as he reaches over his back, grabs a fistful of his T-shirt and peels it off.

"That's better," I murmur as I revel in his glistening skin. His big fingers fumble with the button on his khakis. I drop to my knees, release the button and tug down his zipper. His hand goes to my hair, and he fists it tight. The little tug sends sensations straight to my pulsing core.

"Mmm," I moan as I free him. I take my time to admire his length and girth.

"Like what you see?" he asks, his voice a tortured growl.

Instead of answering, I stick my tongue out and hold it there. He tugs my hair, and our eyes meet.

His breath hitches as he grips his cock and cants his hips forward, rubbing the crown over my tongue.

"That is the hottest damn thing I've ever seen," he says.

"More," I say.

He pushes against my tongue, and I widen my mouth to accommodate his thickness. My fingers slide around to cup his beautiful ass, gripping him tight as I take him deeper than I've ever taken a man.

He pumps into me, his cock swelling as I eagerly suck. I've never been into giving oral sex like this before. My nipples tingle, anxious to feel his mouth wrapped around them, and my sex is so needy, I'm sure the second he touches me I'm going to soar higher than ever. He pulls out of my mouth, and I whimper at the loss.

"I'm about to come down your throat, Khloe."

I lift my chin and meet his eyes. "I want that," I protest.

"You'll get it," he says, shoving his thick thumb between my lips. I suck on him, lick him, and he lets loose an agonized cry.

"On the bed. Right now," he growls. I bite back a smile, and he reaches down, lifts me from the floor and sets me on the bed.

"I was fighting a losing battle, wasn't I?" he asks, and just to be bad, I flip over so he's looking at my ass as I crawl to the center of the bed.

"You tease," he says.

"Who, me, sir?"

"I should tie you to that bed and make you pay for what you've been doing to me."

"I believe that's covered in rules nine and ten." I flatten myself on the bed and roll onto my back.

"My God, you'd like that."

"I'm merely pointing out a rule, Will."

"I want you so goddamn much, I can't think straight. You bending over in that little French maid outfit…"

I bite on my finger. "I had no idea what I was doing."

A sound of disbelief rumbles in his throat. "This might not be slow or easy."

"Did you read anywhere in the rules that I wanted slow or easy?"

"I want you so damn bad, I might just wreck you."

"Yes please," I say, and run my tongue over my lips. "Can I taste you again first?"

He tugs his shorts and boxers off, climbs onto the bed, and straddles me. He not-so-gently shoves his thumb back into my mouth. "You want me to come in here, Khloe."

Since my mouth is full, I nod, and he strokes himself. In a fast move, he pulls his thumb out and replaces it with his erection, filling my mouth. My entire body quakes, and I suck hard as he rocks into me. I reach for him, run my hands over his sides, but he takes my arms and puts them over my head, positioning my body so I'm entirely open to him. He slides deeper into my throat, and I moan around his cock.

"Fuck," he cries out. I make a move to reach for him when he pulls back, but the intensity in his eyes as he slowly shakes his head stops me and fills me with a new kind of excitement. I take a fast breath.

He repositions between my legs, his eyes going from my wet mouth, to my breasts, to the needy juncture aching for his fingers...for him.

"This sweet pussy. I'm going to own it."

"Yes, sir," I say.

Falling over me, he takes my breasts into his big palms. He tugs at my nipples and squeezes my breasts to form a channel.

"You have the nicest tits."

I reach down and take hold of him. "You're not so bad yourself."

He grunts as I stroke him, but I lose purchase as he backs up and sucks a nipple into his mouth. A moan erupts from the depths of my throat, and I squirm, arch into him, giving him everything. He backs off and lightly flicks his tongue over my nipple.

"Oh, yes," I cry out, and put my hands back over my head, gripping the headboard. The heavy weight of his body presses down on me, fueling the need between my legs as his cock presses into my outer thigh. Pleasure sweeps through my veins, burning me from the inside out.

He strokes my clit, and I rock my hips shamelessly. His chuckle vibrates around my nipple.

"Are you laughing at me?" I ask, as I take deep

breaths. As long as he keeps doing what he's doing, I don't much care.

"Nothing to laugh at here, Khloe. No, this sweet pussy is something to admire, appreciate and enjoy." He slides a finger into me, and I swear to God my eyes roll back in my head.

I lift my head, but he's not looking at me. He's staring at my pussy like it's the most fascinating thing he's ever seen. When was the last time this man had sex? Then again, when was the last time I did?

"Spread your legs wider," he commands, and I do. He grips my inner thighs and opens them a bit more, putting me on full display. "Jesus."

His head slowly lifts, and his gaze collides with mine. "I knew you'd have a nice pussy, Khloe. Christ, when you bent over and I could see your panties hugging you, your sweet lips, I knew. But this—" he rubs his finger down my lips, spreading them "—is so fucking pretty. The hottest pussy I've ever seen."

My throat tightens with the way he's admiring me like I'm a national treasure. I like it. A lot. Holy shit, if my ex could see me now, see the way Will is worshipping my body. Wait, no. I don't want to think about that jerk.

"You know, if you come into my office and bend over like that again, you'll probably be sorry."

Okay, so I'm definitely doing that. "You have a problem with me bending over?"

"I sure as hell do. How am I supposed to work

with my cock standing up to take notice every single time?"

I grin.

"You like that, huh?" he asks, and slides another finger in.

"Will..." I murmur.

"Khloe," he says, "we shouldn't make this sweet pussy wait a second longer." He slides down my body, and my hips rise with that first delicious swipe along the hot length of me. Hot sensations fill me as the soft blade swirls around my clit, coming close but never touching. "Is this what you wanted?" he asks.

"I'm going to add no talking to the list," I say, and he chuckles softly.

"But don't you want me to tell you how much I love your body, the taste of you?"

"Yeah, okay. Just don't stop."

"Khloe, I'm not going to stop until you come."

"Thank you," I murmur, my head going from side to side as delicious waves course through my body. He goes quiet, licking, probing, doing magical things between my legs until I'm shaking mindlessly. He moans and works his fingers inside me, his tongue taking me higher and higher.

"You've been in need of attention," he says, his voice raspy.

"Yes..." My breathing changes as he returns to his task, and it becomes almost impossible to fill my lungs as everything in me focuses on my building climax. "Will... Will..."

He sharpens his tongue, applies more pressure to my clit, and like a damn bursting, I let go. His moan of approval sends a tingle down my spine.

His head lifts, his breathing rough.

"Come here," I say.

He climbs up my body, his weight pressing down on me as his lips hover over mine. My lips part automatically. Shit, no kissing. "I'm not the only one in need of attention," I say, and shove until he's on the mattress beside me.

I roll over and crawl across the bed. The position isn't all that different from when I'm dusting.

"What are you doing?" he asks. The gruffness in his voice brings a smile to my face, and I glance at him over my shoulder.

"Getting a condom. I just assumed you had them in your nightstand."

I turn, give an extra wiggle of my ass and pull open his nightstand. I tug out a condom, and I'm about to hold it up, but Will is right there, his body pressed over mine, his hard cock between my thighs. His heat burns my skin, and my heart gallops like I've just run a marathon.

"You're such a tease," he whispers into my ear as he slides his hands around my body, covers both breasts and lifts me until I'm upright on my spread knees. I slide my hand down, capture his cock as he pivots forward, and I give it a stroke, wishing I could taste it. My God, this man brings something out in me—something wild and adventurous, something I was too afraid to allow myself to feel with my ex. Knowing Liam, he'd simply have shamed me, reprimanded me for my behavior. But I'm done with that. I've accepted my body the way it is, and now I'm going to accept my needs, too.

I bring my fingers to my mouth and taste Will on my tongue. He growls against my ear, the heat of his breath caressing my bare flesh.

"Jesus Christ that's hot," he growls.

"Good. I want to try everything with you."

He stills for a second. "Try?"

"Will," I begin, deciding if I'm going to have the best sex of my life, then I need to be open and honest. I go down on my breasts, press them into the sheets and keep my ass in the air.

"I've never been fucked like this."

He goes quiet, thoughtful for a moment, like he's struggling to make sense of my words. Hesitation tightens my gut. Maybe I shouldn't have taken this position, or opened up so readily. Maybe it's too soon to admit my inexperience. Will it scare him away? But all worry evaporates when he grips my ass, squeezes my cheeks.

"No?" he asks, his voice a bit shaky.

"No," I say. "I've never even been on top. Sex was never something my ex and I excelled at, and he was kind of my…"

"First?"

"First and last."

He slides a finger into me, and we both groan. "Not your last, Khloe. Not your last by a long shot."

"No, not my last," I say, even though I'm sure once my time here with Will is over, my sex life will go back to dormant. I'm still sure no man out there is right for me, and I refuse to change who I am to suit someone else. Besides, when I return I have a career to focus on. But I can't think about that when Will is ripping into the condom and sheathing himself.

"That's something I want to do, too," I say as I look over my shoulder, note the way he's rolling on the condom.

"You want to suit me up?"

"Yeah, is that weird?"

He grins. "Not weird at all. In fact, I think you should write out a list of all the things you want. Put it in the rule book. We'll work our way through it and check things off as we achieve them."

I smile at him. "I like that idea."

"And here you thought I was insane for having a rule book."

"I never used the word *insane*."

"Khloe," he says in a commanding voice that tugs at my clit.

"Yeah."

"You can keep talking if you want." He presses his crown to my wet pussy. "But I'm going to put my cock in you. Right now."

"Okay," I say, and let loose a breath.

"This position is going to allow me to go deep. It might hurt."

"I like a little pain, remember?"

He runs the rough pad of his thumb along my spine. "Baby, I don't think you know what you like," he says in a tone so soft and so full of genuine concern, it nearly knocks me off my knees. "But when you leave this island, you're going to know what you want and what you love. I promise you that."

"Yes," I say as he pushes inside me. I grip the sheets, curl them around my fingers as he slides in, going deeper and deeper, stealing the breath from my lungs with every delicious, glorious inch. My walls spread, clench, tighten around him. My God. "This is what I've been missing out on," I say.

"Feels good, right?" he moans, his hands gripping my hips harder, biting into the flesh for leverage. He slides in so deep I lose all train of thought, can't even answer his question. He pulls almost all the way out, and in one swift movement, he's filling me again. I gulp.

"Khloe," he says in a soft voice, his thrust slowing.

"Yeah," I manage to say when I get my voice working again.

"You with me?"

His thoughtful check-in does something weird to my insides. "I am," I say.

"I don't want to hurt you."

I move my body, back up against him, wiggle

and encourage him to take me the way he needs to. The way I need him to, even though I'm not sure I know what I need.

"Talk to me." His grip loosens and he draws circles with his thumbs. "Tell me how this feels."

"Good. So good."

"Too deep?"

"No, Will. I want all of you in me. I want everything."

"I'll give you everything." He lowers himself over my back, once again seated high inside me, pushing on my walls, brushing the sensitive bundle of nerves inside. He moves slightly, rotates his hips, and I groan. "Thattagirl. Tell me how you like it."

He pulls out and pistons into me. Hard. My nipples scrape against the mattress, and the tingles spread to my sex as the headboard bangs against the wall. Pain mingles with pleasure, and so help me God, I love it.

"Like that, Will. Yes, please," I whimper.

"You should see the way I'm sliding in and out of you. I've got an amazing view, Khloe."

My sex clenches. "I want to see."

"You will, but not tonight. Tonight I'm just going to keep fucking you like this until you come. That's what I want, I want you to quiver around me when I come inside you," he says. Beneath his even tone, there's a hint of tension, a shakiness that I'd easily miss if my attention wasn't on everything he was doing to me, everything he was saying. Will Carson is teetering on the edge, and I've done this to him. Me. Khloe Davis. He grips my ass cheeks and massages.

"You've got the nicest ass." He slides a pillow under my hips and pulls my knees out from under me. I fall until I'm flat on the pillow, my ass slightly raised.

"You're going to like this," he says, and when he slams into me, my clit rubs against the soft pillow-case.

"Oh, God, Will. More, please. Harder."

"Greedy girl. I like that about you." He traces my curves. "I like this about you, too."

As he touches me, worships me, I lift my ass a bit more, a shameless move I never would have tried in the past, and I'm rewarded with a deep groan and a smack to the ass.

He changes angles, thrusts, going deeper. Hard. Pounding. Every purposeful slide stimulates my breasts and clit until I'm drowning in heat and need. An erotic throb crashes over me until nothing exists but pleasure.

"Will!" I cry as my muscles clench around him, each determined drag in and out of my sex causing more friction, more sensations. I lose all control of my muscles as he coaxes orgasm after orgasm out of me. I whimper, fist the bedding, and I know he's reached his limit when he seats himself high, goes still and calls out my name. Nothing has ever been more satisfying than hearing my name on his tongue as he reaches his ultimate pleasure. The sweet, beautifully seductive sound wraps around my closed-off heart.

He falls over me, his hot body moist and hard. His rapid breath flutters my damp hair. "You good?" he asks, and I smile, taking a moment to enjoy the post-orgasm bliss. He rolls off me fast, his brow pinched as he moves my body around like I weigh nothing. Our eyes meet.

"Khloe?"

Oh, crap. He's worried he hurt me. I touch his face, enjoy the feel of his bristles against my hand. I'm guessing it's a rare day when he forgets to shave. "I'm good," I assure him. He examines my face a moment longer, then a slow smile curls his mouth. My lips tingle, but no, I'm not about to kiss him. I can follow the rules—my own rules, anyway. "There is one little thing, though."

His brow pinches again, and the muscles in his shoulders grow taut. "What?"

"If we check this position off the list, does it mean we can't do it again?"

He laughs, relaxing. "We can do whatever you need, however many times you need it."

"I mean, I have to be sure, right? Have to nail down what I like and don't like."

"Yeah, we're going to nail it down. Over and over again…"

CHAPTER TEN

Will

I TAP A finger against my desk as I wait for my call to Granddad to connect. Outside my door, Khloe is struggling to figure out how to get the new vacuum to work. I can't help but grin and shake my head. Yesterday, having her beneath me in my bed, should have helped get my thoughts off her. But now that I know what her soft body feels like, the way her tight walls squeeze an orgasm from me, I only want more.

I turn to the window, and in the near distance, I spot Vin, the groundskeeper, a man I entrust with my place when I'm back in New York. He comes once a week to do the shrubbery and does a walk-through of the house every day in my absence. Since he knows everyone on the island, he's also my go-to guy for everything from furnishing the villa to repairs on the house. He glances up as if he feels my gaze and waves to me. As I wave back, an idea takes shape, and I can't help but grin. If Khloe wants to experience everything, then I'm damn well going to make that happen.

"Hello...hello..."

"Oh, hey, Summer."

"Everything okay? I said hello like four times."

"Yeah, I was just distracted."

"What's her name?" she teases.

"Summer—"

"Oh, we have the same name."

"You are not funny."

"So this call is not to say you finally found someone and you're getting married."

"No, I was distracted because of work. Nothing more," I lie.

I stare at the open computer on my desk, the algorithms that need my attention. I just can't seem to focus lately.

Summer chuckles, and it pulls me back. "Something funny?"

"Nothing funny at all." Her voice takes on a serious tone. "What's up?" she asks, and I can hear Jules squealing in the background.

"How's Jules?"

"Good. Granddad is showing her a rope trick. Remember the one where he threads it through his fingers and you put your arm through a couple times?"

I laugh softly. "I remember," I say. He used to do that with me when I was sad, missing my dad. "Can I speak to him?"

"Hang on." From the muffled sounds on the other

end, I suspect she's put her hand over the phone. "Ah, he said he's busy with Jules right now and asked if he can call you back later."

"What is going on with him?" I frown and rub the center of my forehead. "I've been trying to reach him for days."

"What about?" Summer asks.

"I just... I guess I wanted to know more about Khloe."

"Khloe?"

"The woman he hired to assist me on this trip."

"Is it not working out?"

I lower my voice. "She can't even cook, plus she broke the vacuum and numerous dishes."

Summer laughs. "Meaning she's making your life chaotic. I like her already."

"Not funny." I eye the door to make sure she's not within earshot. "I'm not sure how Granddad thought she was good for the job."

"Are you disappointed in his choice?"

"No."

Shit, that one word jumped to my lips rather quickly. And I'm sure I hear Summer chuckling again.

"Well then, what's the problem?"

"You know I like things done a certain way."

"Oh, I know, Will. Believe me, I know."

"There's a reason for that, Summer." I sit back in my chair and watch a yellow bird perch on the shrubbery outside. The sky is a perfect blue, the sun shining brightly, and for some reason it takes me back to a time when I used to enjoy the outdoors. Enjoy life.

"I know that, too. Look, why don't you try to enjoy yourself while you're there. This Khloe sounds like a breath of fresh air. Take her out, show her around. She's probably breaking things because you're an ogre and she's intimidated. I know how you are."

"Believe me, she's not one bit intimidated by me," I say quickly.

"Oh? I thought all your assistants were afraid of you."

"Not this one."

"Are you saying she likes you?"

"I wouldn't go so far as to say that." We might be physically attracted to each other, and she might be seeking lessons, but twice now, in her most disgusted voice, I heard her say something about men in power all being alike. I'm not sure what she means by that and I hope she's not lumping me into the same category as her last asshole boss, who wanted more than she was willing to give. What's between us is consensual. That much I'm sure of. I wouldn't make her do anything she didn't want to, and the French maid outfit was her doing, not mine. I must say I'm growing quite accustomed to her attire.

"That doesn't change the fact that you should get out of the house, go do something fun."

Yesterday I did something fun...and I didn't even have to leave the house.

I chuckle softly.

"Something funny?" she asks.

"No." I quickly straighten. "I do have to go check on the middle school and get to Granddad's resort. There are some staffing situations I need to look into."

"When are you going to take that stick out of your ass?"

My head jerks back. "What the hell, Summer?"

"Motherhood. It changes you." She laughs. "What I'm trying to say is checking progress at the school and the resort is not fun."

"It needs to be done."

"Lots of things need to get done. I need to bake a zillion cupcakes for Jules's party. It'll happen but not today. Get it?"

"I don't like to procrastinate."

"And you like rules. I know, I know." I can almost hear her rolling her eyes at me. Oh yeah, motherhood has definitely changed her. "But sometimes rules are made to be broken. Sometimes really good things happen when they are," she says, a hint of mischief in her tone.

"Summer—"

Her exaggerated sigh cuts me off. "Do we want to talk about the stick again?"

"No."

"Okay, then. Go do something that doesn't *need* to be done. What about running the ninety-nine steps at Charlotte Amalie? Granddad said you used to love to do that. And take Khloe with you. She deserves fun for having to put up with you. That in itself is just cruel."

"Why don't you tell me what you really think," I say, and shake my head.

"Fine then. Get your pasty white ass out of the house, and go do something fun for a change."

"Pasty white ass? Jeez, I love you, too."

"Love you, Will. Now go, do what I say. Doctor's orders."

"Fine, fine." I end the call and drop my phone onto my desk.

Curses reach my ears along with a lot of banging and clanging.

"Khloe," I call out.

She appears at my door, blinking innocently. "Yes, sir?"

I take a deep breath and work to keep the blood in my brain. "I have to run some errands. It's a beautiful day. I thought I could show you around Saint Thomas. Unless, of course, you prefer to stay here and abuse the vacuum."

"Your vacuum hates me."

"Vacuums can't hate, and it's brand-new. You broke the last one, remember?"

"I remember." She plants a hand on one hip and sticks it out. "Then why won't it turn on?"

"I don't know. How about I look at it later?"

"Why not right now?"

"Because right now I'm thinking about all the

ways I need to reprimand you for breaking the first one."

Her mouth goes slack, and her chest rises and falls at her fast intake of breath. "Oh, I see. Don't let me interrupt you, then." She makes a move to go, but stops when I push from my chair.

"Want to get out of here? Go for a drive, get some fresh air?"

"And ice cream?"

That brings a smile to my face. "Sure, we can get ice cream."

"Let's go then."

"I…uh…think you might want to get changed first."

She glances down and laughs. "Good catch."

"Khloe." Christ, I sound like I've just swallowed sand.

"Yeah."

I scrub my face. "You don't have to wear that around here. You can wear whatever you want. Yoga pants. Whatever makes you comfortable."

What are you doing, dude?

Being the goddamn gentleman I should have been from day one.

She blinks up at me. "Really?"

"Yeah"

"But the rules…"

"We can write new rules."

"We could…" She sticks one leg out and her skirt lifts to reveal the garter belt holding up her stocking.

Whoa.

She makes a soft, throaty noise that instantly takes me back to yesterday afternoon, and all the little moans I pulled from her. "I've grown rather fond of these suits, actually."

"Yeah, me, too," I grumble.

"Then it's settled." She straightens, and her beautiful tits jut out. "I'll continue to wear them."

"And I'll continue to be rock hard all day long."

She grins and magically pulls a feather duster out from behind her back. "I think I missed a spot." She bends down, points her ass directly at me, and swipes at some imaginary spot of dust on the baseboard. I have zero control over the hungry growl that crawls out of my throat.

"Sir, is there something wrong?" she asks.

"I just asked if you wanted to get out. Bending over isn't conducive to that plan."

"Oh, I apologize, sir."

My dick thickens. "Actually, since you have that duster in your hand. I think I do have a spot on my desk that needs some attention."

"Of course." She walks across the room, my gaze latched on the sexy sway of her hips. "Oh, yes, I see it right here."

She leans over my desk and concentrates on a spot, all the while gifting me with an up-close view of her gorgeous tits.

I stand, circle the desk and grip her waist. She yelps as I spin her, lift her from the floor and set her ass on my desk. I cup her chin, press my thumb to her lush lips, and since kissing is off the table, I slide my thumb inside her mouth. She sucks on me, and the sweet sensations wrap around my dick. Her legs envelop me, and she pulls me against her until she's pressed against my cock. She's so goddamn hot between her legs, my mouth waters for a taste.

I reach around my back, lock my hands on her ankles and remove her legs. She whimpers, but I step back, take one foot and brace it against my stomach. Her breathing changes as I run my hand along her thigh and unsnap the garter holding up the lace.

"What are you doing, sir?" she asks, and I love the role she's playing.

"We're going out, and you can't go out dressed like this. You're so goddamn sexy it will draw attention, and I like to keep a low profile, as you know."

"I do know."

"I thought I'd help you out of these clothes. That is, if you want me to."

"Oh, I do. I do," she says quickly, and I love her enthusiasm.

I grip the band and slowly roll the lace down, tossing it away. I repeat the motion with the other leg, and step back to admire the woman before me. Her dark eyes are ablaze, her thighs wide.

I'll never look at that desk the same way. I step around her and clear my desk, my hands shaking with need. She's practically quivering when I circle back, widen her legs even further and position myself in between them. I cup her breasts, run my thumbs over her nipples until they're poking through the thin black material. She shivers.

Her hands lift, but I grab her wrists and place them at her sides. "Keep them here. Only I get to touch. That's your punishment."

"Yes...sir."

I unzip her outfit from the back, and it falls to her waist, showcasing those gorgeous full tits.

"Fucking beautiful," I grumble, and give her shoulder a light nudge until she's flat out on my desk, spread wide open, mine for the taking. I push the skirt up, exposing a flimsy pair of lace panties. With the pad of my thumb, I brush her clit through the material, and her whimper curls around me, tugs at my cock.

"Ever been fucked on a desk?" I ask, pretty sure of her answer.

"No."

"You want to be?"

"So much..."

I chuckle at that, and in one fast movement tear the lace from her hips.

"Oh God," she moans.

"So pretty," I say, and bend forward to lick her. Her hips writhe restlessly as her heat reaches out to me. She's so damn responsive, it fucks with me in the strangest ways.

I suck on her clit and slowly slide a finger into her tight channel. She clamps around me. "Look at you, so needy and wet and ready for me."

"Yes…" she murmurs and tosses her head from side to side.

I stroke her until she's whimpering, but I don't make her come. I want to be inside her, to feel her contractions around me. I push my shorts to my knees, and she goes up on her elbows, watching as I tear open a condom.

"I want to do it," she says.

"Yeah?"

"Please, sir."

I take her arm and sit her up. "Make it fast, okay?"

Her teeth dig into her bottom lip as her small hand takes hold of me. Her soft fingers glide over my shaft as she fits me with the rubber, and I curse under my breath.

"That wasn't so hard."

I laugh. "Yeah, not hard at all." I nudge her a little. "Go back on your elbows so you can watch."

Her breath catches, and the excitement in her eyes thrills and infuriates me. I'd like to hunt her ex down and punch him. It pisses me off that he never properly cared for her in the bedroom. Then again, I kind of like it that I'm the guy giving her lessons and letting her explore her body and fantasies. Yeah, I like that a lot, and I want to make this great for her.

I rub my crown over her clit, get it nice and wet. Her moans vibrate through me, and the heated look in her eyes is a thing of beauty. "You like the idea of that, Khloe."

"Yes," she moans. "I want to watch."

I press my head to her opening and give her an inch.

"More," she says.

I give her more and grip her legs. My fingers dig into her lush thighs as I widen them. I thrust forward, sliding deeper.

"Will," she says, "that is so hot."

"Yeah, you got that right," I murmur, a grunt catching in my throat as I clench my teeth. Watching her take every inch of me into her body, watching her watching me…oh yeah, for the rest of our time on this island, this woman is mine. I move, rock into her, my body curling toward hers.

"No visitors, Khloe," I say without thinking.

"What?" she asks, her lids falling closed, ecstasy written all over her face.

"No visitors, for either of us. Just you and me while we're here, okay?" Christ, why would I want to be with anyone else when this beautiful woman has dropped into my lap. The truth is, in the past I've brought a woman to my bed while here, for physical release, but I've lost interest in one-night affairs. This three-week affair, where I'm helping a beautiful woman blossom, that's where it's at.

"Okay," she agrees, and I don't want to think too hard on how happy that makes me.

Her hand slides down her body, and she tentatively strokes her clit. Holy shit. My gaze flashes to hers, and for split second I catch the vulnerability in her eyes, the uncertainty. Everything inside me softens.

"You never touched yourself with your ex, did you?" I ask.

"No," she says.

I slide in and out, and her finger stills. "You like it?"

She nods.

"Then keep doing it, because baby, that is so damn hot."

Her eyes widen a little. "Yeah?"

"Oh, yeah. Do it, Khloe. Rub yourself. Let me watch."

Her finger moves faster, her inhibitions ebbing, and I fuck her the way I think she needs to be fucked. Hard. Fast. Strokes that hit all her hot spots. One of these days I'll go slow, show her the pleasure in a softer touch. But for right now, we fuck.

Her gorgeous tits jiggle with each thrust and her ass slides on the desk. I grip her hips, pull her back to the edge of the desk, and let her rub herself a little more. But I need to touch her, too, so I join her, my fingers mingling with hers as I play with her clit, and her gaze flashes to mine. The admiration in her eyes, the appreciation at what I'm doing, the freedom I'm giving her to explore, messes with me a bit.

She removes her hand, giving me full access, and leans on both elbows. Her head falls back slightly, and I touch her body, learn her likes from her sexy little noises. I change the pressure on her clit, experiment with my touch until I get it just right.

"Like that, just like that," she says, and a second later she's tightening around me, squeezing and milking me as she gives herself over to the pleasure.

"Khloe," I groan, and every muscle in my body tightens as I let go. I feel so goddamn happy it's a little strange. When was the last time I was this happy? I open my eyes to find her staring at me, a smile on her pretty face.

"Wow," she says, and I can't help but laugh. "Sex on the desk wasn't even on my list. Maybe I should get you to make the list."

"I can help you add to it, if you like." I brush a strand of hair from her face and swipe my thumb over her wet bottom lip.

"I like," she says, and we both chuckle. We stay like that for a long time, both basking in the afterglow.

"Come here." I pull out of her, quickly discard the rubber and stand back between her still-open legs. "Let's get you out of this." I tug at the dress bunched around her hips. "It must be cutting off circulation." I peel the outfit over her head. "You made the…?" I begin, but my gaze drops to her beautiful breasts.

"Made the what?" she asks.

"I can't remember what I was going to say." I cup her breasts. "Do you have any idea how beautiful these are?"

"Breast man, are you?" she jokes.

"Khloe, with you I'm every kind of man. Ass, legs, breasts…" Her mouth parts slightly. What would she taste like?

Wait, no. Can't go there. It's in the rule book.

Rule book, right. That's where I was going earlier, until her beautiful breasts sidetracked me.

"Did you make your list already?"

"Yesterday, after we had sex."

I shake my head. "I like a girl who gets right at her tasks."

"I thought you might."

"Oh, you think you know me now, do you?" I say.

"I watch, learn, listen."

While I like to keep a measure of distance from, well, everyone, I'm not as upset as I should be, normally would be, to know she's been observing.

"So do I," I say.

"I like the way you watch, learn and listen," she says in a teasing voice.

"How about tonight I take a look at your list, see if you missed anything?"

She runs her hand over the top of my desk. "I'm guessing I did." Her grin is slow, seductive. "What other tricks do you have up your sleeve?"

"We have lots of time for me to show you," I say, and make a mental note to talk to Vin before we leave the house.

CHAPTER ELEVEN

Khloe

MY BODY IS blissfully sore, my mind still a bit woozy from that glorious climax, but I'm not complaining. I loved every minute of it. I stretch out my legs in the passenger seat as Will drives us to town. The windows are down, and I breathe in all the fragrant scents from the local foliage and blossoming flowers. I slowly turn my head his way, take in his freshly shaven face. It's late morning, and he's dressed in cargo shorts and a T-shirt. He suggested I dress in casual clothes and wear comfortable footwear, yet he never said where we were going. Not that I care. I'd go bungee jumping if it meant getting away from that mutinous vacuum cleaner.

I sigh contentedly and rest my head against the leather seat. It's odd how comfortable I am with Will after such a short time. Yeah, okay, so he's an asshole. At least, according to Steph. Although, outside of scolding me for my appearance and tardiness, he's been pretty decent. But of course, I can't forget he admitted he's a cheater. And when it comes right down to it, I don't *really* know him. It's possible he only took care of me when I was sick because his granddad would kill him otherwise.

Do you really believe that, Khloe?

I'm not sure. He did ask me to be exclusive for the next few weeks. I said yes in the heat of the moment, but do I expect him to keep it in his pants? Not really, and I don't care one way or the other. I have no ownership over him, and vice versa. We're just having fun. Things will go back to normal when we return home.

"We're a long way from New York," I say, pulling my phone from my bag to shoot a picture, then send it off to Steph. After I'd left James's mansion, I texted her to tell her about the job. She was both thrilled and worried for me, but I assured her I could handle any entitled millionaire. And handle him I did. I snicker quietly.

Will's hand slides across the seat and gives mine a squeeze, and I turn my attention to him as he drives.

"What are you doing?"

"Sending a picture to my best friend."

"Khloe, no one is supposed to know you're here in Saint Thomas."

As his brow furrows, panic invades my gut. Shit, I'd forgotten all about that in the nondisclosure agreement. I wasn't supposed to give away the location. There's nothing I can do to get the picture back.

"I'm sorry, Will. She's trustworthy. She won't tell anyone." Worry creeps into his eyes, and a chill goes up my spine.

"I understand that, but things have a way of getting out."

He's not wrong about that. "Am I fired?"

He winks at me. "Not this time, okay. But if you break the rules again…"

There's a teasing note in his voice, but beneath it I understand he's serious. His life had been put under a microscope, and it was a horrible invasion of privacy that resulted in a lot of loss. Yes, he did something wrong, but was it the world's place to dissect and judge? No. It was no one's business but his and Naomi's. It's certainly none of mine.

"It won't happen again, I promise. And I'll tell her not to share my location."

"You're sure she's trustworthy?"

"Yes, best person I know. You'd like her a lot. Not that you'll ever meet her. I'm just saying—"

The jerk of his chin cuts off my rambling. "Look."

Up ahead I see two gigantic cruise ships in dock. I sit up a little straighter.

"My God, those are magnificent. Look at the size of them. How do they even float?"

"They float because the gravitational force is less than the buoyancy of the upward force."

"Ah, okay. I'll have to take your word for it. I was an English major. If you want to know how to fix a dangling modifier, I'm your girl."

He chuckles. "I'll be sure to remember that. Have you ever been on a cruise?" he asks.

I shake my head, and a few loose tendrils fall from my ponytail and slide down my neck. His eyes follow, and the hairs on my nape tingle under their appreciation.

"Nope, never even been out on a sailboat," I say.

"Let me guess, motion sickness."

I crinkle my nose at him. "Funny, and no," I say, and in that instant, I realize how different we truly are. But I'm not about to bring up that I had only the basic necessities in life, and unlike the people in his social circle, I never went on elaborate trips, flew in private planes, sailed in fancy boats and cared only about getting richer—no matter who got hurt in the process. I'm not resentful that I never had material things. Hell, I'm a strong, independent woman because of it, and I like who I am. Instead I say, "The opportunity just never presented itself."

He arches a brow. "You know I have a sailboat, right?" He points downward. "Right here on Saint Thomas."

"How would I know that?" I ask, even though I'm not one bit surprised. The man has everything he wants. Well, except for a wife. Does he still want that? My guess would be no, considering the lifestyle he lives.

He follows the winding road. "I guess you wouldn't."

"No one knows anything about you, Will. You take privacy to the extreme."

"You know why that is, right?"

"Yeah," I say, a measure of guilt worming its way through me. I consider the front cover spread again. Yes, Benjamin insists we sensationalize. But the fact is, Will was caught with his hand in the cookie jar, so to speak. It seems out of character for him, though.

"I'm sorry about Naomi," I say.

"I'm sorry I hurt her, too, but she deserves better than me."

"Are you…" Ugh, how can I word this?

"Still in love with her?" he asks.

"Yeah."

"I'll always love her, Khloe." He casts a quick glance my way, his blue eyes showcasing pain and regret. "We had something great. I ruined it, and something like that doesn't come along every day."

I stiffen at that admission, jealousy zinging through me. What the hell? No way should I be feeling anything other than sadness for this whole situation.

"Maybe something better will come along." Not that he'd ever know. He's locked up tight and not about to open himself to love.

He grunts a response.

"Do you still keep in contact?"

He runs agitated fingers through his dark hair. "No, and I don't read the tabloids, either, but the last I heard she was in Milan and seeing some guy there. I have no idea if it's serious or not, but I want her to be happy."

I'm totally shocked by his maturity. He loves the woman yet wants her to find happiness with another man. Not quite the asshole everyone says he is…but the pictures. I press my hand over my stomach as it takes that moment to tighten, and I make a mental note to do a little research of my own.

"Where are we going?" I ask.

"I need to stop at Granddad's resort."

"James has a resort here? I knew about the one in Saint Moritz because he showed me pictures of Megan and Alec's wedding, like I mentioned. Actually he showed me a picture of you at the wedding."

"Why did he do that?"

"I guess he wanted to show me the ogre I would be working for."

"Ogre, Khloe. Really? Do you want to go talk about how I took care of you when you were pro—"

"Okay, not an ogre," I say, laughing. "Tell me about James's resort."

"It's called Great Bay Resort. I think he bought it because the first time we came here, I fell in love with the place. Granddad's like that. And he's always been there when we needed him." He chuckles, staring into the distance like he's remembering happier times.

"What's so funny?"

"I'm just thinking back to when he told Tate he wanted to gift half of his million-dollar estate to

Summer Love. And Tate thought she was a con art-ist out to steal millions from him, so he flew to Saint Moritz to take her down." He chuckles again. "She took him down instead."

"What do you mean?"

"He fell in love with her. Sometimes I think Granddad orchestrated the whole thing, but other times I realize he's in his nineties and probably couldn't pull off a scheme like that even if he had a team working for him."

You're perfect for Will.

For a moment, James's words ping around inside my brain. During our meeting he seemed so lucid at times; other times, I thought he was dozing off. Is it possible that he was trying to find a wife for his grandson? No. The man barely knows me. What would make him think I was perfect for his grand-son? He wouldn't, simple as that.

"That's a great story, Will. So romantic."

He makes a noise—a half laugh, half groan. "It's crazy how it all played out, if you ask me."

We pull up to the resort, and my eyes go wide to take in the opulence. "It's beautiful."

"It was practically destroyed in the hurricane."

"The damage and loss broke my heart when I heard about it on the news. So much devastation."

"You remember Bevey?"

"How could I forget her?"

He chuckles again. "She's head chef at Granddad's resort. Her husband, Samuel, was injured in the hurricane."

"I'm so sorry to hear that."

"Her daughter's school was destroyed, too. The kids are in an old school that's been waterlogged. It's dirty and mold-ridden. Not healthy for them at all."

"My God, I had no idea. I wish I could help out some way," I say. "I don't really have anything to offer, though."

He casts me a quick glance, and I can't quite figure out his expression. He drives under a roofed-in area, pulling up in front of the grand resort.

"It's even more amazing up close." I examine the sprawling resort painted in bright yellow, orange and blue. Each room has a balcony overlooking the emerald waters.

"How come you don't stay here when you visit?" He arches a brow and reaches for his door handle. "Right, privacy," I say, answering my own question. "This doesn't look like it was destroyed by the hurricane."

"We rebuilt quickly."

"I'd imagine that really cut into the bottom line," I say under my breath.

He opens his mouth to speak, but the valet steps up to the driver's side.

"Good morning, Mr. Will."

Will smiles at the valet and turns back to me. "I have some things to take care of. Do you want to wander around, check out the pool and gardens?"

"Sure, but I thought you said we were getting ice cream."

"We are, soon."

Will opens his door, and the valet gives him a big smile. "Mr. Will, it's so good to see you."

Will shakes the man's hand. "Anthony, my friend. It's been too long. How is Hannah?"

He sticks his stomach out. "Another little one on the way," he says, his big brown eyes beaming.

"Congratulations. Is Hannah well this time?"

He holds his hand out flat and wavers it a little bit. "Just slight morning sickness. Not like last time."

"No hyperemesis, then?"

"No, thankfully."

"Glad to hear it."

I stand there and listen to the exchange. Not only does Will know the valet, he appears to know his wife and the circumstances surrounding her last birth. I'm beginning to believe there is more to this man than meets the eyes.

Will looks my way. "Anthony, this is my assistant, Khloe. Khloe, if you need anything at all, Anthony is your man. You can trust him to help you." Anthony appears to grow two inches taller at Will's compliment. I exchange pleasantries with Anthony, and Will hands his keys over. He circles the front of the vehicle, puts his palm on the small of my back, and leans in. "I'll only need about thirty minutes, I think. I have some staffing issues that need my attention."

"Who are you firing?"

He shakes his head. "I love the high opinion you have of me." Before I can say anything, he holds out his hand. "Pass me your phone?"

I reach into my purse. "What do you want my phone for?"

"I'm going to put my number in, call myself, and then I'll have yours."

He takes my phone, puts his contact in and a second later his rings. "Don't venture off the resort, okay?"

"Why?" I shoot a glance over my shoulder. "Is it dangerous?"

"It's safe enough, but easy to get lost. Although I'm pretty sure you can handle yourself," he says with a smirk.

"You know I can." He gives me a nudge and the double glass doors open, inviting us into the posh lobby. I glance around, take in the buttery yellow sofas, the chandeliers, the curving staircase that leads to a restaurant on the next level.

"Through those back doors, you'll find the garden, the pool and the bar. Grab yourself a drink. Charge it to me."

"I can buy my own drink," I say, and frown as I recall the meager amount of money at the bottom of my purse.

"You're my guest, Khloe." His blue eyes narrow, go serious. "You'll charge it to me."

"You're kind of bossy."

"Which is why you call me sir," he says, but the

heat behind that one word fills me with luscious memories.

My gaze travels back and meets his. "Right, thanks for the reminder, sir," I tease, and I'm rewarded with a groan. With an extra little shake of my ass, I head toward the back door, not bothering to glance over my shoulder. My cell pings. I lift it and read the text from Will.

Will: You're going to pay for that.

Khloe: Looking forward to it.

His growl follows me outside, and the sound is muted as the double doors close behind me. In the courtyard, men, women and children lounge at the pool. There are a few people sitting at the bar, nursing things that look quite refreshing. The fragrant foliage fills my senses as I walk the brick path to the outside bar. I slide onto one of the stools, and the bartender comes right over. He looks to be in his midthirties, a light beard covering his jaw. He's handsome, but let's face it, he's not Will Carson handsome. Few, if any, are.

"I'd like something fruity and refreshing," I say, and tap my chin as I look past his shoulders at the chalk menu listing the drinks.

"Strawberry daiquiri?" he suggests.

"Perfect." The man two stools over picks up his icy beer and begins to spin my way. "Oh, and please put it on Will Carson's tab. I'm his assistant," I add, as per Will's request. The man does an about-face, sets his drink back down and stares into the glass like it holds all the answers to the universe.

Wow, it's almost like the simple mention of Will invokes fear in others. Maybe he actually is an ogre to the staff working here. In all seriousness, he's been nothing but a perfect gentleman to me. Well, okay, maybe that's pushing it. Other than ensuring I'm having a good time and climax first, he's no gentleman between the sheets. But I wouldn't want it any other way.

I pick up my drink and wander around, taking time to smell the flowers and smile at the child laughing in the pool. The longing pulsing through my body doesn't go unnoticed. Here I used to think Liam and I would marry and have a family of our own. Now I'm convinced there is no right man out there for me. And that's okay. I don't need a man to make me happy. Kids? Well, if I do decide to have them someday, there's always in vitro.

The warm sun beats down on me as I meander through the gardens, greeting guests and staff. My phone pings and I grab it.

Will: All done. Meet me out front? Let's go get you that ice cream.

Khloe: On my way.

I tuck my phone back into my purse, take my empty glass back to the bar and head toward the front of the resort. Will is leaning against his car talking to Anthony. I don't want to interrupt, so I open my door. Will turns at the sound, and a smile touches his mouth, like he's extremely happy to see me. Weird thing is, my heart is speeding up a little, too.

"Hey," he says turning to me. "Did you get a drink? Enjoy a walk?"

I nod. "Did you get your staffing situation straightened out?"

He nods, says something to Anthony and slides into the car. I drop into the passenger seat next to him.

The drive is a short one, and the next thing I know he's parking on a street.

"Where are we?"

"Historic downtown. Have you heard of the ninety-nine steps at Charlotte Amalie?"

"I've been busy wrestling a vacuum into submission, so I haven't had time to do much research."

That brings a smile to his face. "Well, you're about to get a firsthand look, and I'm going to race you to the top."

"So this is why you told me to wear comfortable footwear."

"Yup." He unbuckles and slips from the car.

I do the same, and the heat beats down on me. "I am not running up ninety-nine steps, Will. I'll die."

"It's fun, trust me."

"Trust you? I don't trust anyone, remember?"

He briefly looks past my shoulders, his smile faltering. "First one to the top wins."

"Wins what? A drive to the hospital in an ambulance, or worse, to a funeral home?"

He laughs out loud, circles the car and steps close to me, very close. His warm breath feathers over my face.

I plant one hand on my hip. "I thought we were getting ice cream."

"You can have ice cream and anything else you want. If you beat me."

I spin around and glance up and down the busy street. A man with a cart full of coconuts stops to hack the top off one with a huge knife and hands it over to a customer, who dips a straw inside. I make a mental note to try one. Then I see the brick stairs. My gaze goes from the bottom to the very top.

"That looks like a lot more than ninety-nine steps to me."

"Only by four. They added some cement steps."

I eye Will. "You've done this before, right?"

He rolls one shoulder. "Sure, numerous times."

"Okay, since you have an advantage, I get a head start."

He thinks about it for a second. "Fair enough."

"You have to count to ten before you can start up."

We walk toward the stairs, our knuckles brushing innocently, but damned if it doesn't send shock waves straight down my body. Maybe the rush of adrenaline will help me beat him. We reach the bottom step, and I glance up to see the green wooden rail on the right, and foliage popping with bright purple flowers on either side of the steps.

"It doesn't look so bad up close."

His mouth is close to my ear when he says, "It's not."

"What does the winner get?"

"Whatever they want."

I take a second to think about what I want. But the vision of myself living happily ever after in a cozy house with a family, writing articles I want to write, is a dream not even Will, a man with all the resources in the world, could fulfill.

"Go," he says.

"What?"

"One, two…"

"Oh, shit," I say, and dart up the stairs. Will is laughing from the bottom. "Count slow," I yell, but when I look back he's already closing the gap between us. I start laughing so hard I can barely climb, but I'm competitive, and clearly Will is, too. I pick up the pace and hurry onward.

I push harder, but his long, strong legs have no trouble reaching me. His breath is hot on my neck, and I do everything to block his way. I spread my arms, but he grabs me by the waist, picks me up and spins me until I'm behind him.

"That's cheating!" I yell at his back, but my gaze quickly drops to his ass as he easily negotiates the steps. I reach the top, panting like a Newfoundland dog…in Hawaii. Will doesn't appear winded at all. Jerk.

"I won," he says.

"You cheated."

He takes my hand, leads me through a crowd I hadn't noticed from the base of the stairs, and my breath catches when I see the spectacular view below.

I turn to see Will's reaction to the view, but it's me he's looking at. I swipe at my damp forehead. I must look a mess, but from the appreciation in his eyes, you wouldn't know it.

"Fine, you won. But I want a rematch after I get in shape."

"You're in great shape, Khloe," he says, and despite the crowd of tourists at the top, all standing by the rail taking pictures of the most breathtaking view of Saint Thomas, he comes close and puts his hands on my curves. For a private guy, this public display of affection surprises me. Then again, the place is full of tourists who don't know either of us.

"Want to know what I want?"

CHAPTER TWELVE

Will

"What do you want, Will?"

I open my mouth, about to tell her how I plan to take her tonight, when my pants start pulsating. She glances down, arches a brow.

"Ah, you're vibrating down there," she says, and grins at me. "Maybe instead of asking you what you want, I should be asking what kind of kinky things you're into." Her voice is playful, and if we weren't in public, I'd strip her bare and show her exactly how kinky I like it.

I grin. "Since I won, you'll soon find out."

A visible shiver moves through her as I pull my phone from my pocket. I hope it's Granddad. When I see it's Alec, I frown.

"Hey, bro, what's up?" I ask.

"Not much. Just wondering how things are going in Saint Thomas."

Why the hell is everyone calling and checking in on me?

"Since when do you call me when I'm here?"

"Never. Just missing my big bro is all." My gaze slides to Khloe, who is wiping her brow with the back of her hand. Her big eyes are full of awe and wonder as she steps away to give me privacy and takes in the view below.

"Have you been talking to Granddad?" I ask.

"Yeah, I was with him yesterday. Brianna is back from Italy. She was hoping to see you. Megan wants to have a big family barbecue."

Shit, it's been months since I've seen my cousin and her husband. "How long is she home for?"

"Just a couple weeks."

A thread of worry weasels its way down my spine. There was no talk of Brianna coming home. Is her marriage breaking up? "Is she...okay?"

"Why wouldn't she be okay?"

I step away from the chatter of the crowd and lean against a tall tree. "If she's back suddenly and Luca isn't with her..."

"That's where your mind goes?" Alec asks. "Straight to divorce?"

"You know we've seen a lot of it."

"We're a new generation, Will," he says, his voice full of conviction.

I snort. "Yeah, well, tell that to Naomi."

"She was never right for you anyway."

"Alec—" I begin.

"Listen, Luca is flying in next week. He had some work commitments. So you see, they're still happily married like the rest of us, and we're hoping for a big family reunion."

I don't miss the dig. "I probably won't be back in time."

"You could come home early." I let my eyes travel Khloe's length, admiring her curves in her V-neck T-shirt and the shorts that show off her curvy ass and hips. I suppose I could cut this trip short, but do I want to? "I'm ah, not sure that's possible."

Alec snickers. "Yeah, that's what I thought."

"What are you talking about?"

"Work comes first over everything for you," he says, humor gone from his voice.

"You're one to talk."

"Priorities change when you're married. You'll see."

"No, I won't see, and we're not having this conversation again." Why the hell can't they all just leave me alone? I'm married to my job now, and I'm content. Happy.

I'm also having the best sex of my life with Khloe.

"Come on…" Alec goads. "Humor me. You, of all of us, wanted to get married."

"Things have changed," I say. "When you see Granddad can you please ask him to call me? Also ask him to check the staffing agency. Leonard Elementary needs English teachers. Surely there must be one unemployed teacher on the list."

"Will do, bro."

I end the call and step up to Khloe, my chest to her back. She leans against me.

"Hey, are you okay?"

"Fine, why?"

She turns and presses her hand over my heart. "It's beating a little fast."

I shake my phone before shoving it into my pocket. "My brother."

"You two get in a fight?"

Not really wanting to get into it, I hedge with, "Something like that."

"I always wanted siblings," she says quietly, a look of longing in her dark eyes.

"You can have mine." I snort. "My brother and my cousin and his wife are driving me crazy."

"I love that you're all so close."

"You'd love them, Khloe. I think you'd really hit it off with Summer." I laugh.

"What's so funny?"

"After Summer had Jules, she lost all her filters. She tells it like it is."

"Then I probably would like her."

"She told me I needed to get you out of the house today, that you deserved to do something fun for having to put up with me."

"You have been doing something fun for me."

I grin. "Yeah, it has been fun." I put my hand

around her waist and lead her back to the stairs. We descend slowly, and she runs her hand along the wooden rail. But my grin turns to a frown as I go over my conversation with my brother. Khloe studies me, concern etched in her eyes.

"Are you sure you're okay?"

"Yeah, it's just. Alec and Tate and even Summer are on me about getting married."

"Ah, I see."

"I don't need a wife to make me happy."

"Just like I don't need a husband," she says.

I eye her. "Do you still love him?"

"My ex, you mean?" I nod, and she exhales.

"No, I don't. I'm glad I woke up before I found myself in a controlling marriage."

"But someday you'd like to get married?"

She gives me a very unladylike snort, and it makes me smile. I like that she's herself around me, doesn't pretend to be something or someone else. I'm used to pretense from the women in my circle, especially the ones looking to marry up. It's hard to know who's real and who isn't. I appreciate Khloe's honesty.

"I've given up on the idea. Besides, right now, after my last job, I need to concentrate on me."

I give her a nudge. "Maybe while you're here, you can write that book you talked about."

"I would." She pauses and gives me a seductive smile. "But I think my boss is about to start keeping me up late at night. He's an ogre, you know."

I laugh, the tightness in my chest easing a bit, as we talk openly. I'm not usually like this with women. But she's not any woman, is she? She's open and real, and I kind of like that we have this easy banter. I chuckle inwardly. Christ, with the ease she can get things out of people, she'd make a good reporter.

"You know, I have a lot of connections in the publishing ind—"

She holds her hand up to stop me. "Will, I appreciate that but—"

"But you need to do everything on your own."

She nods. "I want to get there on my own merit, you know. I want the validation that I can do it."

"I understand." Her dark eyes are serious as they move over my face, like she's not sure if I really can understand. "I get it, Khloe. Sometimes, though, it's okay to get by with a little help from a friend."

She smiles. "Is that what we are?"

"Friends?" I nod. "Yeah, I like that. I like the idea of us being friends."

"With benefits," she says, and nudges me.

"I like that, too," I say, and laugh. "Come on, let's get that ice cream, and I have one more stop to make before I take you home and have my way with you."

We go down the rest of the stairs, the noonday sun beating on us. We find an ice cream stand and both get double scoops. A few minutes later, we're in the car, headed to the middle school. We finish our cones as I drive.

"Where are we?" Khloe asks, as she takes in the old school and the new one in construction behind it.

"This is where Bevey's daughter goes."

"Oh, you wanted to say hi to her?"

"Something like that." I look into a field where the kids are seated at picnic tables. "Do you want to wait here?"

"No, I'll come."

We slide from our seats and walk toward the kids, who are all dressed in the same uniforms and eating boxed lunches. When they see me, they jump up and run our way.

"Whoa," Khloe says, as they huddle around me. "I guess you're well known here."

"Kids, kids," Amelia says, and claps her hands. "Come finish your lunches." After a few grumbles the kids all file back to their seats.

Khloe casts me a curious look. "Aren't you popular?"

"I have a way with kids," is all I say.

"Uncle Will. Uncle Will," Chardane says, and waves me over.

"Come meet Bevey's daughter."

"She calls you Uncle Will?"

"I've known her since she was born." Khloe follows me across the sunburned grass, and I note all the girls at the table are coloring as they eat their sandwiches. I go down on one knee to talk to Chardane. She gives me a hug, and I introduce her to Khloe.

"Is she your girlfriend?" Chardane teases in her

childlike voice. All the girls around the table chime in and rib me about my "girlfriend."

"She's my friend," I assure them.

"Good, because Chardane wants to marry you," one of the girls says.

Chardane turns red and glares at her friend. "Annie!" she cries out. "That was a secret."

Beside me, Khloe is muffling a laugh, and I catch Amelia's eye as she looks on with concern. I scrub my hand over Chardane's head.

"I'm an old ogre," I say. "Just ask Khloe." I look past Chardane's shoulders. "Besides, I think that boy two tables over might like you." Chardane spins and then makes a face.

"Chad is a butthead."

"And he picks his nose," the girl to Chardane's right adds.

I laugh at that and stand. "I need to go talk to your teacher. Will you girls take care of Khloe for me?"

They snuggle together to give Khloe room on the bench. "Will you be okay for a minute?"

"Coloring is my favorite pastime."

I walk with Amelia until we're out of earshot.

"It's good to see you, Will." Amelia pushes her thick dark hair from her shoulders, her brown eyes full of concern.

"You, too. How are things?"

"Overcrowded classrooms and overworked teachers."

"I'm waiting to talk to Granddad, to see if he can

find someone at the staffing agency that can take the position."

"Even one more teacher will make a difference," she says.

"No sicknesses, with the mold?"

"We keep the window open and the school ventilated. The new school will be ready before the rainy months, and we have you to thank for that."

"You don't have to thank me. It's the least I could do."

She looks beyond me, and I follow her gaze to see Khloe laughing with the kids. It brings a smile to my face.

"Bevey told me you had a new friend. That her?" She fiddles with the bright pink scarf around her neck, lifting it over her head to block the sun.

I laugh. "Oh, is that how she put it? And yes, that's Khloe."

"Bevey is just happy to see you enjoying more than work."

"Why is my love life suddenly everyone's concern?"

"It's not right for a man to be alone."

"I'm fine alone, and Khloe is nothing more than my assistant."

Who I sleep with.

"Uh-huh," she says, and I shake my head, letting it go.

"I need to speak with the foreman." I nod toward the new schoolhouse.

"You go. I'll take good care of your assistant until you get back."

"Amelia," I warn, and she laughs and brushes me off. I head to the new school and stand back to take in the progress.

"Will." I turn at the sound of Lyron's voice. I extend my arm and his big palm closes around mine, squeezes with a firm handshake.

"Lyron, my friend. It's good to see you."

Lyron takes off his ball cap and uses his arm to wipe away the moisture on his forehead. "She's coming along good, no?" he says, his accent much like Bevey's. "Right on schedule."

"That's good to know. The sooner we get those kids out of that old school the better."

He shakes his head. "Not healthy at all."

"How's the family?" I ask.

"Raeni is no longer coughing, now that we've moved into the new housing complex. Clean running water and no mold. It's heaven."

I put my hand on his back. "Glad to hear it."

"How is your family?" he asks in return.

"Doing well. Granddad is still as stubborn as ever." I wink.

"And a wife for you?" he asks. I just shake my head.

"I can't get away from it," I say, and he laughs.

"It's not natural, Will," he says.

"You've clearly been talking to Bevey."

He whistles innocently. "Come, I'll show you through."

I follow him into the building, and I'm pleased to see how fast it's come together. After the inspection, I bid him a farewell and make my way back to the girls.

My girl.

Whoa, where did that come from?

Khloe glances up when I block the sun from her table. Her eyes are alive, full of happiness.

"You really do like coloring," I say, and she sets her crayon down.

"The girls were just telling me a funny story about the time you went scuba diving and panicked when you thought you saw a shark, but it turned out to be a sea lion." The girls all laugh again, and Khloe joins in.

"My goggles were foggy."

"Sure," Khloe teases.

I shake my head, defeated. "I'm going to have to have a talk with your mother, Chardane." I say, and she just grins up at me. "No more talking about me." I turn to Khloe. "And you…didn't you have your own incident where you thought you encountered a shark?"

Khloe stands. "All righty then," she says quickly, a grin playing on her mouth. "Thanks for letting me color with you, girls."

I put my arm on the small of Khloe's back, and we head back to the car. "Sweet kids," she says. "I'm glad they're getting a new school."

"Now we just need to find teachers to fill the classrooms."

"There's a shortage?"

I nod. "I've been trying to get a hold of Granddad, to check the staffing agency for qualified English teachers."

"Will," she says quickly, and touches my arm to stop me.

"What?"

I turn toward her. "I can help out. I have an English degree, remember?"

"Yeah, I remember." I stare at her for a moment, and see nothing but open honesty on her face.

An odd lump settles into my throat. "Are you serious, Khloe?"

Her eyes widen like she's excited by the opportunity. "Very serious." But then her demeanor changes, her enthusiasm waning, and she frowns. "Oh, but wait. I already have a job here."

"Well, so far you're pretty shitty at it," I tease.

"Hey," she says, feigning offense. A second later a grin pulls at her lush lips. "Okay, well, maybe you are right. But your granddad—" She stops talking, like she's about to say too much.

I frown and narrow my eyes. "What about him?"

"I don't want to let him down."

"Okay, so maybe you can't cook, and you break things, but he is going to lose his mind when he hears you're going to help out in the classroom."

"I think he's already lost his mind," she says.

"You're probably right."

Her teeth dig into her bottom lip, and it draws my attention. Once again, I can't help but wonder how her lush mouth would taste. "Would you mind? I could work around what you need."

"You could take a few hours in the afternoon to help while you're here. If that's what you really want."

"I do," she says, a new purpose about her. I start the car and can't help but feel this woman is too good to be true.

Could I be right?

CHAPTER THIRTEEN

Khloe

I STEAL A glance at Will as we drive back to his villa, feeling excited. I've never taught school before, but at least I'll now be doing something useful. I study the man who has given me this opportunity—he has a strange, unreadable look on his face.

"Hey," I say.

He smiles. "What?"

"You never told me what you wanted for winning the race." I lift my chin. "Although I do want a rematch."

His hand slides across the seat, and there is a new kind of tenderness, a mellowness in him I've not seen before.

"How about I show you instead."

"Ooh, I like the sound of that," I say, as the heat from his hand seeps under my skin and arouses my body.

"There's a festival coming up. Have you heard anything about it?" he asks.

"No, what's it about?"

"It's a cultural fair with a mix of food, drink, plants. Things like that. It's a fundraiser for the church and schools. They play traditional games, and nightly performances by schools and organizations display various aspects of Virgin Islands traditions and culture."

"That sounds like fun."

"We should go."

I eye him carefully. "As long as it's not a date. Rule number three."

He frowns at me. "I know the rules. And it's not a date. I just thought since we both want to go, and we're going in the same direction, we might as well go together."

"Good. Then okay, let's go." He looks ahead as he navigates a turn, and my gaze settles on his mouth. Why, again, did I say no kissing?

Because it's too personal.

Yeah, maybe, but damned if I don't want to feel his lips on mine. They've been pretty magnificent on other parts of my body.

I sink back into my seat and enjoy the scenery as we make our way home. I'm a little sleepy by the time we reach Will's villa. But I sit up straight when I see a big truck pulling out of his driveway and a man standing on the path waving the driver off.

"What's going on? Who is that?" I take in the stocky man dressed in long white pants and a long white shirt that contrast with his dark hair and skin.

"Right, you haven't met Vin yet."

"Vin?"

"He's the caretaker when I'm not here. He was overseeing a job for me today while we were gone."

The mischievous smirk on Will's face raises my curiosity. "What kind of job?"

"Oh, just a little something I thought you'd like."

I frown at him. "What have you done?"

"You'll see."

I give him a warning glare, but he just laughs and exits the car. I hop from the passenger side, and Vin comes to greet us.

"Vin, meet Khloe. She's my new assistant."

"Nice to meet you, Khloe."

"You, too," I say, and shake his outstretched hand, noting the warmth about him. Most people here on the island are so laid-back and welcoming.

"Everything is in order?" Will asks.

"Exactly as you asked," Vin answers.

"Excellent," Will says, and puts his arm on my back to lead me inside.

"What is going on?" I demand when we're alone.

"Come with me and find out."

He guides me down the long hall into his bedroom, and when I step inside a gasp climbs out of my throat.

"No. Way."

Incredulous, I spin to face Will, my cheeks flaring hot.

He arches a brow at my reaction. "You don't like it?"

"Vin," I begin. "He knows." I cover my face with my hands. "This is so embarrassing."

Will chuckles, puts his arms around me and backs me up until we're standing in front of the huge floor-to-ceiling mirror he had installed beside his bed. "Don't be embarrassed."

For some reason, with Will I have no problem being open. But maybe deep down I'm still scarred from my ex, still shy and embarrassed about my needs. "What must he think?"

"That we're adults, doing what adults do. I'm pretty sure he's not judging, Khloe. Even if he is, so what?"

As his words sink in, my hands drop from my face. *Fuck you, Liam.* "You're right, Will. I'm a grown woman, single, and what I do is no one's business but my own. No one has any right to judge me."

"Especially your asshole ex," he says, and that's when I get that he really understands me and where I'm coming from. I'm a little—okay a lot—touched by his insight and what he's trying to do here. My heart beats just a little faster.

Careful, Khloe. You don't want to start feeling things for this man.

"Especially him," I say.

He brushes his knuckles over my cheeks, and the touch is so tender and sweet my pounding heart races just a little faster. Dammit.

"I only hire trustworthy people. People who respect my privacy. What we do here stays here."

"Did he have to sign a nondisclosure agreement, too?" I tease.

He gives me a lopsided grin. "What, did you think you were special?"

He's joking. I get it, so I shouldn't feel like I've just been slapped in the face. I freaking hate that I do. But in all seriousness, his words are a good reminder that what's between us is sex, and I'd be wise to remember that. But everything from the way he cared for me to the fun we've been having—even running the stairs and getting ice cream together—makes it a little hard to keep my head on straight. Is it any wonder women throw themselves at him?

"Well, good. Because I don't want the world to know my business, especially in the bedroom."

He cringes. "That makes two of us."

I soften. "I'm so sorry that happened to you."

"You know what I'd rather talk about?" he says, and repositions me until I'm looking at myself in the mirror.

Light shines in through the open curtains and slants off the wall, lighting up our bodies as we admire each other in the mirror. "I think I might know."

He walks around me, his fingers lightly touching my stomach, hips and back as he circles. I let loose a feathery breath, my legs a little shaky. I have to say, I'm a bit surprised that he went to the trouble of installing a mirror so I could get the full experience, see exactly what we're doing to each other. There's a thoughtful side to Will. Have reporters been judging him too harshly?

He was caught on camera, Khloe.

But it had never sat right with me before, and after spending time with him, even less so.

I can't think about that right now, though. Not when he's gripping the hem of my T-shirt and running rough knuckles over my flesh.

"Hands up," he commands, and grins when I physically react to the direct order.

I lift, and he ever so slowly peels my shirt over my head, tossing it onto the bed. I wet my lips, and his gaze drops from my mouth to my breasts, which are cresting over the top of my bra, almost like they're eager for his touch, his tongue.

He cups them, weighs them in his hands. "I'm going to fuck these," he says with conviction, and a moan catches in my throat. He meets my eyes. "I'm going to fuck you everywhere. That's what I want for winning." He waits for me to react, and I nod. "You want that, don't you? You want to figure out what you like and what you don't."

"Will, I'm pretty sure I'm going to like everything you do to me."

That brings a smile to his face. He steps closer, slides his hands around my back and unhooks my bra. He tosses it away and stands beside me. We both look at my half-naked body in the mirror.

"So beautiful," he says, and I appreciate that he loves my curves.

"When you look at me like that, Will," I say, wanting to be completely honest with him, "it truly makes me feel beautiful."

"Good, because there are two things I want you to feel when you're with me. One is beautiful…" He steps behind me, and his hard cock presses against my back as he slides his big hands around my body and palms my breasts. His thumbs brush my nipples, and as they harden even more, his low groan reverberates through me.

"From the moment you stepped onto the plane, I haven't been able to stop thinking about these. Then… Jesus, Khloe…then when I saw you in that sexy French maid outfit, I knew I was a goner, knew I'd have to have you or risk a bad case of blue balls for the duration of our stay."

"I wasn't going to wear it. I mean, of all the things to make your—" My words fall off when one hand leaves my breasts and dips into my shorts. His finger finds my swollen clit and brushes lightly. "Will," I moan. "That feels so good."

"Yeah, and this is the second thing I want you to feel when you're with me."

"I like those rules," I say as he slides a thick finger into my body. My head falls back, rests against his shoulder, and he puts his mouth to my ear.

"Take your shorts down, Khloe, and look in the mirror. Watch me touch you."

I grip the button on my shorts, rip it open, and bend forward slightly to shove them down my legs. My ass connects with Will's cock, and his groan turns me into a tease. I stay bent, like I'm having trouble with my shorts. But what I'm really doing is wiggling my ass against him. His groans grow louder when he clues in.

"You're such a tease."

"Who, me?" I say, and blink my lashes at him in the mirror. He backs up an inch and gives my ass a whack. I jump, secretly delighted by the sting left behind.

"Now watch," he orders, and puts his finger inside me. I spread my legs, catching his eyes in the mirror before my gaze drops to his hand. I move my hips, grind against his palm and moan without care. I love what this man is doing to me, the way he's freeing me and taking me to new heights as I get to watch it all.

"Like that, baby?" he asks, his breath hot on the shell of my ear.

"You know I do," I say, and cup my breasts. I pinch my nipples.

"Yeah, like that," he says. His lips slide over my skin, and he buries his mouth in the crook of my neck, kissing softly as he slides a second finger into me.

"God, yes," I groan. My hips move faster, and his fingers go deeper, stroking the hot bundle of nerves inside me. I can barely catch my breath as I take in the action in the mirror. I swear to God this is the hottest thing I've ever seen.

"Like what you see?" he asks, his breathing a little rough, too.

"I'm so close, Will," I cry out, my body quivering, all sensations centered between my legs, where his deft fingers are about to make me come.

"Take what you need, baby," he says, and my body lets go. I gasp, and he puts one hand around my waist to hold me upright. "I got you," he murmurs into my ear. My body shudders around his fingers as he slowly brings me back, lightly stroking in a soothing motion.

He guides me to the end of the bed and sits me down. His blue eyes are drenched with lust as he pushes my hair from my shoulders. "Comfortable?" he asks.

I nod, touched by his check-in, and turn my focus to the big bulge before my eyes. Eager to touch him, taste him, I unbutton his shorts and shove them to his knees. His gorgeous cock springs free, and I open my mouth to take him in, wishing I could swallow every inch but knowing it's impossible. Still, I'm not a girl to go down without at least trying.

"Oh God yes," he sighs, and I take his balls into my palm to massage gently. I move to the very edge of the bed and tilt my head as he slides in and out of my mouth. "So damn hot," he growls.

Moisture drips from the tip of his cock, and instead of licking, I dip my finger into it and rub it between my breasts for lubrication.

"Oh, yeah," he says when he realizes what I'm doing.

"I want you here," I say, and squeeze my breasts together. "Right here."

"Baby, I want that, too."

He bends and thrusts upward, easily sliding between my breasts, and I open my mouth to give him a lick with each motion.

"I must have died and gone to heaven."

If my mouth wasn't full, I'd laugh at that. He reaches behind me and fists my hair, and I steal an upward glance and catch the way he's watching the action in the mirror. Wanting to give him the best show of his life, I rub my breasts around him and suck him into my mouth. He grows harder, blood filling his veins, and that's when I know I've got him right where I want him, and my efforts are about to be rewarded.

"Khloe, I'm going to come," he says and tries to back up. But I squeeze my breasts harder, locking him in place. "Oh fuck, yes."

Now that we're on the same page, I loosen my hold, and he thrusts once, twice, and slides into my mouth the second he lets go. I lift my eyes to find Will's face twisted like he's in sweet agony as I drink him in. I swallow every last drop and let my breasts go.

When I do, he holds the back of my head and

brings my cheek to his stomach. I bask in the warmth, the soapy scent of his skin. Contentment falls over me as he rakes his fingers through my hair. It falls over my back, tickling me. My eyes close, sleep pulling at me.

"You're incredible, Khloe."

The hitch in his voice, the waver in his words, combined with the intimacy in his touch pull me wide awake. I glance up to see his eyes closed, his head tilted back. If I didn't know better, I'd think what just happened has touched him on a whole different level, too.

Too?

Oh, Khloe, don't go there.

CHAPTER FOURTEEN

Will

I WAVE TO Vin from the window over the kitchen sink, and he waves back. A week ago I gave him a big bonus—a thank-you for taking care of the mirror installation—and it had put a huge smile on my face. Similar to the ridiculous smile I'm currently sporting as my mind goes back to all the fun Khloe and I've been having inside the bedroom and out. Sex with her has been phenomenal, and the way she opens to me, the way she's game for everything, is mind-blowing. I had fun adding to her to-do list, and we've rapidly been making our way through it, but there is one thing, one act, I didn't add. One I knew better than to add. This is sex, with no emotions, and the last thing I plan to do is make love to her.

We only have a little over one week left here in paradise before we go back to the grind of New York. I have no idea how the time went so fast. Then again, what is that old saying? Time flies when you're having fun. It's strange, because normally I'm happy to return home after being away for an extended period, but this time is different. I'm not sure I'm ready for this trip to be over. Oh, and why is that?

Khloe.

Simply put, I've become totally obsessed with the woman who is wide-open and honest in the bedroom. The same woman who is currently giving her time to a classroom full of elementary school kids. She's been spending a few hours there every day for the last week, and I've never seen her happier.

I step away from the window, take the steaks from the fridge and flip them over in the marinade. A laugh bubbles up in my throat. Here I hired Khloe to take care of the household chores while I worked, yet I've been cooking for her every night and damn well loving it. I especially love all the gratuitous moans she makes when she slides the fork into her mouth as she savors a home-cooked meal. The women I know love to eat at fancy restaurants, but Khloe prefers home cooking. Probably because before this week she lived on takeout pizza and nuked food. Something she confessed to me earlier in the week when she burned my eggs. Which once again takes my thoughts back to Granddad and why he hired her in the first place. Not that I'm complaining. I chuckle quietly to myself as I think about thanking the old man.

While Khloe and I have stuck to the rules for "fucking your assistant," it's getting harder and harder to watch her leave my bedroom after my lips have been all over her body, save for her mouth, and my cock has been inside her. Christ, I might be cashing in my man card here, but I kind of like the idea of her snuggling in next to me, and more importantly waking up next to her in the morning. I shouldn't be having those thoughts, but there doesn't seem to be a damn thing I can do to stop them.

I put the steaks back in the fridge and wander outside. Warm air falls over me, and I step up to the deck to glance at the pool and ocean below. Papers rustle on the table near the pool. Shit, Khloe must have forgotten her journal.

I make my way down the stairs and pick up her hard-covered journal. I consider opening it, but that would be a huge invasion of her privacy, and what kind of man would that make me when I go overboard to protect my own? I carry it into the house and deposit it on the kitchen table. Perhaps she's started work on that novel she's talked about. The sound of my car pulling into the driveway reaches my ears, and I nearly bolt to the door like a lovestruck teenager.

Jesus, I can't fall for her. I'm not looking for more, and neither is she. Even if I was, I've already proven I can't stay committed, and I'm not about to hurt her the way I hurt Naomi. Khloe put important rules in place for a reason, and that reason was to ensure we keep this physical. So I'd be wise not to get any notions that she might want more.

I force myself to walk slowly and pull the door

open to find Khloe jumping from the passenger seat, a wide smile on her face. Goddammit, I like her. I like her a lot.

"How was your day?" I ask, my heart picking up tempo at the mere sight of her. I let my eyes skim the length of her, admire her T-shirt and skirt, which both hug her curves.

"Amazing," she says. I can't help watching her mouth as she excitedly goes on to tell me all about today's lessons and how well the kids are doing. She never did tell me what her last job was, and it's not important, but I have to say, I think she's found her calling here. Would she like to stay on permanently? I mean, she could live in my house, use my car, and I could fly here often, maybe even move—

Jesus, what the hell am I thinking?

I shut those thoughts down quickly, and as she talks, I lead her into the kitchen. She comes to an abrupt halt, her voice falling off when she spots her journal on the kitchen table. She points at it, worry backlighting her brown eyes.

"What's that doing down here?"

I jerk my thumb toward the deck. "You must have left it by the pool earlier."

Her eyes widen. "I did? That's not like me."

"Guess you must have had other things on your mind." I step up to her, put my hands on her hips and pull her against my body. "Don't forget, these past couple weeks you've been doing all kinds of things that you don't normally do." I hope to pull a smile from her, but her startled expression doesn't go away. I soften my voice and ask, "Hey, are you okay?"

Her eyes flicker to mine. "Did you...read it?'

"Of course not," I say, a little offended that she thought I would. "I would never betray your trust like that, Khloe."

"Yeah, I know," she says, and it calms me. She visibly relaxes, and my mind briefly goes back to the way I betrayed Naomi's trust. It seems like a lifetime ago now.

She glances at me like she wants to say something, then closes her mouth again.

"What?" I ask, and step back to examine the way she's still staring at her journal. "Do you have the secrets to the universe in there?"

"Something like that," she says, and picks the book up. She jumps at the sound of her phone ringing in her purse. She pulls it out, checks the caller and casts me an apologetic glance. Over the last week, I've gotten used to that look, considering her phone has been ringing like crazy, and she'll only ever answer it in private. It's possible she's lining up work for when we return, but I don't ask, and she doesn't supply. That's rule number seven for "fucking your assistant." No exchanging personal information.

"I'll be right back." She darts upstairs, and my curiosity deepens. I fully understand and respect that whatever she has between those pages, and whoever it is calling her, is none of my business. It shouldn't bother me that she's being secretive and almost cagey.

Why then does it feel like she just kicked me in the teeth?

I light the barbecue, and when it reaches temperature, I place the steaks on the racks. Khloe has a strange expression on her face when she comes back downstairs and steps outside.

"Everything okay?" I ask.

She hesitates for a second, and I can't help but get the feeling, again, that she wants to tell me something. "Yeah, sorry about that." She jerks her thumb toward the kitchen. "I had to take that call."

I eye her for a second. "You sure you're okay?"

She briefly looks down, like she's considering that, and when her head finally lifts her demeanor changes. "Positive," she says, and gives me a big smile that's obviously forced. "Should I make a salad?"

"Already made." She turns to go back inside, and I follow.

"You always think of everything," she says, her smile genuine this time. Her dark eyes light up, "Speaking of thinking of everything, this girl at school told the funniest story..."

I smile to encourage her to continue as I grab the bottle of white wine I've been chilling, pour us each a glass and head back outdoors. The whole time Khloe is following me around and talking animatedly with her hands.

We both laugh at the end of her story, and she takes a sip of wine. That gives me a chance to pipe in. "Khloe, have you ever thought about becoming a teacher?"

Her brows pull together, and she stares into her wineglass. "Actually, no. I never considered it before. Never thought I'd like it."

"You're so good with the kids."

She smiles. "I'm having fun. I can't deny that."

Before I can help myself, I say, "You could always stay on here." Shit, what am I doing? "I mean, if that's something you'd want. You said you loved it here, and the school is desperate for help."

She sets her drink down and stares past me, like that thought had never occurred to her—and why would it?

"I...don't know." She flips her hand over until it's palm up. "My life...friends... New York."

"Sorry. I don't know what I was thinking," I say. "You once asked me why I didn't live here, and I gave you the same answer."

"Yeah," she says so quietly I have to strain to hear. She fiddles with the stem of her glass and takes a deep breath as she looks out over the ocean. "The truth is, Will, I don't really have a reason to go back." Without looking at me, she continues. "I lost my dad and have no family to speak of, other than my best friend, Steph. I used to think I was going to be a part of Liam's big family." Her smile is shaky, and her eyes are a bit glossy as she looks up at me. "I've always wanted that, you know. I always wanted to be a part of something great like that. I think I liked the idea of belonging to his family more than anything."

I step away from the grill and sit facing her. Sliding my hand across the table, I take her palm in mine and lightly brush my thumb back and forth over her flesh. "You should have that. Just not with him, because you shouldn't change yourself for anyone. You're perfect just the way you are."

She chuckles. "Look at that. The one guy who likes me the way I am is an anti-marriage recluse."

"Khloe—"

She holds her hand up to stop me. "It's fine, Will. I'm not asking you for anything."

And now why does it feel like she kicked me again, except this time lower?

"Anyway, I'm far from perfect, but thank you for the compliment." She gives a humorless laugh and glances at our enclosed hands. "Steph is in my corner, but..." Her head lifts. "But we could always visit each other, I guess." She looks at the ocean. "The people here are much nicer, more accepting." She shrugs. "I said there was no right man for me in Manhattan, but here in Saint Thomas you never know, right?"

An ugly burst of jealousy tightens my throat. The thought of another man's hands on her curvaceous body...hell no.

I swallow. Hard. And I try to sound normal when I say, "You're a beautiful woman, Khloe. The right guy for you is still out there. You just haven't found him yet."

"What about you, Will? You've locked yourself away in this villa. Do you really believe the cheating gene runs in your family?"

"I did a bad thing, Khloe. Now I'm paying for it. I deserve to pay for it."

"You made a mistake. People make mistakes, and most times they get to deal with them in private. What happened to you, *Starlight* broadcasting your mistake all over the newsstands, it wasn't fair. You deserve happiness. You're a good guy, whether you think so or not."

"Do you know something I don't?"

Her entire body stiffens. "What do you mean?"

Jesus, what is going on with her? Her body language is a clear giveaway that she *does* know something I don't. But what? "You said I'm a good guy. Many think differently."

"Ah..." She takes a sip of wine and meets my eyes. "Amelia told me everything."

Unease worms its way through my veins. "What are you talking about?"

"She told me you personally funded the new school. And the lunches that are delivered to the kids every day come from your granddad's resort."

I frown and go back to the barbecue. With my back to her I ask, "Why would she tell you that? That's not information I want out there."

"At first I thought you wanted to get the repairs

done on James's resort fast because it affected your bottom line, but you care about these people, don't you? You wanted them back to work for their sake, not yours."

"I don't like people knowing my business," I grumble.

She stands up, and when I turn to her, she walks over to me. Her palms lie against the sides of my cheeks. "Why don't you want people knowing about all the good you do?"

"I just don't like it. My business is my business."

"After the spread in *Starlight* it might—"

"I don't need adoration, Khloe. I just need privacy."

"You have so many secrets, Will."

"Don't we all," I say, and her lashes fall quickly, hiding her expressive eyes.

"I suppose," she says, then goes quiet for a few seconds. "Wait, we're breaking rule number seven here, and I know how important rules are to you," she says. She sniffs the air. "How are those steaks coming?" she asks, changing the subject.

"Medium-well, right?"

"You got it."

"Then we're good to go." I take the steaks from the barbecue and set one on each plate as she disappears into the house and comes back with a salad. But when she sets it down, I see that look on her face again, and I'm convinced she wants to tell me something but isn't exactly sure how. And I have a feeling I'm not going to like it.

CHAPTER FIFTEEN

Khloe

WE STAND BEHIND a barrier and watch the adult parade make its way down Main Street. Honestly, I've never seen a carnival quite like the one they throw here in Saint Thomas. Women dressed in pink boots, colorful bikinis, headpieces and fluffy angel wings dance down the street to the music of "Soca Kingdom." Another troupe comes behind them, and I gasp when I see the women bending forward, twerking, and the men holding their hips, simulating sex.

"Whoa," I say to Will, who turns and grins at me.

He playfully wags his eyebrows. "A little racier than you thought?"

"Definitely not the kind of parade I'm used to."

He jerks his head to the left. "Want to go?"

"Nope."

Chuckling, Will puts his arm around me, and the guilt circling my stomach jumps into my throat. For the past week, I've been making secret phone calls, gathering information. And just the other night, I finally got hold of Avery Roberts, the journalist who'd caught Will with his pants down.

I sort of told her I was doing a follow-up story, a small lie, and asked how she managed to get him in such a compromising situation. I hinted that I wanted something just as racy for the headline. She was reluctant to talk at first, but when she mentioned that she had a hatred of rich, arrogant men and I fully agreed, she loosened up a bit and admitted she once hit on Will and he stone-cold rejected her. That's when it occurred to me she was out for blood, and I was determined to get to the bottom of it. Those pictures had always felt a bit off to me, and now I know why.

The more we talked, the more she let slip, and I eventually learned she was behind the pictures—she'd personally set Will up to fall. Apparently, she'd contacted the girl who was to dance at Will's bachelor party and paid her off to slip a roofie into his drink. Later that night, the stripper had led him to the bedroom and left a window open in the back of the house so Avery could get in to take the illicit pictures.

The sheer horror of what she'd done—that she could destroy a good man's life on purpose—left me speechless, and that never happens to me. Avery hadn't just been out for a headline, she'd been out for revenge. As I mull that over now, my heart aches for the man and all he lost simply because some reporter wanted to get even.

As my stomach cramps, I once again try to figure out how to tell him. I can't keep that information to myself, but I'm not sure how to say it. I nearly blurted it out the other night when he was barbecuing, but something horrible and selfish had stopped me. I'm stupidly falling for the man—how could I not—and once he knows the truth, he'll go back to Naomi, the woman he's never stopped loving. I hate myself right now, and I have to figure out how to tell him because he's a good man, and he deserves the truth. He deserves the happiness he was denied.

My phone buzzes, and I unzip my purse to grab it. My damn heart jumps into my throat when the word *Starlight* lights up my screen. Crap, it's my old boss. I angle the phone so Will can't see it and shove it into the back pocket of my shorts.

"Aren't you going to answer?" he asks.

"No, it's not important."

He looks at me for a moment, his eyes narrowed, and I'm grateful when he doesn't push. In a few short days, we'll be headed back to the real world, and I'll deal with Benjamin then. For now, I'm going to ignore his calls. But I can't deny that I am curious. Why is he suddenly reaching out to me? Has he had a change of heart? Even if he has, I'm not going back to *Starlight*. I'd rather starve. But that won't happen for at least a couple of months. Assistant to Will Carson pays well. One of his rules is he never hires the same woman twice. But I wonder if he'd make an exception. Bend the rules for me.

Good God, girl, get it together.

He doesn't want more, and once he finds out he was set up, he'll be begging Naomi to come back.

Why, oh why, did I go and fall for him?

We watch the parade until the end, and when the crowd begins to disperse, Will puts his hand on my back and leads me down the street.

"How about we try some local cuisine?" he says as music blares from a band playing on the corner nearby and people bustle about. Will pulls me closer before I get lost in the hustle.

"Sounds like a great idea," I say, trying to push a little enthusiasm past the lump in my throat.

His eyes narrow in on me. "Are you okay?"

"Yeah, fine." I give him a little nudge. "Just thinking about what we might cross off the list tonight." He laughs at that, and we make our way to the food tables. Will points out all the traditional food— everything from fungi, which is made with salted cornmeal, water and okra, to callaloo, a soup made from leafy greens, okra and meat. He stops at the table serving deep-fried pastry stuffed with chicken, beef, fish or vegetables. He rubs his stomach.

"Pâté. Mmm. My favorite."

"They look yummy."

"Want to try?" Since I can tell he does, I nod. "I'll grab us a couple," he says, and pulls his wallet from his pocket. He hands over a stack of bills and in return receives six different pastries. "There's a free table over there." He gestures with a nod. "Grab it, and I'll get us a couple painkillers."

"Painkillers?"

He laughs. "It's a local drink made with rum, pineapple juice, coconut and orange juice."

"All things I love."

I take the plate from him, weave my way through the loud, excited crowd, and drop down into a chair. I push my hair from my face and wonder how I'll be able to eat when my stomach is a roiling mess. I almost laugh at that. I feel as ill today as I did when I first met Will—all those years ago in the back seat of the car. The truth is, we've been having sex, and it's been great, but as I sit here, I actually miss his presence. I miss his tenderness, the gentleness in his touch. I spent my entire adult life taking care of myself, doing for myself, and this is all so…nice.

"I thought that was you."

I glance up at the sound of a woman's voice. "Bevey, it's so nice to see you," I say, and gesture for her to sit across from me. She readily accepts the invitation and sinks into the café chair.

"I'm so glad I ran into you. Chardane talks about you nonstop."

I smile at that. "She's a wonderful girl."

"I wanted to thank you for all you're doing." She makes a tsking sound. "It's a shame you can't stay on permanently."

"My life…well, New York," I say, and she nods like she understands. Once again, I think of the offer

Will made. I'm sure that offer will be rescinded once I tell him the truth and he goes and finds his true love. "If the circumstances were different," I say.

"Where is that man of yours?" she asks, and runs her hand over her pretty yellow-and-blue head scarf as she searches the crowd.

"He's not my—"

"Oh, girl." Her gaze flies to mine, and she waves a dismissive hand. "Don't even go there with me." She gives a big laugh. "I see the way you two look at each other." She leans in. "Between us girls, I've never seen the man happier."

"Not even when he was with Naomi?" I blurt out without thinking, and then slam my mouth shut, wishing I hadn't brought her up. I probably sound like a jealous teenager. Which wouldn't be too far from the truth. Except I'm a twenty-seven-year-old woman, and I knew what I was getting myself into when I wrote the rules for having sex with your assistant. I just never knew at the time Will was so sweet, loving and caring. I'd once told him I trusted no one. He'd said the same. Things have changed for me, and after everything we've been doing, is he capable of letting down his guard and trusting me?

Bevey taps a long finger on the table. "Not even with Naomi," she says with a slow shake of her head. "No one makes him smile the way you do."

My stupid heart jumps in my chest, and a smile I have no control over shapes my lips. My God, I must look like a fool.

Bevey laughs again, confirming my suspicions that I do look like an idiot. "That's what I thought. Girl, the first time you answered that door in that outfit, I knew you were going to give him a run for his money."

I cover my face. "I can't believe he makes all his assistants wear such ridiculous outfits."

"Excuse me?"

I drop my hands at the surprise in her voice. "I said I can't believe—"

"I know what you said." Her brow furrows, and she briefly looks down. "Who told you he makes all his assistants wear those outfits?"

"His grandfather, James. He told me Will had a strict dress code and that my closet would be full when I arrived. Why?"

She grins like she's privy to something I'm not, then lets loose a hoot of laughter. "That old son of a bitch, and two sizes too small at that."

"What?"

"Nothing. Ignore me, I've had too much sun."

She turns from me when a shadow falls over our table. "There you are," Bevey says, and stands to give Will a hug. He sets the drinks down and pulls her into his arms.

After a quick embrace, she says, "I have to get back to my table. Raising good money with my johnnycakes." She squeezes Will's hand and gives him a wink. "You take good care of this one, Will."

He frowns thoughtfully as she leaves. "What was that all about?"

I shrug and my phone rings in my back pocket. I continue to ignore it and take a sip of my drink. "Wow, this is delicious," I say, and try not to think too hard on what Bevey told me. She can't be right. Will can't be happier with me than he was with Naomi, right? He pretty much said he still loves her.

Will takes a bite of the pastry and moans. "You have to try this." He holds it out to me, and his eyes focus on my mouth as I bite into the pastry. For a second, I can't breathe or even chew. All I can do is stare back as heat and energy arc between us. My pulse picks up tempo, and I finally manage to chew and swallow.

"You've got…" He leans toward me and brushes a crumb from my lip, and before I realize what's happening, he's leaning closer, then his mouth is on mine. Tender, exploratory at first, tasting, testing. But when I lean toward him, he deepens the kiss, and his tongue tangles with mine. His hand slides around my head and he grips a fistful of my hair. We exchange hot, hungry kisses born of need and frustration, but he halts abruptly when someone catcalls and tells us to get a room.

He pulls back, and we're both breathless. Silence falls heavy, our heated gazes locked. I bring my finger to my kiss-swollen lips and touch them lightly, the burning imprint of his mouth still there, ruining me for any other man. I am in so much trouble.

"The rules," he says, his voice rough and gruff. "We broke rule number five."

My brain races, spins, and I work to quiet it. "Remember how we replaced your rule for not sleeping with your assistant with ten new rules?"

"Are you suggesting we replace the no-kissing rule with something else?"

"Yes."

"Okay, what do we replace it with?"

"No expectations," I say. He doesn't flinch, doesn't even bat an eyelash. If he wanted more from me, wouldn't he have reacted? Bevey can't be right.

"Fine," he says. He continues to stare at my mouth, and I resist the urge to squirm. What is going through his head? His gaze lifts slowly, and as the black in his eyes bleed into the blue he asks, "Want to get out of here?"

Before I can answer, he's standing and taking my hand. People blur around me as he quickly guides me through the crowd, and I'm not sure I've ever seen him so intense before. We get in his car, and less than ten minutes later, we're entering his villa. As soon as I step through the door, he locks it and pushes me against it.

"This mouth," he says, and runs his thumb over my still kiss-swollen bottom lip. "It's been making me crazy. I've wanted to taste you for so damn long now."

"Why didn't you?"

"Rules."

"Right," I say, barely able to fill my lungs as his entire focus falls to my mouth. Adoration, affection, worship dance in his eyes, and my heart crashes harder against my chest. I swipe my tongue over my bottom lip, and the groan that follows trickles through my body and settles deep between my legs.

I place my hand on his hard chest and slide it down until I'm cupping his swelling erection. His eyes briefly close, and I reach for his zipper, but he stops me. I frown, and he steps into me, scoops me into his strong arms and carries me to his bed. He sets me down on the edge of the mattress and steps back, his gaze roaming over me, a slow, leisurely inspection. There's a change in him, but it's so slight I wouldn't have noticed if I wasn't familiar with all his nuances. Over the past couple of weeks, I've gotten to know this man...have fallen in love with him.

"We go home soon," he says.

"I know," I answer, and hold my breath, praying he wants more after we leave paradise but knowing it's impossible. I fight the tears in my eyes, and while I should blurt out the truth and stop this before it goes any further, I can't. I want—need—this one last night with him.

But instead of asking more from me, his eyes scan my face, and he sinks to his knees. He lightly traces my chin and dips his head until his lips are on mine, tasting softly, exploring thoroughly. And I shut down my thoughts, wanting to enjoy this moment for what it is.

"Baby, you are so beautiful," he murmurs into my mouth, one hand pushing my hair from my shoulder to expose my neck. He runs a soft finger down my neck until he reaches my T-shirt. He tugs it from my shoulder and slides my bra strap with it. His lips leave mine and brush lightly over my skin, and goose bumps follow in the wake of his wet mouth.

I put my hands on his broad shoulders and touch him, my fingers moving over his skin in much the same way he's touching me. His mood is mellow yet deeply intense. Normally our sex is frantic as we try out new, fun positions. I have no idea what he intends this time, but I like this slower, softer version of him.

He nudges my arms and I lift them, knowing full well what he wants. He strips my shirt away and unhooks my bra. His gaze drops, and a quiver goes through me as he takes my breasts into his hands, leans in and presses soft, openmouthed kisses to my nipples.

My heart misses a beat and then another, and I try to swallow down the things this man makes me feel with every touch, every kiss, but this time I can't. I can't smother the love blossoming inside me, filling me up and making me whole again.

"Will," I say quietly, and his eyes lift.

"Yeah."

I swallow again and cup his cheek. "I…I…"

"I know," he says, everything in his gaze softening. But what does he know? How I feel about him? Will it scare him or… "Come here." He stands and tugs me to my feet. I go up on shaky legs, and he slides his hands around my body, cups my ass and pulls me to him.

His lips find mine again, and one hand burrows into my tousled hair. I grow wet between my legs as his tongue delves deep, tasting all of me, savoring, exploring until I'm moaning and arching my back, wanting more…wanting everything.

I slip my hands under his T-shirt, and his muscles clench as I spread my fingers, unable to touch enough of him at once. His mouth is at my ear, and the hungry sounds curl around me, take me to a higher state of passion. I go higher and higher until I reach a place where I'm free-falling without a net. Will I fall or will he catch me?

"I fucking love the way you touch me," he says, and releases the button on my shorts. He inches back, and my hands fall to my sides, a whimper catching in my throat at the loss. But then his mouth is on me again, my grumbles turning to a moan, as he gently swipes the soft blade of his tongue over my hard nipple.

"Yes," I moan, and move against him.

His lips trail lower, and he drops to his knees as he slides my pants down my legs, his heated breath scorching my skin. My hands go to his hair, and I fist it to hold on as he buries his mouth between my legs and pleasures me with soft, gentle licks that vibrate through my entire body. If he weren't holding me, I'd drop to the floor, a quivering mass of need.

"Oh, yes." Sensations are pulling me under, making it harder and harder to think.

He glances up, his eyes the darkest shade of blue I've ever seen. "I love how wet you get for me."

"I love how hard you get for me."

He grunts and gestures to the mirror. "You've seen yourself, right?"

My heart squeezes. "You always make me feel beautiful, Will."

"You are beautiful, Khloe."

I look in the mirror. The sight of Will on his knees, loving every moment of what he's doing to me, nearly pushes me over the edge. My muscles tremble, and Will chuckles softly between my thighs. And somewhere in the back of my mind, I register that my phone is ringing, but then it stops. It's not like I was going to drop everything and answer it anyway, and I'm not even sure Will can hear it over his hungry moans.

My thoughts shut down, go completely blank as he slips a thick finger into me, to tease the sensitive bundle of nerves. My hips involuntarily jerk forward, my clit smashing against his face.

"Will!" I cry out as I come, shattering completely. His tongue continues circling my sensitive clit as he slowly swirls his finger inside me. I wobble on shaky legs, and he backs me up until I'm on the bed, his mouth still between my thighs, his fingers still buried deep.

"I want you inside me," I whisper.

His head lifts. "Now there's an invitation I can't refuse." He stands, and I admire all six feet of hard muscles.

I point my finger. "Naked. Now."

He grins. "You are a woman who knows what she wants."

I'm about to roll over, but he puts his hand on me to stop me. "Center of the bed, on your back."

I eye him. Is he seriously telling me he wants to do this missionary? But that position is boring and has never brought me to orgasm. I open my mouth to protest but he stops me. "Do it, Khloe."

I do as he says, and he sheds his clothes, grabs a condom from the nightstand, and quickly sheathes himself.

"Open your legs. Show me your sweet pussy."

My thighs widen, and I slide a hand in between. He grins. "You can remove your hand. Your pussy is all mine tonight." He kneels between my legs, grips them and bends my knees, opening me even more. His eyes drop, roam over me. With the lightest of touches, he pets my pussy.

"So pretty," he says. I turn my head to watch in the mirror. "Eyes on me, Khloe," he commands in a soft voice. My head jerks back to his as his gaze bores into me, like he can see into the depths of my damn soul. I pray what he sees doesn't scare him off.

He strokes himself, and balances on one arm as he lightly rubs his crown over my clit. A whimper catches in my throat.

"Right here," he says. "This is where I need to be." His hips power forward, and he fills me with one hard thrust.

"Will," I cry out, and slide my hands around his

back. His eyes never leave mine as he moves in and out of me, sliding easily into my slickness. An odd little lump settles into my throat as his lips find mine. His kisses are soft, wet, a deeper hunger, like he's seeking something more, something we've yet to share. My hands circle his back, and my knees brush his sides as he thrusts, stretching my walls and stimulating me all over again.

His mouth leaves mine, and he kisses my nose, my eyes, my cheeks and chin before he buries his face in the sensitive hollow of my throat. I turn toward the mirror to see his body moving over mine, and there is a part of me that can't believe this man—one with a kinky side—is taking me in the missionary position.

But it's unlike any missionary position I'm familiar with. No, the way he's taking me feels anything but vanilla. In fact, it's deeply profound, incredibly moving, and I can't help but wonder if we're… making love…with our hearts involved. Could Bevey be right? Could Will be the happiest he's ever been, because of me? The way he's kissing me, touching me, loving me… I've never experienced anything quite like it. Is it possible that I was wrong, that there is a man out there for me and I'm currently in bed with him? If so, does that mean when I tell him my findings, he won't run back to Naomi?

He inches back and places a hand on my cheek, and his heat seeps below my skin, wraps around my trembling heart. His hips rock, rotate, his pelvis stimulating my aching clit, his eyes moving over my face. But there is something in that gaze, something that I've never seen before.

"Will," I say as I hold on to him harder, afraid if I loosen my grip, I'll tumble into the unknown and never be able to find my way back...from loving him. My flesh ignites, pleasure pinpoints between my legs, and all the air leaves my lungs as the most powerful orgasm I've ever had tornadoes through me. I gasp, clench around him and scratch at his back. His mumbled curses whirl around me, the room fading to black. Wetness coats him as he continues pulsing in and out.

"I feel you," he murmurs. He pumps into me, slow movements that prolong the pleasure and bring on another orgasm. My inner walls quiver, pull him in deeper, until he's touching me on a whole different level.

"Oh my God!" I cry.

"Khloe, look at me."

I crack my lids open, and our eyes meet and lock. His nostrils flare, and with the utmost tenderness, he cups my face in his big warm palm. That's when I understand why he wanted this position. He wanted to see my face, my expression. He wanted to see me, and he wanted me to see him as we tumbled over the edge together. As I stare at him, I struggle to breathe, to understand the true depths of what is happening between us. He lets out a loud growl and pulsates inside me. My lids feel heavy, but I don't dare blink or close them. I want to remember this moment, to memorize every curve of his face. But a second later, the vision before me is gone, and he's collapsing over my boneless body.

I link my fingers together behind his back, and catching me by surprise, his mouth is on mine again. His kisses are so slow, so achingly tender tears prick my eyes, and I squeeze my lids together to fight them back.

"This…" he begins, and lifts his head, his eyes searching my face. "This was everything," he whispers.

"Yes," I say, and he's kissing me again. A long time later, he rolls off me and pulls me to him. I snuggle into his warmth, breathe in his familiar scent, never wanting to break this moment between us. I trace his nipple, and his body quivers. His hand closes over mine, and he brings my fingers to his mouth, kissing them one by one.

I close my eyes and bask in the euphoria of post-orgasm bliss. My heart slows and sleep pulls at me, until something Bevey said jumps to the forefront of my mind.

"Will," I say sleepily.

"Yeah." His voice is as groggy as mine.

"Do you make all your assistants wear French maid outfits?"

"What are you talking about?"

My head clears a little more as my heart beats faster. "I'm talking about all the outfits in the closet when I arrived."

"Khloe, baby. I have no idea what you're talk-ing about."

My mind races back to my meeting with James. What the hell is going on? If Will doesn't make his assistants wear the sexy outfits, who does? Surely to God, a ninety-year-old man couldn't be behind this.

You're perfect for Will.

"You said you thought your grandfather set Tate and Summer up, right?" I ask.

"Yeah, I think so," he says, his voice fading. He shifts in the bed until we're facing each other, and from the strange way he's looking at me, it's easy to tell he has something other than James and Tate on his mind.

He cups my face. "Khloe..."

Just then my stupid phone rings, and Will stiffens.

"Ignore it," I say, dying to know what it was he was about to say to me.

"It's been going off for a while. Whoever is try-ing to get a hold of you is not going to stop anytime soon. We'll talk after you answer it."

Before I can stop him, he's out of the bed and fish-ing the phone from the back pocket of my shorts. His gaze lazily goes to the screen as he's about to hand it to me, but then he goes still...too still. His mel-low expression changes, his features morphing from confusion to anger, and in that instant, my entire life comes crashing down around me.

CHAPTER SIXTEEN

Will

"WHAT THE FU—"

My gaze goes from *Starlight* written in bold letters on the screen to Khloe as she jumps from the bed and nearly falls on her face when her foot gets stuck in the tangled sheets. Her hair is a wild mess, and her eyes are huge as she reaches for the phone and snatches it from me like it's on fire. It might as well be, considering someone from the magazine from hell is calling.

"It's not what you think," she says quickly as she puts the phone behind her back to hide it from my view.

"Seriously, Khloe?" I shake my head and almost laugh—manically. "I can't unsee what I've already seen."

"It's not what you think," she repeats, a measure of panic in her voice as she blinks rapidly.

The room spins around me, and I scoop my pants

and shirt off the floor. As I tug them on, I say, "Tell me what I think."

"Will," she begins, and reaches for her own clothes. She holds them in front of her body like a shield. "You think I'm working for *Starlight*."

My nostrils flare as I suck in a fast breath. "Are you?"

"I...used to."

"You used to?" I rake my hands through my hair, trying to wrap my brain around this unexpected turn of events. Khloe worked for *Starlight*? Of all the... I sift through the information, and in a calm voice that belies the storm going on inside me, I ask, "You're a reporter, then?"

"I..." She stops speaking and jams her teeth into her bottom lip, answering me without words. And this time, I do laugh, like a goddamn crazy man. Hasn't *Starlight* screwed with me enough already?

"Yeah, okay. You're a reporter. I get it."

"Technically, I am," she finally says. "But you don't get it."

I gesture to her arm, the one still behind her back. "Who's calling?

"Ah, it's Benjamin Murray."

I stare at her, incredulous, and my head rears back. "The fucking owner of *Starlight*?"

She waves her hand. "But it's not what you think."

"So you keep saying." What the ever-loving fuck. I stare at her, hard. "What the hell have you done?"

"The story…the story Avery did on you," she says as she comes toward me.

I back up. I can't be close to her right now, not when all signs lead to one thing. Khloe is here to get a story on me. "What about it?"

"None of it was true." She tugs on her T-shirt and slips into her shorts as she says, "I talked to Avery this week. She said she set you up."

"What are you talking about?" So those were all the secret phone calls? To Avery? Then why the hell is the owner calling her? None of this really adds up.

"She set you up. She knew the dancer and had her slip something in your drink. You were drugged and tricked, all for a headline."

I take a deep breath, hold it for a second as I process, then let it out in a loud whoosh. "And you were going to tell me this when?"

"I wanted to tell you, I just—"

"Wanting to and telling me are two different things," I blurt out, cutting her off as rage rockets through me.

"Will, listen. Benjamin wanted me to do a follow-up story on you—"

"Fuck." Anger spikes my blood pressure, and a headache begins brewing at the base of my skull. The bedroom starts to close in on me, each breath getting harder and harder to take. I gulp but can't fill my lungs. "I need air."

I step from the room, hastily make my way down the hall and open the back patio door. Outside, I lean over the railing and work to sort things through as I glance at the pool and the stirred-up ocean beyond. The sight is fitting, really, matching the state of my stomach.

Khloe worked for *Starlight*?

Wait, how do I know she doesn't still work for them? I briefly close my eyes and go over everything that happened between us since the second she arrived on Granddad's plane, sick with the flu.

"Will..." Her soft, tentative voice has me spinning around. "I wanted to tell you, but—"

"Why should I believe anything you say? How do I know you're not just telling me that to get me to trust you?"

"I guess..." She stops and shrugs, like she's working hard to come up with an explanation that's believable. "Maybe because of the time we spent together."

"That's it? That's all you've got?" I stare at her, my gaze moving over her face. "Why did you go see Granddad? After all these years, why did you suddenly pay him a visit?" I can't ask Granddad myself since he's yet to call me back. My stomach coils, and my shoulders are so tight the strain goes up through my neck. Khloe moves toward me again, and I hold my hand up to stop her.

"I went to see James because my boss wanted me to do a story on you."

I pinch the bridge of my nose, the tumblers all falling into place. "And you needed to find out where I was and what I was doing. I keep my private life private, my whereabouts mostly unknown, but you used your connections to get the inside scoop. Wow, I didn't see that coming."

She winces. "I can see how you'd think—"

"It's common sense. It's two and two." I swallow past the knot in my throat. "I can't fucking believe this." I turn around and stare at the ocean.

"Do you really think I'd do that, Will?" she asks, her voice low…offended.

She's the one who's offended?

I spin around and glare at her. "How did you talk him into it?"

"Talk him into what?" Her hand is as shaky as her voice as she sinks into one of the chairs at the small café table. I laugh again, thinking about all the private conversations we had at that table. All the things we shared.

"How did you get Granddad to hire you?"

"He offered me the job. I didn't ask for it."

I spread my arms, grip the edges of the handrail and squeeze until my knuckles turn white. "How fucking convenient." I shake my head. How the fuck did Granddad not see this coming? Not see *her* for who she really is? Oh, maybe because she's such a great con artist and has no trouble lying or doing whatever it takes—even sleeping with me—to get the headline. Granddad is old and slipping, which is probably why he didn't recognize a con for a con. But what excuse do I have? Why didn't I see through it?

Because you were too busy having the best sex of your life and falling in love.

Fuck me.

My gaze leaves hers, goes to her journal on the table. I'd caught her writing in it earlier this morning when I joined her for coffee. A sound crawls out of my throat as I gesture with a nod.

"Have you been writing about me?"

Her face pales. "I… Will… I…" She swallows hard. "Yes, but it's not what you think."

"Of course not. Do you seriously take me for a fool?"

"I don't think you're a fool at all," she says.

I consider that for a moment. "Yeah, well, then you'd be wrong. I am a fool." I'm a goddamn dumbass who was duped by a reporter. Again. If she's telling the truth about Avery, that is. I shut my eyes, my thoughts going to Naomi. "My life was ruined because of that article."

"I guess you can go and get her back now." Her voice is low, pain edging her words.

My lids open slowly, and when I see Khloe gripping the journal—clearly not wanting me to see what's inside—my stomach plummets. "You should go."

"Go where?" she asks.

"Back home. You should go, Khloe. No, you *need* to go. I'll call for a car. It will take you to Granddad's jet, and I'll arrange to have you flown back to New York."

"So that's it? You're just sending me away?"

Anger coloring my words, I say, "What choice do I have?"

She goes quiet for a long time. "I guess you don't have any. You see what you want to see. You hear what you want to hear. I obviously can't change any of that." She turns and is about to walk back inside the villa.

"The journal stays," I say in a hard voice that stills her. "It's in the nondisclosure agreement you signed, remember?"

She spins, gives me a long, hard glare, but in the depths of her eyes there's a profound sadness. What? Is she sorry she's not going to get the headline? For a second, I think she's going to protest, but then she tosses the journal onto the table, and her face tightens. "Just so you know, Will. You're not a cheater. You see, there is no cheating gene, and you *do* have staying power. You were just screwed over. Go ahead and take that information to Naomi. I'll confirm it for her."

"How do I know you're telling the truth about that?"

"Spend a few minutes thinking about the events of that night," she says.

I blink, that night a blurry haze. "I don't remember much."

"How much did you have to drink?"

"It was my bachelor party. I drank a lot."

"Let me guess, you felt like hell the next morning."

"Yeah."

"Different than a regular hangover?"

"Much worse," I answer, and she opens her mouth, only to close it again. "Go ahead and say what you want."

"It's none of my business, but why didn't you look into it? Why did you so readily accept that you didn't have staying power?"

I scoff. "Because none of the men in my family do."

"What about Tate?" She arches a challenging brow. "What about your brother? What about James?"

I laugh at that. "James had numerous women in his life over the years."

"Before your grandmother passed away?"

I look down, search my memory. "Well, no, not that I remember."

She takes a big breath and lets it out slowly. "I think you need to spend some time asking yourself *why* you just accepted what the papers wrote about you."

I fold my arms, lean against the railing. "What are you trying to say, Khloe?"

Her chin nudges upward, her intense gaze locked on mine, unwavering, challenging. "Maybe you didn't really want to marry Naomi."

Before I can voice an argument, she steps into the house and disappears. I stare at the spot where she'd been standing, my blood draining to my toes. Jesus, could she be right? Yeah, sure, Granddad had been pressuring me into marriage, but I loved Naomi, didn't I?

Then why didn't you fight?

Doors slam inside, and my brain shifts direction. I pull my phone from my pocket and make a few calls to arrange for Khloe to be picked up and for the staff to be waiting for her on the plane. I'm about to shove my phone back into my pocket, but once again I'm thinking about Khloe's parting words. Naomi was deeply hurt by my actions and deserves to know I wasn't unfaithful. While this truth won't change things between us—do I even want it to?—I pull up my contacts and find her number.

I turn to face the ocean, my world a goddamn mess. I swallow as my phone vibrates against my ear. It rings three times before I hear her breathy voice. "Naomi," I say, and spin when a bang reaches my ear. I turn to find Khloe standing there, staring at me. "What?" I ask.

Glossy eyes meet mine. "Never mind," she says, and as she darts toward the front door, I have half a mind to go after her. But she's a reporter who went undercover to take me down, right? Why is it that I'm suddenly not sure of that now? Spending time with Khloe reminded me I hadn't been living, only surviving. I loved talking to her, doing things with her, taking her to my bed and making sweet love to her, and she'd blossomed under my touch. She'd been so honest and open with me, and the look on her face after working at the school had been pure bliss. No one can fake that. And putting herself out there was all about her, not me. She was volunteering and helping out from the kindness of her heart.

As that thought rings inside my brain, Naomi's voice pulls me back. "Will," she says. "It's been a long time. I'm glad you called."

"We need to talk." I drop down into the chair, and run my fingers over the leather binding of Khloe's journal. A warm breeze washes over my damp skin as I tell her everything. We spend the next hour talking, getting caught up, and I hear a new lightness in her voice. As we talk I learn she's engaged, and I'm genuinely happy for her. She asks me about my love life, but I gloss over it. The woman I'm in love with played me for a fool. After a long time, a ding alerts me that there is another call coming through. I glance at the screen to see that it's Granddad. About time.

"Naomi, there is a call coming in I have to take."

"It was good talking to you, Will."

"You, too."

"I hope you can come to the wedding."

"I wouldn't miss it."

"I'll look forward to an invitation to yours when it happens."

I laugh at that, end the call and switch over to Granddad.

"Granddad, finally."

"What's going on, Will? I got a call that my plane is on its way back."

"I sent Khloe home."

A moment of silence, and then, "Why is that?"

"Because she's a reporter. She was here to do a story on me."

Ice rattles in a glass and then, "I think you're mistaken, son."

"I have proof, Granddad." I push to my feet and fist my hair, the gorgeous view below doing little to calm the storm raging inside me.

"What kind of proof?"

I turn, lean against the rail and catch my unkempt reflection in the glass door. "She's been writing about me in a journal."

"Do you have the journal?"

"In my hand."

"Open it."

"I'm not opening it. I don't want to see the lies she's written in there." Restless, uneasy, I pace to the patio door and back to the rail. "How could you have hired her?" I ask, not wanting to make him feel old and senile but needing to get to the bottom of matters.

"Because she's perfect for you," he says smugly.

"Perfect for me?" As his words sink in, my mind takes me to our conversation about the French maid outfits. What was that she asked? If I made all my assistants wear them. My gut tightens. "Granddad, tell me you didn't…"

"Didn't what, son?"

I swallow. "Did you arrange for all those French maid outfits to be in Khloe's closet?"

A hoot of laughter follows my question, and then what sounds like him slapping his leg. "That was Summer's idea. She's a brilliant one."

Holy fuck.

"You were...matchmaking?"

"Of course I was."

"She's a reporter. Did you know that?"

"Yes, boy. I knew that."

I shake my head and try to wake myself up from this nightmare, but no, I'm not dreaming. This shit is really going down.

"Then why did she keep it a secret?" I ask.

"I asked her to. I know how you feel about reporters."

"Then why her, Granddad? Why hire her if you knew how I felt about reporters?"

"She came to me to warn me that her boss wanted her to do an exposé on you, but she was fired because she refused. Just as well she left *Starlight*. Her dream is to write for the *New Yorker*. That place was only holding her back. But she's too proud, too much like her father to let anyone give her a leg up, even though she's talented."

My fuzzy brain spins. Wait, what was that she'd said about being out of work?

My boss wanted me to do something, and when I refused, he canned me.

Christ. I'd thought it was about sex. But it was because she'd refused to do a story on me? I grip the journal harder, my world sinking around me.

"Open the journal, Will."

I slowly peel the cover back and begin to read. I skim the page and read faster. My heart leaps into my throat. "Jesus."

"What's that, boy?"

"It's...it's all about me, all about my kindness and the community services I do here on the island. She wrote a whole article on me."

The sound of Granddad slapping his knee again reverberates through the phone. "I knew it."

"But I don't like my business known. You know that."

"Who says she was even going to publish it?"

A knock on the door reaches my ears, and my heart leaps. Has she come back?

"Someone's at my door."

"Go check. Might be her."

I hurry down the hall, pull the door open and find Bevey standing there, a plateful of johnnycakes in her hands. "It's Bevey," I say.

"Hey, don't sound so disappointed," Bevey says.

Ice clinks in Granddad's glass again before he says, "Tell her I said hello."

"I'm not disappointed. Come in. Granddad says hi," I say, and turn back to my conversation with Granddad. Even though Bevey is listening, I say, "I...fucked up. I said cruel things. I sent her away, and I don't think she's coming back."

"Then go fix this."

"How?"

"You're a smart boy. You'll figure it out."

Bevey follows me into the kitchen as I resume pacing. "But what if…what if she doesn't feel the same way about me as I do about her?"

"Oh, she does," Bevey says with a big smile.

CHAPTER SEVENTEEN

Khloe

IT'S BEEN A WEEK since I've returned from Saint Thomas, seven whole days that have felt more like four hundred and twenty-seven days and a whole bunch of hours and minutes. I haven't been sleeping or eating very well since coming home, and forget about functioning properly. Only problem is, if I don't pull myself together, I'm going to lose this temporary gig that's going to keep me afloat until I can secure a permanent position. I refused to deposit the check that arrived at my apartment and refused to take James's calls. The man had no right sticking his nose into our business. *Around Town Magazine* isn't where I ultimately want to work, but I'll take anything thrown my way. And I'm just filling in while one of the reporters is off on maternity leave.

It's funny, Will said to me that by the time I left Saint Thomas I'd know what I wanted and what I loved. He was right. It's hard to believe how my priorities have shifted. I didn't know what I wanted in life until I spent time in Saint Thomas. I think it would surprise everyone, Will included. But now Will thinks I was out to sabotage him, and he's back with Naomi, which means my dreams will never be fulfilled. Not in this lifetime.

Stupid tears prick as the bell over the front door jingles. I swipe the moisture away and glance up from my desk to see Steph bouncing in, a smile on her face as she checks the rows of desks in search of me.

"Over here," I say with a wave, and she bounds over to my side of the room. I lower my voice, not wanting to disturb those working close by. "What are you doing here?"

"I wanted to check out your new workplace."

"Well, I'm only here temporarily, so don't get used to it."

"Look on the bright side, you're not a pod person anymore."

I stand and take in her fashionable attire as I give her a hug. "Look at you. All dressed for your new position at the *Cut*. It's always been your dream to write about fashion and trends. I'm so proud of you. I told you that, right?"

"Only a million times." She jabs her thumb into her chest. "And this girl with the fancy new clothes and office wants to go out to lunch with her best friend."

I crinkle my nose. "I can't really—"

She cuts me off. "It's on me, girlfriend. When you're rich and famous, you can buy."

I snort. "Like that's ever going to happen."

"Maybe sooner than you realize," she mumbles.

I eye her. "Have you come off your meds?"

She laughs out loud, and I close my laptop and reach for my purse. "I could eat. I think. One condition. We don't talk about *him*."

At the mention of *him*, her eyes travel the length of me. "Have you been taking care of yourself?"

"Yes, Mom," I lie.

"Okay, I'll shut up, but you're ordering one of everything." I link my arm with hers, and we step out into the sunshine. People bustle by, one man with his face buried in his phone nearly mowing me down.

"I sure miss Saint Thomas."

"I bet you do." She steals a glance at me. "Do you think you'd ever go back?"

I give her a look that suggests she's insane. "Not now. What reason would I have?"

"I don't know. You said you loved working with the kids." Her eyes light up. "Hey, maybe you could get a job here teaching."

"Since it doesn't look like I'll ever write for the *New Yorker*, maybe I should," I say, even though, strangely enough, the *New Yorker* isn't where my heart is anymore.

"Why can't you do both, part time?"

I stop walking and stare at Steph. "Who are you, and what have you done with my best friend?"

She laughs. "Come on, before lunch I have to make a quick stop."

I glance at my watch. "I don't have a long lunch hour."

"Yeah, well. I think it might be longer than you realize."

I grab her arm. "Oh my God, please don't tell me I'm getting fired again."

"Come with me," she says, and I once again go over the few bills left in my wallet. I ate the Mentos in the bottom of my purse, so there goes my backup.

We step into a bookstore, and I furrow my brow. "What are we doing here?"

"Oh, you'll see." She takes my hand and leads me to the stack of newspapers. "I wanted to check out the papers."

"Don't you get like every newspaper known to mankind already?"

"I do, but you don't."

I grimace. How's a girl supposed to write for the *New Yorker* when she had to cancel her subscription because she couldn't afford it? Heck, I can't even afford the cheaper digital version. A saleslady walks by me, a grin on her face. Okay, why is she looking at me like that? I turn to see her switch the sign on the door from Open to Closed.

I nudge Steph. "We need to go. She must be closing up for lunch."

"Hang on, I heard there was an article on Will Carson in today's paper."

Blood drains to my toes. "Oh, God, no. Who wrote it?" Did Avery find him after I called her? If so then I'm the one responsible for whatever is written about him. I swallow and lean against the stack of books as my legs weaken.

Steph blinks at me. "Khloe, you've gone white."

"What was written about him? Oh, Steph, please tell me it's nothing bad. He's a good guy. Yeah, okay, he was a jerk who accused me of some nasty things, but I can see how it all looked to him. He doesn't deserve any of this."

"A jerk, huh?" The familiar voice comes from behind, and I gasp as I spin around and nearly sink to the floor. My gaze rakes over Will, who is dressed in a perfectly tailored suit, looking as handsome as he did the first day I met him on the plane.

"Will, I didn't—"

"You're right, though. I don't deserve any of this," he says.

I point to the paper that Steph is riffling through. "I…I don't know…anything about it." Wait, why is Steph so calm, flipping pages without even acknowledging Will or my burst of panic. What is going on?

"Will, it's not what you think."

"You keep saying that to me, and I have to stop you because you need to know what I do think. But before I say anything, you should read the article."

Steph's grin is wider than I've ever seen it when she folds the paper and hands it to me. My eyes go big when I skim the article—my article. Oh no, these are *my* words.

"Will," I croak out. "I never meant for anyone to see this. I have no idea how my journal ended up in the wrong hands, but—"

"What I think is that I'm the world's biggest idiot." Feet shuffle behind him, and before I know it, there are numerous people lined up watching us—including James. I recognize Tate, Summer, Brianna, Luca, Alec and Megan from the tabloids. What the heck is this, a Carson family reunion?

"What…what's going on?"

Will laughs. "Family. They don't know when to mind their own business."

I grip the edge of the bookshelf, the room closing in on me. "Will—"

"I don't agree with my granddad's meddling, and for the record, Summer was the one responsible for the French maid outfits." I glance past him to see a pretty woman with long strands of honey-blond hair piled on the top of her head. She gives me a small wave and coy smile. "But how can I be mad?"

"Mad? What? The article… I didn't…"

Will steps up to me and takes my shaky hands in his. And the second he touches me, tears fill my eyes. I blink through the haze, take in his handsome face, the way he's looking at me with pure adoration.

"I know you're an independent woman who likes to do everything herself, and that's one of the things I admire most about you."

"Thank…you. But… I just can't understand—"

"I submitted the article, Khloe."

My jaw drops, and filling my lungs with air becomes an impossible task. "No, you're a private guy." I shake my head hard. "You don't want anyone knowing anything about you."

"But your dream was to write for the *New Yorker*. Granddad told me."

As understanding dawns, tears spill from my eyes. "Wait, you…you did this for me? You put yourself out there, let the world know your private life… for me?"

"Of course."

But Naomi. After he accused me of trying to sabotage him, I'd run back to the patio to fight for him, to tell him how wrong he was about me, but he'd been on the phone with Naomi. He'd called her the second he sent me packing. So why is he doing this? Maybe because I told him the truth, and he wanted to do something nice to thank me? Maybe that's all that's going on here.

"Naomi," I begin quietly. "Did you get back what you had with her?"

"I'll never get back what I had with Naomi."

"I'm sorry."

"Don't be. I don't want that."

"You don't?"

"No, because you were right about everything. I didn't really want to marry her, and something better did come along."

Steph shrieks beside me, and I catch the way she's holding her hands in front of her face like she's trying not to shout. I make eye contact with every person standing behind Will. My God, why is his entire family here?

"Will?"

"This time, this time, Khloe, I'm not going down without a fight. When I said I didn't deserve this, what I meant is I don't deserve you. Not after the way I treated you. But if you let me spend a lifetime making it up to you, I will."

He pulls something from his suit pocket and drops to one knee.

"Oh my God," I whisper.

"I love you, Khloe. I think I fell for you the minute you boarded Granddad's plane all flustered and beautiful, and…your independent, wild self. Will you marry me? Will you make me the happiest man in the world?"

Our gazes meet and hold, and my mind races with everything that's happened—how much I've changed, how much my wants have changed.

"It's not what I want anymore," I blurt out, and the room grows so quiet I can hear the clock behind the counter tick.

He swallows so hard it echoes in the room. "Khloe, I'm sorry about everything. I'm sorry I didn't trust you. I'm sorry I jumped to the wrong—"

"The article," I say, and drop the paper. "You shouldn't have done that."

"I might have sent it to a buddy of mine, but he wouldn't have printed it if it wasn't great, Khloe. You did this on your own merit. Isn't that what you always wanted?"

"No, you don't understand."

"Make me understand."

I drop to my knees. "What you've done, exposing the private side of yourself for me, that's just about the nicest thing anyone has ever done for me, but it wasn't necessary."

Confusion fills his features, and the muscles in his neck are so tight I'm sure they're going to snap. "Isn't it your dream to write for the *New Yorker*?"

I shrug. "Used to be, but things have changed."

As his eyes roam my face, so lost and vulnerable, the love I feel for him bubbles to the surface. "Do you remember telling me that when I left Saint Thomas I'd know what I wanted and what I loved?"

My eyes drop to his pulse hammering against his neck. "What do you want?" he asks.

"My dream used to be to write for the *New Yorker*, but now I want to be with the children in Saint Thomas." His eyes light up. "I want to go back. I want to help, to be a productive member of the Saint Thomas community." I shrug. "And you know what, if I want to write the odd article for the *New Yorker* I can do that, too. Maybe I can even write the book I've always wanted to write."

"Bevey and the kids will be happy to hear that."

I cup his face, and my heart crashes against my chest. "You also told me I'd know what I love."

"What do you love, Khloe?"

"I love you, Will Carson, and the answer is yes."

Cheers erupt behind us as a huge smile tugs at his mouth and lights up his eyes. He lets loose a breath. "You know you had me scared there for a moment."

I grin at him. "And maybe for a moment you deserved it."

"You might be right." He takes the ring from the box and slides it onto my finger. I examine the huge rock for a second and lift my gaze to his.

"I love you," I whisper.

"I love you, too," he says, giving me a kiss so full of warmth and adoration that my heart overflows with all the things I feel for this man. "I'm so happy you decided to take the job in Saint Thomas."

"I realize you can't always be there with me." I cast a quick look at James. "You need to be close to family."

James slams his cane onto the floor. "Don't you worry, child. I'm not going anywhere soon." He taps his head. "Still as sharp as a tack." Everyone nods in agreement. "You two go live your lives. You're only a flight away."

"He's right," Brianna says, putting her hand on Luca's chest. "We live in Italy, and I see Granddad more now than when I lived in New York."

I pull Steph to me. "Everyone, this is Steph, my

best friend. My sister." I hug her. "Clearly she was in on all this, too."

James glances at Steph, checks out her empty ring finger. "I was wondering if you could do me a favor—"

"Oh, God, James, no," I say. "Your matchmaking days are done!" As everyone laughs, I inch away from Will and glance at his family. "Speaking of matchmaking." I glare at the men and women watching me carefully. "Who was behind this?" I wave my finger back and forth between Will and me.

"Uh, well," James says, and the rest of them shift from one foot to the other, all of them looking around the room sheepishly. I point my finger. "Let me just say one thing." My gaze falls to Will, who has a worried look in his eyes. I wink at him, look back at his family and say, "Thank you."

Before I even realize what is happening, his family is hugging and kissing me and introducing themselves as I'm passed from arm to arm. They even include Steph, and for that I'm grateful. Once the hugs are done, Will comes to my rescue.

He pulls me into his arms, places a soul-stirring kiss on my mouth and says, "Did I mention I come with a big, crazy family?"

I laugh and hug him. "I wouldn't want it any other way."

* * * * *

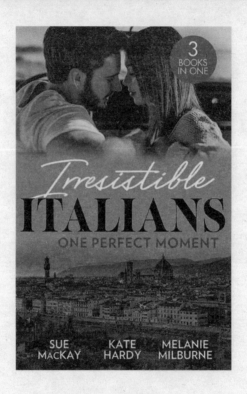

GET YOUR ROMANCE FIX!

Get the latest romance news,
exclusive author interviews, story
extracts and much more!

MILLS & BOON

Desire

Indulge in secrets and scandal, intense drama and plenty of sizzling hot action with powerful and passionate heroes who have it all: wealth, status, good looks...everything but the right woman.